LAW MATTERS

Twelve Stories Based on Actual Legal Principles

By Rick Dantzler

Artwork by Paul Schulz

"Justice, sir, is the greatest interest of man on this earth. It is the ligament which holds civilized beings and civilized nations together."

Daniel Webster, September 12, 1845

Published by
Florida Classics Library, ISBN 0-912451-61-0
P.O. Drawer 1657
Port Salerno, Florida 34992-1657

Printed by
The Maple-Vail Book Manufacturing Group
Binghamton, New York

Book designed by Debbie Gorsuch

DEDICATION

This book is dedicated to my wife, Julie, the most patient person on the planet. She's let me run down one rabbit trail after another as I've searched for the rabbit, never leaving my side.

Notable Quote:
"In respect of civil rights, all citizens are equal before law. The humblest is the peer of the most powerful."

Honorable John Harlan, Associate Justice,
United States Supreme Court,
dissenting, Plessy v. Ferguson, 163 U.S. 537, at 559 (1896).

Acknowledgments

Many people have supported me in my writing pursuits, but none more than Helene Schulz. She edited the stories found herein, as she did in my first book, "Under the Panther Moon." She has also assisted me with various columns and guest editorials that I've submitted for consideration. She's done all of this for free, and I'm not the only person she has helped. Countless others have benefited from her tutelage, and she's received nothing more than the satisfaction of knowing she has been of service. She's meant so much to me professionally that the day she quits editing my work may be the day I quit writing. Thank you, again, Helene, for all you've done for me.

The Honorable Cecelia M. Moore is a friend and retired circuit court judge. She volunteered her time to read every story with an eye towards accuracy of the law and judicial process. I have little trial experience, so it was comforting to have Celie's oversight as I was writing this book. She encouraged me when I needed it and corrected me when I required it, helping to bring this project in for a smooth landing.

My father, Richard Dantzler, read an early draft and caught many inaccruacies and errors. Thanks, Dad, for your help with this and in so many others things.

The final editor of all my work is Julie, my wife. She makes sure I don't embarrass myself or write things I shouldn't. After 22 years of marriage, I've learned to trust her instincts.

Paul Schulz' artwork brings a wonderful dimension to the book. This isn't the first project we've worked on together, however. He provided the artwork for "Under the Panther Moon," and turned that compilation of stories into a beautiful "coffee table book." He's done the same thing with this writing, and I am grateful. He also gave the stories a good review towards the end of the writing process, and his keen mind caught many poorly structured sentences and grammatical mistakes. "Don't end the sentence with a preposition!" he wrote more than once in the margins. Thanks also to Paul's wife, Carole Ann, who kept a backup copy of the book updated on her computer.

Debbie Gorsuch at Crown Printing in Lakeland, Florida organized and formatted the book, preparing it for the manufacturer. She did a great job, and suffered through my taking over her computer for hours at a time as I made changes. I also want to thank Mark Rust, owner of Crown Printing, for allowing me this accomodation.

Keith Donnelly of Maple-Vail Book Manufacturing Group guided me through the book manufacturing process for both of my books. I'm afraid I've worn him out at times with quotes, but that's what happens when one is on a limited budget. He was patient and professional through it all.

Last but not least, I'd like to thank the fine lawyers at Frost Tamayo Sessums & Aranda, P.A., especially John Frost, for allowing me to work on several major civic endeavors at the expense of time spent in the office, and for supporting me while I ran for governor and then lieutenant governor of Florida. I've tried to capture that spirit of public service in both of my books.

Notable Quote:

"Progress generally begins in skepticism about accepted truths. Intellectual freedom means the right to re-examine much that has been long taken for granted. A free man must be a reasoning man, and he must dare to doubt what a legislative or electoral majority may most passionately assert. The danger that citizens will think wrongly is serious, but less dangerous than atrophy from not thinking at all. Our Constitution relies on our electorate's complete ideological freedom to nourish independent and responsible intelligence and preserve our democracy from that submissiveness, timidity and herd-mindedness of the masses which would foster a tyranny of mediocrity. The priceless heritage of our society is the unrestricted constitutional right of each member to think as he will. Thought control is a copyright of totalitarianism, and we have no claim to it. It is not the function of our Government to keep the citizen from falling into error; it is the function of the citizen to keep the Government from falling into error. We could justify any censorship only when the censors are better shielded against error than the censored."

Honorable Robert H. Jackson, Associate Justice,
United States Supreme Court, concurring and dissenting, each in part,
American Communications Association v. Douds, 339 U.S. 382, at 442, 443 (1950).

INTRODUCTION

To better understand the legal issues presented in the book, it is helpful to have a basic understanding of our constitutional form of government, the law and the courts. The following is a summary that will provide context to many of the stories contained herein.

Law is driven by constitutional principles. The Constitution of the United States of America is the supreme law of our land; nothing may conflict with it. To understand the theories behind the Constitution, it is important to recall the circumstances of its writing.

The nation's independence had only recently been won from England in the Revolutionary War of 1776. The primary reason for the Americans seeking independence was to escape the oppression of Great Britain's iron-fisted central government. The precipitating event for the war came when England imposed a new tax on tea, giving rise to the Boston Tea Party.

The memory of the strong central government of Great Britain was fresh in the minds of the Founding Fathers when they wrote the Constitution. Therefore, the first constitution, the "Articles of Confederation," granted virtually no power to the federal government and almost unlimited power to the states. Soon the Fathers recognized that the document was inadequate to govern an emerging nation like the United States, so it was scrapped, and the current constitution was written to take its place. The goal was to fashion a federal government strong enough to coalesce the states and provide enough central control for matters like security and commerce, but weak enough not to overwhelm the states and cause them to lose their sovereignty. Consequently, the new constitution expanded the power of the federal government, but limited that power only to the powers specifically authorized by the document itself.

But who would decide if an action taken by the federal government was authorized? The Constitution didn't specifically answer that question, but it was decided nonetheless early in the nation's history, in the year 1803, in the case of Marbury v. Madison, 5 U.S. 137 (1803). The United States Supreme Court, with Chief Justice John Marshall writing for the majority, established the doctrine of "judicial review," a process whereby the Court would review acts of government for the purpose of determining their constitutionality. The Court in <u>Marbury</u> concluded that the Constitution was law, and that it was the power of the Supreme Court to determine what the law was. Consequently, it was the Supreme Court that would determine the constitutionality of actions of the other branches of the federal government. Subsequent Marshall Court cases established that the Supreme Court could review state acts.

<u>Marbury</u> is widely recognized as the most important court case in the nation's history. By establishing that the judiciary would decide if the actions of legislative and executive branch officials were constitutional, the Court ensured that legislators and administrators could not operate with disregard for the Constitution, and that the Constitution would be the supreme law of the land. That is, statutes and executive branch actions could not supersede the Constitution.

This was not a popular decision, at least at first. Members of Congress and the president didn't like the idea of the Court second-guessing their decisions. Indeed, over the years the doctrine of judicial review has been scorned by many because it has served as the basis for the Court overturning many laws involving sensitive subjects (like abortion). Nevertheless, rightly or wrongly, the doctrine allowed the Court to create parameters within which legislative bodies and the executive branch had to operate.

Critics of judicial review have said that it has led to untoward "judicial activism" where judges stray from a strict interpretation of the Constitution to essentially "legislate from the bench" by either declaring legislative acts unconstitutional or by declaring laws unconstitutional and then substituting policies in their place that they deem constitutional. Those who oppose this kind of judicial activity are known as "strict constructionists." They believe the words of the Constitution should be given their literal meaning, consistent with the context of the times when they were written by the Founding Fathers. Furthermore, they believe that, however meritorious or virtuous the Court's decision in a case may be, it is not the Court's place to second-guess lawmakers. Their view is that setting policy is solely a legislative function. Legislators stand for election, so if the people disagree with what they've done, they can elect new legislators. It is a way for the voters to stay in charge. Strict constructionists believe that a judge is constrained by the original meaning of the words in the Constitution, and that unless a law conflicts with this understanding it should not be declared unconstitutional.

Those who support "judicial activism" believe the Constitution is a "living document," and that it must be flexible to keep up with the times. They believe that, because it was impossible for the Founding Fathers to anticipate the future needs of the country, concepts like due process and equal protection must be flexible so that new interpretations are possible. They assert that majorities can suppress minorities, so the judiciary must guard against what has been described as the "tyranny of the majority." They contend that a judge must be free to factor in context when deciding cases, and that a judge must not be so constrained by the literal meaning of the words of the Constitution that justice towards individuals suffers or the welfare of society as a whole is damaged.

Nevertheless, how is the Constitution of the United States structured, and whom does it affect? Like all good constitutions, it is short and doesn't establish policies. Instead, it focuses on matters of governance and governmental behavior. For example, Article I creates the legislative branch (a Senate and a House of Representatives), outlines the governance of each, and spells out the powers of the Congress. Article II creates the executive branch, vesting power in the president and vice president and saying how they are to be elected. Their duties and powers are detailed, as well. Article III creates the judicial branch, requiring a Supreme Court and allowing lower-level courts as the Congress shall establish. For the purposes of this book, the other federal constitutional provisions worth noting are the first ten amendments and Amendment Fourteen.

The first 10 amendments are known as the "Bill of Rights." They are *restrictions* on the *federal* government. As mentioned earlier, the Founding Fathers wanted to guard against the federal government becoming too powerful relative to the states. They also wanted to prevent the federal government from having the potential to terrorize citizens. Therefore, they built restrictions on the federal government into the Constitution. It is in these amendments that are found the freedoms most essential to self-governance and liberty.

The Bill of Rights gives Americans religious freedom, free speech, a free press, the right to peaceably assemble, and the right to petition the government for a redress of grievances. It allows us to keep and bear arms, to be secure in our homes and to be free of unreasonable searches and seizures. We can be tried only once for the same offense and cannot be required to incriminate ourselves. Americans cannot be deprived of life, liberty or property without due process, nor may private property be taken for public use without just compensation. If charged with a crime, we are guaranteed a speedy public trial by a jury, the right to confront our accusers, and the assistance of counsel. Bail may not be excessive. If convicted, the fines may not be excessive, and punishment may not be cruel and unusual.

The Tenth Amendment is known as the "States' Rights Amendment." It gives to the states (or to the people) every power not delegated to the federal government by the Constitution, so long as the Constitution does not prohibit the power from going to the states. This is why state law more often affects the citizenry than federal law. Criminal cases, traffic infractions, civil lawsuits, divorces, wills, probate…these and other areas of the law are most always governed by state statutes.

To repeat, the first 10 amendments were restrictions on the *federal* government; they did not apply to state or local governments. Early in the history of the United States, if a state legislature passed a law restricting speech, for example, the Supreme Court couldn't declare it unconstitutional even though it clearly violated the Free Speech Clause of the First Amendment in the Bill of Rights. Then in 1868 the Fourteenth Amendment to the Constitution was ratified. Section 1 of that amendment states: "…nor shall any State deprive any person of life, liberty, or property, without due process of law; nor deny to any person within its jurisdiction the equal protection of the laws." Over the years, the Supreme Court used these words to make the most important protections of the Bill of Rights – the ones most important to liberty – applicable to state and local government. Using the example above, the Court could now strike down a state law that violated the Free Speech Clause of the First Amendment. Of course, this required a little creativity, a little "judicial activism" if you will, but it's a good example of how the Court gives new meaning to the Constitution in order to address issues and create change.

Few people today would disagree with these instances of "judicial activism," but the Court also used these words to declare many laws in sensitive areas unconstitutional. State laws restricting abortion and contraception, for instance, were stricken using this methodology, and this

Amendment – and these words – are still used in many civil rights cases, like those involving the care of prisoners and the legality of same-sex marriage. The Fourteenth Amendment has been used by the Court more often than any other amendment to address social issues and bring about social change.

If judges have so much power, how are they kept in check? What remedy do the people have if a judge usurps his or her authority?

In Florida, trial court judges are elected, although in the year 2000 the state constitution was changed to allow a judicial circuit to convert to a system of merit retention instead of election. Merit retention means that a judge does not stand for election in the sense that a candidate may run against a sitting judge. Instead, the judge's name appears on the ballot and she must receive a favorable vote by a majority of the voters to stay on the bench.

The governor appoints appellate court and Supreme Court judges, as well as circuit court and county court judges when there are vacancies. When new judgeships are created, some are filled by appointment and some by election. Whenever the governor appoints a judge, the appointment must come from a list of three to six names given to him by the Judicial Nominating Commission, a committee of lawyers and lay people who first interview the applicants to determine their suitability and qualifications for the office. Appellate court and Supreme Court judges are subject to merit retention.

All judges in Florida must retire at the age of 70, so there is constant turnover. Judges may be removed from office by a process involving the Judicial Qualifications Committee, a committee of lawyers and lay people and other judges, and the Supreme Court. The budgets of the courts are determined by the Legislature, as well, so if legislators determine that judges have gotten too far out of line there are ways for legislators to get the attention of the judiciary.

Still, the power of the people, legislatures, governors and presidents over judges is not absolute, but that is by design. A healthy amount of judicial independence is critical to our country's wellbeing. If judges are subject to too much political influence, their ability to stand up to an overbearing legislature, governor, Congress or president could be compromised.

The federal court system is similar to Florida's in that there are trial courts, appellate courts and a Supreme Court. But there are differences. The president appoints all federal judges, and they are subject to Senate confirmation. The most striking difference is federal judges are appointed for life; there is no mandatory retirement age. Only by impeachment by the United States House of Representatives may federal judges be removed from office.

How are the courts organized? In Florida, there are 20 judicial circuits. Each circuit has county court judges and circuit court judges. County court judges handle smaller cases, circuit court judges larger ones. County and circuit court is known as "trial court," and it is here that trials are held and where all judicial actions start. Trial courts establish facts and the official records of cases.

A decision of the county or circuit court may be appealed. Appeals from county court are conducted by the circuit court. Appeals from circuit court go to one of five of Florida's appellate courts, known as District Courts of Appeal. However, appeals in death penalty cases and certain other enumerated matters go directly to the Florida Supreme Court. Appellate courts review cases to determine if the law was properly applied to the facts. Appellate courts don't establish new facts, but, instead, take the record of the case as established by the trial courts.

Everyone is entitled to one appeal. Beyond that, appeals are made under a "Writ of Certiorari," a mechanism in which the Court exercises its discretionary jurisdiction to accept cases.

In addition to following the law, courts follow precedent, a practice known as "stare decisis." That is, lower courts are bound by the decisions of higher courts. However, the appellate court in one part of the state may decide a similar matter differently than the appellate court in another part of the state. When that happens, sooner or later the Supreme Court will take a case that involves the issue that has been decided differently by the appellate courts and resolve it, and that becomes the law statewide. Until that happens, each judicial circuit abides by the decision of its appellate court.

The process is similar for the federal courts in that there are trial courts and appellate courts. However, the subject matter is different. Federal courts take cases involving federal law, or cases where a state law conflicts with a federal law. The United States Supreme Court has jurisdiction over all appeals from the federal courts of appeal. If there are conflicts between different federal appellate courts, the United States Supreme Court will take jurisdiction and make a decision and that settles it for the entire country.

The United States Supreme Court has Writ of Certiorari jurisdiction over other cases, too. It may elect to hear appeals from the highest state courts where the constitutionality of a federal or state law is at issue, or where a state law is alleged to violate federal law.

Federal law trumps state law. If a state constitutional provision or statute is inconsistent with a federal constitutional provision or statute, federal law prevails.

If the Constitution is largely a limitation on the federal government, why do we read of Congress passing laws that affect so many subject matters? It is true that the federal government is restricted to passing laws only in the subject matters authorized by the Constitution, but there are several clauses in Article I, Section 8 that are very broad. It is here that Congress is given the authority to tax, "provide for the common defense," to regulate commerce among the states, and to make all laws "necessary and proper" to execute the foregoing powers. These are not the only powers granted in Section 8, but they are the ones that have been broadly construed by the courts.

There are four kinds of law: constitutional law, statutory law, case law, and administrative law. Constitutional law is that which is derived from the Constitution, either federal or state (states have constitutions too). Statutory law is law passed by a legislative body like Congress or the state legislature. County commissions and city councils adopt ordinances and codes. Case law is the body of court decisions that creates precedent. It is used to predict how courts will rule in a given situation. Administrative law is promulgated by executive branch agencies to implement legislative directives. These laws are called "rules." Executive branch agencies don't have the authority to pass rules that aren't authorized by the legislative branch. Rules are usually much more detailed than the statutes that provide the authority for the rule.

Overseeing all of this, of course, is the judiciary, adding the third leg of our government's three-legged stool. The legislative branch passes the law, the executive branch administers it, and the judicial branch interprets it. This forms the heart of a concept known as "checks and balances." Each branch operates as a check and balance on the other two. These checks and balances prevent huge policy swings, creating relative stability in society, and it is here that the true genius of the Founding Fathers is manifested. None of the three branches is allowed to get too strong. Each branch has ways to slow things down, or correct an errant governmental body or arrogant public official.

By its very nature the system of checks and balances is inefficient, but that is by design. Having three branches of government stirring the same pot of stew can make the implementation of policy frustratingly slow, but it is important to remember what is at stake. Laws are infringements on liberty. They prescribe behavior, either allowing or preventing persons from doing activities. When a legislative body meets and laws are passed we usually become slightly less free. With stakes this high, having three bites at the apple is a good thing, but it works only if all three branches have the authority to perform their role. If one were to become neutered, the model would break down, and that is why it is important to keep each branch strong.

The system of checks and balances can be exasperating. When the judiciary declares an act of the Legislature unconstitutional, it sometimes angers legislators, but it shouldn't. In fact, they should be thankful that an independent judiciary – with power – is there to act as a backstop. We should trust the model; the Founding Fathers knew what they were doing when they created it.

Notable Quotes:

"Those in power need checks and restraints lest they come to identify the common good for their own tastes and desires, and their continuation in office as essential to the preservation of the nation."

Honorable William O. Douglas, Associate Justice,
United States Supreme Court.

"Between these alternatives there is no middle ground. <u>The constitution is either a superior, paramount law, unchangeable by ordinary means, or it is on a level with ordinary legislative acts, and like other acts, is alterable when the legislature shall please to alter it.</u>

If the former part of the alternative be true, then a legislative act contrary to the constitution is not law: if the latter part be true, then written constitutions are absurd attempts, on the part of the people, to limit a power in its own nature illimitable.

Certainly all those who have framed written constitutions contemplate them as forming the fundamental and paramount law of the nation, and consequently the theory of every such government must be, that an act of the legislature repugnant to the constitution is void.

This theory is essentially attached to a written constitution, and is consequently to be considered by this court as one of the fundamental principles of our society. It is not therefore to be lost sight of in the further consideration of this subject.

If an act of the legislature, repugnant to the constitution, is void, does it, notwithstanding its invalidity, bind the courts and oblige them to give it effect? Or, in other words, though it be not law, does it constitute a rule as operative as if it was a law? This would be to overthrow in fact what was established in theory; and would seem, at first view, an absurdity too gross to be insisted on. It shall, however, receive a more attentive consideration.

<u>*It is emphatically the province and duty of the judicial department to say what the law is*</u>*. Those who apply the rule to particular cases, must of necessity expound and interpret that rule. If two laws conflict with each other, the courts must decide on the operation of each.*

So if a law be in opposition to the constitution: if both the law and the constitution apply to a particular case, so that the court must either decide that case conformably to the law, disregarding the constitution; or conformably to the constitution, disregarding the law: the court must determine which of these conflicting rules governs the case. <u>This is of the very essence of judicial duty</u>."

Marbury v. Madison, 5 U.S. 137, 177-178 (1803) (Emphasis added).

TABLE OF CONTENTS

Notable Quote:

"The very purpose of the Bill of Rights was to withdraw certain subjects from the vicissitudes of political controversy, to place them beyond the reach of majorities and officials and to establish them as legal principles to be applied by the courts. One's right to life, liberty and property, to free speech, a free press, freedom of worship and assembly, and other fundamental rights may not be submitted to vote; they depend on the outcome of no elections."

Supreme Court Justice Robert H. Jackson,
West Virginia Board of Education v. Barnette, 1943.

FOREWORD

The law is of noble purpose. It is the great equalizer, the glue that holds together our republic, and its fair administration the difference between civility and anarchy.

Devotion to the ideals of law makes us high-minded and raises our commitment to equality. It gives us a sense of place among God's order in the natural world, making us better stewards of the land and helping us see more clearly our responsibilities and obligations. It helps us be a better neighbor.

Justice Oliver Wendell Holmes said, "A law embodies beliefs that have triumphed in the battle of ideas."[1] Inherent in a law's passage in the legislative arena and implementation in the executive branch are political considerations. Overseeing this process, though, operating as a check and balance, ensuring that the ambitions and egos of Man don't override the Constitution, is the judiciary. The United States of America is governed by the rule of law, and it is the judiciary that preserves the environment for democratic self-governance.

I've worked in the law my entire professional career, first as a member of the Florida House of Representatives, then as a member of the Florida Senate, and now as a private sector attorney. In these capacities I've had the chance to work with some of the most talented lawyers in Florida, and my hat is off to them. Attorneys lead tough, demanding, and pressure-filled lives, but without them chaos and vigilante justice would be the rule instead of the exception.

I've also gotten to know many judges and Supreme Court justices. Make no mistake about it – they are among the most important officials in government. Unlike a legislator who works as part of a legislative body, thereby minimizing the possibility of a single person's mistake hurting someone, a judge often acts alone, and a poor decision can ruin lives. The judges and justices I've known take their jobs seriously and are committed to justice.

I say this to state clearly that a goal with this book is to exalt attorneys and judges. I enjoy a good lawyer joke as much as anyone, but I also recognize the critical role they play in our society and salute the attorneys who strive to serve their clients well. And anyone who has ever stood before a judge knows the awesome power judges possess. The legal right to take away one's liberty and to even impose death is as much power as one can have. Thank goodness the vast majority of judges and justices understand the responsibility that goes along with their authority.

Another goal with this book is to teach the basic principles of law in areas that the readers will find interesting. I've only hit a few of the main points, but it's enough to provide a sense of the law in that particular area. A word of caution, however. The law changes frequently and is often different from state to state. What is "good" law today may not be good law tomorrow, and what is good law in one state may be totally incorrect in another.

Finally, the overriding purpose of the book is to explain how important it is to our country that we preserve an independent judiciary. Contrary to what many assert, an independent judiciary doesn't mean that a judge is free to do what he or she wants. As Justice Anthony N. Kennedy said, "...the connotation sometimes comes out as judicial independence so the judge can do what he wants. It is just the opposite. Judicial independence exists so that a judge can do what he *has* to do or what she *must* do."[2]

If I have failed in these goals I hope you will use the stories' shortcomings as cause for your own independent study. They are but a teaser of the vast body of law that exists, and a modest attempt at portraying the great importance of the judicial branch of government.

[1] "The Supreme Court in American History," by Marjorie G. Fribourg (1965).

[2] Honorable Anthony N. Kennedy, Associate Justice, Supreme Court of the United States, 2005 Florida Bar Annual Meeting, General Assembly, June 25, 2005.

Notable Quote:

"The law, in its majestic equality, forbids the rich as well as the poor to sleep under bridges, to beg in the streets, and to steal bread."

Anatole France (Jacques Anatole Francois Thibault),
"The Red Lily," (1894). www.quotegarden.com

DISCLAIMER

The law as described in these stories is stated in general terms. Legal theories have been simplified to fit the format of the book. Do not rely on the law as represented herein as a guide for any actual legal situation. Consult your own attorney for legal advice. This book is a work of fiction.

Notable Quote:

"As nightfall does not come at once, neither does oppression. In both instances, there's a twilight where everything remains seemingly unchanged, and it is in such twilight that we must be aware of change in the air, however slight, lest we become unwitting victims of the darkness."

Honorable William O. Douglas, Associate Justice,
Supreme Court of the United States.
www.brainyquotes.com

Chain of Lakes Sunset
Winter Haven, Florida

MALCOLM TITTLEBAUM
The Intent to Commit Crime: Mens Rea

Preface: In common law, one had to have "mens rea," the Latin word for "criminal intent," in order to be guilty of a crime. That is, one had to intend to commit the crime in order for the action to be deemed criminal. However, the law has evolved to impute intent as a way of holding persons responsible for certain acts, like getting drunk and then getting behind the wheel of a car. If a drunk driver injures someone while driving, he can be held criminally liable even though he didn't consciously intend to hurt the victim.

MALCOLM TITTLEBAUM grew up in Umatilla, Florida. With two brothers, a sister and wonderful parents, he had an idyllic upbringing. He played football, basketball or baseball, whatever was in season, fished on the Harris chain-of-lakes and hunted in the Ocala National Forest.

He was a gifted athlete, identified at the age of 10 by his hometown's high school football coach as one possessing unique talent. The coach began working with him at that young age, teaching him to keep his arm high when throwing a football to keep the pass above the arms of the rushers, and showing young Malcolm arm-strengthening exercises to maximize throwing distance. He taught Malcolm to see the entire defense when he came to the line of scrimmage so that he would know which receivers were more likely to be open. This early training slowly inched Malcolm in the direction of football over the other sports, and it was there that he would focus.

Malcolm loved his name and thought that the first part of his last name – Tittle – must have been an omen that he would follow in the footsteps of the great New York Giants quarterback, Y.A. Tittle. Indeed, everything about his life in football indicated that he was headed in that direction. At the age of 12 he began attending the best quarterback camps in the country each summer. Not only did this develop his physical ability, but it also put him on the radar screen for colleges and universities all over America because of the great number of coaches who visited the camps. By the time he graduated from high school, he had enough offers for scholarships to pick the one that offered him the best opportunity to distinguish himself, the school that would give him a starting position and the kind of offense that catered to his fantastic passing ability.

That college turned out to be Alabama Colonial University, an institution rich with tradition bestowed upon it by the late legendary coach, Roger "Bear" Ridley, and flush with excitement over a new head coach, T.E. "Booger" McClure, who promised an offense that would emphasize the pass over the run. Malcolm had a good feeling about the Colonial Red Riders, and was convinced it was the perfect school for him. Colonial alumni were ecstatic about Malcolm's decision. With him leading the team's talented corps of receivers, Malcolm rode into Birmingham as the one who would take the Red Riders back to their former glory.

From the very beginning it was obvious that Malcolm would deliver. In his first year he led the team to a conference championship. Sportswriters all across the country commented that they had never seen a freshman with so much poise. Malcolm's ability to read defenses and make good decisions on the field was unprecedented for someone so young. He had the world by the tail. His walks across campus from class to class drew stares and autograph seekers. They also drew beautiful co-eds, and before he knew it he was doing things he had been taught were to be left for later.

He pledged a fraternity and the fun continued. He made friends, and life was good. Friday afternoon basketball games at the frat house were played to music blaring from huge speakers set outside. This usually led to beer parties that would go late into the evening. The fraternity's little sisters were always there and sometimes an entire sorority was invited over. "Man, this is fun," Malcolm thought.

Over the course of that first year, these beer parties sometimes turned into a time for drug use for a few of Malcolm's fraternity brothers. Drugs had always been a temptation he had been able to resist, but the freedom of college, the music, and the stardom he was enjoying made them very alluring, a natural progression he thought, so he tried them. First it was marijuana, then ecstasy, and finally cocaine. He liked their effects but wasn't worried. He was using them only recreationally, and they weren't interfering with football.

Summer arrived, and the players were given a rigorous training schedule for their time away from the university. Malcolm worked hard, and it was good being home with his family. His father had been very demanding when Malcolm was growing up, but now that Malcolm was in college and doing well, he had chilled out a lot. Malcolm was especially close with his mother, and they sat on the porch most every day that summer visiting. Soon Malcolm began thinking of the fun he was missing at school, though, so he returned to Birmingham earlier than required.

Football took up most of his time, of course, but he still made it over to the fraternity house for much of "rush week," that time when new recruits were coming through hoping for a "bid," or offer, to join the fraternity. Some students were just coming through for the parties, but that didn't matter. Everyone was having a good time, and for a solid week it was beer, music and girls until nearly midnight each day.

Except for a team meeting on Wednesday evening, Malcolm was at the frat house every night, not until midnight because that would have violated curfew, but he made it over to enjoy his share of beers. Though he stayed away from the drugs because the players were subject to random drug tests during the season, Malcolm found himself thinking of them more and more.

Malcolm had another great season at quarterback. Over the last year his body had fully developed, and his speed and arm strength had never been better. He had all the physical tools of the trade, and was quickly developing the mental prowess required to be a top quarterback.

As good as his year had been for him personally, it had been even better for the team. Not only did they repeat as conference champions, but they also went to the national championship bowl game. Even though they lost to the hard-running Nebraska Cornshuckers, the spirit of "Bear" Ridley had returned. The athletic program's financial supporters were giving at record levels and Colonial football was back. In just two years, Coach McClure had turned the team into a national powerhouse, largely due to the stellar play of Malcolm Tittlebaum.

With this fame and notoriety came near celebrity status for Malcolm. He appeared on all the weekend sports shows and was a sure pick for pre-season All-American the next year. Many were even predicting he would win the Heisman Trophy, the award recognizing the most outstanding college football player, becoming one of only a few non-seniors to be awarded such an honor.

His fraternity brothers treated him like royalty. Many of the brothers' families owned huge tracts of land in the Black Delta region of Alabama, a place with rich dark soil that grew monster-sized whitetail deer, so he was taken to some of the best hunting spots in America. Fishing along the coast and quail hunting in fancy lodges were other sporting opportunities made available to him.

And then there were the drugs. Not many of his fraternity brothers indulged, only a couple actually, but the drugs were always there for him. Malcolm knew in which rooms to find them, and it bestowed status on the parties for him to be with the few brothers and their dates who were getting high.

Imperceptibly to him, Malcolm began gravitating towards these rooms and these brothers. At the Friday evening parties he would find his way there and rarely come out until it was time to return to his dorm where the athletes stayed.

These nights of partying made for difficult Saturday mornings, but the players had Saturdays off so he had the entire day to recover. He wasn't the only player doing drugs, either. Almost subconsciously, he found these players and they found him. He often brought them with him to the fraternity house to the great delight of the brothers who were having the drug parties. These additional athletes attracted more women to the brothers' rooms, and this enhanced their status, or so they thought.

With more people learning of Malcolm's drug use, it was only a matter of time before word got back to Coach McClure. The coach didn't believe it at first, but the more he thought about it, the more he realized that he had seen a change in Malcolm. He hadn't been as committed to his weight lifting and fitness program as he had been, and he was spending less time in the film room watching game films of the opposing teams. Malcolm's grades had also begun to slide. If Malcolm were doing drugs, McClure knew it would be better to find out earlier instead of later, so he called Malcolm into his office.

"Son, you've got a great future in football if you want it," he began.

"Of course I want it, Coach. I always have. It's what I've been working towards for all these years," responded Malcolm, a bit confused by the coach's statement.

"You have it all – speed, great arm, quick-thinking mind. I've never been around anyone who I was so sure would make it to the pros," Coach McClure continued. "Not everyone makes it to the next level, though. Few do, really, but that's not what coaching is about for me; it can't be when I see so many players come and go. I'm trying to make good men with my football program, people who will become credits to their communities. In the end, that's what's most important."

Malcolm knew that something was up, but he also knew not to interrupt.

"Some of my players haven't done well, however. A few are in prison, and a few are even living on the street. It breaks my heart because I care a lot more about them as a person than I ever did as a football player. I coach them to play football, but I teach them how to live."

"Coach, why…"

"I'm not through, Malcolm.

"Most of my players who haven't done well began believing they were bulletproof, that nothing could hurt them. They thought they were invisible, that no one was seeing them when they were behaving as they shouldn't. They ran around with loose women, drank, a few even did drugs. Stardom is an interesting thing, an interesting thing indeed."

At this point he stopped and stared straight at Malcolm. Silence. He kept staring and didn't say another word. Malcolm's upper lip began to sweat and his hands began to tremble.

"Coach, I don't know why you're telling me this," Malcolm stammered, looking down. "I'm playing well and making decent grades. I don't get it."

Coach McClure continued to stare, not saying a word. The silence was deafening.

Malcolm had to move so he got out of his chair and paced around the room. Coach McClure said nothing, but when Malcolm moved towards the door, he broke his silence.

"Pee in the cup."

"What?"

"Pee in the cup," McClure repeated, pointing to a white plastic cup on the corner of his desk.

"Coach, you don't think…no! No way I've been doing drugs."

"Pee in the cup," Coach McClure said more forcefully.

"Coach, I haven't been doing drugs."

"Then you shouldn't mind subjecting yourself to a urine test."

"No. I won't do it. It's not football season so I don't have to."

"You do if you want to play for me. Now pee in the cup."

By forcing a drug test, Coach McClure knew he was running the risk of losing his best chance for a national title. Without Malcolm, the hopes of the Red Riders would be dashed. He knew also that Malcolm would have no problem signing with another team, so he just might leave, even if he had to "redshirt," or sit out for a year. His stock would be as high as ever. He could even choose to go pro. If he did, Malcolm would surely go in the first round of the draft and sign for millions, assuming, of course, that he didn't have a drug problem.

"Malcolm, I have it on good authority that you've been doing drugs and you know my policy. I will not make exceptions. If you have done drugs, you will sit out from football for three months. You will also participate in a short-term drug treatment program to analyze the extent of your problem, if you have one. If you do, you will drop out of school during the time required for treatment. After treatment, if you have been successful, you will be re-admitted to this university and allowed back onto the football team. But unless you do these things, you'll be through for good, at least for as long as I'm the coach. Now what's it going to be?"

Malcolm knew he was busted. The urine test would surely prove that he had been taking multiple illegal drugs. He quickly did the math in his head, figuring the time he would be out and how much of his third year he would miss. Not much, really – only Spring Practice. He'd be back in time for the regular season, but it would expose him to his fans as one who used illegal substances, and a few people would even believe he was a dope addict. Would they still love him, or would they think of him as no different than the countless drug users found on the streets of any inner city in America? But of course he was not like them, or so he thought. He was the starting quarterback of a major university, and one who could play with the best of them. His drug use was only recreational and he could stop whenever he wanted. No, he couldn't take the chance that he would be lumped together with the hopeless souls who were living from one score to the next. That would knock him off the pedestal he saw himself on. He couldn't risk the loss of the status he now enjoyed.

He also didn't believe Coach McClure would actually kick him off the team for not taking the urine test; too much was riding on his play for him not to be given some accommodation. Perhaps the coach would ask for the test in a month and he would stay clean, allowing the drugs to wash from his system. Or maybe he would drop the issue entirely.

"Sorry, Coach. I'm not peeing in the cup. We were told that random urine tests might be given during the season and here you are asking me to subject myself to one during the off-season. I won't do it. It's a matter of principle."

"It's not a matter of principle, Malcolm, and you know it. And for the record, you were not told that random tests would not be given during other times of the year, just that they might be given during the season. That really doesn't matter, though. What matters is you were told that illegal drug use was not allowed – period, and no exceptions.

"Look, Malcolm, if you have used drugs and you cooperate, I'll see that you are back as soon as possible and spin it so the media doesn't blow the story out of proportion. We can make your pro-active treatment appear heroic because it would be, and your stock would rise. But I will not ignore this matter, and I won't make exceptions for you, no matter what it may cost the team. Letting you off this time wouldn't be in the team's best long-term interest, and, believe it or not, it wouldn't be in your interest, either. Now what's it going to be?"

"Coach, you need me. Can't we work something out?"

"The only thing we can work out is what we have already discussed."

Malcolm's mind was racing now. Coach McClure seemed serious but how could he be? He had to be bluffing. Surely he would cave in and the two of them could reach some accommodation.

"In that case, I'll go pro, or transfer, but I won't take the drug test."

"You're making a big mistake, Malcolm. You have an incredibly bright future, but now you're running the risk of throwing it away."

"No I'm not. The college teams that wanted me before will want me again, or I may just declare myself eligible for the draft and see what happens. That could even turn out to be better. If I stick around here, I run the risk of breaking a leg or incurring some other injury, and that would hurt me with NFL teams. It could cost me millions. I'll take my chances."

"Okay, Malcolm. The choice is yours and you've made it. In three days, at 10:00 a.m., I'll have a press conference announcing that you are no longer with the team. I won't give specifics; I'll just cite disciplinary reasons. There will be plenty of questions, and word will somehow leak out as it always does, but that will give you three days to announce your intentions to transfer or go pro. It also gives you three days to reconsider, which I hope you do because that's the best choice.

"You are at a crossroads in your life, son. Don't worry about what others might think. Put your ego aside and deal with this problem. Your resistance suggests to me that the problem is greater than you think. If you don't do it now, sooner or later you will have to. This won't go away on its own."

"You're wrong, Coach. Even if I have been doing drugs it's not a huge deal; it's only a recreational thing. I can stop whenever I want." Then he walked out of the office and closed the door behind him.

The day before Coach McClure was to have his press conference, Malcolm Tittlebaum declared himself eligible for the NFL draft. Word of the announcement spread like wildfire. Angry financial supporters called the athletic department wanting to know what steps Booger McClure had taken to try to keep their star quarterback from leaving the university. Because of his commitment to Malcolm, he wouldn't say anything to defend himself, which fueled talk of replacing McClure. One influential booster in particular, Jerry Wingo, even started a website called www.FireMcClure.com. Wingo was a football alumnus, having played at Colonial 20 years before, and had a daughter there who was a cheerleader, so he was Red Rider through and through.

Malcolm's walks across campus now drew angry stares instead of looks of admiration. Occasionally a student would shout "Traitor!" or "Money monger!" This unnerved Tittlebaum, and caused him to hustle to the safety of the classroom.

He was also surprised at the reaction of some of his fraternity brothers who had loved having him in their rooms for drug parties. He became "persona non grata," no longer wanted and essentially ignored. No longer treated like a celebrity, he had lost his refuge.

These were his friends, fraternity brothers no less. How could they be so fickle? Before his big announcement he was the hit of their parties. Now he was just another body in the room trying to get high for free. This disoriented him even more.

Other brothers continued to treat him well and didn't question his motives for going pro. They accepted him at face value and looked beyond whatever problems he might have. They remained his friends.

But no matter how he tried, he didn't feel like he fit in any more. Being an ordinary guy was difficult for him. He didn't think he said the right things or acted the right way. He felt out of place.

He was also bored. There wasn't much excitement to a life without celebrity status. Instead, he felt a desire deep in his gut for the high he got from drugs. The pull wasn't strong at first, but it was there.

His scholarship would last until the end of the semester so he could still stay in the athletic dorm. It was very awkward being with the other players, but what else was he to do? It didn't make sense for him to drop out immediately and not get the class credits.

Several weeks after announcing his intention to turn pro, on a Friday afternoon, he wandered towards the fraternity house for some basketball and maybe a late-night party. Just before getting there, however, he thought of how the druggie brothers treated him and how he didn't fit in with the others, so he veered around the house and headed towards a bar called "The Sixties."

There, several men drinking beer recognized him and called him over. They put their arms around his shoulders and bought him a drink. The rum and coke sure felt good going down, warming his chest and stomach. He settled in with these guys and soon had four drinks under his belt.

These men were scruffy looking and drunk, but they laughed a lot and told Malcolm how much they had enjoyed watching him play. They said they were sure he'd made the right decision to go pro and would soon make millions. It was the kind of talk and adoration he hadn't heard in nearly a month and he liked it, so when they asked him to step out into the back alley to smoke a joint, he agreed.

In the back alley there was a person who lived on the streets playing the blues on his old nylon-stringed guitar. Many years of a hard life showed on his face and skin. Unkempt hair stuck from beneath an old fedora, and his salt and pepper beard indicated he hadn't shaved in weeks. He lived on the streets, surviving on the generosity of passersby who tossed tips into the case of his weathered guitar.

"Willie Rebel's his name," one of the guys from the bar said. "He's nothing but an old drunk, but he sure can play that ax."

"I *am* a drunk, but I'm not an *old* drunk," Willie Rebel said. "I just look old. I'm really a middle-aged drunk!"

Everyone laughed at his joke, especially Willie.

"I wasn't always a drunk, though" he continued. "Used to be a football player. Real good one, too."

"Sure you did, Willie," a guy from the bar said. "And I used to fly Air Force One."

"I *did* play football. Wrote a song about it too. 'I'm on the 15-yard line. Give me the ball and you'll be mine'…"

Malcolm and his new friends eventually walked away laughing and shaking their heads, the words of Willie Rebel ringing in their ears.

When they reached a quiet spot, one of the men lit a joint and passed it around. Malcolm had not tasted marijuana in some time and it tasted good, especially on top of the rum and coke. The pungent smell enveloped him, and he felt the tension of the preceding month drifting away with the smoke.

"I don't know who you guys are, but I'm enjoying myself," he said.

"We're enjoying being with you, too," a man replied. "It's not every day that we get to party with a person like you."

"*A person like you,*" Malcolm repeated in his head. "That sounded good. *A person like you.*" Thoughts of stardom and celebrity status rushed in around him, and he thought of the world that was once so familiar. The booze and drugs were taking their full effect and he was conscious of swaying slightly, his eyes closed.

The night wore on. More alcohol and pot, until finally a goodbye to his new buddies. Malcolm was making his way across campus, focusing on walking in a straight line, laughing as he went. When he reached his dorm, he leaned against the wall with one arm and pushed the "Up" button of the elevator. When the door opened, staring directly at him, was Coach McClure.

Tittlebaum tried to compose himself. "Coach! You're up late!" He couldn't help but chuckle at what he thought was the cleverness of the reply.

"You are, too, Malcolm. I'll help you get into bed."

"Oh, you don't need to do that. I'm fine."

"No, I'll help you; I want to."

"Whatever suits you," Malcolm replied, bobbing a little as the elevator began moving.

They rode the elevator in silence. When the doors opened, Booger walked Malcolm to his room. Malcolm fumbled with the key and dropped it. "Fumble!" Malcolm called out, laughing at the joke. When he leaned over to pick it up he lost his balance and fell forward, hitting his head on the wall.

"Let me help you," Coach McClure said, picking up the key. He opened the door and led Malcolm to his bed. He took Malcolm's shoes off and turned to leave. When he got to the door he stopped and looked at his star player who was now fast asleep.

"What a pity," Coach McClure said to himself, as he closed the door.

The Sixties bar turned out to be a comforting spot to Malcolm. For the next several weeks he met his new friends there every Tuesday and Thursday night for partying. Alcohol, pot, even a Quaalude or two made for adventurous nights.

Malcolm had recently contracted with an agent to represent him in the NFL draft that would be held in three months. The agent had arranged several visits to teams for a tryout of sorts. There, he was given strength and speed tests and socialized with the coaches and a few of the players. Dinner at a fine restaurant was usually on the schedule and everyone noticed that Malcolm drank more than he should. They also noticed he left for the restroom occasionally and suspected that he was doing more than relieving himself. Malcolm Tittlebaum had discovered that cocaine made him even more entertaining than usual. What he didn't realize was that he was hurting his stock with each team he visited. Soon word spread that Malcolm Tittlebaum might have a drug problem.

During this same period, Coach McClure was in more hot water than ever with the Colonial alumni. Led by influential alumnus Jerry Wingo, creator of www.FireMcClure.com, Booger McClure was on the verge of getting lynched. His refusal to discuss Tittlebaum's departure frustrated the Red Rider faithful, and Wingo went on a tear about firing him. He began a media campaign complete with newspaper, radio and television ads calling for the dismissal of McClure. He was convinced that Tittlebaum was leaving because of a personality conflict with McClure, and that if McClure left, Tittlebaum would stay.

Malcolm made things worse by saying he and McClure hadn't seen eye to eye on a few things, adding speculation that it was McClure's fault, not Tittlebaum's, that Malcolm was leaving. Through it all, Booger McClure never said a derogatory or hurtful thing about Malcolm, and instead only wished him well in his new endeavor.

The day after Malcolm returned from his last visit, this time to the Green Bay Packers, he couldn't wait to get to The Sixties bar. It was March, and the weather in Green Bay had been cold with a late-season snow coming in while he was there. In Birmingham, it was a "Chamber of Commerce" spring day. The sky was blue and the air was warm. As he walked across campus he noted that the co-eds were wearing halter-tops, and smiled when he heard their charming southern accents.

Malcolm was pleased to find his two drinking buddies at the bar so early in the afternoon, and they were spellbound as they listened to him speak of the Green Bay Packers and lore of Vince Lombardi, Bart Starr and Lambeau Field.

The afternoon wore on, and Malcolm made a trip or two to the bathroom to do some drugs. He was flying high, happy that the draft was only a month away and sure that he would soon be rolling in the kind of money he had dreamed of since he was a boy.

By evening he was hungry and offered to take his two partners to dinner at Louie's, a fine restaurant with delicious Italian food. Never mind that his friends weren't dressed for anything fancy, he was Malcolm Tittlebaum, a soon-to-be millionaire, and his friends would be extended an allowance for their appearance.

The 10-minute walk across campus to get Malcolm's car was very telling of his condition. Malcolm's testosterone and machismo was running wide open, and he blatantly propositioned several young women who passed them. His friends laughed as the women walked away in disgust. Malcolm's next stunt was to drop down into a three-point football stance and hit a garbage can with his forearm as he came up, knocking it over. Again his friends laughed, and that egged him on even more.

When they left in Malcolm's Camaro, the car screeched off and fishtailed around the first turn. His friends were screaming now, not out of fear but out of the thrill of the ride, and Malcolm was pouring it on, enjoying every minute.

Their route took them by the football stadium. "You'll be sorry you asked me to pee in that cup, McClure!" Malcolm shouted out the window, laughing. He was having a blast now, and his friends loved it.

Passing the stadium, they neared a vacant field used for cheerleader practice and fraternity intramural sports. It was that time between dusk and dark when visibility was poor. Malcolm was glancing at the stadium out of his rearview mirror, still yelling something about the fans of the Red Riders missing his Saturday afternoon heroics, when he felt a "thud" hit the car.

"What was that?" he wondered out loud. He slowed and looked out the right side mirror, but saw nothing and kept on going. Whatever it was, it had the effect of quieting the group. But when they pulled into the parking lot of the restaurant, pandemonium broke out.

Three police cars pulled in behind him, their lights flashing and sirens blaring. The officers leaped from their cars and pulled open the doors to Malcolm's car, snatching him and the other men from inside. They threw Malcolm and his friends against the hood and kicked their legs apart. The officers patted them down and took Malcolm's wallet from his back pocket. They looked at his driver's license.

"What is this about?" Malcolm screamed.

"Malcolm Tittlebaum, you're under arrest for leaving the scene of an accident," an officer announced, as he looked at Malcolm's driver's license. He then began reading Malcolm his Miranda rights. "You have the right to remain silent…"

"What are you talking about?" Malcolm interrupted.

"Come over here," the officer said, leading Malcolm to the passenger side of the car. "See that dent?" the officer asked, pointing to a dent on the right rear side of Malcolm's car. "Do you know what did that? I'll tell you what did that: the body of a beautiful young woman. The woman you killed! 'Leaving the scene of an accident' is not all you're going to be charged with."

"What? I didn't hit anybody! Ask those guys; they'll tell you. This is a mistake."

"It's *not* a mistake!" the officer thundered. "The entire Alabama cheerleading squad saw it happen. You killed a cheerleader – Kerry Wingo – daughter of number one alumnus Jerry Wingo. You're going to need a very good lawyer!"

Kerry Wingo and the rest of the cheerleading squad had been leaving the practice field when the accident occurred. Malcolm had turned too sharply when going around a curve and the rear of his car had dragged across the grass, hitting Kerry who was waiting to cross.

Malcolm's problems were just beginning. A blood test revealed that his alcohol level was .31, more than three times the legal limit, and there were trace amounts of amphetamines in his blood. When this was determined, he was charged with vehicular homicide, facing a lengthy prison sentence.

So began an 18-month odyssey through the court system for Malcolm Tittlebaum. He was, of course, passed over in the draft, and his career was, for all practical purposes, over.

"But I didn't mean to kill her!" Malcolm yelled. "How can they charge me with manslaughter, which is essentially murder?"

His attorney, Franklin Hurst, answered. "For the one-hundredth time, the law transfers your intent to get drunk and high to the action that causes injury.

It makes you responsible for the consequences of what you do!" He and Malcolm were meeting in his office.

"Responsible for the consequences, yes, but murder?" Malcolm asked. "No way! I thought you had to have 'criminal intent' to be guilty of a crime. You know, the 'mens rea' thing. You've mentioned it several times already."

"Generally you do, Malcolm, but with something like this, the law imputes intent. When you made the decision to drink and then get behind the wheel, the law presumes you knew you might very well cause an accident, so you are considered to have had the intent to kill. The standard is one of strict liability."

"But I didn't intend to kill!"

"But you intended to drink and take drugs, and then you intended to drive. You were aware, or at least you should have been, that you might cause an accident. Because someone was killed, you are deemed to have had mens rea, or criminal intent...a guilty mind."

"But that's not fair! Cold-blooded killers get the kind of time they're trying to give me."

"Malcolm, a young woman is dead and you caused it. Does it matter to her or her parents how she died?"

"It *should* matter. It was an accident. I didn't mean to kill her. I'm heartbroken about this. But still, it's different than if I had shot her with a gun or stabbed her with a knife. Now that's criminal intent!"

"Maybe so, but in the eyes of the law you have committed a very serious crime. And worse for you, the law gets you another way, too. Certain acts are wrong because they are prohibited; 'mala prohibita' is the Latin phrase. Committing one of these offenses is punishable regardless of intent. The Legislature decided that drunk driving is wrong and should be prohibited, so it passed a law to make it a crime, and there are severe penalties, regardless of intent.

"Look, we're going in circles," Hurst continued. "I hear what you're saying and there *is* a qualitative difference between your crime and other murders, but you are going to go to prison nonetheless; it's just a matter of how long. I suggest you quit harping on trying to beat the charge and help me minimize the penalty."

"But it's just not right," said Malcolm. "I didn't mean to hurt her. This can't be happening. How did it get to this?"

Malcolm drifted off, thinking of his last conversation with Booger

McClure. "If only I had peed in the cup," he thought. "No, if only Coach McClure hadn't given me the ultimatum. Regardless, McClure had given me a very direct warning, and even mentioned prison!"

The time leading up to the trial was surreal to Malcolm. The media attention was huge, and he still couldn't believe he was the focus of such a crisis.

Obviously, there were questions about substance abuse. Malcolm's lawyer suspected that Malcolm had a drug problem, and actually thought it could help the case if he did. If he could prove that Malcolm was an addict, it might mitigate his culpability in the eyes of the jury. It wouldn't excuse him from getting behind the wheel, but it would explain why he was so impaired.

Malcolm would have no part of this. He didn't want to be portrayed as a drug addict. Besides, he didn't believe he had a problem. He had simply made a mistake, a terrible one, admittedly, but a mistake nonetheless. He also still believed he would not go to prison and would miss only one year – this year – of professional football. But with the media frenzy surrounding him, he knew it would be hard enough to convince a team to take a chance on him. Branded as an addict, he could forget it.

The irony of Kerry Wingo being the one killed was not lost on anyone. In fact, it was downright eerie: As a cheerleader she had cheered Malcolm on for several years, and she was the daughter of Jerry Wingo who had been the most upset about Malcolm leaving the program.

Jerry Wingo took his grief public, speculating that if Booger McClure had not caused Malcolm to leave the team, the accident would never have occurred. This cut deeply at Coach McClure's heart. Still, he kept his promise to Malcolm to stay quiet even though he was under enormous pressure to speak out. It was also a devastating allegation for McClure with the Alabama alumni. They could not understand why he wouldn't defend himself, and his silence had the effect of giving credibility to the claim. Many grew to believe it.

From the night of his arrest, Malcolm was receiving an education on how the criminal justice system worked. Bond was set at his "first appearance" proceeding, a hearing held within 24 hours of one's arrest. A week later he was "arraigned," and entered a plea of "not guilty." Once the plea was entered, the "discovery" phase of the trial began to determine what happened. Depositions (oral questions) and interrogatories (written questions) were taken or received from those with knowledge of the case. There were also several hearings before the judge on points of law.

Once the discovery and the hearings on the questions of law were completed, several informal meetings between the attorneys occurred to discuss a plea bargain. The state's best offer to Malcolm was six years in prison. His attorney recommended that he take it, but Malcolm kept repeating that he hadn't intended to hit Kerry Wingo, and that he wouldn't have left the scene of the accident if he had known he had.

Malcolm would not accept the plea bargain, determined to fight the charges all the way because he was convinced the jury would see that he hadn't intended to do these awful things. Besides, the possibility of playing football would be over if he were sentenced to such a long time in prison. He couldn't – and wouldn't – give up his lifelong dream of playing professionally.

The Oakland Raiders took Malcolm Tittlebaum in the ninth round of the NFL draft, nearly the last. It was a far cry from being one of the first players picked, the likely scenario had he stayed for his last year with the Red Riders. However, given that he was awaiting trial on a charge of vehicular homicide, Malcolm was happy just to have been drafted. He tried to stay in shape and negotiate his contract with the Raiders, but with the trial looming it was hard to focus on anything else. As a result, the pressure built, and he needed something to take the edge off.

Out on bond, one evening he wandered over to the fraternity house and played basketball. Most of the brothers were nice but few were supportive; he had done a terrible thing and they knew there would – and should – be a price to pay. Malcolm could feel this attitude towards him, so he drifted off to The Sixties bar. His two drinking buddies, the guys who had been in the car with him at the time of the accident, weren't there. It wouldn't have mattered; they had cut their deals with the prosecution and agreed to testify against Malcolm, so they weren't allowed to speak to him. Malcolm took a seat at the bar by himself and ordered a scotch and water. His attorney had warned him to stay away from booze and drugs while awaiting trial, but Malcolm promised himself that he would only have one drink.

Sipping the drink, he felt the tension of the last few months begin to slip away. The Rolling Stones were playing on the jukebox and the air was heavy with cigarette smoke. He liked it here, and he was feeling relaxed for the first time in a long while.

The first drink led to a second and third and the alcohol took more of a hold of him. He would occasionally turn around and look across the room, wondering if his two "friends" had come in. His tipsiness turned to drunkenness, and by the time the bar closed, Malcolm was wasted.

He stumbled out the back door and came upon Willie Rebel who was strumming his guitar and singing the blues. "Hey, you're the guy I met a while back," Willie said. "I know who you are, too. Sit down and I'll play a song for you."

"Willie, you're the only person on Earth who's happy to see me," Malcolm said.

Malcolm sat down and Willie strummed a few chords. Malcolm made up simple lyrics: "I'm Oakland bound, man I like that sound. I say I'm Oakland bound, man I like that sound. Gonna find me a new town, man I'm Oakland bound."

"Hey, I like that," Willie said. "Let me try a verse. 'My friend is Oakland bound, oh I like that sound. I say my friend is Oakland bound, man I like that sound. Gonna find him a new town, my friend is Oakland bound.'"

They laughed and kept at it well into the night. Willie passed his bottle of cheap rock-gut whisky to Malcolm and between them they soon had drunk it all.

"What are we going to do now?" Malcolm asked.

"I don't know what *you're* going to do, but *I'm* going to lay down and go to sleep, just like I do every night."

Willie wadded an old sweater and put it under his head. He had been sitting on a blanket that he now pulled over him. He closed his eyes and went sound to sleep.

Malcolm wanted to leave, but he was suddenly so tired he had a hard time standing. He slumped back down and leaned on his side. "I just need to rest for a minute or two," he thought. "Then I'll walk home." He closed his eyes. He was so sleepy. "Just a minute or two, that's all I need…"

"Get up, man. Are you okay?" Malcolm heard someone ask. He opened his eyes to see a newspaper delivery man shaking him by the shoulder.

"What time is it?" Malcolm asked.

"Four in the morning. Have you been here all night?"

"I don't know. I guess so," Malcolm answered through squinting eyes. He was having a difficult time focusing. His head was throbbing and his mouth was cotton dry. Willie Rebel was still there, snoring loudly.

"You must have really tied one on," the newspaper person said, looking at the empty bottle of liquor. Malcolm didn't answer as he slowly got to his feet. When he stood, the fellow saw with certainty what he had suspected.

"You *are* Malcolm Tittlebaum. I thought that was you, but I wasn't sure. Of all the people to find sleeping in an alley with this guy. I see him all the time when I fill the bins in the front of the coffee shop down the street, but you? No way I would have guessed this."

"Do me a favor, will you?" Malcolm asked. "Don't say anything to anybody about this. This isn't normal behavior for me."

"Oh, I know that. I won't tell anyone. I promise. I'm a Raiders fan."

Malcolm smiled. "Thank you. Now, I'll just head on back to the dorm."

"You do that, and have a nice day. Sorry, man."

Malcolm looked at him, aware that something didn't seem right about the tone of his voice. "Sorry, man," the person had said, almost sadly. Sorry about what? The guy then smiled, threw the bound stack of newspapers over his shoulder and walked away. Malcolm headed in the other direction, but not without looking at the scene. Willie Rebel, the alley, the empty bottle…how had it come to this? He leaned against a telephone pole and vomited.

Malcolm was awakened by a telephone call from his lawyer, Franklin Hurst. It was six o'clock in the morning, two days after Malcolm's drunken night with Willie Rebel.

"Have you seen today's paper?" Hurst asked.

"Of course not," Malcolm replied. "I'm still sleeping, or was."

"Well, you should see it. It's not pretty, and it's not as though we don't have enough problems already. You've complicated things for me enormously."

"What are you talking about?" Malcolm asked.

"The front page of the newspaper. You and some drunk sound asleep in an alley with an empty bottle of liquor next to you. The caption reads, 'Two Former Stars Sleep It Off Together.' How could you do such a dumb thing?"

Malcolm was confused. Who could have taken the picture, and what does it mean, 'Two former stars…' A sick feeling in his gut began to creep in as the events of that night back came to him. "I'll get a copy of the paper and call you right back," was all he could think to say.

"You do that, Malcolm. This is bad, real bad."

Malcolm hung up and darted from his room. As he ran through the building's door, he passed Coach McClure who just looked at him, shaking his head, a newspaper folded under his arm.

The picture was worse than the lawyer's description. Malcolm Tittlebaum and Willie Rebel asleep next to each other, in such a wasted state they looked dead. The empty bottle was tipped over between them, the fingers of Malcolm's hand just touching the label as though he was reaching for one last swig. But there was nothing peaceful about this scene.

The blood rushed from Malcolm's head and he had to sit down. His face flushed, and he could feel the thumping of his heart as panic set in. His mistake was fully registering. His panic soon turned to rage, however, as he thought of who had done this to him.

"That newspaper guy! It had to be him. I knew there was something strange about his voice as he was leaving, and now I know what he was sorry about…he snapped the picture before he woke me up!"

Actually, Malcolm was only partially correct. The fellow had recognized Malcolm when he came upon the two of them sleeping, but it was a sports editor at the paper who had recognized Willie Rebel, and it was this editor who realized the irony of the picture. To Malcolm's disbelief, the story was worse than the picture.

Willie Rebel's real name was Willie Haines, and he had, in fact, been a star football player for the Red Riders many years before. Malcolm thought of his first meeting with Haines and how Haines had said he had once played football. Reading on, Malcolm learned that as a freshman, Haines had gained 220 yards and scored four touchdowns against the Ole' Miss Rebels. This gave him status, and his teammates began calling him Willie Rebel because of how he had all but single-handedly beaten one their chief rivals. Willie liked the significance of the new name, even calling himself that on occasion. The press picked it up and it stuck.

Haines went on to have two good football years with Colonial, but he had received virtually no education when growing up so he struggled academically. His family situation was rotten; he had never known his father, and his mother had been abused by a long list of live-in boyfriends. Consequently, he had been taught few social skills and had no idea how to cope with the university environment, especially when faced with the adoration that went with being a football star. He was ill equipped to handle the fame and notoriety and it became too much for him. He turned to the bottle, and by his third year he was done with football. His addiction had taken hold of him and no one was there to help. He dropped out of school and began living on the streets.

The story contained this line: "How sad and ironic that two former star football players for the Red Riders would find camaraderie with each other in an alley behind a bar, one with an addictions problem that everyone acknowledged, the other with one that few even recognized." Malcolm was furious, but instead of calling his lawyer, he called the newspaper and got an associate editor on the line.

"Who does your writer think he is, saying that I have an addictions problem!" he shouted. "He doesn't know anything about me or what I do. And that picture! You just opened yourself up to a lawsuit with that one. I'm not a bum! One night, just one night, I have a hard time and go to sleep in an alley and you portray me as a Skid Row drunk!"

On and on Malcolm went, sounding more irrational the longer he spoke. The associate editor, Howard Nickens, stayed quiet for the most part, but by the time Malcolm quit talking, he was certain that Malcolm had serious drug and alcohol issues. More than that, he was certain there was a big story about Malcolm Tittlebaum that had not yet been told. When the executive editor arrived, Nickens sought and received permission to begin digging. Later that morning, he went to work.

Nickens' first call was to Coach McClure where he received the standard response of "No comment." Towards the end of the call, though, McClure, sensing that he could trust Nickens and thinking that the end for Malcolm was near, told him that if there came a time when he could comment, Nickens would be the one he would call. "That's good enough for me, Coach. My commitment to you is to be accurate and sensitive with whatever you have to say."

"That's all anyone could or should expect," McClure responded.

Later, Nickens wandered over to Malcolm's fraternity house where he spoke to several brothers. They were cordial but offered little. Malcolm Tittlebaum was, after all, their fraternity brother, so they were reluctant to speak of his personal habits. Nickens asked if it was okay to wander around. They were a little apprehensive, but agreed.

Nickens hung around the basketball goal for a while, hoping to speak to some of the young men waiting to play. He didn't get much, so he went inside where he found several of the fraternity's "little sisters." After introducing himself he realized he wouldn't get much from them, either, so he left a card with each, and said that if they thought of anything they'd like to share, he'd love to hear about it.

He soon left, but later that afternoon he received a call from one of the girls. She said she had information he might find interesting. Apparently, Malcolm had led her on, and, after getting from her what he wanted, moved on without a word of explanation. She was deeply hurt and very angry.

Nickens met the young woman at the Brown Hat Eatery the next day. They talked for two hours, and the woman told Nickens everything she knew about the character and personal habits of Malcolm Tittlebaum. The drug parties, the womanizing, the frequent drunken nights…she told it all. But what really peaked his interest was a comment she made about a fight Malcolm had had with Booger McClure. Something about a drug test he had refused to take that had led to "the end." She said he told her about this late one night, a comment that she doubted he remembered making. Nickens thanked the young woman and drove off, sure that he was going to unravel the true story of why Malcolm Tittlebaum had left Alabama Colonial University.

After screaming at the associate editor of the newspaper, Malcolm called his lawyer, Franklin Hurst. They scheduled a meeting for later that morning where Hurst laid it out in plain terms to Malcolm.

"You will not win this case. If you go to trial and lose, you may get as many as 18 years in prison. My strong recommendation is that you take the six-year plea bargain offered by the state attorney, assuming it's still on the table in light of the picture and story in today's paper."

"Why should that make a difference? They can't use that in court!" Malcolm stated angrily.

"No, but the state attorney will view it as evidence that you haven't learned your lesson, that you aren't sorry enough about the accident to change your behavior."

"But Franklin, I got drunk and fell asleep in an alley. I didn't drink and get behind the wheel. I *have* learned my lesson. And besides, I didn't intend to hurt that cheerleader!"

"Oh, for crying out loud, Malcolm! There you go again, thinking that your lack of intent to hit that girl matters. It doesn't. How many times do I have to explain that to you?"

"But it should! It should matter. It does with nearly every other kind of crime. There must be "mens rea," remember? Without criminal intent, one can't be guilty, right? You learned that in your Criminal Law course in law school, didn't you?"

"I did, and you're right," Hurst said. "It *should* matter. In my mind you're not as culpable as one who kills intentionally with a gun or knife. But the law is the law. You are going to prison; it's just a question of for how long."

"You just admitted that it should matter!" thundered Malcolm. "Maybe the 12 jurors will think the same way."

"Malcolm, the jury will only decide your guilt or innocence. The judge will decide the sentence."

"Well, if the jury knows that I'm facing 18 years, they may not convict me," Malcolm said.

"You are not thinking rationally," Hurst stated emphatically. "The instructions given to the jury will prevent them from considering the possible penalty. The judge does the sentencing. The jury will be told only to determine if the facts constitute a crime as defined in the law."

"What is it with this criminal justice system? It's unfair! This is America!" Malcolm exclaimed.

"You're right, Malcolm. It *is* unfair in some ways." Hurst was exasperated. "The system isn't perfect, but it's the one we have. Listen to what I'm saying. Let me go to the state attorney and make the deal for six years."

Malcolm slumped in his chair, thinking hard. Guilty or innocent? Six years or 18? Football or no football?

"Franklin, it's fourth and long," Malcolm said, using a football metaphor. Do I play safe and punt, or go deep and try to score?"

"Play it safe and punt, Malcolm. Think with your head, not your heart."

"That would be good advice if punting got me anything," Malcolm answered. "As it is, I'd still go to prison for a long time and football would be over. Punting is not an outcome that works, not in this situation. I hired you because you were the best criminal defense lawyer around. Now earn your fee. We're going to trial."

Based on this directive from Malcolm, Franklin Hurst put on his game face and began fine-tuning his trial preparation.

The charge he had the most chance of beating was the one involving leaving the scene of the accident. How could Malcolm be guilty if he hadn't known there had been an accident? If the two occupants of the car corroborated Malcolm's explanation that he didn't know he had hit Kerry Wingo, he could beat this charge.

It wouldn't be easy, though. Malcolm had clearly felt something hit the car and wondered out loud what he had felt. The other men must have suspected something, as well, because it became quiet in the car for the rest of the ride.

Malcolm wouldn't be required to testify because of his right against self-incrimination, but Franklin couldn't count on the men who had been in the car to say the right thing. They had become witnesses for the state. As it turned out, both were on probation for petty offenses, a condition of which was to stay sober. They obviously weren't at the time of the accident, and this was confirmed by a blood alcohol test. The law allows even passengers to be tested if a person is killed or injured in an automobile accident. In exchange for their testimony against Malcolm, the state had agreed to not violate their probation. These guys would not want to say anything that could jeopardize this arrangement.

Hurst would have to be careful in the manner in which he questioned these witnesses. Their testimony would help Malcolm if it were clear that he was impaired when he left the scene, but if the situation were overstated, it would hurt him on the vehicular homicide charge. The more impaired Malcolm had been, the greater the likelihood that he wouldn't have known he had hit Kerry Wingo, but greater impairment made his decision to get behind the wheel even more derelict.

Of more concern to Hurst was the fact that several cheerleaders who had been with Kerry Wingo said they saw the brake lights of the car go on right after Wingo was hit. All in all, even though it would be difficult, Hurst felt he could exonerate Malcolm against the charge of fleeing the scene. But the charge of vehicular homicide was another matter.

Malcolm's behavior clearly fit the definition of vehicular homicide. His actions were willful and wanton and made with a callous disregard for the welfare of others. Malcolm was going to get nailed, and Franklin knew it. But three weeks before the trial, Howard Nickens' newspaper story hit, and what Hurst did really didn't matter any more. It was all over but the shouting.

The story painted a picture of Malcolm that few people had seen. Nickens reported everything, including the allegations of drug and alcohol abuse,

Malcolm's lack of respect for women, and the suggestion that Malcolm had left Colonial because he wasn't willing to take a drug test required by Coach McClure. Despite repeated attempts to get Malcolm to respond in detail, all he would say was that the accusations were lies. Without a plausible explanation contradicting the many unnamed sources, the readers were left with the belief that Malcolm Tittlebaum was not the man they thought he was.

In the story, Coach McClure did not comment on the assertion that Malcolm had left the Colonial program because he had refused to take the urine test. Jerry Wingo was quoted, saying again that if McClure had done more to keep Malcolm from leaving, his daughter would still be alive. This hurt Coach McClure deeply, but again he honored his commitment to Malcolm and stayed quiet.

The story was so damaging that, when he read it, even Malcolm knew the case would lose. Even though Hurst could get jurors who had not seen the story, the prosecution had, and they could find witnesses who would speak to Malcolm's propensity to party and get behind the wheel while impaired. More than that, he now saw himself differently, fully appreciating the import of his actions. The full measure of his remorse for causing the death of a beautiful young woman hit him. Whether or not he intended to hurt her no longer made any difference to him. What mattered was that he had gotten high and then driven a car, a "dangerous instrumentality" in the eyes of the law, and a person was killed as a result. He would admit his guilt, ask for forgiveness from the Wingo family, and throw himself on the mercy of the court.

Of equal impact to Malcolm was the reaction of his mother. All along she had been supportive, not wanting to believe the rumors about her son. Now the truth was undeniable, and she told him so. Her son's problems extended beyond one careless afternoon of partying. Malcolm finally saw that his desire to use drugs and alcohol was more than recreational; it was a craving he felt in his chest and stomach.

It is said that an addict must hit bottom before recognizing the need for help. That's the way it was for Malcolm Tittlebaum. Not until he saw the full measure of what his addiction had cost him did he see the hold the drugs had over him. It was like he had to become disconnected from his body in order to see himself.

Malcolm called his lawyer, and the lawyer called the state attorney. An agreement was reached for Malcolm to plead guilty to the charge of vehicular homicide in exchange for an eight-year prison term. The state would drop the 'fleeing the scene of the accident' charge.

Three weeks later, Malcolm Tittlebaum, one-time star quarterback of a major university, stood before a judge and admitted his guilt. He apologized to the family of Kerry Wingo, accepted his sentence stoically, and left the courtroom in handcuffs, bound for state prison for the next eight years of his life. On the way out, he noticed Coach Booger McClure sitting on the back row, letting Malcolm know that he would always be there for him. It was then that Malcolm's stoicism gave way to the grief he was feeling, and tears welled in his eyes.

The bane of prison life is boredom. Jobs and work programs inside and outside the institution walls aren't adequate to keep the vast number of inmates busy. As a result, most inmates sit around all day.

Malcolm was lucky. For part of his stay in prison he was given the job of helping the park rangers in a nearby state park. Still, there was plenty of down time, so with little else to do, and because Malcolm's desire to transcend himself into a better person was genuine, he applied himself diligently to the 12-step Narcotics Anonymous program. When he finally realized he was powerless over his addiction, healing began.

One year led to two, and two led to three. After six years, Malcolm was released two years early for good behavior.

Seeking to get totally away from the life that had led him astray, he left Alabama and returned to his hometown of Umatilla, Florida. Because of the experience he had gained working at a state park while in prison, he was able to get a job working as a maintenance worker in Ocala National Forest. It was very different than the jet-set life for which he was once destined, but the solitude of the woods was just what his regretful and forlorn spirit needed. He had little desire for crowds, traffic or city life. The sandy scrub flats and hills of the 383,220-acre forest were his playing field now, and he felt most at peace when he was there.

Three years after his release from prison, an old blue pickup truck pulled up to the maintenance barn where Malcolm was working. Out stepped Coach Booger McClure.

Malcolm turned up the mask of the welding helmet he was wearing and then took it off. The men stared at each other for a few moments, then smiled.

"We're both a long way from where we once were partners," Malcolm said.

"Yes, but not a long way from where we first met. I remember walking into the living room of your parents' house and meeting them – and you – for the first time. What was that, 12 years ago?"

"Something like that. I had just finished my senior year in high school. As long ago as that was, it seems like just yesterday in many ways."

"That it does. Where has the time gone?"

The sentence hung in awkward silence.

"Well, what brings you to Ocala National Forest," Malcolm asked.

"You. I came to see you," McClure answered softly.

"What in the heck for? I'm hardly worth a special visit, especially after all I've put you through." Malcolm was thinking of how Coach McClure had ultimately lost his coaching job at Colonial, largely because of his silence about why Malcolm had left.

"We never know why things work out the way they do, Malcolm. Some things aren't revealed to us until later. But I'm doing all right. Don't worry about me. How about taking me for a ride through the woods?"

"Sounds great," Malcolm replied. "Climb in."

As they pulled away in Malcolm's dark green Forest Service truck, Malcolm was suddenly overcome with emotion. He choked on the lump in his throat and he had trouble speaking. Coach McClure put his hand on Malcolm's shoulder and said, "It's okay, son. It's okay."

"I blew it, Coach. I had it right there in my hand and let it slip away."

McClure didn't say anything, instead letting Malcolm say out loud what he had said to himself thousands of times before.

"If I'd peed in that cup like you told me...if only I'd done that! Everything would be different now. I had a problem. You suspected as much but I wouldn't believe it."

Coach McClure didn't comment. He didn't say, "I told you so," and that would have been easy to do. Great coaches aren't like that. They build people up, not tear them down.

Malcolm talked for 30 minutes, telling of his addiction to drugs, his life in prison and his new life on the outside. He talked of Kerry Wingo, the beautiful young woman he had killed, and how sorry he was for that. He also told Coach McClure how much it had meant to see him in the courtroom the day he was sentenced.

Coach McClure told Malcolm how he came to leave Alabama Colonial University. He wasn't fired. On the contrary, the university president never wavered in her support, giving him total deference in how to run the football program. She was the one person whom McClure had told of Malcolm's refusal to submit to a urine test.

Jerry Wingo was obsessed with his calls for McClure's firing. He was still convinced that his daughter was killed because McClure forced Malcolm out of the Colonial program. As an influential alumnus, Wingo had the wherewithal to make it uncomfortable for McCure. Nevertheless, McClure was certain he could have withstood it. Wingo's ravings, however, had become a distraction to the team and were hurting recruiting, the lifeblood of any athletic program. McClure saw that he should leave. But there was another reason that ultimately led Coach McClure to resign. After two years, he saw that Jerry Wingo could never have peace about his daughter's death until he was gone, so he left. McClure had always known that life was about much more than winning football games.

From Birmingham, McClure moved to Winter Haven, Florida to become the head coach of the new Division Three football program at Lake Country College. Even though it was a much smaller school than what he was used to, he was drawn to the challenge of building a team from scratch. He also enjoyed the atmosphere of a school that placed less focus on winning and viewed its athletes as very visible examples of the kind of character expected of its students. McClure made the conscious choice to recruit men of character first and ability second. Not surprising to him, this approach had the interesting and ironic effect of building a team that won games. After just three years, the team went undefeated and won its conference title.

Malcolm listened intently, and thought of how his life might have been different if he had focused on his character first, and his ability as a player second.

They drove all through Ocala National Forest with Malcolm explaining the numbering system of the roads. He pointed out camps that had been in families for generations, begun in a time when receiving a lease from the government to hunt on public land was not difficult. There were also hunting camps just outside the perimeter, built on lots purchased from the private sector, giving easy and quick access to the Forest.

Malcolm and Coach McClure had a few laughs, too. When they drove by the former site of "Tommy Bartlett's Deer Ranch," a fenced-in petting zoo with scores of tame deer, Malcolm told of a hunter who once threw about a dozen of his deer dogs (dogs used by hunters to run deer) over the fence. These dogs went crazy, thinking they had landed in "Deer Dog Heaven." While not at all clear why the hunter had done this or how he would get the dogs out of the fenced-in property, he and his buddies went to dinner. When they returned, law enforcement vehicles with their flashing lights were everywhere.

"What's going on here?" the hunter asked.

"Someone's deer dogs have gotten into the deer ranch!" the officer answered as he and other officers were trying to catch the wayward dogs.

"What name's on the collar?" the hunter asked. A deer dog wears a collar with the name of its owner and contact information so the dog can be returned if lost, a common occurrence when a dog gets on the hot trail of a deer.

Several of the dogs had been caught, so the officer reported the name of the dogs' owner. When the hunter heard the name, *his* name, he said, "I know that guy and where he hunts. I'll get them to him."

With that, he and his friends began helping the officers catch the remaining dogs, *their own dogs*, and then drove off with them, promising to return them to the "rightful" owner.

For two hours Coach McClure and Malcolm drove, swapping stories and talking of life. Finally, Malcolm could stand it no longer.

"Why are you here, Coach?"

Coach McClure turned and looked at Malcolm.

"I'm here because I want you to come to Lake Country and coach my quarterbacks."

For a mile or so Malcolm drove without speaking. Then, "After all these years and all that I cost you, you would ask me to be one of your coaches?"

"That's right. You're too good of a football man to be away from it forever."

"But there are a lot of good football men out there. Why me?"

"I don't know for sure, but it may be because we have unfinished business with each other and you know how I dislike that. I've thought about you a lot these last years, wondering if I was unreasonable in insisting that you pee in that cup. If I hadn't done that, Kerry Wingo would probably still be alive."

"Oh, Coach. Don't blame yourself for that. We both know who was at fault."

"I know, but we make decisions in life that touch people in ways we can never predict or even know. I made a decision that day that started a chain reaction and a woman ended up dead and you ended up in prison. Maybe I see your coming to work with me as a way to start over."

"Are you doing this only for yourself, or for me too?" Malcolm asked.

"Both. For me, I need a Quarterbacks' coach, and giving you the chance to get back into the game that you once loved strikes me as the right thing to do and that makes me feel good. So in those ways I guess I'm doing it for me. But I think I'm doing it for you, too. I'm sure it gnaws at your gut every day, what happened to that girl. You'll feel that for the rest of your life, I guess, but getting back onto the field might be a way to move on. My guess is that Jerry Wingo would even find it helpful. If he sees that you and I have reconciled, maybe it will also help him find greater reconciliation with this whole tragic mess."

"I don't know, Coach. I have a comfortable life here, and keeping it simple makes it easier for me to stay sober. All the excitement of college football could bring back the old demons."

"It could, that's for sure," McClure answered. "But it provides a wonderful platform for a powerful testimony about the pitfalls of stardom, booze and drugs, especially to young athletes. And who knows? Sharing your experience with others might be a way to strengthen your sobriety. Isn't that part of your 12-step program?"

"Not exactly," Malcolm chuckled. "It actually says, 'Having had a spiritual awakening as a result of these steps, we tried to carry this message to addicts, and to practice these principles in all our affairs.' But I hear what you're saying. Constantly admitting that I'm powerless over drugs and alcohol reinforces my sense of vulnerability and that helps me stay clean. And maybe there *are* those who would listen to me if I were more public with my struggle with addiction and the lifestyle that let it in."

"I'm sure there are, Malcolm. You were larger than life when you were in your prime."

"I guess so, but I may actually be happier not being that 'larger-than-life' guy. I'm doing okay now in this simple life."

"That sounds like a great message, and if people hear it from you, it'll stick," McClure said confidently.

Malcolm chewed on those words, and soon a tear ran down his cheek.

"I can't believe you're here asking me this. You had made it to the big time, coaching one of the great college teams and contending for the national title, and I took it from you. What really kills me is you could have saved yourself by ratting me out. All you had to do was tell Jerry Wingo why I left, and he never would even have gotten started with his campaign to fire you. Why didn't you?"

"Because I told you I wouldn't," McClure replied. "A coach's first responsibility is to teach his players character. I wouldn't gain the respect of my guys if they didn't believe I meant the things I said, or if I broke my word."

"But, why are you giving me this chance after what I've cost you?"

"Because the second responsibility of a coach is never to give up on his players, to be there for them always if he is needed."

Malcolm Tittlebaum stopped the truck, pulling over into an area shaded by the outstretched arms of a live oak. He got out and walked a short way. When he returned, he was wearing a big grin.

"Okay, Coach. I'm in."

"That's great, Malcolm. I'm really glad. Thank you!"

"No. Thank you," Malcolm replied, as he smiled and shook his coach's hand. "Now let's go get our national title, and finish what we started so many years ago."

Author's Note:

Black's Law Dictionary defines strict liability crimes as "unlawful acts whose elements do not contain the need for criminal intent or mens rea." Black's Law Dictionary, Sixth Edition, p. 1422. Injuring someone while driving drunk is such an act, but what constitutes drunk driving has been the focus of many legislative debates, and I was involved in a few of them.

I voted for the bill that lowered the legal blood alcohol content while driving from .1 to .08. The initial proposal was to lower it to .02, and some wanted it to be illegal for any alcohol to be in one's system while driving, but that was considered as going too far.

I also voted to raise the legal drinking age to 21. There were many arguments put forward. One was that younger people simply reacted differently to alcohol than older people, and were more likely to become "problem" drinkers. A second argument, and it was probably the deciding factor for many legislators, was that Congress passed a law saying that a state couldn't receive federal transportation money if it didn't raise its drinking age to 21. A final argument was that with the legal drinking age at 18, it was easier for a 16-year old to get alcohol. Since 16-year olds were brand new drivers, even a small amount of alcohol was especially dangerous. I'm not sure the experience has been that a drinking age of 21 has made it more difficult for 16 and 17-year olds to get alcohol, but that was one of the arguments.

Finally, I supported laws that stiffened penalties for drinking and driving. However, there are occasions when I believe the laws miss the mark of justice. Double-digit prison terms sometimes seem inappropriate for those who act totally out of character and who are truly remorseful over causing an accident. On the other hand, I've met with members of Mothers Against Drunk Drivers, parents who have lost a child because of a drunk driver, and their grief, anguish and anger were palpable. Still, there should be a way to punish and deter in a way that reflects the seriousness of the crime without such long prison sentences.

One thing is undeniable. These laws have helped to change the attitude of many towards drinking and driving. When I turned 18, the drinking age had just become 18. It was common to get a six-pack and "cruise;" that is, drive around town and look for friends. Thank goodness that doesn't seem to be as common today. The drinking I hear about now seems to take place at someone's house, in a grove or around a campfire. Getting back from these settings is certainly problematic, but at least there are other people there to help, or maybe they're at a place where they can stay and not have to drive. The use of "designated drivers" is a common practice today also, and it was almost unheard of 30 years ago. The law can and does change behavior.

After this story was written, I had the chance to coach junior varsity football at my alma mater, Winter Haven High School. I loved it. I'd been away from the game for many years so I was rusty, but it was a super experience. I saw the importance of coaching from a new perspective. Something as easy as calling an injured player to see how he was doing meant a great deal to the player and parents. Teachers knowing that the coach would support them when they were having problems with players went a long ways towards enhancing the academic performance of the players and increasing teacher morale. A coach sharing a life experience with the team seemed to get through. Most former players (or most anyone, for that matter), can't tell you who the Vice President of the United States was four years ago, but they can tell you the name of every coach they've ever had. More than anything, the experience gave me a better appreciation of the awesome responsibility coaches have to be good role models because the players are always watching.

On page seven, Coach McClure tells Malcolm of how stardom makes some people believe they are invisible. That thought came from T.E. "Red" Holcum, a longtime Tallahassee lobbyist.

In 1982, when I was first elected to the Florida House of Representatives, Red was retired and living in Lakeland. He took an interest in me, and I sat in his kitchen frequently, drinking coffee and listening to stories of the Legislature. I was far from famous, but he cautioned me about a disease he called "egoism," a malady he said afflicted many legislators. These legislators, he remarked, went to Tallahassee and began believing they didn't put their pants on like everyone else. He said they thought they were invisible, believing that no one was seeing them drinking too much or cheating on their spouses. He cautioned me about such behavior, saying it caught up with the transgressor sooner or later.

Red Holcum is no longer with us, but his advice is as good today as it was back in 1982.

THE LAW: Definitions and Explanations:

Mens rea: As an element of criminal responsibility: a guilty mind; a guilty or wrongful purpose; a criminal intent. Guilty knowledge and willfulness.

Black's Law Dictionary, Sixth Edition, page 985.

Notable Quotes:

"Laws that do not embody public opinion can never be enforced."

Elbert Hubbard / www.worldofquotes.com

"To make laws that man cannot, and will not obey, serves to bring all laws into contempt."

Elizabeth Cady Stanton / www.worldofquotes.com

"The first duty of society is justice."

Alexander Hamilton, Federalist Papers,
as noted by Miles McGrane, 2003 president of the Florida Bar,
in The Florida Bar Journal/December 2003.

"If one man can be allowed to determine for himself what is law, every man can. That means first chaos, then tyranny. Legal process is an essential part of the democratic process."

Honorable Felix Frankfurter, Associate Justice,
United States Supreme Court
www.worldofquotes.com

"We may win when we lose, if we have done what we can; for by so doing we have made real at least some part of that finished product in whose fabrication we are most concerned: ourselves."

Honorable Learned Hand, Associate Justice,
United States Supreme Court
www.brainyquotes.com

"The man of character, sensitive to the meaning of what he is doing, will know how to discover the ethical paths in the maze of possible behavior."

Honorable Earl Warren, Chief Justice,
United States Supreme Court
www.brainyquotes.com

"I always turn to the sports pages first, which records people's accomplishments. The front page is nothing but man's failures."

Honorable Earl Warren, Chief Justice,
United States Supreme Court
www.brainyquotes.com

Catch of Blue Crabs

FRUIT OF THE POISONOUS TREE
Search and Seizure: The Exclusionary Rule

Preface: Few judicially created doctrines have evoked as much praise – and scorn – as the exclusionary rule, a doctrine that forbids evidence from being used at trial if it was obtained in violation of the search and seizure protections of the United States Constitution. Some commentators believe it is an essential brake on law enforcement, preventing over-zealous officers from trampling the constitutional rights of people accused of committing crimes. Others consider it a millstone around the neck of those who are trying to apprehend criminals.

JOEY PETRUCO was New York through and through. Son of a Sicilian immigrant, raised in Queens, Yankees fan, New York accent, he was the total package.

He cherished his heritage and loved his city, and couldn't imagine living any place else. But then he visited Daytona Beach, Florida in 1978 during Spring Break his senior year in college and from that point on, knew exactly where he wanted to retire. Driving on the beach, visiting the Boardwalk and pier, watching the young ladies in bikinis, and frequenting the many shops had been a blast. He had bodysurfed in the ocean and stayed in the sun too long. All in all, it was the most fun he had ever had.

Before retirement he'd need a career, though, and there was never any question as to what he would do. His goal from the time he could remember had been to become a police officer for the New York City police department. He would follow in the footsteps of his father, Louie Petruco. As a small boy, Joey was mesmerized by the sight of his dad putting on the blue police uniform. He liked nothing more than to walk down the sidewalk holding his dad's hand. His father – "The Cop" – had been a source of immeasurable pride for him.

Then a dealer of illegal guns ruined it all.

Officer Louie Petruco and his partner had answered a call in Astoria about a domestic disturbance. A neighbor had called, saying a woman was screaming. "It sounded like she was being beaten," the caller had said.

It was the dead of summer, hot and muggy. Walking up to a little row house, Petruco noticed that he was sweating more than normal.

Knocking on the door, the cops waited. They knocked again. Finally, the door opened slowly. Standing before them was a woman, crying softly and cowering.

"Ma'am, do you need help?" Officer Petruco asked.

"No, I'm fine," said between her sobs. "Please leave."

"You don't look fine. May we come in and have a look around?"

"No. I'm okay, really."

Silence.

Pulling a small notebook from his pocket, Petruco wrote, "If you need help, close your left eye." He held it up for her to read and she closed her left eye.

Petruco motioned for his partner to go around the building to cover the rear. He then stepped in, his hand on his gun.

The house was old and rundown, the air stale and deathly quiet.

Petruco walked from room to room. Nothing.

He slowly pushed open the bedroom door and peeked inside, looking to his left and right. He walked in.

The wind blew, causing the sheer white window curtains to flutter. The window was open.

"Whoever was here is gone now," he thought, dropping his hand from his gun.

He turned to walk back to the woman, but standing in front of him was a rough looking man with a long scar on his left cheek. He had been hiding behind the door when it opened. "How dumb could I be?" Petruco thought.

The man was pointing a long-barreled pistol with a screw-in silencer at Officer Petruco. The gun flashed twice, making hardly a sound. Petruco fell to his knees, two small red spots on his chest soaking through his police shirt. In the 1960s, officers rarely wore bulletproof vests. Another shot, and Petruco grabbed his neck. He pitched forward, landing on his face, dead.

The gunman ran through the front door out of the house, disappearing down the street. The woman – his girlfriend – stood in the doorway, too scared to make a sound. She ran into the bedroom, saw Petruco lying on the floor, and then screamed.

Officer Petruco's partner ran back around the house and darted into the bedroom. When he saw his partner, he called for an ambulance and reported the shooting. Black and white units blocked every street to try to catch the shooter, but he was gone.

Petruco's partner later found 48 military-style Chinese Model 56 SKS rifles in the bedroom closet. The assassin was a dealer of weapons.

Joey was devastated. He was 12 years old and never fully got over it, thinking of his father every day for the rest of his life.

This event had another effect on Joey: it caused him to go into detective work for the NYPD. He did the required amount of "beat" time, but it was detective work that really motivated him. He wanted to work on cases that were difficult to solve because he knew the anguish felt by family members of victims.

Joey was driven in his pursuit of suspects who committed violent crimes, and he was good at finding them. He was often recognized for his work, and won five special citations from the mayor for solving very difficult cases. At each ceremony, he began by asking for a moment of silence in memory of his father.

Joey married once but the marriage lasted just two years. He took his job so seriously, and worked so hard at it, that he didn't have time to share his life with someone else.

Twenty-five years on the police force took its toll. By the time he was eligible for retirement, he was burned out and ready for a more relaxed lifestyle. He had started with the NYPD when he was 24 years old, so he was just 49 when he retired, young enough to have another career if he wanted one.

If Joey wasn't sure what he was going to do with the rest of his life, he was sure where he was going to spend it: Daytona Beach. He packed up his belongings and headed to Florida.

His first night there he dined at the Inlet Harbor Restaurant at Ponce Inlet. After ordering, he walked outside, casually milling about as he waited for his food. A dock extended well out into the inlet. Moving over it, Joey noticed that the dock had a fence running underneath that actually enclosed part of the inlet, creating a giant outdoor holding tank. In it were many fish that would later become part of someone's meal. The fried grouper Joey had just ordered might very well have come from the tank.

"This is good. This is good. I'm gonna like it down here," he thought, looking around.

For the first year, Joey did little but fish and hunt. His favorite fishing trips were those to the "Party Grounds," a rock-ledge reef system found well offshore. In three outings, sharing an offshore charter with several other guys, he caught one blue marlin, two wahoo, 12 dolphin, three bonito and eight kingfish.

He joined a hunt club near the little town of Samsula, not too far from a small racetrack where stock car racers honed their skills, hoping someday to race at Daytona International Speedway down the street. The hunting in the area wasn't nearly what it used to be, though. The woods had once been thick and full of game. Now the growth along Highway 44 was causing a decline of everything except new houses. Still, it was woods, and Joey managed to get his buck for the year, a small four-pointer.

But it was a chance encounter with a person who would later become his best Florida friend that brought Joey the activity he liked best: crabbing. While walking along the Boardwalk one evening a couple of years after he'd settled in Florida, Joey came upon Jack Brown, a Daytona Beach police officer who was trying to talk two guys out of fighting. One was holding a 2x4 board, the other a power saw that was plugged in.

"It's over. Now put the board down," Jack yelled at one of the guys.

"Not until he puts the saw down," the other answered.

"Okay you, put the saw down!" Jack said to the other.

"Not until he puts the board down!"

Joey ran over. "Looks like you could use some help," he said. "Joey Petruco, retired NYPD."

"Yeah, I could! Thanks," responded Jack. "You get in front of the guy with the board, and I'll get in front of the guy with the saw. Maybe if two people are between them they'll walk away."

"That's it, men. Put your weapons down right now or you're both going to jail. It's now or never," Jack said. "There won't be another chance."

Slowly the guys put their weapons down.

"Good. Now each of you back up and leave...in opposite directions. I don't want to see you back here anytime soon."

The men ambled away, stealing glances over their shoulders.

"Another Friday night at the Boardwalk," Jack said, introducing himself. "But if you're from New York, I bet you've seen it all."

"I've seen a lot, that's for sure," Joey answered.

"Hey, my shift's over in 30 minutes. We have a police hall a few blocks from here. How about going with me for a beer or two? You'll like the guys there. A few of them are even from New York."

Joey thought for a moment. "Okay, great. I'll meet you here."

"Sounds good."

So began a friendship that grew steadily. Jack, a native Floridian, was fascinated by Joey's stories from his police work in New York City. Likewise, Joey was impressed with Jack's knowledge of natural Florida. As a native Floridian, Jack could hunt and fish with the best of them, and one thing he taught Joey was how to crab.

"Take this chicken neck and tie it onto the string. Good. Now tie the other end of the string onto this big rock. Throw the chicken neck out and have a seat. In 15 minutes we'll pull it in and see if we've caught anything."

It was midnight in the dead of the summer, and Joey and Jack were on land underneath a bridge that crossed the Intracoastal Waterway, a 1,095-mile stretch of water that runs from Norfolk, Virginia to Miami, Florida. For most of its 380-mile trek along the entire eastern coastline of Florida, the Intracoastal separates a sliver of land from the rest of the peninsula. In the Daytona area, this waterway lies between the beaches and the downtown district.

"You need to go back to work," Jack said to Joey in the quiet stillness of the night. The only sounds were cars crossing the bridge overhead. Heat lightning was flashing in the distant sky. "You can't do this for the rest of your life."

"I don't know. Fishing, hunting, crabbing, an occasional round of golf... not bad," Joey answered.

"No, but there's more to life than that."

"True, but what in the heck would I do? Police work is all I know."

"Then how about police work? We have a need for a part-time investigator. It could be right up your alley."

"No way. I've had enough of that. It's someone else's turn to catch the bad guys," Joey said, thinking of his many years chasing those on the wrong side of the law.

"I understand, but we could use you. Just think about it."

"I will, but first let's check these chicken necks."

"Pull in the line real slowly," Jack said. "If there's a crab eating, it will stay with the chicken neck. If you pull too fast the crab will let go. That's right. Now, when the neck gets close to the surface, I'll shine a light on it. If there's a crab there, I'll slip the dip net under it."

Joey pulled the line in slowly, and sure enough, there was a big blue crab tearing at the chicken neck with its claws. Sam put the net under the crab and brought it up.

"Hey! Nothing to it, is there?" Joey laughed.

"Nope, there's not much to it. The trick is knowing where the crabs are."

After a few hours, they had 24 big crabs. Cooked with spicy sausage, potatoes and corn, it was enough for five or six guys at the police hall. Of course, a meal like this would require a few beers to wash it down, so they were in for a fine time of good food, drink and fellowship.

On the way home a few hours later, Joey asked Jack a question he had been pondering. "What kind of detective work do you need?"

"You've been here for nearly three years, Joey, long enough to know there are some pretty rough people around. We've discovered there may be a network of gun smugglers working out of here."

"Gun smugglers. What do you mean by that?"

"People taking guns from Florida into New York illegally. New York's gun laws are so strict that many people aren't able to buy a gun, so they find someone to bring them one from Florida. Most of these people just want a revolver or semi-automatic for personal protection, but it's still illegal, so we have to try to stop it. What has us real concerned, though, is a few of these smugglers have begun bringing in assault weapons like UZIs, MAC-10s and Street Sweepers. These guns are going to gangs, the Mafia and terrorists."

"Did you say 'assault weapons?'" Joey asked.

"Yeah, new ones as well as old ones like the Chinese military rifles from the Vietnam era. We think there's actually a gun smuggling ring that's doing this."

Assault weapons, Chinese military rifles…he was suddenly re-living that awful day when the police chief and the mayor walked into his house and told his mother that his father was dead.

"Why are they bringing the guns into Florida?" he asked Jack.

"Because Florida has 14 deepwater ports. Most of these guns are made in other countries and sea freight is how they get into the U.S."

"But why Daytona Beach?"

"That we don't know. Maybe it's because the bigger cities are more focused on stuff like this as a result of 9/11. Or it may just be that a few bad guys were living here and saw a business opportunity. We just don't know, but that's one of the questions we'd want you to answer."

"Gun dealers. Why did it have to be gun dealers?" Joey thought. "Why couldn't it be drug dealers or pornography dealers or some other kind of dealers. But gun dealers?" All the old ghosts were coming back.

"We really need you, Joey."

Joey looked at Jack, then thought of his father.

"All right. I'll be in Monday morning. We'll talk to the chief."

Joey began working for the Daytona Beach Police Department three days a week. He was assigned the gun smuggling case, just as Jack thought he would, and he went to work. Another detective had already done some work on it, but hadn't gotten anywhere. Joey was starting almost from scratch.

He learned that a small-time drug dealer named Ricardo Montero had recently been convicted of possessing a dozen "Street Sweepers," revolving-cylinder 12-gauge shotguns capable of firing 12 rounds in three seconds when converted to fully-automatic capability. Montero wouldn't say what he intended to do with the guns, or even if he was planning to take them to New York. He simply took his five-year sentence without putting up a fight. Joey suspected it was because he'd rather do that than share information about anyone else involved.

When checking into Montero's background, Joey discovered that he had a cousin who worked as a mechanic at Samsula Race Track southwest of Daytona Beach. This cousin, Jorge Rodriguez, would arrive at the track on Fridays to help any driver get his racecar ready for the races that night. Jorge was a super mechanic and had no trouble getting work. Still, it was just part-time for him; the rest of the week he worked at a service station at the intersection of Highway 44 and Interstate 95. It was here that Joey paid him a visit.

"Mr. Rodriguez, I'm Detective Joey Petruco of the Daytona Beach Police Department. I'm conducting an investigation that may involve your cousin, Ricardo Montero." At the mention of Ricardo's name, Jorge grew defensive.

"Why are you asking about Ricardo? He's in jail."

"That's a pretty good reason to ask about him, don't you think?" Joey said sarcastically. "But it's just routine. Trying to clear up a few loose ends, that's all. Where do you live, Mr. Rodriguez?"

"In a trailer, along Hunting Camp Road."

"Is that where Ricardo lived?"

"No…actually, I don't know."

"Jorge. *I* know where Ricardo lived, and you do too. He lived not too far from you. This isn't a good way for us to get started, you not telling the truth."

"Okay, he lived close by. Why does that matter?"

"Just wondering if you saw anyone come by his place. Anyone hang out there?"

"Sometimes, yes. But I don't know who they were."

"Anyone stand out?"

"No, no one."

"Come on, Jorge, you must remember something. Were they Hispanic?"

"Most were, but not all," Jorge finally offered.

"See, you remember more than you thought. What else, Jorge?"

"That's it, really. Now I must be getting back to work."

"Okay, but here's my card. Call me if you think of anything else, will you?"

"Yes, of course."

The way he said it, though, made Joey sure he wouldn't.

Over the next few weeks, Joey made it a point to go to the Samsula races every Friday night. He had a gut feeling that Ricardo had been involved in the smuggling operation, and that the area around Samsula was the epicenter. Chances were that if arms smugglers were around, they would make it to the track sooner or later. Fast cars and guns often went hand in hand. He also wanted to watch Jorge. He didn't think Jorge was involved, at least not directly, but he did believe Jorge knew more than he was saying.

One Friday night Joey noticed a white 500 SL Mercedes pull into the crowded race track parking lot. Being new and expensive, it stood out like a sore thumb. Other vehicles in the lot were new, but they were mostly 4x4 pickup trucks, and they sure didn't cost $100,000.00.

Stepping from the car were two people: a snappily dressed white man and a young woman with bleached blonde hair and bright red lipstick. The parking lot was not paved, and, because it had recently rained, the couple was forced to walk through mud. This dirtied their shoes, something that annoyed them greatly.

They paid their admission and walked into the stadium. Many spoke to the man as he worked his way through the crowd; he was well known. He and his girlfriend made their way up the steps of the concrete bleachers and found their seats. Stock cars were roaring by, making so much noise it was hard to hear anything else.

The man was enjoying the race, but soon he looked to his left and nodded to another guy who was sitting five seats over and one row down. The other person came over and took an envelope from him. He then took it to Jorge who was sitting in an open-sided garage next to the track. Jorge opened the envelope and removed a letter. He read it and looked up. The man seated in the stadium tipped his hat. He was watching every move Jorge made. Jorge became flustered, and left.

Joey ambled out into the parking lot to get the license tag number from the couple's car. Louisiana. "Strange," Joey said to himself as he memorized the numbers. "This car's a long way from home."

The license tag turned out to belong to Bill Brough of Baton Rouge, but Brough's car was a Chevrolet Tahoe, not a Mercedes. His tag had been stolen a month before. "Time to pay Jorge another visit," Joey thought.

"But who was he, Jorge? I'm losing my patience," Joey said.

"I don't know his name, I told you. I'm not lying. I *don't* know his name!"

"*How* do you know him?"

"Don't ask me that, please. I cannot tell you."

"Why can't you tell me, Jorge."

"I just can't, all right?"

"Will he hurt you? Is that what you're worried about?"

"Yes. I'm scared of those people."

"*Those* people. Who are *those* people?"

"Just people! They sometimes come around where I live."

"But why you, Jorge. Why did he send you the note?"

"I'm not going to answer that. I don't have to."

"You will sooner or later. This is the time to talk if you know anything. It won't get any easier for you."

Jorge walked around the car he had been working on when Joey had walked in the garage. He rubbed his head and face, distraught.

"Okay. I'll tell you, but then you must leave me alone. I fear for the safety of my family."

"No guarantees on that one, but I'll do my best. Now let me hear it."

"I drove a car to New York City for him one time," Jorge finally answered.

"What was in the car?"

"I don't know. He told me to never look in the trunk. He said if I did, I'd regret it. I took him at his word. He was a scary guy."

"Where did you pick the car up?"

"At a house near where I live."

"Where your cousin Ricardo lived too, right?"

"That's right. In fact, the house was next door to where Ricardo lived."

"Where in New York did you take the car?"

"A car stereo shop in Queens."

"How did you get back from the City?"

"I drove a different car back."

Where'd you take this car?"

"Tiny's Body Shop, just off the beach."

"Jorge, why did you do it?"

"I needed the money. He gave me $5,000.00, and all I had to do was drive one car to New York and another one back."

"What did the note say, the one you got at the track last week?"

"It said I was needed for another job."

"Have you answered him?"

"No. I've been avoiding him."

"Good, because you're going to do it."

"But I don't want to!"

"Too bad. You screwed up by doing it the first time. Now they won't let you out. Punks like that don't let you do it just once. Besides, you'll do it for me if you don't want it to get real ugly."

"Come on, man! You said you'd let me go if I told you what I knew."

"That's not exactly what I told you. It doesn't matter, though. If you don't do it for me, you'll do it for him. Either way, you're doing it. And when you do, I'll be watching. Call him back and tell him you'll do it. Tell him this is the last time. He'll chuckle and say 'Okay.' Then make the arrangements. We'll be tracking you the whole way when you go."

"Man o' man. How did it come to this?" Jorge said, shaking his head.

"That's the problem with getting started with lowlifes like him. Once you do, they own you."

Jorge made contact with the gangster who had contacted him and received his instructions. He was to walk to the same house as before and drive north to New York in an old Lincoln Continental. A down payment of $2,500.00 would be waiting for him in an envelope in the glove compartment. There was no worry of Jorge absconding with the money; he was too smart for that. If he did, he'd live the rest of his life looking over his shoulder.

After delivering the Lincoln to its destination in the City, he was to drive another car south and deliver it to Tiny's Body Shop. The second half of his $5,000.00 fee would be in the glove compartment as final payment. Again, he was instructed not to look in the trunks of the cars he would be driving, but this time he was also told not to look at any "cargo" that might be in the back seat.

Jorge shared this with Joey before leaving. Joey, in turn, made the police departments from both cities and the FBI aware. As soon as Jorge left New York in the second car, the plan was for the police to storm the house where Jorge picked the first car up, where he delivered it, and Tiny's Detail Shop at the same time. Jorge would be on the road when the raid happened, so it was a way to keep him safe…at least for a while. Simultaneous raids in three locations would also minimize the chance that the bad guys would be tipped off before they were caught. However, it still wasn't known if Jorge would be delivering anything illegal.

But Joey knew in his gut that Jorge would be delivering something illegal and he felt it was guns. Everything was adding up. Joey guessed Tiny's Body Shop was modifying the cars to create bigger storage compartments. By connecting the trunks to the back seats and building a flat area, the carrying capacity of the cars could be doubled. He thought the cars were then driven to Jorge's neighborhood in Samsula to be loaded with guns, and from there driven to New York where the weapons were delivered for distribution.

To prepare for the joint operation between the two police departments, Joey met with the Special Operations officers in New York. Entering the law enforcement building where he had spent so many years of his professional life was weird, a curious mix of nostalgia and anxiety. It was nostalgic because he had spent so much time there, but anxious because when he had left the Big Apple, he had reached a point where he *had* to get away. The heart-wrenching cases he worked had finally gotten the best of him. He couldn't take any more tragedy.

"Joey! It's good to see you again," Detective Sam O'Shaunessy said, shaking Joey's hand hard. He and Joey had started with the force the same year, 28 years ago.

"Good to see you, too. You need to come down to Florida with me, Sam. It's nice down there. I catch really big fish."

"I know, but Lori won't let me go. We have three grandkids here now."

"Hard to think of you as a grandfather, Sam. But you know, the hardest thing for me is to think that I'm not a father. I think about that a lot, wondering what I've missed. "

"I bet you do, but it wasn't in the cards. You were so dedicated to the job that there just wasn't time. Think about how many slimeballs would have gotten away if you'd been at a Little League baseball game. You never know."

"No, you don't, but I don't know if it was worth it or not."

This segued into a conversation Sam knew he must have with Joey.

"If this case really is about guns, we need to review all our past assault weapons' cases, even your father's." He let the sentence hang.

"That was 41 years ago, Sam. How could that be relevant?"

"It may not be – probably isn't – but we should go through it anyway. No telling what we might find."

"I suppose you're right, but that's going to be tough. Do you know how much I've anguished over that murderer never being caught? That's probably what drove me to work so hard all these years."

"Of course it was, Joey. We all knew that."

"I've often wondered what I'd do if I caught him. In some ways I hope I never get the chance. I'd go totally berserk, I'm sure."

"And I'd fully understand it if you did. Now let's get to those files. There are a little over a hundred of them."

The review of the files was an interesting study in the evolution of assault weapons. For the most part, the changing look of these guns mirrored the changing look of military arms. This was understandable because assault weapons were, in fact, guns with the same actions as legal arms but with a military look and a capacity for holding more rounds of ammunition or for accepting sound suppressors. Contrary to popular belief, a gun doesn't have to be a fully automatic weapon to be an "assault weapon." Fully automatic guns had been illegal since 1968.

One trend was unmistakable, however: Assault weapons, like military guns in general, were getting smaller, actions were getting faster, and firepower was getting greater. Many current models were no larger than an ordinary grease gun any mechanic would have, and with clips holding as many as 50 rounds, they could shoot so long without having to be reloaded that one weapon could hold many police officers at bay. It was no wonder that the law enforcement community was working so hard at keeping these weapons out of the wrong hands.

The review of the case involving the death of Officer Petruco was very difficult for Joey. The woman who had let Joey's father into the house that fateful day acted as though she knew little about the assassin. All she gave police was a physical description of him. Detectives thought she was holding back, but they couldn't get her to say anything more. An artist's rendering was the only piece of evidence in the file.

Joey stared at the drawing for a long time. "The man that killed my father," he thought. Joey had known many killers in his time and often wondered if they felt remorse or even cared.

This murderer had a very distinctive look that was sinister and evil. A scar on his left cheek went from the corner of his lips to the top of his jawbone, making his mouth seem very long on one side. He had a ruddy complexion, bushy mustache and long hair.

But there was something else, something that made him look off balance. Joey didn't notice it at first, and only after staring at the picture for a few seconds did he see it. The killer was missing his left ear lobe, the same side of his face as the scar.

"Not a pretty guy, was he?" Sam asked.

"No, he wasn't. So this is the guy who did it, the guy who changed everything for me?"

"That's him. I'm sorry we never caught him, Joey. I'd like to have seen him get a needle in his arm."

"Me too, Sam. Me too."

Jorge was to pick up the car in Samsula at noon on Saturday. He would spend the first night at a designated hotel in Columbia, S.C., the second in a motel in Richmond, Va., and the third in a truck stop in Harrisburg, Pa. before making it into New York City on Tuesday. Joey suspected the bad guys would have lookouts at all stops to see if Jorge was being followed, so the police would leave Jorge alone until the simultaneous raid on all sites.

Jorge did as he was told, picking up the car on schedule. Twenty-five hundred dollars were waiting for him in the glove compartment. Black canvas covered what appeared to be boxes in the back seat.

He made the trip without incident. At 4:00 p.m. on Tuesday, he pulled into the car stereo shop in Queens to drop off the car. Fifteen minutes later he pulled away in a different car, headed back to Florida. When he was just several blocks away, the raids began.

Dressed in riot gear, police in New York stormed the car stereo shop, ordering everyone to lie down on the floor with their hands behind them. At the same time, federal agents in South Carolina, Virginia and Pennsylvania entered the places where Jorge had stayed, and questioned the proprietors. A common link existed between them: all the managers were of Middle Eastern descent.

While this was going on, Daytona Beach police officers rushed into Tiny's Body Shop, and Volusia County Sheriff's deputies rushed the home in Samsula where Jorge had picked up the first car.

The time leading up to any coordinated police action was a time of great anxiety for Joey. This was *his* operation, and he felt an enormous responsibility to the officers involved. It was critical that the suspects be totally surprised to maximize the chance for a successful outcome and minimize the risk of injury to the officers. He also felt an obligation to the suspects. If he was wrong, and they weren't criminals, their businesses could be ruined.

Joey was not wrong about this one, though. The car Jorge delivered to New York turned out to be loaded with eight wooden crates full of MAC-10 and MAC-11 assault weapons. At a thousand dollars apiece, the street value of the 180 guns was $180,000.00.

Joey's suspicion about Tiny's Body Shop was correct. Regular automotive bodywork was done there, but also cars were converted to hold more cargo like the one Jorge delivered to the City. At the time of the raid, there were two stolen cars in the bays being converted in such a fashion.

The house in Samsula was dry, however. No one was there, and nothing was found that would indicate it was used in the operation. The deputies turned the place upside down and dusted for fingerprints, but it was as clean as a whistle.

By all accounts, the operation was a big success. Nine people were arrested on the day of the raid, and subsequent investigations led to the arrests of four others. Six hundred assault weapons were confiscated, and Joey was sure that a severe blow had been dealt the smuggling network. Still, something was missing. It didn't make sense that nothing was found at the house where Jorge had picked up the car. Joey was convinced that a significant part of the criminal enterprise – or those who ran it – had escaped, so he stayed with the case, following every possible lead.

Title to the house was in the name of Glenn Harding of Kalamazoo, Michigan. When interviewed later, Harding said he inherited it from a deceased uncle and had only visited it once. He had intended to put the house on the market soon. Joey was convinced he wasn't involved.

The wooden boxes the guns had been packed in were coffee crates. The weapons confiscated were manufactured in the United States and legally sold to the government of Columbia, South America. They had then been stolen or corrupt officials had sold them to a third party. From there, they were packed in coffee crates and shipped to the Port of Jacksonville, Florida, with other coffee crates full of coffee beans headed for the Cup O' Joe Coffee plant in that city.

Upon arrival in Jacksonville, the crates were off-loaded into semi-trucks. Somewhere along the way, the crates containing the guns were taken out and delivered to Daytona Beach while the crates containing coffee beans continued the journey to the Cup O' Joe plant.

Joey ran down all of these rabbit trails, and over the next few months several more people were arrested. Still, he learned little of what happened to the weapons once they reached Daytona Beach. Where were they stored, and how did they get loaded into the cars?

Once or twice a week he found himself driving through the Samsula neighborhood where Jorge had picked up the car filled with the guns. Occasionally he would walk down the street, speaking to the local residents he met. Most who lived there were either Hispanic or native to Samsula, so he stuck out like a sore thumb. Consequently, few would engage him much, and the best he could get was a polite "hello" from most people.

One day, however, he passed an elderly woman shuffling down the street. She accidentally dropped a bag full of fruit, and Joey knelt down to pick it up.

"Good afternoon, ma'am," he said as he handed her the bag.

"Oh, you think so, huh?" she replied. "You ain't from here if that's what you think."

"What's wrong?"

"This used to be a good neighborhood," she said as they walked slowly along. "Now it's a dump. People here were poor, but proud and good. Not no more. It's gotten so bad I don't dare go outside at night."

"Are you afraid?" Joey asked, helping her put a few oranges in her bag.

"Darn right I'm afraid. Half the people here are illegals, so what do they care? They'll do anything."

"Like what?"

"Drugs, prostitution, drinking until all hours of the night...it's a regular rats' nest around here, I'll tell you. Who are you anyway, and whatcha doin' here?"

"I'm a police investigator with Daytona Beach."

"You're a good ways from your territory, ain't you?"

"I am, but I've been working a case that may have a Samsula connection."

"What kinda case?"

"Guns. Have you ever heard any shooting?"

"Ain't heard no shots 'cept an occasional rifle shot out in the woods. People 'round here hunt deer year-round," she said, laughing. Joey grinned but he wasn't amused, thinking of the problem they had with poachers at his camp nearby.

"I saw a guy carrying a gun once, though...a scary one too," she continued. "The kind you see in the movies. It was early Saturday mornin'. I was walkin' to the jiffy just like I do ever' day. He looked at me kinda funny, like I'd seen something I weren't supposed to see. But he didn't say nothin'. "

Joey was keenly interested now.

"Can you tell me about the man?"

"Don't know nothin' 'bout him, 'cept he lives in that house." She pointed to a small wooden clapboard structure across the street. "You gonna pay him a visit?"

"I think I will," Joey answered.

"I thought you would," she said with a grin. "Don't tell him I sent you, though. Might not be good for my health, iffen' you know what I mean."

"I do, and I won't say a thing. Thanks for the information."

"Okay. Hope you find what you're lookin' for. This neighborhood ain't gettin' no better 'til we get rid of the riffraff."

Joey waited until the woman turned the corner then approached the house. He walked up two steps to the screen door of a porch. He called out, "Anyone home?"

No sooner had the words left his mouth than a dog exploded from the crawlspace, a mean-looking pit bull/cur crossbreed. It ran at Joey, barking wildly. A chain was connected to its collar, but Joey didn't know how much chain there was, so he opened the screen door and jumped inside the porch, slamming the door behind him.

"Son of a gun that was close!" Joey thought, his heart beating fast.

When the chain drew tight, the dog was still five feet from the door, growling, saliva dripping from its mouth.

Joey straightened his clothes and wiped his face with his handkerchief. "Anyone home?" he called again as he knocked on the door. Still no one answered.

He peered through the window of the door. He could see pretty clearly with sunlight shining in from a side window. There was an old photograph on the mantle of a fireplace, an 8"x10" picture of a man and a woman. They looked to be in their early 20s. "What is it about that man?" Joey thought. He didn't know him, he was sure of that, but there was something familiar about the person's face. "What could it be?"

Then it hit him like a ton of bricks. The blood rushed from his head and he grew dizzy. He steadied himself against the wall.

The man in the photograph had a long scar on his left cheek from the corner of his mouth to his cheekbone, *and he had no left ear lobe!*

There was no doubt. It was the man who'd killed Joey's father!

Joey instinctively drew his gun. He turned the doorknob, but the door was locked. He backed away and left the porch, walking the other way from the dog that was still growling menacingly. He slipped around the house, checking the windows as he went. They were all locked…except for one, a bathroom window. Joey opened it and climbed through.

The floor creaked each time Joey stepped, the old wooden floor giving a little under his weight. From room to room he went, holding his pistol in front of him. His nerves were on razor's edge.

Nobody was in the living room, dining room or kitchen. "The bedroom," Joey thought. "The room where, in another house, he killed my father."

Walking towards the bedroom he felt like a death row inmate walking towards the electric chair. "Is he going to get me, the same way he got my dad?" Joey wondered.

He pushed the door open slowly and looked to both sides. He stepped inside. The window was open, a gentle breeze blowing the sheer curtains. He spun around, gun raised, thinking someone was behind the door. Nothing. No one was in the house.

When the reality of that sunk in, he grew weak and sat on the edge of the bed. He was having difficulty getting his breath. He lowered his head and leaned over, trying to get blood back to his brain. It was then that he saw the stock of the rifle lying on the floor, protruding slightly from underneath the bed.

He jumped to his feet thinking someone was there. Realizing there was not enough space for that, he knelt to investigate. What he found was unbelievable. Lying side-by-side, attached to a board by hooks and Velcro, was a sampling of top-of-the-market assault weapons. There was an Israeli-made UZI, a Soviet AK-47, a TEC-9, a Chinese SKS rifle, a Street Sweeper, a MAC-10, a MAC-11 and a Colt AR-15. There were also banana clips and flash suppressors. This was a display case! The guy who owned them had to be into some really serious stuff.

Joey slowly moved the material out from under the bed so he could get a good look at it. He then pushed it back under and slowly moved away. He peeked out the windows to see if anyone was watching the house. Seeing no one, he quickly walked from the house to his car, the fierce dog growling and barking the whole time.

He immediately called his boss at the police station, who then alerted the Sheriff's office and the Florida Department of Law Enforcement (FDLE). Undercover officers then began a stakeout of the house. Three days after the operation began, the guy in the photograph above the fireplace mantle – a person who now appeared to be about 60 years old – showed up. Joey was there, and he was finally able to confront his father's killer.

As soon as the man was out of his car, the officers were on him, their guns drawn. They weren't going to take any chances with this lowlife.

"Put your hands on the hood and spread your legs," an FDLE agent shouted, spinning the man around and pushing him against the car.

"What's this about," the man yelled back. "I haven't done anything."

"You've done plenty," Joey said, getting in the guy's face, his hand gripped tightly around the back of the man's shirt collar.

"We got it, Joey. Back up," one of the deputies injected. "You'll have time with him later."

Joey wouldn't leave. "What's your name," he said, his voice shaking with rage.

The man wouldn't answer.

"I said, what's your *name!*" Joey said more forcefully, twisting the man's collar until his face turned red.

"Come on, Joey. That's enough," one of the FDLE agents said. They were all aware that this might be the killer of Joey's dad, so they gave Joey some latitude, but they weren't going to let him do something he might regret later. Joey slowly loosened his grip.

"Lincoln Diablo," the man finally said. "My name is Lincoln Diablo."

"You live here?" the FDLE officer asked.

"Yeah, why?"

"Because we found a nice little bundle under the bed in your house. Whose are they?"

Diablo didn't say a word.

"Whose are they, Diablo?"

Diablo spit over his right shoulder. It was clear he wasn't going to give them anything.

"Okay, that's it. Lincoln Diablo, you're under arrest for the possession of illegal assault weapons and accessories. You have the right to remain silent…"

As Diablo's Miranda rights were read to him, Joey walked around the car so that he could look straight into his eyes. Diablo stared back just as hard, each searching for something.

"What do you want of me?" Diablo asked Joey.

Now it was time for Joey to stay quiet. Diablo was quickly dragged from the scene by the other officers and shoved into the backseat of a deputy's car. The car pulled away and Joey watched until it disappeared. He no longer felt the rage as he had at first. In fact, he felt strangely disconnected from the scene playing out before him, as though he had left his body and was looking down from above. He had thought of this moment so many times before; now that it was here, he didn't feel anything at all.

Joey participated in the interrogation of Lincoln Diablo. Sitting next to Diablo was his attorney, William Roundtree, a criminal defense lawyer from Miami who was recognized as one of the country's best. Roundtree wasn't cheap, $400.00 an hour. From the shabby appearance of Diablo's modest house, it seemed unlikely that he could afford an attorney like Roundtree. Joey was sure others were bankrolling him.

Roundtree would not allow his client to answer any questions about the guns or accessories.

"Whose guns were they, Diablo?" a FDLE agent asked. No answer.

"You're not even going to tell me if they belonged to someone else?" Nothing.

"*Help* yourself, Lincoln. Tell us about the guns. Who did you get them from? Now's the time to talk." Still no answer. The agent walked away angrily.

Joey and the other officers had decided not to bring up the murder of Joey's father at the beginning. They didn't want him to know they suspected him. Joey took a turn at questioning him.

"Where are you from, Lincoln," Joey asked.

Diablo looked at his attorney, who nodded. "New York."

"Were you born there?"

Again his attorney nodded, indicating it was okay for him to answer.

"No. I was born in Costa Rica, near Quepos."

"Quepos, huh. Did you fish?"

"Doesn't everybody in Quepos fish?" Diablo responded smartly.

"I guess they do," Joey said, smiling. He thought briefly of a trip that he had taken there to catch sailfish, but quickly dismissed such thoughts. He was determined to give this interrogation his best shot, and that required focus. "Is that all you did?"

"No. We also farmed."

"Who's 'we'?"

"My family and everyone who lived near us. Crops grow year round, so everyone farms."

"When did you move to New York?"

"When I was 15. My parents sent me there to live with an aunt and uncle."

"Why?"

"They wanted me to learn English and get an American education. My mother said it was the best way to live better. She didn't want me to stay in Costa Rica and just scratch out a living."

"Did you go by yourself?"

"Yes, but others from our area went too. We called our street in New York 'Little Quepos.'" Joey had never heard of that, but made a note to call about it.

"How'd things go in New York?"

"Not too bad, I guess. I got by."

"How'd you get that scar?"

"Okay, that's enough," injected Roundtree. "My client's not answering any more questions."

"And what happened to your ear?" Joey pressed. "Looks like a dog chewed it off. I've never seen anyone who was missing an ear lobe."

"I said he's not answering any more questions. The interview's over," Roundtree said again.

"The other guy got the best of you, didn't he," Joey continued. "Carved you up like a Thanksgiving turkey." Diablo just smiled.

"Don't say a thing, Lincoln," said Roundtree. He turned to Joey as he stood. "I'm leaving and you may not interrogate my client without my being present."

Joey was wound up. He wasn't going to stop now.

"I bet it was over a lady, wasn't it?" he said.

This got to Lincoln, and he began to fidget in his seat. Joey wouldn't let up.

"She left you for him, didn't she, Lincoln? You couldn't keep her in the stable, could you?"

"She did not leave me!" Diablo said angrily. "I left her!"

"Why? Why'd you leave her?"

"I had to!"

"Why, Diablo? Why'd you have to leave her?"

"Don't say another word!" Roundtree yelled.

"You're lying, Lincoln. She left you because you couldn't carry the mail. That's what it was. She found somebody better!"

"She would *never* have left me! She followed me to the United States. She loved me!" Diablo was standing now, his voice quivering.

"Not another word!" Roundtree shouted at Diablo.

Diablo was seething. His face was red and he was shaking. He slowly sat down.

"Why'd you have to leave her, Lincoln," Joey asked again.

"Lincoln!" said Roundtree sternly.

Diablo looked down and crossed his arms. He had gotten the message. He was through talking. It didn't matter, though. Joey had gotten what he wanted.

"What do you mean, 'We have a problem,'" Joey asked Alicia Bell, assistant state attorney.

"Diablo's attorney has filed a Motion to Supress, claiming your search of Diablo's house was unlawful so the evidence found is inadmissible. It's a legal theory known as 'fruit of the poisonous tree.'"

"Oh, that's just lawyer stuff," Joey said in a dismissive voice. "With the weapons Diablo had, no jury in the world would let him off."

"Maybe so, *if* it gets to a jury. But if the Court suppresses the evidence – the guns – we have no case. A Motion to Dismiss will be next and we may lose."

"But the judge wouldn't do that. No way."

"Don't be so sure of that. Judge Clifton is a courageous judge."

"But that wouldn't be courageous. That would be foolhardy! No judge in Florida would get re-elected if he threw out this evidence."

"Perhaps not, but you screwed up. You should have gotten a search warrant," Alicia said sternly.

"Oh, give me a break. I'd like to see how you or any other do-gooder would have handled it. I can't believe this. And I thought New York was bad!"

"It's the law in New York, too, so I don't know what you're talking about. It's a judicial doctrine created by the U.S. Supreme Court so it applies nationwide. What were you thinking, Joey? You're an experienced cop. You should have known better than to enter the house under those circumstances. There was no emergency. You had time to get a warrant."

"Look, I had just been run into a screen porch by the scariest dog in Volusia County, and I'd just seen a picture of an arms dealer who killed my father 41 years ago. I was a little pumped."

"I know, and I'm sorry. But that may not matter to Judge Clifton. He doesn't coddle criminals, but he's a real stickler for the Constitution."

"This man murdered my dad! He shot him twice in the chest and once in the neck!" Joey was angry now, and all the rage that had been missing at the time of Diablo's arrest was coming out.

"Joey, we're on the same side. I'm not going to dismiss the charges voluntarily. I'm just telling you it's going to be a tough sale."

"I don't care how tough it's going to be! You can't let this guy walk! And what about charging him with the murder of my father? You *are* going to do that, aren't you?"

"We don't file charges in Florida for a crime that happened in New York; that's up to the prosecutors up there," Alicia answered.

"But you are going to at least arrest him for that, aren't you? Joey said with a pleading look in his eye.

"In all honesty, we haven't decided. The arrest warrant from New York is 41 years old, and the only evidence we have is an artist's rendering. The only person who could help us, the woman who answered the door, is gone. Soon after the murder she just disappeared."

"But you *have* to arrest him!" Joey implored. His emotions were turning from rage to sorrow, and he was getting distraught. "He killed my father,

Alicia. At least give it a try. Use the artist's rendering if that's all you have, but at least try…please."

"Joey, this is being discussed with New York officials as we speak, but these are team decisions, you know that. My guess is we'll get the okay for the arrest and extradition, but senior staff in the office will discuss it and vote."

"What are you going to do, Alicia?"

"You'll get at least one vote," she said with a kind-hearted grin.

"Thank you. But don't do it for me," Joey replied. "Do it for my dad."

"Your honor, Detective Petruco clearly violated the exclusionary rule. The evidence obtained was in contravention of my client's Fourth Amendment rights against unreasonable search and seizure, so it must be suppressed," argued William Roundtree, Diablo's attorney, to Judge Clifton at the Motion to Supress hearing.

"But Judge, without the guns, there is no case and this defendant was in possession of many assault weapons, including several that had been converted to fully automatics!" Bell responded.

"Your detective should have thought of that before he entered the house," Roundtree replied.

"He didn't know he was going to find guns," she answered. "That isn't what he was looking for."

"He entered the house illegally," Roundtree said. "Anything found in connection with an illegal entry is inadmissible, even that which would have been admissible if derived legally. It's classic 'fruit of the poisonous tree,' Judge."

Alicia knew she was in trouble, so she tried a different tactic.

"Detective Petruco did not enter the house illegally."

"Oh, give me a break," Roundtree murmured.

"Quiet, Mr. Roundtree," Judge Clifton admonished. "Continue, Ms. Bell."

"Detective Petruco chose to enter the house only after he saw the picture of the man who killed his father."

"Who he *claims* killed his father," injected Roundtree. "I've been over this with Ms. Bell. Just for the record, my client strongly denies he had anything to do with that murder."

"Surprise, surprise," Bell said. "You mean he's not confessing?"

"Your honor, the state hasn't even arrested my client for that crime," Roundtree continued.

"But that's because it was 41 years ago and we don't yet know what evidence we can produce," Bell said. "We're convinced he did it, though, and we're discussing the matter with New York authorities."

Judge Clifton stared at her, not reacting either way. "Get back to your argument, Ms. Bell."

"Detective Petruco didn't enter the house to look for weapons, but to look for Mr. Diablo, and looking for him was reasonable. Should he have not looked for a cop killer? Of course not. In fact, one could argue that he had an obligation to do so."

"Your honor, Detective Petruco went to the house because he had been told the occupant had guns," Roundtree argued. "At that point, he should have gotten a warrant to search the house. Of course, we haven't even discussed Detective Petruco being out of his jurisdiction, and you can be sure that will be the next motion I file if we don't win here. A Daytona Beach detective confiscating evidence in the far-reaches of the county? All he had to do was make one call to the Sheriff's office and a deputy would have gotten a warrant and been out there within an hour."

"It's easy to second-guess Detective Petruco, Judge," Alicia Bell said. "But he had just seen a picture of a man who he believed killed his father. He went in looking for him, and that was reasonable."

"Okay, that's enough. I'm prepared to rule. Detective Petruco was out of his jurisdiction, but that's not uncommon in investigative work. And if he had been in 'hot pursuit' in an otherwise lawful case, I wouldn't worry about it. But that question is not before the court now.

"What *is* before the court is the lawfulness of the entry of the house and the seizure of the weapons. Two reasons for entering the house have been put forward. One claims that Detective Petruco entered to search for the defendant, the other that he entered to search for guns. The Fourth Amendment is dispositive of both, but first I wish to comment on Detective Petruco's state of mind.

"I can only imagine the emotions he was feeling. If Diablo murdered his father I hope we can find a way to string him up by his thumbs. But Ms. Bell, there must not be much of a case or you would already have had him arrested for that crime. Regardless, Detective Petruco should have understood that just because a picture of the defendant was on the mantle it didn't prove anything, not even that he lived there. The defendant could have been an uncle or a friend of the actual resident.

"Of greater concern to me was him entering the house to look for weapons, if that was, in fact, why he entered. People say all kinds of things about their neighbors. Law enforcement officers need more than reports of neighbors before charging into a home without a warrant.

"Whether Detective Petruco entered the house to search for the defendant or to search for weapons doesn't matter. Either way, he did so without a warrant and there was no urgency or emergency. This constitutes an unreasonable exercise of police power. A search warrant should have been secured. The evidence – the guns and accessories – constitute 'fruit of the poisonous tree' and shall not be allowed."

"Unbelievable!" Joey said. "This scumbag is going to go free because I didn't get a stinking warrant?"

"We have no choice," Alicia answered. "Without the guns we have no case." Alicia was back in her office. Joey had been waiting for her when she returned from the hearing before Judge Clifton.

"There's nothing you can do?" Joey asked.

"I'm afraid not, but there is one thing *you* can do," she answered.

"Me?"

"Yes, you. There is an exception to the exclusionary rule. If we can prove that the evidence would have come in through another source, we might be able to get the judge to reconsider and allow it."

"You mean, if we can show that someone would have told us of the weapons, something like that?"

"Exactly. If the evidence would likely have come in through some other legal means, the courts will allow it."

"But there's only one way to do that," Joey said. "I'm going to have to show that the investigation of the gun running case would have led to Diablo, and the guns would have been discovered. That's going to require someone to squeal on him. Pretty unlikely."

"Probably so, but it is a way. You have your work cut out for you, though."

"What do you mean?"

"I'm only going to be able to hold Diablo in jail for another couple of days. Roundtree hit me with a Motion to Dismiss this morning. He'll get his hearing soon, and we'll lose. We have no evidence. Also, New York prosecutors are leaning against charging him with the murder of your father because the artist's sketch is the only evidence they have. You'll have to work fast."

Joey was very discouraged when he left the State Attorney's office. His error had led to the evidence against Diablo being thrown out, and the irony of it was almost too much to bear. He finally finds his father's murderer, but his own mistake sets the killer free. It was crushing.

How could he get someone in the gun running operation to rat out Diablo, and how could he do it in a couple of days? The answer was clear: he couldn't. So instead of heading back to his office, he got onto Interstate 4 and headed towards Orlando. He had a plane to catch. He was going to Quepos to look for a young woman who had disappeared a long time ago.

Morning fog was still lingering in the valleys of the mountains between San Jose and Quepos as Joey flew overhead. The beauty of the area with its lush tree canopy and fertile fields was intoxicating as he looked through the window of the small propeller airplane.

The plane broke past the mountains and flew along the coast a few miles before banking hard to the left. It circled wide and then straightened as it shot the gap between two mountains. Then it dove steeply and leveled, coming to a smooth landing on the short Quepos airstrip.

Joey moved quickly through the thatch-covered, open-air terminal and caught a cab headed for downtown. Over a fast lunch of fish, rice and black beans from the El Gran Escape Restaurant, he looked at the harbor where the sportfishing boats were usually anchored. It was January, prime fishing time, so most boats had charters. Joey would love to go out, especially to catch the prized roosterfish, but he had vital work to do and not much time to do it.

Leaving the restaurant he walked to the police station. He showed his identification and asked to see the chief.

Chief Olivo Norriega was nearly 75 years old but still going strong. He was a lifelong Quepos resident but had been educated at the University of Miami. Joey confided in him completely, telling him exactly why he was there. Corruption was so bad in many Central American countries that Joey would normally have had to be more cautious, but not in Costa Rica. The country was democratic and the governmental institutions were stable and honest. Besides, Joey didn't have much time so he had to trust someone.

"Yes, I knew Lincoln Diablo. He was a bad kid, always in trouble with the law," Chief Norriega answered.

"He told me his parents sent him to the United States to get an education and to learn English," Joey said.

"That might have been part of the reason, but his parents could not control him. He was heading to prison if he stayed here; it was just a matter of time and they knew it."

"He said a woman followed him to New York. This may have been the woman who was in the house when my father was killed. Do you know who that could have been?"

"No, but it was probably a person from his neighborhood. Many people from that area went to the States at that time. Why don't we go there and ask around?"

"That would be great."

The drive through the quaint countryside revealed a people who were happy in their simple surroundings. Small schools were full of well-behaved children, farmers were leading horse-drawn carts full of fruits and vegetables, and plump women wearing aprons were standing in front of their houses.

The chief's quick and nimble Toyota Cessna police car marked "Policia" on top passed trucks transporting tourists to Rainmaker Nature Refuge. The trucks had rows of bus seats mounted on the back to provide open-air seating for the guests. Getting to the Refuge was part of the adventure; these trucks would soon be crossing several suspension bridges that would make the passengers suck in their stomachs and grip the guardrails tightly.

The tourists would lose their breath many times that day as they rode "zip" lines through tree canopy. Strapped into a pulley and harness system, they would glide along cables from platform to platform, 200' above the ground. Invariably, some yahoo would let loose with a Tarzan yell.

The travelers would spend the afternoon riding horses back down the mountain, going through streams and seeing fascinating wildlife like two-toed sloths and Howler monkeys before reaching their final destination: a cabana bar serving Costa Rican beer and coconut-rum drinks. They were going to have a good day. Joey wished he could join them. "Maybe later, after all this is over," he thought.

"This is the spot. This is the neighborhood where Lincoln Diablo was raised," Chief Norriega said. "Let's get out and walk around. I know someone who lives at the end of this street."

The yellow house with green shutters was neat and well kept. Chief Norriega knocked. They heard someone shuffling across the floor. An old man opened the door.

"Olivo, my friend. It is good to see you, although it must be serious business for you to come all the way out here to see me."

"It is, Renaldo. May we come in?"

"We? Who do you have with you?"

"A police detective from the United States. I'm afraid one of your former students may have done a very bad thing."

"Then by all means, come in." Renaldo Castille opened the door and offered his guests a cup of strong coffee. Castille had been the superintendent of schools for 48 years. Before that he had been a teacher for 13. An old man now, he remembered Diablo, just as he remembered most of his students.

"He was a bad one, that Lincoln Diablo. I am not surprised he is in trouble. How can I help you?"

"We're looking for a woman who, Lincoln claims, followed him to the States. She grew up in this neighborhood. We're assuming she was about his age, making her about 60 now."

"Let me think," Renaldo answered. "Many people from this area went to New York back then. I do remember a family that lived next door to the Diablos: the Balarts. They had a daughter who was about Lincoln's age. I don't know if they were romantically involved, but she did go to the United States. I remember it clearly because her parents were very distraught about this. They did not want her to go."

"What happened to her?" Chief Norriega asked.

"I have no idea. After she left, I never heard of her again."

"Is her family still around?"

"No. Her mother died years ago. After that, her brother and father left to operate a restaurant in the north, one of those that float on water. I don't know the name, but it's not too far away and there can't be too many of them."

"Renaldo, you have been very helpful. I'm sorry to leave so quickly, but Detective Petruco and I don't have much time."

"I understand how police work is," Castille answered. "But you must come back when you can stay longer. An old man like me doesn't get many visitors."

"I promise I will. And thank you."

By now it was late afternoon, too late to investigate further, so Chief Norriega and Joey drove back to Quepos. They made plans to meet at the police station at 8:00 a.m. the next day.

After checking into a hotel just off the waterfront, Joey walked to the area where the anglers disembarked. He paid his fee to go out onto the dock and watched the boats come in and tie up. Most fishers were worn out and red from a long day of fishing in the tropical sun.

A group of fly anglers were on cloud nine, having taken one of the sea's great fish – a sailfish – on fly. Teasing a sailfish within range for a cast was an art, and a successful fisher could be rightfully proud of the accomplishment.

One guy plopped a 25-pound roosterfish on the dock, its silver body, black stripes and long flowing spines on its dorsal fin shining beautifully in the afternoon sunlight.

Joey was suddenly very tired. The travel and stress of the case had worn him down. He wandered back towards the hotel, stopping in a waterfront bar for a light meal and beer. This was all it took; he was in his bed by nine o'clock, fast asleep.

Chief Norriega and Joey were heading north at eight in the morning. Café Milagro coffee was giving Joey the caffeine jolt he needed after a long night's rest.

Joey would learn that the chief had been busy that night. He had made several calls and discovered that a family with the last name Balart had a floating restaurant about 30 miles north. The patriarch of the family, Juan Balart, had recently died. He had a son who lived next to the restaurant with his family. There was a daughter, too, but she had never married.

The restaurant was on a wide river that wound its way through mangrove islands and jungles, ultimately emptying into the Pacific Ocean. Built on pontoons, the restaurant wasn't big, seating only about 20 guests, but it was cozy and comfortable. The restaurant was moored to a dock and locked. No one was there when Joey and Chief Norriega arrived.

Chief Norriega walked out to the street and stopped a boy who was going to school. Showing him his badge, he asked, "Where are the Balarts?"

"The restaurant doesn't open until eleven," the youngster answered. "The man takes small riverboats out to show monkeys to the tourists early in the morning."

"What about the woman? Where is she?"

"She works at the beach selling jewelry and braiding hair."

"Which beach?"

"Playa Espadilla, the one with gray sand."

"What is her name?"

"Arnhilda."

"What does she look like?"

"Thin, but with curves," the boy said with a smile. "And salt and pepper hair. Very pretty."

"Gracias, amigo."

Playa Espadilla was on the other side of Quepos. It would take nearly an hour to get there.

Along the way, Joey bought two coconut drinks made and served in the coconut shell from a roadside vendor, one for him and one for Chief Norriega. Driving along, sipping his drink with a straw, Joey looked at the richness of the soil and the lushness of the gardens. "No wonder people take life so casually down here," he thought. "If everything else fails, they can always grow a garden and survive. It takes the pressure off."

South of Quepos, Joey marveled at the beauty of the coastline. As they drove through the village of Manuel Antonio, high above the ocean, he was sure he had never seen such a beautiful vista. The azure blue of the sea, white-crested waves and distant islands of rock...it was breathtaking. Back towards Quepos, charter boats were heading to the fishing grounds.

"Once I get this case behind me, I'm coming back, Chief," Joey said. "I've always wanted to catch a roosterfish."

"I hope you do. I'll take you to some of my secret spots. I'll guarantee you a roosterfish."

"Then that seals it. I'll be back at my earliest opportunity."

They were going downhill now, the road leveling off as they approached Playa Espadilla. Within minutes, they were walking among the many vendors set up under shady trees.

The third person they asked directed them to Arnhilda Balart.

She *was* beautiful, just as the boy had intimated.

"Arnhilda Balart?"

"Yes?"

"I am Olivo Norriega, Police Chief of Quepos. This is Detective Joey Petruco from the United States. He has a few questions for you."

"Ms. Balart, do you know Lincoln Diablo?"

Her reaction answered the question. The breath left her lungs. The color left her face.

"Why do you ask?" Her English was good, as though she had learned it in the States.

"Many years ago, we believe he committed a murder...and we believe you might know something about it."

She became very agitated. "Is he here?"

"No. He is in custody in the United States."

"Is he getting out?" she asked nervously.

"Are you afraid?"

Again, her reaction answered the question.

"If you help us prove he committed this crime, he will spend the rest of his life in prison," Joey stated forcefully.

She thought long and hard before answering.

"I followed him to the United States when I was too young to know any better; then I fled the United States to get away from him."

"Why? Why did you flee from him?" Joey asked.

"It was so long ago. What good could it do now?"

"Any man who commits a murder needs to be brought to justice. Please. It's important," Joey said with a pleading look in his eyes.

Arnhilda closed her eyes. Her anguish was palpable. Finally, she began.

"Every day for the last 41 years I have wondered if this would be the day he would come to get me, to make sure I was not around to tell the story. There can be only one reason why he hasn't: he must still love me. I know he used to, and first love lost is hard to get over.

"We were living in New York, planning to be married. Everything was good at first, but then Lincoln got involved with some very bad people. They were members of a gang, and life for them revolved around drugs and women. One guy in particular, Jose Cortez, made advances toward me. Lincoln found out about it, and they got into a fight. Lincoln was knocked out, and while he was unconscious, Jose cut him along his face, leaving a horrible scar. Many people have scars, but Jose did something that would make Lincoln stand out forever: he sliced off his left ear lobe.

"When Lincoln gained consciousness, he went crazy. After he healed, he asked around and found someone on the streets that would sell him a gun. The following weekend, he killed Jose.

"This began a relationship between Lincoln and the person who sold him the gun that led to other things. Soon, Lincoln was so far in that he couldn't get out. I never knew exactly what he was doing, but it had something to do with guns.

"One day, he came home drunk. He kissed me and I pushed him away. He said, "What's wrong? Would you rather be with Jose Cortez?"

Just the mention of his name made him go loco. He started pushing me, slapping me…he had never done anything like that. I was scared, and screamed.

"A neighbor heard me yell. She called the police. Two officers arrived. The one doing the talking was special. I could tell he cared about me. He wouldn't leave. He knew I needed help."

Arnhilda was crying softly now. Joey was biting his lip.

"He came inside and began going from room to room. I wanted to tell him to leave, but I couldn't talk I was so scared.

"He went into the bedroom. In a few seconds there were two shots, then a third, each one making only a 'peeew' sound, not loud. Lincoln ran from the room, carrying a pistol. He slowed down only to say, "I'll kill you if you tell them anything." He disappeared through the front door. I never saw him again.

"I ran into the bedroom and saw the body of that officer who had tried to protect me. I fell to my knees, screamed, and then cried.

"I was so scared I didn't tell police anything about Lincoln. I gave them a description, but that was all. After that, I left the country, returning to Costa Rica as soon as possible. I thought I would be safer here. Still, I have lived in fear all my life. It's probably why I never married and had children."

Arnhilda seemed relieved to have finally told the story. A great burden had been lifted.

"Ms. Balart, will you return to the States to tell this story in court?" Joey asked.

"I can't. I'm too scared."

"Arnhilda, please. The officer who Lincoln killed was my father."

Seated next to Joey on the flight back was Arnhilda Balart, allowed special clearance to travel without a passport. She had just lost her father, so when Arnhilda heard that Lincoln Diablo had killed Joey's dad she knew what she must do. Her father had died of natural causes and that was painful enough. She couldn't imagine Joey's grief, and when she heard his story, knew immediately that she must testify. It would be difficult, though. She had once loved Lincoln and he had apparently continued to love her. Had he not, would she still be alive, or would he have eliminated the only witness who could have led to his conviction?

Joey had called Alicia Bell, the state attorney, before they were airborne, to fill her in and alert her that they were coming. They would be arriving just in time; Diablo's Motion to Dismiss hearing was at 2:00 p.m. that afternoon and the assault weapons' charge would be dropped. Worse yet, unless there was a witness in the country that could provide testimony that Diablo murdered Officer Petruco, she had learned that New York authorities would not charge Diablo with that crime and he would be freed. With the scrutiny Diablo knew he would receive from law enforcement, he would likely go underground and never be seen again. Not only would the murder conviction be lost, but also a critical link in the gun running operation would remain intact.

Arnhilda said little on the trip to the United States; she was anxious about seeing Lincoln. While she had known this day might come, with each passing year the possibility had become more remote.

"I'm worried, Detective," she said.

"I know you are, but I'm not going to let anything happen to you."

"No, you don't understand. I'm not so worried for my personal safety; I'm worried that I'm doing the wrong thing. It was so long ago." She was having second thoughts about testifying.

"Arnhilda, I still think of my father every day. People say time heals, but they're wrong. It still hurts as much as it did the day I found out. The shock is gone and I don't cry as much, but it still hurts. I gave up on closure a long time ago; that's another false concept. But it will settle my soul to know that my dad's murderer is being held accountable, and that's what he is, Arnhilda – a murderer. We also don't know the others he's killed. At the very least he's been trafficking guns that have brought death to countless people."

"Yes, I know. But it's hard," she said. "We had big plans at one time, he and I. We were going to open a restaurant in the City, specializing in Costa Rican dishes. The restaurant was going to be downstairs and we were going to live upstairs. Our kids would work in the restaurant," she said with a smile. "Then he got with the wrong crowd and everything changed. Just a few unfortunate acquaintances wrecked our dream of a great life in a new country."

"It happens all the time, Arnhilda," Joey answered. "Without a father or a teacher or someone to keep a kid like Lincoln straight, it's easy to go astray. But there's another reason why you need to do this: *You* need peace. You've been living with this for 41 years, wondering if the knock on your door was going to be him, or feeling the guilt of knowing that a killer was getting away with murder. You need to do this for yourself more than you need to do it for me."

Arnhilda grew silent, thinking about what Joey had said. She knew in her heart that he was right. She did need peace. She had lived with this long enough.

"Ms. Bell, do you have any additional evidence against Mr. Diablo?"

"No, Your Honor, we don't, but we are convinced he is integrally involved in gun running."

"Then I have no choice. I must dismiss the charges against him."

Diablo and his attorney, William Roundtree, smiled.

"Before you rule, Judge, could we please take a 15 minute recess?"

Roundtree sat forward, concerned.

"Why would I do that, Ms. Bell? If you have no further evidence now, you won't in 15 minutes either, will you?"

The time had come to lay the cards on the table.

"As we have briefly discussed, the People believe Diablo committed another crime, a very serious crime, a long time ago. If you will recess for 15 minutes, you will understand why I make this request."

Roundtree jumped to his feet. "Your Honor, this is highly unusual. If the People have evidence that my client committed another crime, they should produce it now or let him go."

"Not so fast, Mr. Roundtree," Judge Clifton said. "For the record, state the nature of the crime, Ms. Bell?"

"Murder. Murder of a police officer 41 years ago. We discussed this at the Motion to Supress hearing."

"But what's changed, Ms. Bell," Judge Clifton asked.

"We have someone who can testify that Mr. Diablo is the killer...someone who was there!"

The color drained from Diablo's face and he became very agitated, a reaction noticed by the judge.

"This is absurd, Your Honor," Roundtree exclaimed. "Forty-one years ago? If Ms. Bell had any basis to arrest my client she already would have."

"Our practice is not to hold people in jail unless they have been charged or awaiting extradiction," the judge said. "And they can't be charged without any evidence. What basis do I have for holding him in jail?"

It wasn't going well for Alicia, and she was out of answers.

"Ms. Bell, the way I look at it, this defendant's already getting one free pass out of jail," Judge Clifton said. "It's going to chap me no end to do it again, especially since I saw his reaction when you mentioned the crime you claim he committed, but what choice do I have? It's now or never with your evidence, Ms. Bell. Who is your witness, and where is he?"

Suddenly the doors to the courtroom burst open, and in walked Arnhilda Balart escorted by Joey Petruco.

Lincoln Diablo went wild. He leaped over the defense table, stepped onto the rail separating the observers from the courtroom participants, and rushed Arnhilda. "Noooooo!!!" he yelled.

Joey clotheslined him with a forearm to the throat, knocking Diablo onto his back. He then fell onto Diablo's stomach, leading with his knee, knocking the breath out of him. He rolled him over and cuffed him.

"Lincoln Diablo, you're under arrest for the murder of Officer Louie Petruco, my father!" Joey shouted. "You have the right to remain silent. Anything you say can and will be used against you…"

By now the bailiff was there, helping Joey pick Diablo up from the floor. Two more bailiffs from down the hall ran into the courtroom when they heard the commotion. They quickly led Diablo away as he strained wildly to look at Arnhilda.

"How could you?" he yelled as he was being taken through the side door. "I loved you!"

The door closed behind him, and he was gone.

Lincoln Diablo was extradicted to New York for prosecution, accompanied by Joey Petruco. He avoided the death penalty by accepting a plea bargain to serve the rest of his life in prison. At his sentencing, Joey and a dozen detectives, including Joey's detective friend, Sam O'Shaunessy, sat in the audience. Diablo had been brought to justice for the murder of Joey's dad, and the gun smuggling ring had been broken as well. Diablo had been the mastermind, and knowing he was incarcerated gave others with information the courage to speak out and identify the remaining players in the operation.

A corrupt judge and shipping company executives in Columbia, South

America, were arrested for stealing guns from the military and exporting them back to the United States.

The man Joey had seen at the Samsula racetrack was the leader of an auto theft network that stole cars all over the South. He was apprehended in New Orleans, convicted and sentenced to 23 years in prison.

In a small warehouse near the racetrack, hundreds of assault weapons were found. A stakeout caught three men going in late at night trying to remove them. It was here that the cars were loaded with their deadly cargo. From there the cars were taken to Diablo's neighborhood where the drivers who had been recruited to take them to New York began their journeys.

The managers of the three places where Jorge Rodriguez stayed along the way to New York were implicated and faced extradition, if they weren't first prosecuted under the Patriot Act in the States.

This closed the loop on the gun running operation. From smuggling the guns into the United States, delivery of the guns to the Daytona Beach area, to the transporting of the guns to New York, everyone involved was apprehended and prosecuted.

"It couldn't have worked out any better," Sam said. "It was a clean sweep."

"Yes it was," Joey answered. "Yes it was."

They were at LaGuardia airport. Joey was preparing to catch a flight back to Florida.

"But the best thing…the best thing…" Joey's voice cracked. He couldn't finish.

"I know. That *was* the best thing," Sam replied. "You don't have to say it. We all feel that way. It took 41 years, but we got him, and you got to make the arrest. What are you going to do now? Keep working or go back into retirement?"

"Probably quit. This would be a good one to end on, don't you think?"

"I guess it would," Sam replied.

"But I do have a plan," Joey remarked."

"What's that?"

"There's a Costa Rican woman I must take back to her country. After I drop her off, I have a commitment from a police chief to take me fishing – some of his secret spots. He guarantees me a roosterfish."

"That does sound like a good place to think it over," Sam said, smiling.

"That's what I was thinking. I always think better when I have a fishing rod in my hand."

They shook hands and hugged. Joey turned and walked away, disappearing into the crowd.

Author's Note:

I know the Samsula area of Volusia County well. For 30 years or so I belonged to a hunting camp between Samsula and Interstate 95. In fact, one of the stories in "Under the Panther Moon," my first book, is set at this camp. The name of the story is "Crapper Creek," and it and the Author's Note that follows describe some of the great times we had there.

Like all areas, most of the people who lived in and around Samsula were good and fine people. It had a few scalawags, though. I recall pulling into a convenience store one evening on my way to the camp. It was the day <u>before</u> the opening day of deer hunting season. There was a man in camouflage clothes standing next to the counter. I asked him if he was going to hunt the next day. He said, "No, I've already killed 10!"

Unfortunately, population growth hasn't avoided this part of Florida either. Six thousand acres of our camp – including the area of the camp itself – have just been lost to housing development, and I'm aware of a Volusia County developer who built more than a <u>billion</u> dollars worth of homes last year after pre-selling more than two thousand houses.

Growing up, our family vacationed in Daytona Beach most summers. We stayed in a neat place called Elinor's Village, across the street from the oceanfront hotels. Elinor's Village is long gone; I believe it was razed and a condominium complex constructed in its place.

On these trips, my father often took us crabbing beneath a bridge traversing the Intracoastal Waterway. It was great fun being next to the water at night, but I must confess I had a hard time dropping the crabs into hot water to cook them. I still do.

THE LAW: Definitions and Explanations:

Exclusionary Rule: This rule commands that where evidence has been obtained in violation of the search and seizure protections guaranteed by the U.S. Constitution, the illegally obtained evidence cannot be used at the trial of the defendant.

Black's Law Dictionary, Sixth Edition, p. 564

"The right of the people to be secure in their persons, houses, papers, and effects, against unreasonable searches and seizures, shall not be violated, and no warrants shall issue, but upon probable cause, supported by oath or affirmation, and particularly describing the place to be searched, and the persons or things to be seized."

Article IV, Constitution of the United States

Fruit of the Poisonous Tree Doctrine: Evidence which is spawned by or directly derived from an illegal search or illegal interrogation is generally inadmissible against the defendant because of its original taint, though knowledge of facts gained independently of the original and tainted search is admissible. This doctrine is to the effect that an unlawful search taints not only evidence obtained at the search, but facts discovered by process initiated by the unlawful search.

Black's Law Dictionary, Sixth Edition, p. 670; Nardone v. United States, 308 U.S. 338, 341 (1939); Wong Sun v. United States, 371 U.S. 471 (1963)

"Yet, however felicitous the phrasing, these objections hardly answer the basic postulate of the exclusionary rule itself. The rule is calculated to prevent,

not repair. Its purpose is to deter – to compel respect for the constitutional guarantee in the only effectively available way – by removing the incentive to disregard it."

Justice Stewart, writing for the majority, in explaining the rationale of the exclusionary rule, in Elkins v. United States, 364 U.S. 206, 220 (1960)

Selected Quotes on the Exclusionary Rule:

"The criminal is to go free because the constable has blundered."

Justice (then Judge) Cardozo, speaking against the exclusionary rule, in People v. Defore, 242 N.Y. 13, at 21, 150 N.E. 585, 587 (1926)

"The criminal goes free, if he must, but it is the law that sets him free. Nothing can destroy a government more quickly than its failure to observe its own laws, or worse, its disregard of the charter of its own existence."

Justice Clark, writing for the majority, in support of the exclusionary rule, in Mapp v. Ohio, 367 U.S. 643, 657 (1961)

"Our government is the potent, the omnipresent teacher. For good or for ill, it teaches the whole people by its example...If the Government becomes a lawbreaker, it breeds contempt for law; it invites every man to become a law unto himself; it invites anarchy."

Justice Brandeis, in dissent, writing in support of the exclusionary rule in Olmstead v. United States, 277 U.S. 438, 485 (1928)

Notable Quotes:

"The Fourth Amendment and the personal rights it secures have a long history. At the very core stands the right of a man to retreat into his own home and there be free from unreasonable governmental intrusion."

Honorable Potter Stewart, Associate Justice,
United States Supreme Court
www.brainyquotes.com

"If the provisions of the Constitution be not upheld when they pinch as well as when they comfort, they may as well be abandoned."

> Honorable Charles Evans Hughes, Chief Justice,
> United States Supreme Court, in Home Building &
> Loan Association v. Blaisdel, 290 U.S. 398 (1934),
> as attributed in www.home.att.net/~midnightflyer/supreme.html

"It is not enough to know that the men applying the standard are honorable and devoted men. This is a government of laws, not of men…It is not without significance that most of the provisions of the Bill of Rights are procedural. It is procedure that spells much of the difference between rule of law and rule by whim or caprice."

> Honorable William O. Douglas, Associate Justice,
> United States Supreme Court, concurring in Anti-Fascist
> Refugee Comm. v. McGrath, 341 U.S. 123, 178-179 (1951)

"The history of the American freedom is, in no small measure, the history of procedure."

> Honorable Felix Frankfurter, Associate Justice,
> United States Supreme Court
> "Quotes From Supreme Court Justices,"
> www.home.att.net/~midnightflyer/supreme.html

"I cannot say that our country could have no secret police without becoming totalitarian, but I can say with great conviction that it cannot become totalitarian without a centralized national police."

> Honorable Robert H. Jackson, Associate Justice,
> United States Supreme Court,
> in "The Supreme Court in the American System of Justice," by Robert H.
> Jackson, as attributed in "Quotes From Supreme Court Justices,"
> www.home.att.net/~midnightflyer/supreme.html

"There is nothing new in the realization that the Constitution sometimes insulates the criminality of a few in order to protect the privacy of us all."

> Honorable Antonin Scalia, Associate Justice,
> United States Supreme Court
> www.brainyquotes.com

"Life and liberty can be as much endangered from illegal methods used to convict those thought to be criminals as from the actual criminals themselves."

Honorable Earl Warren, Chief Justice,
United States Supreme Court
www.brainyquotes.com

"The police must obey the law while enforcing the law."

Honorable Earl Warren, Chief Justice,
United States Supreme Court
www.brainyquotes.com

"It would degrade our country and our judicial system to permit our courts to be bullied, insulted and humiliated and the orderly progress thwarted and obstructed by defendants brought before them charged with crimes."

Honorable Hugo Black, Associate Justice,
United States Supreme Court
www.brainyquotes.com

Swamp Reflections

Careful What You Ask For
Freedom of Religion: The Establishment Clause and The Free Exercise Clause

Preface: Few freedoms are as cherished as religious freedom. It was, in fact, the reason the Pilgrims came to America in the first place, to escape the control of the state-sponsored Church of England.

A tension exists in the United States, though, between those who assert that their religious freedom is being threatened by those who claim to want nothing more than to be free of others' religious influence. It's a dichotomy that's hard to understand, and poses an interesting question: How can those who want pure religious freedom be guilty of preventing others from practicing their religion? The answer may lie in differing perspectives on what religious freedom means.

To many, religious freedom means that all taxpayer-supported settings should be free of any reference to a deity or to a particular religion. To allow otherwise would, they say, have the effect of promoting a belief in God or one religion over another, violating the Establishment Clause of the United States Constitution. Others believe that to prevent any reference to God or to a particular religion at public functions prevents them from practicing their religion, violating their rights as guaranteed by the Free Exercise Clause of the United States Constitution. As we'll see in this story, however, the courts don't distinguish between gods or religions. If mixing is allowed for one, it will be allowed for all.

TO A DEER HUNTER like Ed Starkes, there was no better sound than deer moving through water. Sometimes it was a faint and delicate pitter-pat as a deer slowly tiptoed through the swamp, raising and lowering each foot gingerly. Other times it sounded like an entire football team was crashing through the bog. Either way, it meant deer were in the area, and if the sound was getting louder, they were getting closer.

Encounters such as these were what kept Ed coming back to the woods. He would be the first to say he had spent entirely too much time in a tree in his lifetime, sitting in a tree stand, hoping the deer coming his way was that monster buck that would take his breath away.

Early in his hunting, when he was a teenager, Starkes could barely sit for an hour and a half. But as he got older, he found that he could stay longer, sometimes all morning or all afternoon. As long as the tree stand was a comfortable one, he could sit for hours on end.

Indeed, Ed loved his time in the woods. His family property along the banks of the Alapaha River in North-Central Florida close to the town of Jennings, nearly in Georgia, was sacred ground to him. His father had bought the 1,200 acres in 1932, and Ed and his two brothers would never part with it. It was there that they had learned to hunt and love the outdoors, a place where they always felt the closest to each other. Their father left it to all three of them when he died, and they decided to leave it exactly as it was.

Ed's favorite tree stand was on the uphill side of a thick "river-bottom" swamp that bordered the Alapaha, a view that allowed him to see down towards the river. Behind him, up the hill, were planted pines. This was a fine place to be on a cold morning in late December, and Ed had taken several great bucks there.

He had a lot of time to think when he was hunting. Sometimes he'd jot down notes of thoughts that came to him, but most of the time he'd just push the thought away after dwelling on it for a while and wait for what would come next.

Some thoughts were recurring themes: his wife and kids, his job, God. This hunting season, though, a new thought had permeated his consciousness, and it was with him constantly. The past year he had found himself in the middle of a controversy that had rattled his conservative beliefs and shaken his political philosophy. He was feeling better now, better than when he had been in the middle of the controversy, but he would be the first to admit that things weren't nearly so clear to him as they used to be, not nearly so black and white...

Ed Starkes had been elected to the Florida Legislature at the age of 52 from Live Oak, Florida. He owned the local franchise of a national electronics store and was very involved in his church. It was a convergence of these two interests that led him to run for office. In his mind, taxes were going up and the morals of the country were going down, so he ran and won, riding a Republican wave into the Legislature in 1994.

A self-described conservative, his religious beliefs blended perfectly with his political philosophy on "cultural" issues like abortion, homosexuality and school prayer. Not that it would have mattered though, because on these issues his positions were driven totally by his religious convictions. On fiscal matters like government spending and taxes, and social issues like affirmative action and school vouchers, his positions were completely in line with national Republican ideology, so he never strayed from the party line. On all fronts he was in the comfortable place of having his personal feelings in sync with his political philosophy, his political party and the people with whom he worked most closely.

He developed a close personal and professional relationship with the newly elected Republican governor, Thomas C. Stimson, often handling the governor's most difficult and controversial bills. This put him in the news often, and he soon became the public legislative face of state Republican politics.

Such a high profile made him the butt of Democrats' snide remarks and the focus of occasional newspaper cartoons. He kept a stiff upper lip and laughed along, but the truth was, such attacks hurt him deeply. His motivation couldn't have been purer: he truly believed his legislative proposals would help people, not hurt them. He also believed with all his heart that his proposals would be good for the morality of the country and reflected a set of values that was divinely inspired. Indeed, he genuinely liked many of his Democratic colleagues even if he disagreed with them, praying for them often, hoping they would see the light. Ed Starkes was a good man, a thoughtful person with good intentions.

He was a wonderful father to his three daughters and a fine husband to his wife of 24 years. He was a pillar in the community, someone the town could always count on to lead well in difficult times. But he was not a man of nuance. In his view, for example, there was no difference between being "pro choice" and "pro abortion." Anyone who claimed a difference was merely parsing words. An elected official who claimed to be against abortion personally, but for choice politically, had a "rump cheek placed firmly on each side of the fence," Ed liked to say. Likewise, Ed saw an unjustifiable inconsistency with legislators who believed that homosexuality was a sin, yet voted to prevent homosexuals from being discriminated against in housing and hiring. If one believed it was sinful behavior, how could one vote to make it protected behavior? And school prayer? If one was truly a godly person, how could he support the prevention of sanctioned public prayer at public-school events just because a few people might be offended? That would discriminate against those who supported the prayer, and that wasn't fair.

This rigid view of right and wrong drove his politics and trumped every other consideration. He didn't let anything get in the way of his support for the "moral" or "conservative" position on issues like this; no other consideration could be more important, not even whether a proposal was considered by most scholars to be unconstitutional. In his view, people "over-thought" issues of this nature. They would be far better off if they just supported the general moral value the issues were prescribing, and not get sidetracked by academic arguments like constitutionality.

After his first term in the House, Representative Starkes was re-elected with only token opposition. When he was re-elected with no opposition two years later, in 1998, the same year the incumbent Republican governor was re-elected, he saw their elections as a mandate for the conservative policies they had begun together several years earlier.

One of these issues was the matter of school vouchers for grades K-12, a centerpiece of Governor Stimson's re-election campaign. His concept was to measure how well a school was doing by testing its students annually with standardized tests. If the school was not doing well enough and was classified as "failing," the students would be entitled to a "voucher," a public stipend that could be used to pay tuition at a private school. Vouchers had been used in higher education for years without controversy, but extending the concept to K-12 was viewed by many as the beginning of the end for public education. Critics believed that siphoning money from a public education system that was already under-funded would push the system even further behind and erode quality to the point that more and more people would choose private school over public school. To the governor, however, the issue was one of conscience. How could anyone in good conscience keep students from the means of escaping such a poor learning environment? Ed Starkes shared the governor's view. They talked about it often, so it was no surprise that the governor asked Representative Starkes to file the bill, placing him front and center in the debate.

"This is about giving parents choices," Governor Stimson said at the press conference announcing the filing of the bill. "It's also about giving students a ticket out of poverty. It is a statistical fact that students who are educationally deficient are several times more likely to be poor.

"More than anything, though, this is a matter of conscience," the governor continued. "Wealthy parents can afford to send their children to private schools, but poorer parents cannot, and it is simply unconscionable to allow students to languish in a learning environment where they are not doing well. I've heard the argument that we should focus solely on improving the entire system instead of providing individual students with a pathway out, but I don't agree with that. Those changes will take years, maybe decades. What do we say to the parents of students who need help now? Do we say, 'We know there is a better school for your child, but we're not going to let him go there. Instead, he'll just have to wait until the entire system improves, and, by the way, he may be grown and gone by then.' As a parent, that would make me crazy. I'm sure you'll have questions, but first I'd like to ask Representative Starkes if he has anything he'd like to add."

"Thank you, Governor. I agree with everything you said, especially the last point. To me, it *is* a question of conscience. It's also a question of fairness. Is it fair not to allow a student with poor parents a way to a better school? No! Is it fair that only students with wealthy parents can escape a school where they are not learning? Of course not! What about a single mother who is struggling to make ends meet – is it fair to force her to send her child to a school where he or she is not learning? No! It's simply not fair to force a student to stay in a school where he is not learning simply because his parents don't have the financial means to escape. With all due respect to those who disagree, how could they defend the status quo? The current system is discriminatory on its face because it does not create equal opportunity. Private school tuition is costly, and, as it stands now, if you can't pay, you can't play, and that's not fair. Thank you."

"We know this will be a hard fight," Governor Stimson said. "But it's a fight worth fighting. Nothing is more important than educating our children. I'll be happy to take a few questions."

"Could the voucher be used in a parochial school?" Tyler Hollis, a reporter for the <u>Miami Post</u>, asked.

"Yes," the governor answered. "Some of the best schools in the state are Jesuit schools, for example, and we wouldn't want to deny students the opportunity to attend them."

"But what about the argument that this would violate the doctrine of 'separation of church and state'?" Hollis continued.

"You're speaking to the issue of constitutionality," the governor replied. "This program gives money to parents, not church-affiliated schools. Besides, the separation of church and state is a judicially created doctrine, and judges sometimes change their minds," he said with a hint of a grin.

Ed Starkes was really keyed up now; this was leading into an area in which he had strong feelings. "If it's good for the kids, why should anyone care?" he was thinking.

Tyler Hollis wouldn't let up. "But the church schools end up with the money. What's the difference?"

"The lawyers say there's a big difference, but I'll let them address that later," the governor answered.

Hollis knew a little something about Jesuit schools, having attended one himself. "Aren't students in a Jesuit school required to go to Mass at least once during the school week? I thought they went as a class on Wednesday mornings? Doesn't that have the effect of 'establishing' a religion with them, and wouldn't that violate the Establishment Clause of the First Amendment?"

"I don't know if an entire class goes to Mass together or not, but it doesn't matter. The students won't be required to participate," the governor answered. "With a note from their parents, they won't even have to attend."

"But, Governor, wouldn't students participate just to not feel different?

Doesn't this have the effect of moving the students towards Catholicism, or at least towards Christianity?" Hollis continued.

"And that's a bad thing?" Starkes was thinking.

"I don't think so," Governor Stimson said. "If their parents helped them think it through, it shouldn't be a big deal. Besides, the bill doesn't force a student to go to a parochial school; it's a matter of choice. If a student is uncomfortable with a parochial school, he or she can go to a private school that isn't parochial."

"Are there many of those schools out there?" asked Hollis.

"There are some, but I don't know how many," Stimson answered honestly. "However, my guess is that, once the lock the public schools have on educating students is broken, there will be many more. This will create competition for the students, and education overall will improve. Look, this isn't about establishing a religion, but about educating kids. That's the goal; nothing else."

The governor's press secretary loved that comment, so she ended the press conference on that note.

Later that afternoon, a group of five Democratic senators, led by Senator Kenneth Washman of Palm Beach County, held a press conference to speak out against the bill. They were standing outside the chapel in the Capitol. Given the importance of the issue, most of the reporters from the Capitol press corps were there, including Tyler Hollis of the Miami Post. There were also political operatives from each party in attendance. The political stakes were high; if a state like Florida could pass this, it was an initiative that could sweep the nation.

"This bill is unconstitutional," Senator Washman said. "Under the Florida Constitution, public money is not allowed to be given to a religious school. It says so in Article I, Section 3: 'No revenue of any state or any political subdivision or agency thereof shall ever be taken from the public treasury directly or indirectly in aid of any church, sect, or religious denomination or in aid of any sectarian institution.' For the governor to say that the money is going to parents, not to religious schools, is a distinction without a difference. The church schools end up with the money, and this violates the doctrine of the separation of church and state." Palm Beach County was rich in Jewish voters who were wary of initiatives that could have the effect of ostracizing Jewish students or imposing Christianity on them.

"But aren't vouchers allowed in church-affiliated colleges?" asked Tyler Hollis. He was an objective reporter who asked tough questions of both sides.

"Yes, but college students aren't as impressionable as students in K-12," Washman answered.

"But isn't the principle the same?" Hollis continued.

"Not really," Washman replied. "If no one is affected by the government's intervention into the area of religion, there is no violation of the Establishment Clause. If students aren't impacted, there's no violation, and students in college aren't impacted, at least not to the degree that secondary students are." Washman wasn't sure about that answer, but he thought it sounded good, and it was the only thing he could think to say. Senator Debbie Congleton of Tampa sensed that the press wasn't buying Washman's answer, so she added that as a mother of young children she was aware of how they soaked up what was said around them like a sponge. "Contrast that with how we were in college where we challenged authority; at least, that's how I was!" she said with a laugh. Several reporters nodded in agreement.

"My strongest concern is that the bill will take money away from our public schools and they are starved for resources already," said Senator Fred Tobin, a senator from Broward County. As he said this, he looked at the representative of the teachers' union who nodded in agreement. The union was adamantly against the bill, and the union was stronger in Broward County than in any other county in Florida.

"But for every voucher given, wouldn't there be one fewer student in the public schools to educate?" Hollis asked. "Why would losing money be such a big deal if the school system were also losing a student?"

"Because it doesn't even out," Tobin answered.

"How couldn't it?" pressed Hollis. "Schools get a set amount of money per student. If they lose a student, why would it hurt for the school to lose the money for that student? Wouldn't it be a wash?"

"The system still has to come up with money to pay for its programs, but we aren't receiving any funding for the student we're losing," Tobin said. Hollis got a slightly confused look on his face, something Tobin noticed, so he continued. "This is not just about money, though. Public education is the true melting pot of America. It's the place where we learn to get along with each other and grow to know different cultures."

"So, would it be fair to say that you place greater value on the intangibles that go along with attending school than the actual material learned from a textbook?" Hollis asked.

"I hadn't thought about it like that, but maybe that's a good way to say it," Tobin answered. "School is about a lot more than reading, writing and arithmetic. It's a collective experience that we should all go through together. It's where we learn to be neighbors and fellow citizens. If schools don't represent America racially, ethnically, economically and socially it would be bad for the country."

The press conference droned on for a while longer, but the Democrats in both houses were such a minority that everyone knew they couldn't stop the Republican initiative. There might even be a few crossover Democratic votes from legislators in rural areas, or African-Americans from inner city districts who saw it as a way for their constituents to receive a better education. The outcome was already determined, and the bill hadn't even had its first committee hearing.

During the session there were heated debates from both sides as the bill was considered. Ed Starkes did most of the talking for the proponents, and it was apparent that he genuinely thought the idea would *improve* public education, not destroy it. He also saw the possibility of more students receiving an education in parochial schools as something that would infuse them with wholesome morals and values that they weren't getting at home. "This is a good thing," he often said, "something to be encouraged, not discouraged."

Representative Elaine Mooney of Orlando argued that the bill would be catastrophic for public education. "If this bill passes, it's just a matter of time before it is expanded and other categories of students are able to use vouchers. Today, it's those students attending a 'failing school,' whatever that is, but next year it will be something else, maybe students with disabilities. The following year it may be those who haven't made straight-As. I'm convinced that some of you want this bill to cover those with blond hair, black hair, brown hair, red hair or no hair. In other words – everybody!

"But think of what that would do to the public schools," Mooney continued. "They'd be left with students who, for one reason or another, couldn't get into a private school. And who might those students be? The ones who are expensive to educate like those with severe disabilities or those with criminal records or discipline problems or those who are low achievers. Remember, unlike the public schools, private schools aren't *required* to take anybody! They can cherry-pick students and leave the 'tough' ones for the public schools, and they will, and the public schools will deteriorate a little bit more each year."

One of the most moving speeches against the bill came from Representative Robert Simon of Aventura in north Miami-Dade County. Simon was an Orthodox Jew whom everyone respected, and in his remarks he led the House through a long history of religious persecution at the hands of otherwise good people. He spoke eloquently of the founding of our country, and how escape from the bondage of the Church of England was a motivating factor in the Pilgrims coming to America. He quoted from the Founding Fathers, making it clear that while Judeo-Christian values formed the backbone of law in America and our constitution, it was the freedom to exercise one's religion as one saw fit and escape from state-sponsored religion that were the twin goals of the First Amendment. He brought some members to tears when he recounted his family's experience with Nazi Germany.

"The Nazis thought they were doing God's work, at least at first," he said. "Before they were stopped, they had slaughtered six million of my people and inked a tattoo of numbers into my father's forearm. He tried to keep those numbers covered for the rest of his life. Do you see why I am so deeply concerned about a bill that would ostracize those who aren't members of the majority religion? Can you understand why a bill that takes tax money from me and gives it to a religion that is not my own is such a worry? No matter how the law tries to protect students from the religious influences of the church-school, the core mission of many such schools is religious training, and that means there will be a coercive effect, even if unintentional. Please do not vote to use my tax money to indoctrinate children into a religion that is not my own. If you can, put yourself in the shoes of one who has firsthand knowledge of millions killed simply because of their religion, and see how I would be suspicious of that. With all due respect, the method in this bill is not brutal and cruel like the gas chamber or the firing squad, but the effect will be the same in one regard: fewer Jews in classrooms and communities to enrich the fabric of this country."

You could have heard a pin drop on the carpeted floor of the House Chamber. Ed Starkes was deeply affected and had difficulty composing himself, but he had to rebut the argument because he was the bill's sponsor.

"I do not question the sincerity of those who have spoken against this bill. I respect them greatly, and know they spoke from the heart. Still, I respectfully disagree with them. This bill is not intended to destroy public education, Representative Mooney, but to save it! If the public schools don't improve, the flight of students from the public schools of which you spoke will occur anyway! Parents with the means to do so are going to take their children to a school where they can learn, regardless of what happens with this bill. What the governor and I are trying to do is make sure that *all* parents have the same choice. And I have a prediction. If this bill passes, you're going to see the greatest renaissance in public education in a century! The public schools will become innovative and aggressive and do the very thing the private sector has been doing since the beginning of commerce: compete! They will compete for students, and they will prosper. But if we do nothing, the schools will not improve, and it will lead to their demise. We must act to save them from themselves.

"Representative Simon, there are few people on this floor whom I admire and respect more than I do you," Starkes continued. "I'm a man of faith, and so are you. My intention is not to indoctrinate Florida's children into a faith tradition not supported by their parents, and I'm certainly not intending to hurt your religion or anyone else's. But I must tell you, if a result of this bill is that more kids get exposed to the values that religion brings, I'm okay with that. In fact, it's a good thing. Our country needs *more* of that, not less. Note that I didn't say expose the kids to a religion, but to the values that the religion brings. In fact, I'll make this promise to you. If this bill has the effect of turning students into 'little Catholics' or 'little Baptists', I'll work with you to help repeal the law."

That was a bold promise on Representative Starkes' part, and he was probably a bit carried away when he said it. Still, it was a statement that had an impact on the House. To no one's surprise the bill passed, but with Representative Starkes' promise, it passed with even more Democratic votes than expected.

After the session, and with great fanfare, the governor signed the bill in a carefully choreographed ceremony that featured poor inner-city women who spoke movingly about the "escape" to a better school the new law would provide for their children. Representative Ed Starkes was very proud of the law. It was his most significant legislative accomplishment, and he went on a statewide tour with Governor Stimson speaking about it. "If I pass nothing else in my legislative career, I will have made a significant positive difference," he told his wife.

It wasn't long before a lawsuit was filed against the new law. The plaintiffs were self-proclaimed atheists who attacked the law on two fronts: First, they saw the law as an unconstitutional violation of the Establishment Clause of the First Amendment. Second, they contended that the law violated the Religious Freedom Article of the Florida Constitution.

Their arguments against the law on the basis that it violated the Establishment Clause weren't novel, tracking the three-pronged test created by the Supreme Court in the case of Lemon v. Kurtzman, 403 U.S. 602, (1971). "Our tax money goes to religious schools so this law has a religious purpose," they claimed. "Furthermore, it has a primary effect of advancing religion, and creates an 'excessive governmental entanglement' with religion," they said. "It fails all three prongs of the test. In addition, this law sanctions a religion by giving money to churches to run their schools. By sanctioning a religion, it subtly establishes a religion, and that violates the Constitution."

The second claim, that the law violated the Religious Freedom Article of the Florida Constitution, was based on a plain reading of the constitutional provision, the plaintiffs said. "The law allows state revenue to be taken from the state treasury in aid of church-sponsored schools, and this is clearly prohibited by the language of the Religious Freedom Article."

"Oh, for crying out loud," Starkes said when he first heard of the lawsuit.

"What are they talking about, this three-pronged test?" he asked Jarrod Banks, a House lawyer in the Speaker's Office. Starkes was in Tallahassee for committee meetings and was waiting to see the speaker.

"The First Amendment says 'Congress shall make no law respecting an establishing of a religion,'" Banks said.

"But the state legislature isn't Congress," Starkes replied. "Why is the First Amendment legally relevant?"

"The first ten amendments contain restrictions on the power of the federal government," Banks answered. "Many of the rights contained within them are central to the concept of liberty. Over time, the courts have used the Fourteenth Amendment to extend these protections to actions of state and local government. That's how the First Amendment is made applicable to the state legislature."

"That makes sense," Starkes said, "but what about what's good for everyone else? Do we deny a kid a good education just because he might get exposed to Christianity? It's not like he's being exposed to something that's *bad* for him."

"I understand," Banks said, "and it is strange in a way. But remember, if the government is going to allow religion into the classroom, it can't play favorites. If one form of religion is allowed in, they all can come in."

"I'm not worried about that," Starkes replied. "You're over-thinking things again."

"Maybe so," Banks answered, "but it's my job to point these things out to you."

"What's our argument?" Starkes asked.

"We have several of them," responded Banks. "First we'll use the same three-pronged test enunciated in <u>Lemon</u>. We'll say the law does not have a religious purpose, but the secular one of educating kids. Next we'll argue that the primary purpose of the law is not to advance or inhibit religion, but to improve education. Finally, we'll show that involvement with religion occurs only if the parents give the check we send them to a church-affiliated school. Our argument will be that we don't have any entanglement with religion, only the parents and their children do, and only if they choose to."

"That sounds pretty strong to me," Starkes said.

"It is," Banks replied. "I think it's a winner."

"What about the state constitution claim, that it violates the Religious

Freedom Article of the Florida Constitution? In all honesty, the law does seem to run afoul of that language."

"That one's close, no doubt about it," Banks answered. "A state constitutional provision can't trump a federal constitutional provision, though, so if we prevail on the federal Establishment Clause argument, we'll argue that the state provision is inconsistent. We'll also contend that the church school is separate from the church, and that the money is not going to the church but to the parents…all the things we've been saying since we started. I think we have a decent shot with this."

"Any other arguments?" Starkes asked.

"We have one more, but I don't think we should use it."

"What's that?"

"Ironically, it comes from the same sentence in the Constitution," Banks answered. "We could argue that if the law is not allowed to stand, it would violate the 'Free Exercise Clause.'"

"How?" Starkes wondered.

"Many believe that attending a church-affiliated school is consistent with their religious practice," Banks replied. "For those who believe this way, if they don't have the money to pay for tuition, they could argue that to strike down this law would partly deny them the ability to practice their religion."

"That's very creative, counselor," Starkes said with a smile. "Will it win?"

"Nope. Not in my opinion, anyway," Banks responded honestly. "The Free Exercise Clause is better suited for issues like prayer in school where prohibiting public prayer at a school event prevents the exercise of religion. It's a stretch to contend that one would be prevented from attending a religious school if this law is stricken."

"But that would be the practical effect for poor parents," Starkes argued. "Without the voucher, they couldn't afford the church-affiliated private school; with it, they could."

"Maybe so, but that's a losing argument in my view," Banks responded.

Starkes' frustration was building. Again, he just couldn't see why the court system let nuances like this get in the way. Couldn't judges see that the country would be better off if the people were more religious?

"Don't let it get to you, Representative Starkes. We shouldn't even use this argument. Our best shot with the Court is to stay as far away from religion as possible. The last thing we want to do is concede that people will use this law to practice their religion. From a legal standpoint, we should distance ourselves as far from religion as possible."

"And that," Starkes thought, "was exactly what was wrong with the country."

The case went to trial, and in a shocker the trial court declared the law unconstitutional. The Circuit Court judge wrote that the law created an "excessive governmental entanglement with religion," and violated the Establishment Clause as interpreted by the United States Supreme Court in Lemon. She did not buy the government's argument that it was the parent who was getting the voucher, not the church school, when the school ended up with the money. Calling that argument "form over substance," the judge concluded that in addition to the student, the church where the school was affiliated was an equal beneficiary, thereby creating excessive entanglement. She also concluded that the law violated the Religious Freedom Article of the Florida Constitution.

The governor's lawyers immediately appealed, and several of the nation's top appellate lawyers came in to assist. The issue of vouchers was central to the national agenda of the governor's political party, so no expense was spared in seeing that it survived.

The strategy worked. The District Court of Appeals reversed the trial court's decision. This time the plaintiffs appealed, setting up a high stakes battle before the Florida Supreme Court.

The day of oral arguments was a madhouse outside the Supreme Court building. The issue of vouchers was the biggest education issue in the country, and the national media understood that the outcome of the case could even affect the next race for president. They were out in full force, and all up and down the street in front of the Court were television trucks and reporters.

Four months after the case was argued, the Florida Supreme Court rendered its ruling. The decision of the District Court of Appeal was affirmed, and vouchers for students in "failing" schools was now the law of the land in the Sunshine State.[1]

Governor Stimson and Representative Starkes were thrilled, not just because they won, but also because they genuinely believed that public education in Florida would improve. They took a victory lap around the state, imploring public schools to buckle down and promising to give them the resources they needed to achieve educational excellence.

Then something happened that was totally unexpected. Several of the nation's top African-American athletes who had converted to Islam announced that they would open a dozen middle schools in Florida that would be affiliated with the Islamic faith. They would target African-American males from inner cities who were attending "failing" schools. Between what money the athletes were willing to put forward and the annual voucher the government was obligated to provide, it would be enough to have locations, teachers and course materials.

When this was announced it raised the eyebrows of Representative Starkes. This was not the kind of religious school he had in mind when the idea of legalizing vouchers was considered. Still, he wasn't too concerned because he didn't think the athletes' plan would get very far. "They won't get many students," he thought, "and even if they do, they'll soon tire of feeding the schools the money."

He was wrong. The schools were a big success. Students liked the rigid structure of the schools and the strong older male figures that ran them. The administrators and teachers all wore suits with bow ties, and were very demanding of their students. They also did something else: they practiced Islam in everything they did, and Islam permeated all activities at the school. They learned about the prophet Muhammad. They kneeled five times a day for prayer, and prayed in the name of Allah at lunch and before athletic games. The students weren't required to participate, of course, but invariably one or two students would, and others would follow. Soon, most students were participating. By the end of the year, their conversion to Islam was complete.

Another thing happened, or, rather, didn't happen to make matters worse from Starkes' perspective. The proliferation of private schools that were not affiliated with a church didn't occur. A few tried, but they just couldn't make it financially. Most church-affiliated schools received significant financial support from the congregation, money that was necessary to keep the doors open. Without it, they couldn't survive. The private schools envisioned by the governor and Starkes didn't have this support so they had to be self-supporting. Most couldn't make it, and soon folded. This was just as well in some cases, because they were schools that Starkes did not support. One had a communist orientation and another was rumored to have an affiliation with a hate group.

With vouchers available, other religious sects came into Florida and opened schools. These were pretty insignificant, though, attracting only a few students, but every day it seemed that Starkes was hearing of some other group trying to get started. But none attracted the following of the Islamic schools, and these were a source of constant concern for Starkes. He recognized that the students were doing well. Indeed, most students completely turned their lives around while attending these schools. Students who had significant criminal histories, or who were angry and unruly were transformed completely, becoming respectful, polite and law-abiding. Students who were barely staying in school academically began making good grades and their scores on standardized tests soared.

What gnawed at Starkes was the religious conversion the students experienced. Most of them were raised in Christian faith traditions. Regardless of whether they practiced Christianity, these students at least called themselves Christians at the beginning of the school year. By the end of the year, though, most had converted to Islam, and Starkes was seriously conflicted by this. Their educational performance was rising greatly, but they were becoming followers of a religion he didn't agree with or understand.

"Can't we do something about this?" he asked Jarrod Banks, attorney for the House of Representatives. Starkes was back in Tallahassee, having decided that he had to get back on the issue.

"No, sir. There isn't," Banks replied. "Not without changing the law."

"But there has to be. This isn't what we intended."

"No, it's not" responded Banks. "But if you'll remember, I told you if one religious school could participate in the program, they all could. Mixing 'church and state' doesn't just mean mixing Cathedral with the state. It also means mixing the state with the Mosque or the Temple or any other bona fide religion. The government can't pick and choose which religions it supports."

"But we aren't supporting religions!" Starkes exclaimed. "We're giving parents a voucher to use as they see fit. Wasn't that our argument before the Court?"

"Yes, it was," answered Banks. "That was the argument, anyway."

"You don't sound like you believe it, Jarrod."

"I do believe it, Representative. But you had to know it would help the schools too. Churches see their schools as extensions of their ministries. If they can get just a little financial help from the government they'll take in a student they otherwise wouldn't."

"But that's a good thing," Starkes said. "It exposes kids to the values that religion brings." He was thinking back to his argument on the floor of the House in support of the bill, and how he had used some of those exact words. "I just never thought it would be used like this."

It was late December, the Friday before Christmas, and Ed Starkes was in his favorite tree stand on his family's property along the banks of the Alapaha River. It was 8:00 a.m. and sunlight was beginning to streak through the trees. It was cold but getting warmer, and there wasn't a cloud in the sky. A soft breeze was wafting through, rustling the leaves around him. A squirrel was leaping from branch to branch, unaware of Ed's presence.

"It's a fine morning," he thought.

He liked where he was. It comforted him, especially after the telephone calls he had made the day before. His first call had been to Representative Robert Simon, telling him he would help him try to repeal the law that legalized vouchers.

"You're kidding! Why?" Simon asked.

"Because I'm a man of my word. I now see how the law can change the religious beliefs of young, impressionable students. I told you if that happened, I'd help you repeal the law."

"Thank you, Ed," Simon said. "It takes a big man to do this. Actually, with a little tinkering, we may be able to come up with something that we can both support. I'm not totally opposed to vouchers, only the way you were allowing them to be used by religious schools. Let's keep talking."

"We will," Starkes replied. "But now I must go. I have another call to make."

Starkes hung up and dialed another number.

"Governor, this is Representative Starkes. I need to tell you something. I've decided to…"

A flicker of movement caught Starkes' eye. It was the ear of a deer above the brush next to the river. The deer was a buck – a good one – and it was coming Starkes' way. The deer's legs were stained black up to the knee from walking in the swamp and sinking down in the ooze. The rut was over, so his neck was no longer swelled. He had survived the hunting season…so far.

"Survived," Starkes thought. "The old buck survived."

Starkes put his rifle down and watched the deer walk right under his stand. Starkes never made a sound, but the buck caught wind of him, spun around and bolted away.

As the deer disappeared, Starkes heard him hit the river with a loud splash and then slosh through to the other side.

"One of my favorite sounds," he thought, smiling. "But that deer made a mistake. He was mine if I'd wanted him. But I didn't, and he survived.

"I made a mistake too," he thought. "I thought I was doing the right thing, but I couldn't see it unfold the way it did. There's nothing to be ashamed of; I'll work with Representative Simon and see what we can come up with. I'm going to have to eat some serious crow and take a lot of grief, but I'll survive, just like that old buck."

---

[1] After this story was written, the Florida Supreme Court ruled that Florida's voucher program for grades K-12 was unconstitutional. Surprising to many legal scholars, however, was the basis of the Court's decision. Instead of ruling that the law violated the Establishment Clause of the United States Constitution or the Religious Freedom Article of the state Constitution, the Court found that it violated the state constitutional provision that requires equal funding of public school districts.

Author's Note:

The issue of education was the most prominent issue in the 1998 governor's race. My education plan didn't touch on vouchers. Instead, it was built around what I called the "Three Ss: Safe, simple and small." My contention was that if we kept the school environment safe, education policy simple, and class sizes small, we would have a good educational outcome for most students.

My campaign for governor ran out of gas and Buddy MacKay, another candidate and our lieutenant governor at the time, honored me by asking that I become his running mate. We became the Democratic nominees for governor and lieutenant governor.

Our Republican opponents, Jeb Bush and Frank Brogan, came out with their education plan. It contained many of the components of the education plan discussed in this story. Students were tested, and, based on the results, schools were graded. If a school received a failing grade for two years in a row, the students in that school could receive a voucher to be used in a private school, including parochial (religious) schools. Also, the schools that received the highest grades received a financial bonus. This latter component became a big point of contention in the campaign. The MacKay/Dantzler team contended that the additional money should go to the schools that weren't doing as well, in an attempt to pull them up. MacKay/Dantzler also took issue with vouchers. Personally, I was willing to experiment with them. For example, since school safety was foremost on the minds of parents, I wondered if there were private schools that would be willing to take unruly students or students who had broken the law in exchange for a voucher. That way, unruly students might receive the attention they needed, and wouldn't be in the regular classroom preventing others from learning. I didn't support vouchers being used in parochial schools, however. I opposed it on philosophical and constitutional grounds, but I also thought the people would turn against the concept in the long run.

We lost the election and Governor Bush pushed through the education plan on which he had campaigned, which was exactly what he should have done. Elections are how the people set the agenda, so it is the obligation of candidates to put forward proposals so that voters will have policy choices. We certainly did that with education in the governor's race; there were two very different proposals that received a great deal of attention on the campaign trail. The people made their choice by whom they elected.

During my time in the Legislature, issues involving religion were always very difficult because the subject was so personal. One of the most difficult was school prayer.

*The Legislature passed a bill in 1996 that allowed voluntary student-led prayer at non-compulsory school functions. The prayer had to be non-sectarian, non-denominational and non-proselytizing. I was in the Senate and voted for it, but I'll never forget a speech Senator Robert Wexler gave on the floor in opposition. It was heartfelt, powerful and moving. He spoke of what it was like to be a Jewish student in a largely Protestant school, asking us to please not force those in the minority to feel ostracized, as would inevitably happen. We listened in rapt silence. When he finished, Senator Pat Thomas, one of my great friends from North Florida and a person who sat in front of me, spun his chair around and said, "**What** are we going to do, Ricko?" That's what he often called me – Ricko. "I don't know, Pat," I answered. "I knew what I was going to do when I came in this morning, but now I'm not so sure." I had discussed this bill with my wife the weekend before when I was home. We were sitting on the deck and she asked, "How are you* *going to vote?" I said, "I think I'm going to let them pray."*

After Senator Thomas and I spoke, I believe I remember Senator W.D. Childers, another North Florida senator who sat next to Pat, turning his chair around and we all stared at each other with anguished looks on our faces, each looking for wisdom or comfort. It was one of those great, few and difficult times in the Senate when all senators were searching their consciences.

The time came to vote. I looked at the red and green voting buttons on my desk. There was no yellow button. It was either green for "yes," or red for "no." I pushed green. When the vote was announced, it remained relatively silent on the floor for some time. I looked down, wondering if I had done the right thing, and not wanting to see Senator Wexler.

The Legislature adjourned and the tension mounted over whether Governor Chiles would sign or veto the bill. Governor Chiles was a person of great Christian faith, but he also had been an elected official in Florida for decades. He knew the state and its people well, so he might have a different idea about what was good for Florida.

The day before the deadline I couldn't take it any more, so I called Governor Chiles' chief of staff, Linda Shelley, and asked her what he was going to do. She said she honestly didn't know, but that she would not be surprised if he signed the bill (meaning that it would become law).

The next day we learned. Governor Chiles vetoed the bill. I was sent a copy of the veto message. It was one of the best-written documents I had ever read. I don't remember its exact words, but it essentially said that a non-sectarian, non-denominational and non-proselytizing prayer wasn't much of a prayer. In fact, he said it cheapened prayer and prevented it from being the personal and deeply spiritual connection with God that it was supposed to be. He also made it clear that he supported prayer, even recommended it, but that the government had to be respectful of those who might be of minority faiths.

When I read the veto message, I was again at home on my deck with Julie. I put the paper down and said, "You know, he might just be right."

I don't know if he was right or not, but I remember something that happened on the floor of the Senate that helped me understand what a Jewish person might feel when the one leading a public prayer prays in the name of Jesus.

The Senate begins each day on the floor with a prayer. A privilege extended to senators is to invite a member of the clergy from back home to give the morning's prayer, but when a member of the clergy is not present, someone else prays. One day in particular, when a member of the clergy wasn't present, a young African-American staff person with the office of the Secretary of the Senate who had a deep and soothing voice that resonated wonderfully, gave the prayer. It was beautiful, and I was listening hard, really feeling it. His ending snapped me from my meditation, however, because he ended by saying, "In the name of Allah, amen." We all looked up, a bit stunned. I remember thinking, "Hey, that's not my god!" I didn't know whether to try to take back the prayer in my mind, or chuckle and ignore it, but from that moment on, I've had a greater sensitivity to those who belong to minority faiths.

Several years later, when I was running for governor, my wife had me read the books "The Chosen" and "The Promise" by Chaim Potok. Julie knew I would be campaigning among many Jewish voters and she said the books would give me a better understanding of what it was like to grow up Jewish in largely a Protestant country. Later in the campaign, Senator Howard Forman arranged for me to meet with 18 rabbis in Broward County to discuss issues and politics. They liked it that I had read these books, but they also spoke of their own experiences. It was very enlightening.

Soon thereafter I went to a meeting with many Holocaust survivors. I believe Bill Nelson, the insurance commissioner at the time and now a United States senator, had called the meeting. Bill was seeking compensation from insurance companies and Swiss banks for benefits and deposits not paid or returned to the survivors of the Holocaust. At this meeting, I met survivors who showed me numbers that had been tattooed on their inner forearms while in concentration camps when they were children or young adults. I thought of the time when Elie Wiesel, a person who has dedicated his life to making sure the horror of the Holocaust was never forgotten, spoke to us on the floor of the House of Representatives imploring us to "never forget."

All of this together was very powerful. It made me realize afterwards that the great value of a contested election is not just what the voters learn about the candidates, but what the candidates learn from the voters. It makes the winner a better public servant.

THE LAW: *Definitions and Explanations:*

Congress shall make no law respecting an establishment of religion, or prohibiting the free exercise thereof; or abridging the freedom of speech, or of the press; or the right of the people peaceably to assemble, and to petition the Government for a redress of grievances.

Article I, Constitution of the United States

Religious freedom. -There shall be no law respecting the establishment of religion or prohibiting or penalizing the free exercise thereof. Religious freedom shall not justify practices inconsistent with public morals, peace or safety. No revenue of the state or any political subdivision or agency thereof shall ever be taken from the public treasury directly or indirectly in aid of any church, sect, or religious denomination or in aid of any sectarian institution.

Article I, Section 3, Constitution of the State of Florida

Church: In its most general sense, the religious society founded and established by Jesus Christ, to receive, preserve, and propagate His doctrines and ordinances. It may also mean a body of communicants gathered into church order; ...organization for religious purposes; religious society or body; the clergy or officialdom of a religious body.

Black's Law Dictionary, Sixth Edition, p. 242

State, n.: A people permanently occupying a fixed territory bound together by common-law habits and custom into one body politic exercising, through the medium of an organized government, independent sovereignty and control over all persons and things within its boundaries, capable of making war and peace and entering into international relations with other communities around the globe.

Black's Law Dictionary, Sixth Edition, p. 1407;
United States v. Kusche, D.C. Cal., 56 F. Supp. 201, 207-208

The issue of school vouchers was addressed by the United States Supreme Court in Zelman v. Simmons Harris, 122 S. Ct. 2460, 2467 (2002). Chief Justice William Rehnquist, writing for the majority: "We believe that the program challenged here is a program of true private choice. The Ohio program is neutral in all respect toward religion. It is part of a general and multifaceted undertaking...to provide educational opportunities to the children of a failed school district...if a government aid program is neutral with respects to religion, and provides assistance directly to a broad class of citizens who, in turn, direct government aid to religious schools wholly as a result of their own genuine and independent private choice, the program is not readily subject to challenge under the Establishment Clause."

Notable Quotes:

"The 'establishment of religion' clause of the First Amendment means at least this: Neither a state nor the Federal Government can set up a church. Neither can pass laws which aid one religion, aid all religions, or prefer one religion over another. Neither can force nor influence a person to go to or to remain away from church against his will or force him to profess a belief or disbelief in any religion. No person can be punished for entertaining or professing religious beliefs or disbeliefs, for church attendance or non-attendance. No tax in any amount, large or small, can be levied to support any religious activities or institutions, whatever they may be called, or whatever form they may adopt to teach or practice religion. Neither a state nor the Federal Government can, openly or secretly, participate in the affairs of any religious organizations or groups and vice versa. In the words of Jefferson, the clause against establishment of religion by law was intended to erect 'a wall of separation between Church and State.' Reynolds v. United States, supra, at page 164."

Everson v. Board of Education of Ewing Tp., 330 U.S. 1, 15-16 (1947)

"The First Amendment has erected a wall between Church and State. That wall must be kept high and impregnable. We could not approve the slightest breach."

Everson, supra, at page 18

"This freedom was first in the Bill of Rights because it was first in the forefathers' minds; it was set forth in absolute terms, and its strength is its rigidity. It was intended not only to keep the states' hands out of religion, but to keep religion's hands off the state, and above all, to keep bitter religious controversy out of public life by denying to every denomination any advantage from getting control of public policy or the public purse."

Honorable Justice Jackson, Associate Justice,
United States Supreme Court, in dissent, in Everson, supra, at pages 26, 27

"The Amendment's purpose was not to strike merely at the official establishment of a single sect, creed or religion, outlawing only a formal relation such as had prevailed in England and some of the colonies. Necessarily it was to uproot all such relationships. But the object was broader than separating church and state in this narrow sense. It was to create a complete and permanent separation of the spheres of religious activity and civil authority by comprehensively forbidding every form of public aid or support for religion."

Honorable Felix Frankfurter, Associate Justice,
United States Supreme Court, in dissent, in Everson, supra, at pages 31, 32

"The right to be let alone is indeed the beginning of all freedoms."

Honorable William O. Douglas, Associate Justice,
United States Supreme Court
www.brainyquote.com

"The major obstacle to a religious renewal is the intellectual classes, who are highly influential and tend to view religion as primitive superstition. They believe that science has left atheism as the only respectable intellectual stance."

Judge Robert Bork / www.brainyquote.com

"Those who made and endorsed our Constitution knew man's nature, and it is to their ideas, rather than to the temptations of utopia, that we must ask that our judges adhere."

Judge Robert Bork / www.brainyquote.com

"There may be times when we are powerless to prevent injustice, but there must never be a time when we fail to protest."

Elie Wiesel / www.brainyquote.com

Caribou Country

CRRRAACK!!
Corporal Punishment: Paddling in Public Schools

Preface: The doctrine of "in loco parentis," a Latin phrase meaning "in the place of the parent," was the original common law concept relied upon by school officials as authority to administer corporal punishment (paddling) to students. It's been weakened somewhat, but it still exists. Inherent in the doctrine is the idea that school personnel are considered to be standing in the place of the parent while the student is at school.

FOR MOST of his 17 years, Reginald Winthrop, II came across to many as a spoiled rich kid with a temperament that cried out for a good paddling. But the truth was, he was basically a good kid. He related to his father, enjoyed hunting and fishing, yearned to play sports, and got along well with classmates who got to know him. It was only when he was around his mother, subject to her attitudes and snobberies, that he was viewed in the same light. It was of little consequence, though, because his family's wealth had managed to protect him…most of the time.

Reginald lived in Twin Lakes, a ritzy development in northern Palm Beach County where a house averaged 6,000 square feet in size. Double security gates and a 10-foot high privacy wall around the perimeter kept out the "riff-raff." Not that he would have been in any danger had undesirables been able to enter, however; his two personal attendants would have seen to that. One, a kindhearted man named Biggsley, had only one responsibility, and that was to wait on young Reginald and meet his every need. The second, a ruddy-faced security expert with the nickname "Jacko," carried enough armament to fight a small-sized war. Anyone messing around with the Winthrops was in for a real battle.

Concern for protection of this sort was prudent because of the family's great wealth. Reginald's father, Reginald Winthrop, nicknamed "Reece," had founded a company that made men's shavers and razor blades. His share of stock put the family fortune in the billions. Still, Reginald's mother, Priscilla, had taken her concern for the family's security to paranoid levels. Reginald was not allowed to go to a movie or even play in the neighborhood without Jacko and Biggsley being present.

Priscilla was a case, but she hadn't always been this way. She had been raised on the "other side of the tracks," the daughter of loving parents who had taught her there was dignity in hard work, no matter what the job was. They also understood that the ticket to an easier life was a college education, so her parents saved and sacrificed so Priscilla would have this opportunity, an opportunity they never had.

Priscilla took her studies seriously. After graduating from a public high school, she enrolled at Palm Beach Community College and earned her Associate of Arts degree. She then attended Florida Atlantic University in Boca Raton in the southern part of Palm Beach County. It was there, while earning college money by working as a waitress at Burgundy's, a trendy Italian restaurant, that she met her future husband.

Reece Winthrop, a 30-year old bachelor, was swept off his feet by Priscilla the first time he met her. He thought he had never seen anyone so beautiful with her angular face, long blonde hair over a well pressed white shirt, and shapely hips in tight black slacks. Winthrop was alone that night, returning from an unsuccessful meeting with yet another investment banker as he sought financing for his startup company, FaceSaver Razors and Blades. Priscilla had not just taken his food order; she had *listened* to him, and that was something he needed that evening. Next door was an all-night coffee shop, and Priscilla agreed to meet him there when she got off work. Later she gave him her telephone number, and their courtship began.

For the next year, while Priscilla completed college with a degree in Business Management, Reece secured seed money for FaceSaver. Priscilla and Reece were married right after her graduation, and she seemed to give him the "hitch in his step" he needed to convince a national chain of retail pharmacies to carry his products. With this in hand, other venture capitalists invested money, and Reece was able to go on cable television to pitch his products. He was soon a nationally recognized business personality, and his company soared.

Over time, the success of FaceSaver changed Priscilla. Little by little she went from having a humble and grateful heart to being haughty. She forgot her simple upbringing and was even embarrassed by her parents' modest means. She convinced them to sell the house they had lived in all their married lives and move into a condominium near the ocean. They didn't want to move, but she made them believe they should. It gave them a "better" address for the many invitations they would receive as the in-laws of Reginald Winthrop.

Slowly at first, Priscilla took on the role of being the wife of one of Palm Beach's richest men, but then she attacked it with zeal. She had a knack for getting into the society page of the <u>Palm Beach Chronicle</u> more than anyone else. She convinced Reece to move to Twin Lakes where they hosted receptions for national political figures that once included the president of the United States. Priscilla became a socialite of the first order.

For his part, Reece never forgot the hard road he had traveled to business success. He had scratched and clawed his way to the top. Despite this hard work, he knew he had been enormously lucky. Many other entrepreneurs had worked just as hard but failed. His wife's concern with social status seemed silly and irrelevant to him, but he was too busy to protest. FaceSaver was establishing a national presence, and it required his full-time attention.

When Reginald Winthrop, II was born, however, Reece forced himself to slow down and spend time with his son. As young Reginald got older, his father introduced him to fine shotguns and quality fly rods. Reece had been raised in Palm Beach County by middle class parents who took him to great dove shoots just west of Military Trail Drive, a virtual wilderness back then, and to a hunting lease near Palmdale, Florida, near Lake Okeechobee. It was on this lease that Reece developed his love for the woods. He liked nothing more than to slip along the edge of a cypress swamp looking for a buck whitetail deer or get into a ground blind and try to call up a long-bearded gobbler. When his son took a genuine interest in hunting and fishing, Reece couldn't have been happier.

Now, however, circumstances had changed so much that security concerns usually forced them to go to commercial establishments when they went to fish or hunt. Gone were the days of being able to walk carefree on a large lease. What's more, Priscilla wouldn't be part of any trip that didn't include the finest in sporting accommodations. She wouldn't stay in a trailer or tent; it was simply beneath her. Whether they were fishing for trophy-sized trout in New Zealand, Atlantic salmon in Nova Scotia, steelhead in Oregon, or pike in Alberta, they would stay in luxury facilities, or they wouldn't go at all; no "roughing it" for her.

Priscilla had an aversion to hunting because she thought it was uncivilized. That was fine with Reginald and his dad, and those days spent together were times they treasured, times when they could be "regular" guys. Of course, not many "regular" guys could hunt red stag in the Black Forest of Germany, ducks in Argentina and moose in Alaska. Still, there was something about hunting that equalized all people in certain ways. Campfires, coffee cooked in a saucepan over an open fire, a warm sleeping bag, or the companionship of a good dog were things to be enjoyed everywhere, not just in faraway and exotic places. These were times when a father and his son could talk about real things, a time for them to become closer. It was that way for the Winthrops, and nothing helped forge a stronger bond between them than an ordeal they faced together on a caribou hunt in the remote interior of Canada's Northwest Territories.

When Reginald turned 16 years old, his father's gift was a hunt in Central Canada for barren-ground caribou. His dad had chosen a "drop hunt" where a pilot would fly them into the hunting area, leave them to hunt alone, check on them on the fourth day, and then pick them up on the seventh.

Their pilot was Mable Hopkins, a middle-aged stocky woman who looked as though she had shot a few caribou herself. She was part Tlingit Indian, and understood the wilderness of Northwest Territories as well as anyone.

Getting to their campsite had been an expedition in and of itself. They flew from Norman Wells, Northwest Territories, for 160 miles over complete wilderness to a flat alongside the Mackenzie River. Looking out the window of Mable's DeHaviland Beaver airplane, a small workhorse aircraft legendary for its dependability and ruggedness, Reginald was sure he had never seen any place prettier. Mountains and tundra stretched out before him in all directions. He saw thousands of caribou walking steadily towards some unknown destination. Behind them were a few bears, waiting to jump the slower animals that lagged behind.

With Mable's help, the Winthrops pitched their tent alongside the great Mackenzie. She then gave them instructions on how to communicate with her without her having to land.

"I'm leaving you with a tarp that is green on one side, red on the other. I'll fly over your campsite on the fourth day. If everything's okay, stake out the tarp with the green side up. If the tarp's not there, or the red side is up, I'll assume you need help, and land. Got it?"

"We understand, Mable," Reece said.

"Good. You should have no trouble finding caribou. I can't guarantee you a *huge* bull, but you should be able to fill your tags. With a little luck, the toughest thing might be deciding which bull to take.

"You have all the supplies you need, but nothing more. No need to put out more scent for the bears than you have to. They're a real threat out here. If you have trouble, help is *not* right around the corner, so be careful. Make some noise as you walk along; if they hear you coming, they'll usually get out of your way.

"That's about it. Enjoy yourselves – I'll see you in a few days."

When Mable took off, the Winthrops watched the plane until it disappeared in the distant sky. They felt totally alone, and for good reason; they were only 250 miles from the Arctic Circle. The area they would be hunting was a 6,000 square mile tract of unspoiled wilderness. If one of them needed help, he would have to rely totally on the other. Reginald was both scared and exhilarated and had to fight his fears, but he felt a kinship with his dad that he'd never experienced.

The fall countryside was breathtakingly beautiful. It was September, and mile after mile of treeless low-rolling tundra was awash in colors of gold, brown, red and yellow. The species of caribou they would be hunting, "barren-ground caribou," was well named given the country in which the animals lived.

On the distant horizon the Mackenzie Mountains rose from the flat country, their peaks jagged and snow-covered. A few miles from the Winthrops' tent was a small creek that converged with the Mackenzie River. This convergence formed a natural "game funnel," directing huge herds of caribou, up to 15,000 in number, into a narrower area as they continued their migration southward towards the flats above Hooks Lake. Ultimately the caribou would have to cross the great Mackenzie, and it was here that grizzly bears and black bears would often wait, occasionally catching a cow or calf that was struggling in the fast moving water. Here, too, was a good place for the Winthrops to hunt. Reginald took his bull in this spot on the third day.

Reginald had never taken such a magnificent animal, awestruck by the majesty and beauty of the bull. The caribou's back, neck and legs were brownish gray, its shoulders and underbelly white. The rack of antlers was very tall and had 23 points on one side and 21 on the other. Hanging from them were strips of "velvet," spongy material that surrounds the new set of antlers the animals grow each year after the previous year's antlers fall off. As the new antlers harden, the velvet peels away in long strips, exposing the red blood-colored hue of the new antlers. Reginald's bull was an old animal that would make a fine addition to the trophy room of the Winthrop's house after being mounted.

Reginald and his dad gutted the caribou and removed its cape and rack for mounting, and its hide for tanning. The animal was quartered for easier transport back to camp. Each quarter was so heavy it would take two trips just to pack out the meat, and another trip to haul back the rack and cape. By the time night fell, the Winthrops were tired puppies.

The following morning, the fourth morning, they staked out the tarp, green side up, for the pilot to see on her fly-over. They also placed the rack and cape on the middle of the tarp so she could see that at least one of them had filled his tag. They wrapped the meat in cheesecloth and placed it in metal containers that were waterproof and bear-proof. The containers were put in a large canvas sack that was sunk in the river where the cold water would keep the meat cool so it wouldn't spoil.

Hiking out that day in search of a bull for Mr. Winthrop, they saw the plane fly by the camp. It made a second pass and disappeared into the far-off sky, the pilot satisfied that the hunters were okay. Again the isolation of their surroundings rattled Reginald, but he was having a fantastic time and was sure he would never forget this day. How true that turned out to be.

The Winthrops were headed to a large mineral lick about four miles away that attracted herds of caribou from all directions. When Reginald and his dad got close, they saw thousands of caribou milling about. Spotting the bull they had been looking for, a magnificent animal whose rack would score nearly 370 points, they positioned themselves for a shot. A half-hour later Reece's 7mm Remington Magnum roared. The mighty bull stumbled and went down. It was over, and the process of field-dressing the animal began.

With the caribou lying on its back, Reece used his razor sharp Randall knife to slice open the caribou between the back legs, down to the pelvic bone. Kneeling beside the animal, he then placed the index and middle fingers of his free hand between the skin and its underlying muscle, and the animal's guts. He put the knife's blade tip between these fingers, and used the fingers to prevent the tip from going too deep and puncturing the entrails. Moving the knife forward, he was able to move up the bull's body towards the chest, slicing only the skin and underlying muscle as he went.

When he got to the brisket, the cartilaginous area between the front shoulders that connects the ribs, he removed his free hand. He then turned around and straddled the animal above its neck, facing the long open belly. Holding the knife as he would if he were stabbing, he placed the blade underneath the brisket and a little bit deeper, and pulled upwards in a strong and fast motion towards himself, cutting a part of the brisket with each stroke. On the third pull he came through the last of the brisket, but the knife cut through easier than he thought it would. Before he could stop the knife, the blade stabbed him in his right inner thigh, just below the groin.

Rolling over and screaming in pain, he grabbed his leg where the knife blade had gone in. When he removed his hands, the severity of his wound was exposed. Through his hunting pants he could see that the gash was three inches long and at least two inches deep. He was bleeding like a stuck pig, and he knew that if the femoral artery were severed, he could be dead in less than four minutes.

Reginald would forever remember his dad's calm and businesslike demeanor. He knew his life depended on dealing quickly and efficiently with the problem.

"Take your belt off, son," he said. "Wrap it around my leg, above the cut, and cinch it down tight."

Reginald forced himself to act, pulling his belt from his pants. His hands were shaking, and he was so scared he was having a hard time breathing.

"Good," Reece said. "Now put one of your hands over the other and press them down onto the gash with the base of your palm. The direct pressure and tourniquet should stop the bleeding."

Reginald gingerly placed his hands over the cut and pushed down. His father grimaced, causing Reginald to jerk his hands up.

"No, son. You must do it. Don't worry about hurting me."

Again Reginald put his hands on the cut and began applying pressure.

"Harder. That's the way," his father said. "I'm going to close my eyes and try to totally relax, slowing down my heartbeat as much as possible. I may look dead, but I won't be," he said with the hint of a smile and wink of the eye. "Just don't let up with the pressure." Reece closed his eyes and became motionless. He did, in fact, look dead.

Reginald's heart was racing, and he was still short of breath.

"Calm down!" he thought. "Dad needs me! This is no time to panic."

His father's color had gone from ashen when he first saw the cut, to greenish-gray when he closed his eyes. But in 10 minutes, when Reece opened his eyes, his color was nearly normal.

"Don't stop with the direct pressure," Reece said. "The bleeding seems to have stopped, but we can't let it start back again. I'm going to stay quiet. We'll talk in a half-hour or so." He closed his eyes again.

His father's words reassured Reginald. Still, these 30 minutes were the longest of young Reginald's life. The wind was blowing and the weather was raw. He was shaking from the cold and anxiety of the moment. The only things warm were his hands, warmed by his dad's blood. Keeping them in the correct spot with the right amount of pressure required his full concentration.

Reginald occasionally felt dizzy and thought he was going to faint. He tilted his head down, directing blood to his brain.

"Why did we ever take this trip?" he wondered. "Mom always said we were foolish to go on such adventures." Reginald was fighting with himself.

"Get a grip!" Reginald thought. "Concentrate on what you must do. Think! Analyze your options!" Slowly he was able to rein in the demons that were tormenting him.

His dad would not be able to walk, that was for sure, or the bleeding would start again. The clean slice of the razor-sharp knife would make it very difficult for the severed blood vessels to fuse shut. And he couldn't be dragged or the jostling would begin the bleeding once more.

The plane was not returning for another three days. That meant staying two nights where they were. Remaining warm and dry would be the key.

"I have to go for the tent," Reginald thought.

A few minutes later, Reece opened his eyes. The bleeding had stopped.

"Dad, this is what we're going to do. I'm going for the tent. We need shelter, and you can't walk or be moved."

Tears welled in Reece's eyes. He knew that pessimism and indecision could kill him because it would result in inaction. Instead, his son was taking charge with confidence and decisiveness.

"I'll leave a note for the pilot telling her what has happened and where we are. I'll return as soon as I can. Dad, you're going to be all right."

Reece nodded. Reginald gently hugged him and then disappeared across the tundra.

Reginald jogged the entire four miles to camp. He didn't carry his rifle so that he would be able to carry back more of a load, and he almost regretted it. When he neared the Mackenzie River, where the brush was nearly shoulder high, he unknowingly ran between a sow black bear and her two cubs. The mother bear roared and charged, but Reginald held his ground, as he had been told by Mable, and stretched his arms upwards so he would appear to the bear to be bigger than he was. He also didn't make eye contact. The bear slowly stopped and wandered off, an agonizing minute later. Shaking, Reginald continued his trek to the tent.

When he arrived, Reginald packed a liter of water, a can of Sterno, a couple bags of tea and a handful of energy bars in a fanny pack. He broke down the tent and packed it in its sack. Next he folded up the tarp and tied it to the tent bag. He then sat down and wrote a note to the pilot, explaining what had happened and where they were. He put it in a zip-lock bag to protect it from the rain that appeared to be approaching in distant clouds, and tied it to a stick that he jammed into the ground where the tarp had been. Using stones he found alongside the river, he then wrote the word "HELP" on the sandy bank.

He strapped the fanny pack around his waist and hoisted the tent onto his shoulders, and began the hard trip back to his father.

When he got back, the ashen color had returned to his father's face, and he was unresponsive. The cut had begun bleeding again. Reginald once more applied direct pressure, and soon had the bleeding stopped. He then got his dad to drink a little water, which gave him strength.

"Did you get the tarp?" Reece asked.

"I did, plus a few supplies and a blanket and a sleeping bag. I need to get you covered up. You must stay warm."

"We'll do that in a minute, but first lay out the tarp, red side up. Another plane may see it. We also need to get the caribou away from us. It won't be long before bears smell it and come to investigate."

"It's too big. I tried already."

"Then cut it into pieces," Reece said. "First drop its guts. If it's still too heavy, quarter it as we normally would. Then haul everything at least a hundred yards away. Be sure to wash your hands afterwards; you'll need to get as much scent off of you as possible. The last thing we want is a bear coming in for us!" he said, forcing a faint smile.

Before dealing with the caribou, though, Reginald pitched the tent and gently dragged his father into it, laying him on the blanket. He then covered his dad with the sleeping bag.

He turned his attention to the caribou. It didn't take long for him to quarter the animal, and it was soon a good ways away from the tent. He then lit the can of Sterno and heated up water for hot tea.

"You got back with the tent just in time, Reginald" Reece said, as his son helped him sip the tea Reginald had just made. "Another half-hour and I'd have been a goner. I'm not out of the woods yet, but I think we're going to make it."

"I *know* we're going to make it, Dad. I won't have it any other way," Reginald said with a resoluteness that reminded Reece of himself when he was building his company.

Darkness came late in the North Country of Canada, but even in the middle of the night it wasn't hard dark. Reginald could see the outline of the distant Mackenzie Mountains and make out the general landscape surrounding him. The air was cold and still, and the night sky was purple-blue. The Aurora Borealis glowed above the mountains to the north, wispy bands of orange, white and red light dancing gaily about as sun particles interacted with gases in the earth's atmosphere. Reginald felt small and insignificant in the presence of such majesty.

He was doing well, though, and he knew it. He had helped stop his dad's bleeding and was doing all he could to save him. His father was going in and out of sleep, but resting comfortably and breathing easily. They were dry, warm, and well nourished. There was nothing more he could do to better their chances.

He thought of his mother and what she would think of their situation. Would she be mad or proud of how her son was handling it? "She'd be mad," he thought. "She would believe Dad was too important to even be this far from civilization, much less without a guide. She'd fail to see that this was the intrigue of it, that the real adventure was in us being totally on our own."

Reginald was a good kid. He longed for a more normal life where his mother didn't force him to be "Reginald Winthrop, II," with all the pretense that went along with such a role. He didn't like the boring socialite parties and political functions he was required to attend, or sitting for magazine and newspaper interviews for stories that profiled wealth and privilege. He was tired of having security guards shadow him wherever he went, and even wanted to go to public high school. He just wanted to be a regular guy. Maybe he could someday talk to his father about this. Maybe someday…

Reginald was jolted from his thoughts by the snapping jaws of bears, two of them, at least. They had found Reece's caribou. In the faint light of the night, he could make out the shapes of several bears bobbing around near the animal's carcass. They were big bears, probably grizzlies.

Reginald could hear bones being crushed and flesh being ripped as the mighty jaws of the bears chewed on the animal. Occasionally a bear would growl, telling Reginald that others were nearby, waiting their turn at the free meal. Reginald chambered a round in his .270 Winchester and laid the rifle across his lap…just in case.

Reece groaned and cried out in his sleep from some unknown nightmare. The bears quit eating, and there was dead silence. They had heard. Reginald tightened his grip on the rifle.

An enormous bear ambled towards the tent. Ten short steps away, it stood on its hind legs and let out a blood-curdling scream, making Reginald's spine tingle. He smelled the bear's breath even at that distance. The hair along the creature's back stood erect, creating a pronounced stripe from its shoulders to its tail.

Reece stirred. He was awake. Reginald put his finger to his lips. "Bears," he whispered.

Slowly Reginald raised his rifle and drew a bead on the bear's chest. Now was the time to shoot. If he waited until the bear charged, he would likely miss, knowing how quickly a bear could move.

Again the bear roared.

Powwwwww! Fire spewed from the barrel as the rifle barked. The noise was deafening.

Dirt sprayed up at the bear as the 150-grain Nosler Partition bullet tore into the earth. Reginald had lowered the gun quickly and shot in front of the bear's feet. The bear spun around and high-tailed it away. All the bears ran from the caribou, but they would return, as soon as things settled down a bit. But in all likelihood they wouldn't come back to the tent.

"Nice work," Mr. Winthrop said through clenched teeth. His leg hurt. "I hoped you wouldn't shoot the bear with that peashooter. It would have killed him eventually, but it wouldn't have knocked him down. He'd have been in this tent in a split second."

"I thought about that, and figured it would be better to scare him than sting him," Reginald said.

"That isn't the only thing you've figured out on this trip, son. You've done everything right so far," Mr. Winthrop said faintly. "I'm proud of you – you're thinking. Good…good…proud of you." He was struggling.

Those words, 'I'm proud of you,' filled Reginald with warmth. The truth was, he worshiped his father, and was amazed at what he had accomplished. He wanted nothing more than to have his dad's affirmation.

"Get some sleep, Dad," Reginald said lovingly as he tucked the sleeping bag around him.

The bears returned in less than 20 minutes, but stayed away from the tent as Reginald had thought. Still, he stayed awake keeping watch.

Day broke with a heavy fog. No planes would be flying in this weather, so Reginald returned to their original campsite for more supplies, this time taking a bag of grits in addition to water, tea, sugar cubes and Sterno. He also opened one of the cans of caribou from the river and cut off a foot-long piece of backstrap. The tenderloin would go well with a bowl of hot grits.

On the way back, Reginald walked by the remains of the caribou killed by his father. The bears had eaten their fill and left. The scraps were being fought over by black ravens and an Arctic fox. The caws and cackles of the birds echoed loudly in the stillness of the North Country. Soon the bones would be picked as slick as a cat's bottom, and mice would move in to gnaw them down to nothingness.

Arriving back at the tent, Reginald heard his father stir.

"Hey, Dad. How do you feel?"

"Not so good. I ache everywhere and I'm stiff as a board. I also need to take a leak. Can you get me a container of some kind?"

After helping his dad take care of business, Reginald started cooking breakfast.

He used one can of Sterno to boil water for the grits, another to heat a skillet for the backstrap. After the food was ready, Reginald cut the meat into small pieces for his father and mixed it into the grits so his dad could eat with a spoon. He leaned his dad up and they sat back-to-back, each supporting the other.

The hot food was just what Reginald's father needed. He really perked up.

"Caribou backstrap and Georgia ice cream. Did you ever think anything could taste so good?" he asked.

"Never," Reginald replied. "This has been a trip with many 'firsts'."

"That it has, son. That it has."

The sentence hung. Reginald thought this might be a good time for the discussion he had been considering.

"Dad, I've been thinking of something for a long time. I know how Mom will react, but maybe you'll understand it better."

"What's that, Reginald?"

"Well, I enjoy lacrosse and all, but I want to play football. That's why I was wondering about transferring."

"You don't like Palm Beach Prep? It's been a good school for you."

"It's not that I don't like it, it's just that I want to play football."

"What about Blakely? They have a football program."

"I know, but...so does P.S. 3."

Public School #3, one of Palm Beach County's oldest public schools in the northern part of West Palm Beach, almost in Riviera Beach.

A few seconds passed.

"Public high school, huh? You're right," Reece said. "Your mother isn't going to like it."

"Dad, I don't want to sound ungrateful, but I'm tired of all this fancy stuff. Fancy private school, fancy neighborhood, fancy cars. I just want to be a regular guy. I also want to play high school football."

"It would be a lot harder than you think, Reginald, going to public school. There are some students who would ridicule and make fun of you, at least in the beginning. 'Rich kid this, rich kid that.' Do you think you could handle it?"

"I know I could."

"And wouldn't you miss your friends?"

"Yes, at first. But I'd make new ones."

"There are legitimate security concerns that would have to be resolved."

"I know, and I wouldn't want to do it if that couldn't be solved."

"The fancy stuff isn't bad, Reginald. My guess is you'd miss it more than you think."

"Maybe so, and if I need to transfer back, I will. But I really want to try this, Dad."

Reece knew exactly how Reginald felt. There were times when he didn't care for all the privilege, either. Not that he'd give it back, but he understood. He'd attended public schools and gotten a fine education. It had also taught him the ways of folks with different backgrounds and how to deal with them, something that had been helpful as he grew his company.

"I'm not saying 'yes,' but I'm not saying 'no,' either. I want to think about it some more. And I'll need to speak with your mother about it. Fair enough?"

"Fair enough, and thanks."

The day droned on. Reginald helped his dad turn from one side to the other, and occasionally sit up. Reece was so stiff it hurt each time, but moving was good for him. Reginald also kept a hot wet towel draped across the gash, thinking it would help keep infection out.

Weather in Northwest Territories could turn bad in a hurry so pilots rarely flew in the afternoon. It was unlikely anyone would be in the air.

"Looks like it's going to be tomorrow before we're rescued," Reece said.

"I'm afraid you're right," replied Reginald sadly. "I was sure hoping it was going to be today." He looked down, then away. A tear ran down his cheek.

"Hey, what's that?" his dad asked.

Reginald couldn't speak without crying. The stress of the last two days was getting to him. The responsibility of being his father's caretaker had taken its toll.

"Come over here and sit next to me," Reece said. Reginald didn't hesitate. He needed to be comforted by his father as much as his dad had needed his help in the last 24 hours. It felt good to be sitting next to him.

"When I was your age, I'd get scared walking through the woods in the dark as I was coming in from my deer stand, so I'd sing. I mean I'd sing loudly, sometimes at the top of my lungs. Figured it would let the other hunters know I was coming through and that it wasn't a deer, and might also drive the snakes away. It made me feel better.

"The strange thing is I'd always sing the same song, 'Sweet Baby James' by James Taylor. I bet that was some sight, me singing out loud at the top of my lungs."

Reginald smiled. "Do you still remember the words? I don't think I've ever heard that song."

"You're making me feel older than I am, you know. But yes, I do remember the words, most of them anyway."

"Can you sing it, Dad?"

"I probably could."

"Then let me hear it," Reginald prodded, "as long as you're strong enough."

"I think I'm strong enough," his dad replied. "And it might keep the bears away," he said with a smile. In a shaky voice, he started –

There is a young cowboy, he lives on the range
His horse and his cattle are his only companions
He works in the saddle and sleeps in the canyons
Waiting for summer, his pastures to change

And as the moon rises he sits by his fire
Thinking about women and glasses of beer
And closing his eyes as the doggies retire
He sings out a song which is soft but it's clear
As if maybe someone could hear

Good night you moonlight ladies
Rockabye sweet baby James
Deep greens and blues are the colors I choose
Won't you let me go down in my dreams
And rockabye sweet baby James

"That's the first verse, anyway." By now they were lying side-by-side.

"That's nice," Reginald said, his voice drifting off. "Sing some more."

Now the first of December was covered with snow
And so was the turnpike from Stockbridge to Boston
Lord, the Birkshires seemed dreamlike on account of their frosting
With ten miles behind me, ten thousand more to go

There's a song that they sing when they take to the highway
A song that they sing when they take to the sea
A song that they sing of their home in the sky
Maybe you can believe it if it helps you to sleep

But singing works just fine for me
So rockabye sweet baby James[1]

Reece looked at his son, sleeping now. He pulled a blanket over him as best he could, being careful not to move his leg too much. Reginald was a young man, entitled to a say in things. "If he really wants to go to public school and play football, he can," Reece thought.

He, too, closed his eyes, the lyrics of "Sweet Baby James" running through his head. Soon he was sleeping, dreaming in deep greens and blues.

At 8:00 a.m., Reginald awoke with a start. His father was groaning. Reginald saw that his dad was fitful and sweating profusely. He looked at the gash, and grimaced. Red streaks were running down his father's leg. Infection had set in.

Reginald crawled from the tent and began heating water for tea. He also dug in his pack for the first aid kit, left for them by the pilot. It contained an antibiotic that Reece had begun taking after the injury to ward off infection. It had not worked, or not worked well enough.

Reginald opened one of the capsules and emptied its contents into a spoon. He then woke his father.

"Dad, wake up."

Reece was groggy and not very responsive.

"Infection has set in. I'm going to pour this antibiotic directly into the cut. It's probably going to sting like all get out, but I think we should try it."

"Do it," his dad said.

The cut was still wide open at the top, but at the bottom the tissue had begun to fuse together. Without disturbing it too much, Reginald pulled the cut apart slightly and poured the medicine into the wound.

It burned – badly, and Reece just about "stood up in the stirrups." But he gritted his teeth and never said a word.

"I don't know if that's going to help, but I don't see how it could hurt," Reginald said. He then made his father a cup of hot tea, putting in a lot of sugar.

The two sat there together, Reece sipping his tea and Reginald wiping his dad's forehead with a damp cloth. Reginald eased his father back down onto his back, and soon he was fast asleep.

Reginald went outside and checked the tarp. It was stretched tight, red side up. "Nothing to do but wait," he thought.

He didn't have to wait long. Soon he heard the drone of an airplane, far off, but getting closer. When Reginald saw the plane, he jumped up and down and waved his arms wildly, trying to get the attention of the pilot. The plane banked left, and headed towards him. The pilot tipped the wing of the plane. Reginald had been seen.

This time, pilot Mable Hopkins was in a DeHaviland Otter, a much bigger plane than the Beaver. Packing out the caribou meat after a successful hunt required more space. Unfortunately, it also required the hard riverbank to land. The heavy plane would dig into the soft tundra, making landing unsafe. Mable would have to land at the original campsite, and walk in. After circling once, the plane turned right and flew away. Two hours later, Mable walked into the camp area, wearing a large backpack and holding a fold-up stretcher.

"I didn't know what I'd find, so I brought as much as I could carry," she said, surprising Reginald.

"Boy, am I glad to see you!" Reginald replied, shaking her hand.

"The 'HELP' sign you wrote with rocks really stood out," Mable said. "When I saw it I decided to take a few circles around. Since the mineral lick was a good place to hunt, I thought you might be here."

"Good guess. Now let me show you my dad."

Mable greeted Mr. Winthrop. "Let's see what we have here." She looked at the cut and checked his vital signs. Unbeknownst to Reginald and Reece, Mable was also an Emergency Medical Technician. "That's a pretty nasty gash. You can tell me how it happened later. First we need to get you back to the airplane."

"Getting him to the plane is going to be difficult," Mable said to Reginald. "We can't drag him or the bouncing will start the bleeding again. We're going to have to carry him."

"Then let's get with it," Reginald answered. "Dad needs to get to a hospital."

The flat terrain made carrying Reece easier, but it was still late afternoon before they arrived.

"Guys, I'm sorry to tell you this but it's too late to fly out," Mable said. "A front is moving in and the last thing I want to do is try to fly through that storm, especially in the dark."

"What do you mean?" Reginald asked.

"I mean we're spending the night."

"But we can't spend another night out here. My dad needs medical attention!"

"Son, we have no choice," Reece interjected. "If the pilot says it's not safe to fly, we don't fly. It's as simple as that. A lot of crashes have occurred because the passengers *had* to get there."

"But Dad. We do *have* to get there! You need to get to the hospital!"

"Yes I do, but that'll have to wait until tomorrow. I'll be okay, though. That little trick of yours of putting the antibiotic directly into the cut seems to have done some good. My fever has broken and the red streaks are not as bad."

Mable had never heard of such a treatment. Still, Reece *was* better. Just to be sure, however, she gave him a shot of penicillin. "I'll put an IV in him if he needs it."

That helped quiet Reginald, and later that evening, when the clouds rolled in and the rain began, he saw the wisdom of staying on the ground.

"I've never been in such a storm!" Reginald said. The wind was blowing 60 mph and the rain was coming down sideways. If they hadn't been inside the tent to anchor it down, it might have blown away.

"Storms get bad around here," Mable replied. "But with all this wind, it should move out pretty quickly."

It did, and the next morning, after the fog had burned off, the plane was airborne. Mr. Winthrop was finally on his way to civilization.

Two hours later, they landed. Reece spent three days in the hospital and received 83 stitches.

"I told you not to go on that trip," Priscilla said to Reece and Reginald. She'd been ragging on them the whole way back from the West Palm Beach airport. "It was too far away, too remote, too many lots of things for Winthrops. We're not explorers for Heavens' sake! You have a company to run, Reece! Thousands of employees depend on you. And you, Reginald Winthrop, II, you have a company to inherit. The same employees, maybe even their children, will count on you some day. This was beyond foolish; it was stupid! Way up in the tundra of Northwest Territories? Who did you think you were, Admiral Byrd trying to get to the North Pole?"

At that, Reece burst out laughing.

"Honey, we had a time we'll never forget. It was a real adventure, nothing fake about it."

"You're right about that. Those stitches in your leg are real, aren't they?" she said. "You're lucky you didn't bleed to death."

"Yeah, I am lucky about that. If the knife blade had been a half-inch more to the left, it would have nicked the femoral artery and I'd have bought the farm. But it didn't, and I'm okay. Besides, Reginald and I had quite a time together, an experience we'll remember for the rest of our lives."

He then grew very serious. "I wish you could have seen him. Reginald kept his cool the whole time. In all honesty, he saved my life. I wouldn't be here if it weren't for him." Reece's voice choked. He reached back and grabbed Reginald's leg affectionately.

"We talked about a lot of things in that tent," Reece continued. "I even sang him to sleep one night." He and his son laughed. Priscilla looked confused. "You know. 'Sweet Baby James,' the song I sang when I was growing up and felt scared. I've told you about it. Yep, we talked about a lot of things in that tent."

Trips away with his father always seemed to change Reginald. This time, he matured. The responsibilities he had been forced to assume during the time on the tundra with his dad made him more serious. The snobbery of his mother didn't have any effect on him, either. He could handle the cruel remarks students in P.S. #3 would likely dish his way.

"Have you lost your mind?" Priscilla asked. "Reginald is a Winthrop, and Winthrops don't go to public school."

"*I* went to public school," Reece answered.

"But times were different then. There weren't all the…"

"Don't say it, Priscilla."

"Say what? You thought I was getting racist, didn't you. I was going to say there weren't all the problems there are today…drugs, teenage pregnancy, gangs, that kind of thing."

"But you think that's because the student population looks different today, don't you?"

"I don't know what it's from, but what difference does it make? The problems are there, that's all that matters. And what about security? How can security concerns be addressed in a public school?"

"I assume the same way it works in a private school. But we'll work through that, and if we can't, he won't attend. I'm not going to agree to something that's too risky. Priscilla, I think we should let him do this. There's a good chance it won't work out, and he'll be back at Palm Beach Prep in less than a month. In any event, he should have a say in this and it's what he wants to do."

"But what if he likes it?" she said with a worried look.

Reece chuckled. "That would be great! Why wouldn't we be happy for him?"

"I guess we would, but…public school?"

"Come on, Priscilla. Let's let him give it a try. We'll keep him where he is until the Christmas break, then he'll start at P.S. 3 when the students return after the New Year. That'll give him two months to get settled before football begins in the spring. If he likes it, he'll return in the fall for his senior year. If not, he'll be right back where he was and never miss a beat. What do you say?"

Priscilla sat quietly for a long minute. "Okay, if you think it's best. But I'm going to be at that school so often they'll think *I'm* a student!"

Christmas came and went, and it was time for Reginald to attend his first day of school at P.S. #3. He and his dad were fine, but his mother was a nervous wreck.

Even though Reginald had his driver's license, she insisted on driving him to school. Despite his protests, she wouldn't have it any other way. But this wasn't nearly as bad as when she walked him in; this was pure torture, and Reginald almost wouldn't get out of the car. He was nearly late, though, so he acquiesced. When they reached the hallway, they stopped. Reginald could feel the stares of other students.

"This is far enough!" he said under his breath.

"I'll be right here when school gets out," Priscilla said seriously. "If you need anything, just yell for Jacko," who was lurking in the background.

"Okay Mom. Will you please leave? You're humiliating me! It's bad enough to have a bodyguard hanging around."

"Don't complain about Jacko. Without him, I wouldn't have allowed you to attend here. Security concerns, you know. That was the deal."

"I know, Mom, I know. Now goodbye!"

Things began uneventfully. The only surprise was how difficult the curricula was, especially mathematics. Reginald was taking all advanced placement (AP) and honors classes, and he had to study as hard as he ever did at Palm Beach Prep. In fact, there was even more homework in some courses. On a light night it still took him three hours to complete his assignments.

He was also very pleased with his classmates. They were friendly, funny and smart. He could see how the regular classes, with so many students who didn't want to be in school, would be a challenge for the teachers and students who wanted to learn. However, his AP and honors courses brought together the school's brightest students into a very effective classroom environment that he really enjoyed.

Having Jacko around was awkward and drew a lot of comments. After the first week, and because of the genuine concern administrators showed in making sure he was safe, Reginald was able to convince his mother that Biggsley could take the place of Jacko. Biggsley was better able to blend with the school staff and appreciated Reginald's discomfort at having a bodyguard at high school. After a month Biggsley even convinced Priscilla that Reginald didn't need any protection at all.

As well as his classes were going, however, Reginald did feel some apprehension about football. He had decent size and pretty good speed, but wasn't solid on the fundamentals. Two years of Little League was the only organized football he had ever played, and that didn't teach him everything he needed to know.

As luck would have it, one of the assistant coaches, Bobby Bell, took a special interest in him. Coach Bell was the Defensive Backs coach, and he saw something in Reginald that told him he could be a good player. More than that, he saw a kid who was nervous and who needed some help, and that was the real reason he had gotten into coaching in the first place.

Working with Reginald before Spring Training began, Coach Bell taught him the correct way to tackle as well as other basics. After a month of individualized training, Reginald was as ready as he could be, knowing that the real test would come when the players put on their pads and began hitting.

Practice the first week was all conditioning. Many players vomited every day until they became acclimated to the heat and got in better shape. But Reginald held his own. He wasn't the best-conditioned player, but he wasn't the worst, either.

The coaches were pleasantly surprised. The team was weak in the defensive backfield, and Reginald was fitting in nicely. He had a good chance of starting in the Spring Jamboree. At the very least, he'd get plenty of playing time.

Every afternoon when he was in town, Reece would park by the fence of the football field and watch practice. Priscilla would have nothing to do with it. She thought football was barbaric. Biggsley would sometimes accompany Reece; it made for a nice afternoon for them.

The Spring Jamboree arrived. P.S. #3 would play a quarter against each of three other teams. Reginald was so nervous he threw up in the locker room before the first quarter of play.

One reason he was so nervous was because earlier that day he was named a starter. His mother, father, Jacko and Biggsley would be in the stands watching. Reginald was also a bit scared. He couldn't help but wonder what the players from these other schools would be like. He was less physically mature than his teammates and likely less physically mature than the players on the opposing teams.

As he left the locker room and walked across the concrete walkway towards the field, he realized he was softly singing the song "Sweet Baby James." He smiled, thinking of how his father had sung this song when he was young and scared. Strangely, it calmed Reginald down, just as it had his dad many years before.

When he stepped onto the field, he and his teammates yelled and jumped up and down and charged through a paper sign made by the cheerleaders as they headed for the sideline. The captains headed to the middle of the field for the coin toss. The other team won and elected to receive. This would put Reginald on the field right after the kickoff.

Head coach Tinker McCollough gathered his players in a tight group on the sidelines. "Let's show these guys from the other schools a little something about P.S. 3 pride! Take charge early! Get off to a good start! Now let's go!" Reginald and his teammates cheered wildly, encouraging each other along.

After the kickoff, Reginald ran onto the field. His dad, Biggsley and Jacko came to their feet and clapped and shouted. Priscilla stayed seated.

On the third play from scrimmage, the opposing side's quarterback rolled to his left and threw back to his right as the split end crossed the middle. Reginald, who was playing right defensive back, broke on the throw and stuck the receiver in the front numbers just as the ball arrived, forcing him to cough it up.

The hard hit fired up the team, and Reginald was pumped. He ran to the sidelines, shaking his fist as the punt returning team was taking the field. Coach Bell was the first to reach him. "Great stick, man! Great stick!" he said, putting his arm around Reginald.

The P.S. #3 fans, especially Reece, Biggsley and Jacko, went wild. Even Priscilla smiled, although she wouldn't stand and cheer. That would show too much emotion for her. Winthrops were supposed to be reserved and calm.

The rest of that quarter, and the next two, went by so quickly that Reginald could hardly believe it was over. He finished the night with three unassisted tackles and one interception. The team won two of the quarter-long games and tied one.

The short bus ride back to the school was fantastic. The team had played well overall, and everyone was laughing and replaying most every play. Reginald had never had so much fun.

The jubilance continued when the team reached their locker room at the school. The head coach, Tinker McCollough, spoke to the team and announced that Reginald was the defensive player of the night. Everyone shouted and cheered. Reginald felt fully accepted as not just a member of the team, but as a full member of the school. His move to P.S. #3 had been a good one.

The fun lasted all weekend. Friday night, Reginald attended a post-game party. There was no doubt that his stature in the school had risen after his great performance. Saturday morning, there was a picture of him in the <u>Palm Beach Chronicle</u> making the hit on the receiver on the third play from scrimmage. The caption read, "Winthrop Sets Tone Early." This made Priscilla feel much better about Reginald playing football. "A photograph in the paper is a photograph in the paper," she said to her husband over coffee. At church on Sunday, several members of the congregation congratulated Reginald on his play. Reginald's football career at P.S. #3 was off to a fine start.

The euphoria crashed on Monday morning, however. Reginald was called to Principal Ed Cagiano's office where he, Vice Principal Bill Pickering, and Coach McCollough were waiting for him. They closed the door behind him.

"What's up, Coach?" he asked.

"You had a great game Friday night, son. But you made a mistake in the locker room afterwards," McCollough said.

"What's that?" Reginald asked, a confused look on his face.

"You left your shoulder pads out of your locker. I came in Saturday morning, and there they were, lying on the floor."

The blood rushed from Reginald's face. He knew the penalty for leaving pads out. Coach McCollough had told the team many times.

"I'm sorry, Coach. I didn't realize it. I didn't do it on purpose."

"I'm sure you didn't, but a rule's a rule. I can't make exceptions. I'm sorry."

Reginald slumped in his chair and thought for a moment. "Okay, what's it going to be?" he asked.

Pickering answered. "Two licks, one for each shoulder or one for each cheek, however you want to look at it," he said, laughing.

Coach McCollough scowled. He didn't like or appreciate the vice principal making light of something he didn't want to do.

"Let's get it over with, Coach," Reginald said.

Pickering took the paddle from the shelf. The business end was about 18 inches long with holes drilled throughout. The holes allowed air to pass through during the swing, helping to keep the board on target. A hit too high could hit the bottom of the spine; a hit too low could bruise the backs of the upper thighs.

Written across one face of the paddle was the word "LightningStick." The other side had a picture of a bolt of lightning.

"Who gets the honors?" the vice principal asked.

"It's my responsibility," McCollough replied, "although I don't consider it much of an honor."

Taking the short handle in his right hand, the coach told Reginald to stand up and bend over. "Put your elbows on your knees, son."

Reginald bent over. Tinker took two slow practice swings to better his aim, pulled the board back and swung hard. Crrraack!! Reginald flinched. "One more," the coach said. Crrraack!!

Reginald stood, rubbing his stinging rump. He was biting his lip. The licks hurt.

"I'm sorry to have to do that," McCollough said.

"I know. I understand" was all Reginald said. He opened the door and walked out, fighting back tears. The other adults in the office didn't look up. Two students were giggling. They had heard the bite of the board.

When Priscilla heard that Reginald was paddled she went ballistic and immediately scheduled a meeting at the school. In attendance were Mr. and Mrs. Winthrop, Reginald, Coach McCollough, Principal Cagiano, Vice Principal Pickering, and Ron Williams, the attorney for the school board.

"A set of shoulder pads costs over a hundred dollars, Mrs. Winthrop. We *must* have a rule against leaving pads out or the football program would go broke just trying to keep uniforms on the kids," McCollough said.

"But paddling? It's so…humiliating! Surely there is some other way."

"Like 'timeout?'" Pickering asked sarcastically.

"That's enough," Cagiano said angrily. "No more comments like that, please."

"Mrs. Winthrop," Cagiano explained, "Reggie knew the rules…"

"Reggie? You call him Reggie? His name is Reginald!" she admonished.

"But, that's what he told us to call him."

"Reginald, is that true?" Priscilla asked.

"Yes, Mom. It's true. Reginald was just too stiff."

"It wasn't when you were at the *other* school," she replied. "It was just fine there."

A silence hung in the air. Everyone looked around, wondering if the true reason for the meeting had just surfaced.

"Your name is Reginald, not Reggie," she continued. "Reginald Winthrop, II!"

"I guess *Reggie* Winthrop, II does sound a little relaxed," Pickering interjected, chuckling. He just couldn't help himself.

"Mr. Pickering. I asked you to hold your comments to yourself," Principal Cagiano said. "Would you please step out of the office? We'll have a private meeting later."

"Mrs. Winthrop, for what it's worth I hated to give Reggie, er…Reginald, the licks," Coach McCollough said. "He's an outstanding young man, and we've really enjoyed having him on the team."

"And at the school," the principal added.

"But I have to enforce this rule," McCollough continued. "You know how teenagers are; they'd lose their heads if they weren't screwed on. A football helmet here, a set of shoulder pads there. Pretty soon it'd add up to real money."

"But why paddling? Is it even legal?" she asked.

Ron Williams, the school district attorney, now jumped into the conversation. "Oh yes. It's legal. It comes from the common law doctrine known as 'in loco parentis,' meaning 'in the place of the parent.' Basically, if it's legal for a parent to do this, it's legal for the school to do it."

"We have never spanked Reginald," Priscilla said, "and you shouldn't either."

"And if you had filled out the form saying you didn't want your son paddled, we wouldn't have," the attorney added. "But there's no form in the file. I checked."

"Do you remember seeing the form, honey?" Reece asked, speaking for the first time.

"Well, yes," she answered. "But I never did anything with it because I didn't think it would be an issue. A Winthrop would never do anything that would justify such punishment. And besides, none of the schools we've ever attended had such a backward practice."

Reece just sat back in his chair, shaking his head.

"Mrs. Winthrop, the law allows corporal punishment in Florida," Cagiano said, "and I've satisfied all the conditions required. I approved it, prepared guidelines for its administration, identified the offenses subject to it, and spelled out the conditions under which it could be administered. I specified which school personnel were authorized to administer it, and there was another adult present who was made aware of why the paddling was occurring.

Still, if you had asked us not to administer it, we would have respected your wishes. In the future, if you would like us not to paddle your son, regardless of the infraction, we won't. But everything was done 'by the book' in this case."

"But what about the welts, the bruising. He showed me."

"Mom, please!" Reginald exclaimed.

"Everything we did was reasonable, Mrs. Winthrop," the principal said.

"We'll see about that," Priscilla said sternly. "Our lawyer will make you regret you ever touched a Winthrop. And all over a piddly set of shoulder pads…"

"Stop it, Priscilla!" Reece shouted. "Just stop it. There won't be any lawsuit. Our son broke a rule and was punished for it. It doesn't matter that he didn't mean to, and it darn sure doesn't matter that he's a Winthrop! You don't hear Reginald complaining, do you? He likes it here! Why can't you accept that?"

The room was deathly quiet. Priscilla's bottom lip began to shake.

Reece's tone softened. "Sure the rules are a little different than what we're used to, but they *have* to be. These administrators are just trying to maintain a little order and discipline. Let's give them a break, not threaten them with a lawsuit. They're being asked to educate more and more students who don't get any positive training or educational support at home. On top of that, a growing number of students who receive proper training at home are going to private school. The public schools are getting hit from both directions; they're getting more students who are tougher to educate, and fewer students who are easier."

"I know that," she said, her voice now cracking. "But we're Winthrops, and Winthrops don't get treated this way."

"Oh yes they do. I had my tail paddled more than once, and my guess is the schools you attended had the same policy."

That did it. Exposed. Her blue-collar upbringing laid out there for everyone to see. She was not a Winthrop by birth, but by dumb luck. Deep down she knew she was lucky, but she'd spent the last 18 years running from that fact.

"Let's go home, dear. These men have work to do."

Reece took his wife's hand. They rose and walked out the door. As Reginald followed them, the coach said, "Hey, Reginald. You played a *great* game last Friday. Are we going to see you in the fall?"

"You bet, Coach. I wouldn't miss it for the world. And by the way, the name's Reggie." Everyone smiled and nodded, even Priscilla.

[1]"Sweet Baby James" by James Taylor, released in February of 1970 on Warner Records.

Author's Note:

Corporal punishment is controversial; some see it as a barbaric practice that conveys many wrong lessons to kids, while others believe it is a helpful tool in preserving order and fostering good behavior. Paddling by teachers and administrators was used frequently when I was growing up. As one who felt the sting of the board a couple of times (once for leaving my shoulder pads out of my locker after football practice, hence, the thought for the story), I can tell you it worked. On the other hand, I'm sure there were other forms of punishment that would have been just as effective.

The threat of lawsuits ended most corporal punishment in the schools. Even though the statutes allowed paddling, teachers and administrators grew rightfully concerned about being sued for child abuse and the criminal charges that might follow. The line between what was considered excessive paddling and appropriate discipline became blurred in the eyes of the law and parents. When I was coming along, the licks I was aware of always bruised at least slightly, and sometimes the discoloration was pretty pronounced, but that wasn't generally considered abuse. Perceptions changed for many, though, so most school officials concluded it just wasn't worth the risk. Many administrators had begun to question its effectiveness, too. For these reasons, most paddling in the schools was stopped.

THE LAW: Definitions and Explanations:

Corporal punishment: Physical punishment as distinguished from pecuniary punishment or a fine; any kind of punishment of or inflicted on the body...

Black's Law Dictionary, Sixth Edition, p. 339

In loco parentis: In the place of a parent; instead of a parent; charged, factitiously, with a parent's rights, duties, and responsibilities.

Black's Law Dictionary, Sixth Edition, p. 787

"Excessive bail shall not be required, nor excessive fines imposed, nor cruel and unusual punishments inflicted."

Eighth Amendment, Constitution of the United States of America

The United States Supreme Court, in the case of Ingraham v. Wright, 430 U.S. 651 (1977), affirmed the use of corporal punishment in the schools. Mr. Justice Powell, writing for the majority: "...At common law a single principle has governed the use of corporal punishment since before the American Revolution: Teachers may impose reasonable but not excessive force to discipline a child. (supra, at 662)...We conclude that when public school teachers or administrators umpose disciplinary corporal punishment, the Eighth Amendment is inapplicable. The pertinent constitutional question is whether the imposition is consonant with the requirements of due process. (supra, at 672)...Elimination or curtailment of corporal punishment would be welcomed by many as a societal advance. But when such a policy choice may result from this Court's determination of an asserted right to due process, rather than from the normal processes of community debate and legislative action, the societal costs cannot be dismissed as insubstantial. We are reviewing here a legislative judgment, rooted in history and reaffirmed in the laws of many States, that corporal punishment serves important educational interests. This judgment must be viewed in light of the disciplinary problems common-place in the schools. As noted in Goss v. Lopez, 419 U.S., at 580: 'Events calling for discipline are frequent occurrences and sometimes require immediate, effective action.' Assessment of the need for, and the appropriate means of maintaining, school discipline is committed generally to the discretion of school authorities subject to state law. '[T]he Court has repeatedly emphasized the need for affirming the comprehensive authority of the States and of school officials, consistent with fundamental constitutional safeguards, to prescribe and control conduct in the schools.'

Notable Quotes:

"Right is right, even if everyone is against it, and wrong is wrong, even if everyone is for it."

William Penn / www.brainyquotes.com

"There is plenty of justice at the end of a nightstick."

Grover Whalen / www.worldofquotes.com

"Treat people right. I don't care who they are, treat them right: high or low or black or white, treat them right. Be good to them. And that will usually help you in the long run."

Honorable Richard W. Ervin, Jr., Chief Justice, Florida Supreme Court. The Florida Bar News, September 15, 2004, p. 5

"Because just as good morals, if they are to be maintained, have need of the laws, so the laws, if they are to be observed, have need of good morals."

Niccolo Machiavelli / www.worldofquotes.com

"Law cannot persuade where it cannot punish."

Thomas Fuller / www.worldofquotes.com

Roots in Old Cuba

GLASS HOUSE JUSTICE
Mandatory Sentencing v.
an Independent Judiciary

Preface: This is the story of Mario Lacasa, a Cuban immigrant who came to the United States at the age of 14 shortly after Fidel Castro seized power in Cuba. After experiencing the upheaval caused by the dictatorial reign of Castro, Mario grows into adulthood in America, totally in awe of the American legal system and the wisdom of the Founding Fathers in creating a government with three separate branches, each a check and balance on the other two.

Mario's fascination with government leads to a career in law. Watch how his idealism, ambition and ego influence his early governmental actions involving minimum mandatory sentences (prison sentences of a required minimum length). These sentences, often called "minimum mandatories," are passed by legislative bodies but they give judges little flexibility in sentencing. Then notice how Mario's deep-seated beliefs in the role of the judiciary conflicts with the administration of justice with a case at hand when a minimum mandatory sentence is required by statute. Finally he comes face to face in a very personal way with the high stakes and grim reality of what can happen when a judge has little discretion to impose a sentence that accurately fits the crime.

Act I: Cuba

Scene 1: The Early Years for the Lacasa Family

Luis Lacasa loved his farm. Six thousand acres of sugar cane, vegetables and tobacco provided him not only wealth, but also an endless source of enjoyment.

He didn't come by this fortune easily, however. With no formal education, he had worked hard for years in the hot Cuban sun to earn enough to buy his first few acres. Slaving away in the farm fields, he had always set aside 20 percent of his income to buy land. By the time he was 28 years old he had enough land to become self-sufficient, and once he had tasted the freedom that went along with being his own boss, he poured himself into his business, amassing vast holdings and great wealth.

Along the way he married Ileana Martinez and they had three boys, each special and unique in his own way. Their oldest was Mario, and he was a perfect oldest son in his father's eye. He was a good example to his younger brothers, worked hard at the private school his dad was able to afford for him, excelled in baseball, and spent many afternoons learning the family business that he would someday inherit.

The feeling of love and admiration was mutual. Mario idolized his father. To him, his dad was the epitome of what hard work could accomplish. Land, wealth, family…all was made possible because of the hard-working, principled man who was Luis Lacasa.

Life in the Lacasa family was idyllic in most ways. Food was plentiful, their health care was the best money could buy, they lived in a magnificent home, and they went to the finest schools. But Mario and his two younger brothers also worked very hard. Their father made sure they got dirt under their fingernails so they would develop a connection to the land that would last forever. The routine of rising early and moving into the fields wet with dew, planting or harvesting crops under balmy skies, retreating from the frequent afternoon thunderstorms, and relaxing in the cool evenings created a rhythm that swallowed them up. Soon their very identities, like their father's, were caught up in the land. Mario would watch his father and sometimes think that his dad would sooner die than not have his farm, that it was as necessary to him as his heart. Mario was beginning to feel the same way.

Scene 2: Revolution

One day in late 1957, Luis Lacasa returned from town extremely agitated. The administration of President Fulgencio Batista was being severely criticized for not responding to the needs of the poor and for widespread corruption. Batista had decided that the best way to deal with this dissent was to crack down hard on those who dared to speak out. Mario's father was convinced this would only fuel the anger of those who wanted change and could even lead to revolution. He had been through one coup when Batista had come into power in 1952, and it was not something he wanted to experience again. In fact, he had nearly lost his farm in that uprising. In a country like Cuba where there were so many poor people, a revolution was always very dangerous to those with substantial holdings. It was entirely possible that when the dust settled, his assets would not be his but the property of the "new" government.

A redistribution of wealth imposed by government was totally repugnant to Luis and antithetical to the way he believed a society should be structured. He had worked hard to get where he was, and it made him sick to his stomach to think that everything could be taken from him by those who he believed had not worked hard enough or been smart enough. Claims of governmental thievery were nonsense, in his view; he simply couldn't believe that political leaders were stealing from the treasury. And the allegations of political patronage were ridiculous. Helping one's political supporters was the way it had always been, and favorable treatment he had received for supporting the Batista regime was just the way of politics.

Luis did recognize the plight of the poor as a serious threat to the country's stability. While he paid his workers as well as any farmer, it still wasn't enough for them to have access to basic health care or decent housing. They were also illiterate; not a single one of them could read. History was replete with examples of the poor rising up in the face of such difficulties, and often they were successful. Political dissent was like wildfire: once it started it was hard to stop, and now it had started again in Cuba. Luis was very worried.

He was also troubled personally by the rampant poverty because he was sympathetic and truly cared about his workers, yet he felt that it wasn't his or the government's responsibility to provide them with the basics of life. It was everyone's obligation to improve his or her own lot in life, not depend on the government for charity. He had started with nothing and made it big. Why couldn't they?

That evening after dinner, Mario's father and mother were sitting on the front porch, gently swinging in a two-seated swing hanging from the ceiling. The air had cooled, and the frogs and insects could be heard making their "night music."

Mario had sensed at dinner that something was on his father's mind. Later, from a sofa near the window, Mario overheard his father telling of a young revolutionary named Fidel Castro who was waging a guerilla campaign from the mountains of eastern Cuba. His father described him as a big man with a barrel chest who had a commanding presence. Luis had heard him speak and he was a powerful orator who could go on for hours. And with his training as a lawyer, he was smart. He was just the kind of person who could lead the masses...and just the kind of person who could incite a revolution.

"It's not his charisma or courage to speak ill of the current administration that has me so concerned," Luis said. "It's that he has a doctrine, a vision for the country, and it is complete with specifics."

"But why is that so dangerous?" Ileana asked.

"Because he can show people where he wants to take them...and it is a much better place than where they are now. The seeds he is planting, once they germinate, will be very hard to stop. Castro is painting a picture in the minds of the people that is very appealing to them. He is showing them how much better life can be, and telling them that all they have to do is follow his plan and they can have it. He's not just filling their heads with empty promises; he's showing them how to get there. That's why he's so dangerous."[1]

Over the next few months, tension between pro and anti-Batista forces grew. The Lacasas could feel it on their farm, and they were miles from the center of the conflict. Like a small thunderstorm that feeds on the warm waters of the ocean, finally growing into a mighty hurricane, the revolutionary movement was gaining strength.

By March of 1958, Castro and other anti-Batista leaders had formed an extensive network of supporters and were growing brazen. Castro led the more organized faction, and he called for a nationwide strike of all workers. It failed, but had it been successful, it would have devastated the Cuban economy and Luis Lacasa personally. Farm products were perishable, and delays of only a few days could be the difference between a crop being able to be harvested and one that was left to fall from the tree and rot.

The stress in the Lacasa family was palpable. Everyone felt it, especially Mario because he saw what it was doing to his father. In six months his father aged six years.

With the failure of his strike, Castro's attempt to bring about change peacefully had failed. Soon, other revolutionaries bombed many governmental buildings and assassinated several Batista officials. This drew an immediate and severe response from Batista's forces, and many of the leading urban revolutionaries were killed. The dissidents who were left rallied around Castro who sent fighters into a battle against Batista soldiers. The revolutionaries won, Batista's regime collapsed, and Batista fled the country on January 1, 1959. Castro was now the de facto leader of the country and became Prime Minister in February.

He wasted little time implementing many of the reforms he had promised. Temporarily closing the schools, he sent students and teachers into the countryside to teach illiterates how to read and write, and opened clinics in rural areas to bring health care to the poor. This gave him populist appeal and he enjoyed broad support among the nation's underclass.

Castro now controlled the army and the elections' process; his power was solidified militarily and politically. He began aggressively transforming Cuba into a socialist state by seizing property and business holdings from the nation's middle and upper class and from foreign companies. For the Lacasa family, life was forever changed when a Castro initiative nationalized farms larger than 1,000 acres, redistributing the acreage as small agricultural plots to the poor. Nearly all of Luis Lacasa's land holdings were taken from him.

Scene 3: Escape

It wasn't long before many of Cuba's people, including hundreds of thousands of well-educated professionals, began seeking exile in other countries. By the end of 1962, more than one million people had left Cuba for Spain, Mexico, France and primarily the United States. Their positions and many of their possessions had been taken from them. Most importantly, though, they had lost their belief that they could be successful in Cuba in the long run. They disagreed with the politicization of education and felt threatened by an educated and literate underclass. They also feared for their safety: any hint of defiance of Castro brought swift reprisal.

Despite this, Luis could not bring himself to leave. Cuba was where his heart lay, and he would not abandon it to a person who had taken every material possession from him. To do so would allow Castro to take the last thing he had left: his dignity. He would bide his time, getting by any way he could, and then he would strike. There was already talk that the United States was training Cubans in exile so they could come back to fight the Castro regime. America could not afford to have a leader like Castro less than a hundred miles from its border. Surely there were nationalists like Luis who would rise up to assist these exiles and take their country back when the opportunity presented itself.

The rest of the family was a different matter. What he was contemplating – an attempt at overthrowing Castro – would be dangerous indeed. If unsuccessful, he would most likely be executed and the firing squad might next kill his family. He was willing to risk his own life, but not the lives of his children. He would defer to his wife's wishes regarding whether she stayed, but his children would leave. He would wait until the last possible moment, but the time would come when he would have to get them off the island.

That time came in the spring of 1961.

Castro had begun an aggressive campaign to indoctrinate the children of Cuba with Communism. As part of this indoctrination, private schools were shut down and military training for all high school students began. In early-1961, Castro sent 1,000 children to the Soviet Union to live on collective farms, learning the ways of the communists. These events confirmed the worst fears of parents that their children would be forced to spend long periods away from them, or be forced into military service and denied an education.

Strangely, the United States intentionally stoked these fears. The Central Intelligence Agency (CIA) believed that the Castro government would lose its populist appeal if people thought their children could become the property of the government, like everything else in Cuba, and families would be split up. Beginning in 1960, American-sponsored radio broadcasts started with messages like, "Cuban mothers, don't let them take your children away! The Revolutionary Government will take them away from you when they turn five and will keep them until they are 18. By that time, they will be materialistic monsters."[2]

The American campaign was more than psychological. Using the services of the Catholic Church, a voluntary program called "Operation Pedro Pan" began, and children were moved from the islands. Working with the State Department of the United States, Catholic officials first secured visas for 500 children. Parents were not allowed visas because they were to stay on the island and fuel the discord for Castro. By the time the program was over, 14,000 children between the ages of five and 18 were shuttled from Cuba to the United States.

Luis Lacasa was caught up in two overwhelming realities. He loved his children and the thought of being away from them was almost more than he could bear, but he would find a way for them to escape if their future in Cuba was one of communist indoctrination and limited educational possibilities. That might mean participating in Operation Pedro Pan.

The second reality for Luis was involvement in an American military plan to oust Castro. The American government was considering a full-scale secret invasion of Cuba. The CIA had begun training 1,500 Cuban exiles in Guatemala to be the invasion force. The theory was that the exiles would be well received by the Cuban people, and the support for their operation would snowball, ultimately leading to the overthrow of Castro.

On April 15th, after the invasion force had been trained and was ready, the CIA launched covert air strikes to limit Castro's air defenses. The next day the CIA was to finish the job, but President John Kennedy, concerned about the United States appearing too involved, halted the strikes. He still supported the operation, however, so the exiles invaded on April 17th, making landfall at the Bahia de Cochinos (Bay of Pigs) on the south coast of Cuba. Unfortunately, word of the invasion had leaked out and Castro was ready, so by April 19th the fighting was over. Popular support for the exiles from the Cuban people failed to materialize, and in just three days Castro's forces killed or captured every one of the 1,500-member invasion force.

Just as Castro had heard of the impending invasion, so too had Luis Lacasa who decided that he would meet the exiles and fight alongside them. He was confident of victory, but he would not risk the lives of his family in the event the operation went badly. This, coupled with fear of his children becoming indoctrinated into communistic thinking and being denied the education he so dearly wanted for them, brought him to a place in his thinking that he and his wife had often discussed.

So on April 8th, one week before the air strikes were to begin, he and his family gathered after dinner for a heart-wrenching talk. It was then that Luis told his children why they must leave for America.

Luis and his wife had been preparing their children for this moment as best they could. But until now, the specifics of why they might have to go were not discussed for it would be dangerous for the children if they knew their father was considering staying behind in order to fight the Castro forces. During these conversations they spoke little of the danger of staying and mostly of the need of going to a place where there was more opportunity. Always there were assurances that the family would be re-united either in the United States, or that maybe the children could return to Cuba. The children held on to these assurances with everything they had, but deep within them they knew that if the time came to leave they might never see their parents again.

So they prayed that day would never come, but it had, and there on the beach Luis and his wife told their three sons – ages 14, 12 and 10 – that the boys would be flying to Miami early the next day. They would be part of Operation Pedro Pan, named after the fairy tale character, Peter Pan, who had taken children away to Never-Never Land. This wasn't a fairy tale, though, but a true nightmare for the families affected.

"But why can't you come with us?" Mario asked.

"I must stay behind. I have business to finish," Luis said.

"But what about you, Momma. You must come, too!" Mario implored.

"Oh, my child. I must stay with your father for now. But it will not be for long. I will come to Miami soon. And once your father finishes his business here, we will all return so that we can be together again – in our homeland of Cuba. That is my promise."

Putting their children on the plane was the hardest thing Mr. and Mrs. Lacasa had ever done. For young Mario Lacasa, the image from that day was etched in his mind. The tearful embrace and final kiss of his parents, and the look in his father's eyes as he hugged his children goodbye, would be with him forever. But through the despair and pain in his dad's eyes was something else: love. Putting his children on that plane was an act of total and complete love, an act of total conviction that America was their best chance at survival and a life worth living. Otherwise, how could he have done it?

Scene 4: New Life in America

Arriving in Miami shortly before noon, the Lacasa brothers stood at the entrance to Miami International Airport holding a small sign they had been given that stated their names and ages, and a note that said "We need help." Meeting them was a representative of the Catholic Church who took the boys to an office at the airport. There they were introduced to Mr. and Mrs. Frank Roberts, a couple who had moved from Ohio to work for Eastern Airlines. They had been unable to have children on their own, so, working through the Catholic Church, they had agreed to become foster parents for the Lacasa boys. Mr. Roberts was a World War II veteran who viewed his support for people like the Lacasas as a modern day example of what the Statue of Liberty symbolized: a beacon of hope for those fleeing political oppression. Mrs. Roberts viewed being foster parents as her ministry, wanting to extend loving kindness on behalf of God.

Mario never forgot the first time he saw the Roberts and how kind they seemed. He was scared, but he sensed that he and his two brothers were in caring hands. The Lacasa boys hoped their stay with the Roberts would be short-lived, but this dream was dashed when they learned of their father's fate.

Luis Lacasa had made his way to south Cuba, to the Bay of Pigs, a few days after leaving his family. There he waited for the 1,500 exiles that had been trained by the CIA at a secluded camp in Guatamela.

When these fighters arrived in small boats and stormed the beach, Luis met them and together they fought the Castro forces bravely. But as they were racing up the sand, a few of Castro's army's planes bombed and strafed them. These planes were supposed to have been destroyed by American pilots two days before, but the pilots didn't get them all. The planes that were left exacted a terrible toll on the exiles coming ashore, and they also managed to take out ships off the beach that were to re-supply the exiles with ammunition and communication equipment. With these ships gone, the exiles were cut off from their lifeline.

Within a few days, the exiles were short on ammunition and easily captured or killed. Luis was wounded in the battle and taken prisoner. He languished for a week in a Castro jail and received little medical attention for his injuries. He died, and once the half-hearted battle effort of the Americans was exposed, Mario and his family were left to wonder forever why the mission was so poorly conceived, planned and supported.

The Roberts were wonderful parents, providing the boys with a house that became a home. They placed special emphasis on education, and one of their first acts was to enroll the brothers in school.

The Roberts insisted that the Lacasas learn to speak English and develop it as their primary language. They were living in America and were expected to assimilate, but the Roberts did not try to take their Latin culture from them. On the contrary, the boys were encouraged to embrace their roots and be proud of their ancestry. The Roberts frequently took the boys to mass on Sunday where the homily was conducted in Spanish, and they ate out often at restaurants that served only Cuban food.

Mr. and Mrs. Roberts each had their own special impact on the Lacasas. Mr. Roberts' perspective on America molded in them an ardent belief in the principles of freedom outlined in the United States Constitution. Mario was so impacted by this that he later chose a career in law to help safeguard these freedoms for others. Mrs. Roberts, through the example of the generous life she lived, helped shape the boys' views of the need to be benevolent and charitable. Again, Mario was especially moved. Over time, he committed himself to finding a way to help others.

Scene 5: Getting settled in a New Land:

The Roberts and their three charges lived near a section of Miami that would grow to be called "Little Havana" because of the high number of Cuban immigrants living there. Mario's brothers were relatively shy. They got by in school but didn't have the same drive and ambition as Mario, who threw himself into his studies and the entire Little Havana scene. For the rest of their lives the two younger brothers would stay in Little Havana to work, and they never went to college.

Mario, on the other hand, saw his life in Little Havana as training for something much larger. Throughout high school, he worked most afternoons as a "runner" with one of the large law firms on Biscayne Boulevard. It wasn't glamorous work, taking documents to the courthouse and post office and helping with clerical jobs, but it exposed him to a number of very talented lawyers who possessed a high respect for the law. One attorney in particular, William Warren Hightower, III, took a special liking to Mario and would occasionally take him to court hearings or let him sit in on depositions and other matters. This fueled Mario's interest in the law even more.

Perhaps because of their experience with Fidel Castro, or perhaps just because of their Latino blood, Cuban-Americans took their politics seriously, and Mario was no exception. On weekend nights, respected community leaders would meet in great restaurants like The Versailles to discuss government. Having seen first-hand the ascendancy of a dictator like Fidel Castro, Cuban-Americans were aware of how tenuous democracy was and how it could be taken from the citizenry in relatively short order. For that reason, they seemed to spend most every waking moment discussing Cuba and public policy. Mario loved it, sitting for hours listening to these elders.

Mario's favorite time of the year was the fall of the even-numbered years because that meant state and federal elections. One of the issues discussed heatedly by candidates was their hatred towards Castro. Listening to Cuban-American radio station hosts whipping up the electorate was great fun for Mario. What genuinely amazed him, though, was that everyone in America was free to criticize those in office. People were executed in Cuba for this. Countless Cubans had simply disappeared for not showing allegiance to Castro and his surrogates who ran the country. For anyone to openly criticize an incumbent – even the president – and not be punished was a modern day miracle to Mario.

Mario did well in school, finishing 18th in his high school class. This was quite an accomplishment for someone who spoke only a few words of English when he arrived in the country just four years before. This qualified him for an academic scholarship at the University of Miami where he graduated in just three years.

He took a job as a manufacturer's representative selling household products to grocery stores. Since he was bilingual, he was positioned in Tampa where there was a sizeable Latino population.

It didn't take him long to find one of the true political epicenters of Florida, the area of East Tampa. Here, politics was taken just as seriously as it was in Little Havana, but the orientation was usually towards the Democratic Party.

Mario sometimes wondered how the Cuban-Americans of Little Havana had become so rabidly Republican when it was President John Kennedy, a Democrat, who had tried to topple Castro with the Bay of Pigs invasion and force Russian missiles out of Cuba. But then he would think of his father lying wounded on the beach and President Kennedy's tepid commitment to the Bay of Pigs mission, and he would snap out of it. Later he would recognize the charisma of President Ronald Reagan, the first president to firmly announce his total opposition to Castro, as another force that steered Cuban-Americans to the Republican Party. Regardless, East Tampa Latinos were serious about politics, and Mario could just as easily have been sitting in The Versailles restaurant in Little Havana.

Mario's interest in the law grew until he finally enrolled in law school at his alma mater, the University of Miami. There he excelled, especially in courses involving constitutional law, criminal law and judicial process. The more he learned, the more aware he became of the extraordinary wisdom of the Founding Fathers. The creation of the separation of powers among the three branches of government was truly visionary. A legislative branch that created the law, an executive branch that implemented it, and a judicial branch to make sure the law was constitutional was sheer genius. Each branch operated as a check on the other, so no branch could become too powerful.

But what astounded him more than anything was that the entire United States Constitution was built around the theory of limited government. By spelling out the rights guaranteed each citizen in the first 10 amendments, and by making them applicable to actions of the federal government, they could never be lost to a dictator like Fidel Castro as long as the Court was free to protect them.

It was this last thought, that the judiciary had to be independent from control by the executive or legislative branches for personal liberty to be protected, that Mario grew to believe was the most important of all constitutional principles. He understood that judges must be free to interpret the law and decide the legality of the actions of the other branches of government if personal liberty was to be protected. Otherwise, an improperly motivated president, governor, congress or state legislature could run roughshod over the people, especially those in the minority. An independent judiciary was the linchpin in the American experiment with democracy and self-governance. Around this principle all else would revolve.

The court case of Marbury v. Madison, 5 U.S. 137 (1803), established the principle of an independent judiciary. Mario read this case over and over again. Writing for the majority, Chief Justice John Marshall deftly stated that it was the prerogative of the Court to decide the constitutionality of acts of the other branches of government, a process called "judicial review." Without a judiciary to oversee the actions of the other branches, fundamental liberties could be eroded. Such swings of bedrock principles would create instability, instability would create unpredictability, and unpredictability would lead to chaos. It was a decision that might well have saved the country in its infancy, but it was decided to the great consternation of Congress and the president who didn't want their power reduced. He wondered if he would have the wisdom, vision and courage to write such an opinion if he were ever a judge.

Upon graduating from law school, Mario stayed in Miami to work for the huge firm of Denmark & Day, PA, where he made partner in just four years. The firm's office was on Biscayne Boulevard, but Mario returned to Little Havana to live because he wanted to be a permanent part of the community that had been so good to him when he was beginning his life in America.

Even though he was extremely busy establishing his law practice, his interest in politics and public policy was as strong as ever. He began following the Florida Legislature closely, and when a new reapportionment plan gave him a good shot at a legislative seat, he took it and won. At the tender age of 30, he was already in the Legislature and a partner in a statewide law firm, a firm with vast political connections. Pundits saw him as one of Florida's leading up-and-coming political players.

Scene 6: Career Begins to Fly

Mario and his wife, Carmen, had a son and two daughters. Their son, Luis, was named after Mario's father and was the apple of Mario's eye. Mario and Luis had the kind of close relationship that Mario had had with his dad.

Mario and his two brothers also had a prayer answered. After 10 long years, their mother was allowed to immigrate to America where she moved in with Mario and his family. She was joyful at being with her sons but she always missed her husband, and a great melancholy stayed with her for the rest of her life. This was not lost on Mario, furthering his lingering heartache over the breakup of his family and making him experience in a new way the fallout from the totalitarian regime of Castro's. His mother died a few years later.

Mario's career in politics soared. After serving in the House for six years he was elected to the Florida Senate where he earned a reputation for being a strong fighter of crime. He chaired the Criminal Justice Committee and championed a plethora of "get tough on criminals" measures, including the creation of many mandatory sentences. Mandatory sentences, often called "minimum mandatories," left little room for a judge to impose a lighter sentence. If a crime was committed, the offender was sentenced to whatever the Legislature said the prison term for that crime should be, regardless of the attenuating circumstances. "They did the crime, so they'll do the time," was how Mario would end many of his speeches.

This played well with a public that rightfully feared for its safety. Crime was up across the board and people were looking for answers. Taking a tough stance with those who committed the crimes was a logical place to start, and Mario became the public voice in Florida for requiring those who broke the law to serve longer periods of time in prison. Since a relatively small percentage of criminals committed most of the crime, this made sense; if they were in prison, they couldn't commit more offenses.

He took special aim at the practice of allowing an inmate out before the expiration of the entire sentence, a practice called "early release." Early release was the result of an inmate receiving "gain time" for behaving well. It was a practice decried by Mario. "We're rewarding them for behaving the way they're supposed to behave," he would often say. True enough, his critics conceded, but such categorical statements showed a lack of sensitivity to prison guards who were tasked with maintaining order; inmates were more likely to behave properly if they had an incentive to do so. Also, because of a lack of prison space in Florida, it was a management tool used to make room for new inmates.

Another form of early release was even tougher to justify. Because of this lack of prison space, all inmates were given time off their sentences as long as they didn't behave so badly that it was taken away. This "unearned" gain time had the effect of freeing up prison space for newly convicted prisoners. Mario ranted and raved about this, saying, "We're letting prisoners out the back door because we have new prisoners coming in the front door." He was right, but talk was cheap. Finding money to build new prisons required either a cut in existing programs or passing new taxes, neither of which Mario was quick to advocate. "There's plenty of fat in the state budget," he would say. "It's a matter of setting priorities," conveniently omitting to identify the fat or rank priorities.

Tragically, some of the inmates who were released early would re-offend and commit terrible crimes. When this occurred, Mario would never fail to call a press conference to bring attention to the criminal justice system's failure. He would use these incidents to call for more minimum mandatories for everything from violent offenses like murder and rape, to non-violent offenses like minor drug use…and the public ate it up. With the high profile this gave him, everyone expected him to someday run for governor and win, becoming the first Hispanic to be elected to a statewide office.

Mario's motivation was not just political, however. Portions of his legislative district included areas so crime ridden and decrepit they resembled Third World countries. Every week someone was shot or stabbed, gangs were rampant, and drugs could be bought on most any street corner. Prostitutes walked the streets, automobiles were stolen and taken to "chop shops" where they were stripped to their parts and shipped out in boxes within 24 hours, and break-ins were so frequent that people were afraid to open their doors.

Mario believed that drug use was the cause of most of the crime so he took a hard line with not just the sellers of the dope, but also with the users. "If the pushers don't have any customers, they won't be in business for long," he often said, "and the best way to eliminate customers is for the buyers to know they'll do hard prison time if caught and convicted." This was well received by a public worn down by the constant news reports of drug-related crime. Slayings, overdoses, automobile accidents caused by impaired drivers and innocent by-standers shot in drive-by shootings galvanized the citizenry. They demanded a response from their legislators, and Mario was more than willing to provide leadership.

Intellectually, Mario knew the response to the drug problem should be more comprehensive than simply giving more prison time to those who sold or used drugs, but the public was angry and had little patience for softer approaches like more drug treatment programs. Voters also had little interest in going deeper and looking at the social environments that seemed to breed a disproportionate number of persons who used or sold drugs. It was no accident that areas with high poverty rates, high unemployment and poor educational performance had higher than normal drug-related problems. Going deeper still, areas with high rates of out-of-wedlock birth were inextricably connected to these same social barometers. Mario couldn't help but wonder if the drug problems of an area would be cut in half if the out-of-wedlock birth rate were cut in half. But improvement from measures of this sort took time, and the public wanted action now.

Using his chairmanship of the Criminal Justice Committee, he held meetings in each judicial circuit of the state. The meetings were carefully choreographed to begin with a statistical presentation by staff on the rise of drug use. The state attorney would then show that the great majority of cases in criminal court involved drugs. The testimony would end with an emotional appeal from a parent who had lost a son or daughter to drugs, or from kids who talked of how drugs were changing life in their schools or neighborhoods. The meetings would conclude with a discussion among the committee members who, led by Mario, would announce their intention to file legislation to create tough new minimum mandatory drug penalties for those caught using or selling drugs.

Missing from the meetings was testimony from judges, the very ones who worked with offenders every day and who would be burdened with implementing these tough new sentences. Their job was to impose a sentence that fit the crime, and that required the judge to be able to weigh the circumstances of a case. But with minimum mandatory sentences, a robot or computer could conduct sentencing because Tallahassee legislators had predetermined the outcome.

At one meeting, a new and idealistic judge, on his own, testified that he sometimes had to impose a sentence that was too harsh for the circumstances of the case because of minimum mandatories, but members of the committee quickly attacked him. One member accused him of wanting to coddle drug dealers – "purveyors of poison," he called them. Another conceded that there would be cases where the defendant would receive a penalty that was too harsh, but that was "an unfortunate reality, the way it had to be until the scourge of drug use was erased from the face of the earth." An African-American House member suggested that the judge wanted to perpetuate a system where black defendants received stiffer penalties on average than white defendants did. When the poor judge limped back to the courthouse, the chief judge of the circuit, fearful of budget cuts from angry legislators, admonished him for stepping beyond the role of the judiciary and attempting to usurp the role of the legislative branch.

Scene 7: Career Takes a Different Turn

Legislative sessions came and went and Mario carried on with his crusade against crime. Legislation he sponsored created new minimum mandatory sentences, made it tougher for defendants to escape conviction by claiming insanity, and put prisoners back to work on the roadside cleaning ditches and picking up trash. He essentially ended the practice of early release by sponsoring a constitutional amendment, which the people of Florida approved, requiring inmates to serve at least 85% of their sentences.

Campaign consultants were salivating to run Mario's race for governor, a race everyone expected him to make during the next election cycle. However, just before the optimum time for announcing his candidacy, he stunned the political establishment by accepting an appointment to the circuit bench by the current governor. In a hastily called press conference the afternoon of the announcement, Mario stated that his reason for becoming a judge was simple: his love of the law and belief in the American court system. He movingly recounted his experience as a boy escaping a country where there was no rule of law. He spoke of his amazement at the majesty of our democracy and the genius of the Founding Fathers of their creating in the Constitution the balance of powers between the three branches of government.

"The law's purpose is noble," he said. "It is to guarantee equal justice for all, and to make clear the rules that would govern society."

At his investiture, Mario's comments were a curious mix of conservative philosophy and judicial activism. He expressed great deference to legislators, and at the same time also reflected a sensitivity to a judge who found herself, motivated purely out of conscience, incapable of rendering an unjust decision simply because a statute that should be changed was still on the books.

"It is the judiciary that is often required to bring about social change," Mario said. "When change is slow to come from the legislative branch, or when legislators bow to an improperly motivated majority and erode protections of the minority, it is judges who must step in and act. Schools would have stayed segregated longer if the judiciary had not intervened. People who were falsely accused would have been coerced into confessing to crimes that they didn't commit if the judiciary hadn't acted. I could go on and on, but you get the point.

"Many people object to judges forcing change in this manner. They call this behavior 'judicial activism,' and they're correct; a judge who acts like this is an 'activist' judge. These critics believe it is the sole prerogative of the legislative branch to make such changes. But it's curious that, looking back on most of these decisions, few of these critics would today disagree with the result. They may object to how the changes came about, but they don't disagree with the changes themselves. Jurists who made these wise decisions found themselves incapable of acting otherwise, for to do so would have led to an unjust result, and the goal of the court system must be to achieve justice."

Mario's words were powerful. He understood the dilemma a judge would face when confronted with a law that was not clearly unconstitutional but would lead to an injustice. Mario made it clear that a judge who rendered a popular but unjust verdict was a disgrace to the office. Those in attendance left believing that he was well suited for the responsibilities attendant with wearing the black robe.

Scene 8: Life as a Judge

Mario began his work on the bench and worked hard to earn the respect the office commanded. He was always prepared for his hearings and was courteous to the attorneys and parties who appeared before him. He ruled quickly and explained his decisions thoroughly. He found the right balance between enforcing the law and still being compassionate to offenders who deserved it. He became an outstanding judge.

After seven years, he ranked very high in every judicial ranking in the circuit. He took his job seriously, and it showed. Attorneys respected his knowledge of the law, and the local media was impressed with his willingness to issue unpopular rulings when he believed the law or circumstances warranted. Indeed, there was just one criticism that had come his way, and it was from a courtroom watchdog who had a very personal interest in the conduct of judges.

Her name was Beatrice Davis, an African-American who had found her life's calling from a sad event involving her son, Trent. Trent had been a straight-A student and star athlete. He was active in his church and president of the student body in middle school.

Trent adored his father, Willie Davis, a valued and trusted city employee. Willie and Beatrice were happily married and Trent was their only child so they poured their heart and soul into his upbringing. They never allowed Trent to sell himself short and gave him the self-confidence to believe he was capable of doing most anything he desired.

Trent's goal was to attend the U.S. Naval Academy at Annapolis after graduating from high school. There was something about the white uniform that impressed him, and he could see himself in one. He understood the honor that would go along with attending one of the military academies and the important role they played in the welfare of the country.

For several years everything was on track. He made outstanding grades, scored very high on the Scholastic Aptitude Test, and early in his junior year was contacted by the football coach regarding playing at Navy. By April, he had secured a nomination required for entry from one of his U.S. Senators and even the Vice President of the United States. Then tragedy struck: his father contracted liver cancer. For nine difficult months he fought the disease, but it beat him, and he died in January of Trent's senior year.

During the last month of his father's life, Trent learned that he had been accepted to the Naval Academy. Trent's admission was his dad's last great source of joy before he died. He went to his grave more proud of his son than ever.

Trent was devastated by his father's death. He was so distraught that his friends didn't think he would make it through the days before the funeral, not to mention the funeral service itself. The week afterwards, Trent never left the house. When he returned to school, he was quiet and sad, no longer the outgoing guy he had been before.

A few well-meaning friends invited him to go out with them, but he always refused; he wasn't ready. Finally, a guy from down the street, Joe Smith, convinced him to go to a high school basketball game. Their school's team had made the regional playoffs, and the game was against last year's state champions.

It was a real thriller. The gym was packed and Trent's school won. It was a blast, and Trent agreed to go to a party afterwards. Trent wasn't crazy about going, but Joe wanted to, so he went along.

The party was great fun, even for Trent. He enjoyed socializing with his friends again, but the best thing was that he met a girl named Betsy Clinton. They hit it off, and Trent asked if he could see her again. She agreed, and the next Friday night they went to a movie. Soon, they were dating regularly.

Betsy was a year older than Trent and a student at the local community college. She was from another town, so she lived in a rented apartment within walking distance of the college. After a few dates, she invited Trent over to cook him dinner.

"Hey Trent, while this is cooking you want to try some of this?" she asked, holding up a marijuana joint. She lit it, took a drag, and held it out for Trent.

"Um…I don't know," Trent stammered. He had never smoked dope before.

"Oh, come on. It won't hurt you," she said. "Besides, it might lead to something exciting," she said seductively.

Trent wasn't exactly sure what she meant, but he found out later that night when she led him to the bedroom and he experienced sex for the first time.

After that night, he began going to Betsy's apartment several evenings a week. They often got high, and during these times he never thought of his father. It was the one place he could go to forget his grief.

Beatrice was very worried about her son. She sought help from a guidance counselor at school, her pastor, his friends, but nothing could jolt him from his melancholy. She talked to Trent nearly every day, but he always said he was okay and that his relationship with Betsy wasn't serious. He kept up with his homework and seemed to be scoring well on his exams, so Beatrice could only hope that he would pass through this phase and get to the other side of his inner struggles.

One night when he was at Betsy's apartment she sent him to purchase marijuana. She told Trent where to go, what to do when he got there and who to contact. Trent didn't want to do this; he had never purchased drugs before and was scared to death, but she gave him $50.00 and sent him out the door. When the door closed behind him, he stood for a moment, knowing that he should go back inside or go home or go anywhere other than the place where she was sending him. But the anticipation of what might be waiting for him when he returned was too much to resist, and he got in his car and drove off.

When he arrived at the correct location, the middle of a quiet street only two blocks from his high school, he pulled over and turned off his lights. He waited exactly one minute and drove away. He returned in precisely five minutes and pulled over again. Within 30 seconds he saw a man come from a house across the street and walk towards him.

"Who sent you," the man asked when he neared the car window.

"Betsy," Trent replied.

"Right answer. Do you have something for me?"

"Yes, sir. I sure do," Trent answered nervously as he handed the man the 50-dollar bill.

"Perfect," the man replied. He then gave Trent an envelope containing a couple of marijuana cigarettes.

As Trent drove away, he was pumped. He knew he had just done a very stupid thing but he was strangely exhilarated. His exhilaration turned to horror, though, as he saw two police cars approaching him from different directions, their lights flashing and sirens blazing.

In an instant, the cars hemmed him in, and he was immediately dragged from the car by one police officer while two others stood next to him with their guns drawn. He was frisked, handcuffed and put in the backseat of one of the patrol cars. In less than a half-hour he was being admitted to the county jail.

Scene 9: Trent Davis and the Criminal Justice System

So began a four-month process with the criminal justice system for Trent. The stakes were high indeed because he had purchased the marijuana within a thousand feet of a school and the Legislature had made this an offense that carried a three-year minimum mandatory sentence. The bill's sponsors had contended that the law would help keep drugs from schools, that pushers wouldn't sell drugs to students or students wouldn't buy them if the penalty was so severe. In actuality, few students knew of the law, and pushers who did would step beyond the thousand-foot limit, so its deterrent value was virtually zero.

Trent wanted an early resolution to his case. If he could get it behind him quickly, he had a chance of convincing Naval Academy officials to allow him to begin in the fall. From the beginning he had been totally candid with them and fully explained what had happened. They certainly weren't pleased and made it clear that this could be a fatal blow to his admission, but committed to keeping an open mind pending the outcome of the case.

Trent's lawyer, Randolph Underbrink, believed that a full-blown trial would not be in Trent's best interest because the facts of the case were not contested. Trent had made a serious mistake and needed to admit it to the Court. The legal strategy would require Trent to stipulate to the facts on the officers' reports and then demonstrate that the incident was totally out of character for him. The goal was to convince the judge that the law was unconstitutional or find a way for the judge to set it aside. Either route would be a tough sell because the judge assigned to the case was also the one who had written the law when he was in the Florida Senate, none other than Mario Lacasa.

Scene 10: The Hearing before Judge Lacasa

Randolph Underbrink had several lines of attack. The first and most obvious was to allege that the facts didn't fit the minimum mandatory scenario. However, the facts weren't disputed and Trent was stipulating to them as alleged in the charging document. He had purchased drugs within 1,000 feet of a school, so this was not going to succeed with a strict interpretation of the mandatory sentencing requirement.

A better angle was to convince the judge that the law was unconstitutional, and there were two constitutional violations alleged. The first was that the law violated the Eighth Amendment prohibition on cruel and unusual punishment.

The Eighth Amendment, like all of the first ten amendments, was a restriction on the federal government. However, the Supreme Court had decreed that the Fourteenth Amendment made the provisions in the first ten amendments that dealt with essential liberties applicable to the states. The prohibition on cruel and unusual punishment was considered an essential liberty, so the state statute could be trumped by the Eighth Amendment via the Fourteenth Amendment. The second constitutional issue was the Fourteenth Amendment itself, specifically its guarantee that states shall make no law denying due process to persons.

Trent's final argument was that a sentence of this length for the facts of this case would amount to a miscarriage of justice. This would involve the court transforming itself into a "court of equity," where the judge would essentially ignore the law and do "what was right." Ignoring the law was very extreme, however, so courts were loath to sit in equity, but it was occasionally done.[3]

Because of Judge Lacasas' history with the three-year minimum mandatory law, Randolph first asked the judge to recuse himself. For Trent to prevail, Judge Lacassa would have to declare a law he had written to be unconstitutional. Trent's lawyer thought this presented an obvious conflict for Lacassa and that he would readily recuse himself. He didn't. In fact, Lacassa offered a spirited defense of his ability to remain objective. Lacasa was adamant that he could rule fairly. Yes, he had supported minimum mandatory sentences while a lawmaker and he still believed they were a deterrent to crime, but he would listen with an open mind. Besides, there would be little room for judgment anyway. The facts of Trent's case either fit the minimum mandatory scenario or they didn't. If they did, neither he nor any other judge could do anything but impose the sentence; the law was clear and judges must follow the law.

"But Judge, that's our point!" Randolph exclaimed. "Such reasoning completely negates the theory of our case!" Without saying it directly, he was asking for a judge who would think long and hard about the case in an attempt to serve the interests of justice, and not act like a robot by automatically giving out the three-year sentence if the facts fit the statute. Unfortunately, this was the very kind of judicial conduct and thinking that minimum mandatories prevented.

"Motion denied, Mr. Underbrink," Lacasa said sternly. "I am fully capable of performing my duties objectively."

Randolph then asked the chief judge of the judicial circuit to remove Judge Lacasa, but the chief judge refused. He concluded that Mario had been involved in the writing of so many laws that if he had to be removed for all of these he would be too restricted in the cases over which he could preside. So Trent and his lawyer were forced to accept his ruling and hope Mario could, in fact, render a fair ruling.

Scene 11: The Sentencing of Trent Davis

Trent was fortunate in that the assistant state attorney who was prosecuting this case, Linda Lupo, agreed that a three-year prison sentence did not serve the interests of justice. Trent had never been in trouble with the law before and had a promising career in the military before him. He had admitted his mistake and was willing to freely accept some form of punishment. Lupo also knew that it made no sense to take up a prison bed for three years on a first-time offender who had committed a non-violent, minor drug offense.

Over the next three weeks, Lupo and Underbrink worked out a plea agreement that would punish Trent, but not ruin him. Trent would serve three years of probation, but he could serve it while in Annapolis attending the Naval Academy – *if* the Academy would agree. This was a big "if," but if Judge Lacasa would go along with the deal, at least it would give Trent a chance.

At the sentencing hearing, Trent's lawyer put on many character witnesses who spoke eloquently and honestly of how this incident had been totally out of character for Trent. His scholastic and academic records were shared; letters from school administrators and teachers were entered into the record; evidence of his admission to the Naval Academy was presented; and psychologists explained how Trent's bizarre behavior was not uncommon for an 18-year old who had just lost his father. Judge Lacasa listened carefully.

Lupo then explained the plea agreement and why she thought it was fair.

"The defendant did not buy the marijuana with the intention of bringing it onto campus or sharing it with classmates" she said. "He was acting at the direction of his girlfriend, and that can't be underestimated," she said with a wry smile.

Judge Lacasa was not amused. He began questioning her on the specific facts of the case. Did he buy drugs? Was he within 1,000 feet of a school? Was he sober, and did he appreciate what he was doing? The judge made sure that all the material facts were entered into the record.

He then asked her if the crime was being prosecuted under the statute that called for a three-year minimum mandatory sentence. She explained that technically it was, but the plea bargain was a better fit for the crime. This made Lacasa angry. He began a philosophical soliloquy about his understanding of the "separation of powers" doctrine and how judges should apply the law as it was written by lawmakers.

Seeing that this was going nowhere, Randolph Underbrink then entered the fray, asking the court to sit in equity. He argued that it would be a miscarriage of justice to sentence this young man to a three-year sentence. "Manifest injustice" was how he described it.

This request, that the court sit in equity and essentially ignore the penalty prescribed in the statute, really set Lacasa off. He began lecturing the parties on how the law could not make exceptions, that everyone must be treated exactly the same, that "no man was above the law," as Chesterfield Smith, then president of the American Bar Association, once said of President Richard Nixon in 1973.[4] If anyone was going to get a three-year sentence, everyone had to get a three-year sentence. If Lacasa had known of Chesterfield Smith's deep commitment to justice, he would have seen how wrong it was to use his quote in this context.

Trent's lawyer asked if all crimes involving the same transgression were equal. "Shouldn't individual circumstances, all nuances, be factored in? Shouldn't an offender with prior convictions be treated more harshly than a first-time offender? What about one who was truly remorseful for what he had done compared to one who wasn't the least bit sorry? Weren't value judgments of this kind the very things judges were to consider? Was it even possible for lawmakers to craft a specific penalty that would be fair in all cases involving the same core facts, or was it better to leave that to judges who could analyze circumstances, weigh evidence, watch the demeanor of witnesses, and determine whether a defendant was contrite. In a word, shouldn't judges think?"

Judge Lacasa was furious. "Using the judgment you are advocating is why a poor black defendant often receives a longer sentence than a rich white person even though they committed the same offense."

"But Judge, here we are asking for a reasonable approach for a black man!" the lawyer retorted.

"Mr. Underbrink, you know what I mean. There is disparity of sentencing between the races. Just look at death row. A black murderer is more likely to receive the death penalty than a white murderer, and you know it!"

"But Judge, that's no reason to treat someone else unfairly. What you're saying is just because one person might get a sentence that is too severe, we'll do the same thing to someone else just to maintain consistency. That is not logical!"

"Drug use takes a terrible toll on society," Lacasa said, shifting gears. "Violent crime and lost productivity follow drug use. Minor offenses lead to major violations. Marijuana users graduate to hard drugs. Don't you think lawmakers were thinking of this when they passed the three-year penalty? Maybe they knew more about what they were doing than you give them credit for.

"I've heard enough," Lacasa said. "Your client's crime fits the statutory definition of the required three-year minimum mandatory sentence, so that's my ruling. You have the right to appeal, of course. Bailiff, take the defendant into custody."

The hearing was over. Trent turned and looked at his mother who was sobbing quietly. "I'll be all right," he mouthed to her as he was led away.

It was at that moment, as she saw her son disappearing through the side door, that Beatrice Davis found her life's purpose. She soon started an advocacy group called "Mothers Against Minimum Mandatories," or MAMM for short. The mission was to eliminate minimum mandatory sentences, and to support families dealing with travesties like what she had just experienced. Her group also began monitoring judges and scoring them on how they dealt with situations like her son's. Did judges carefully weigh the circumstances of a case and administer justice accordingly, or did they mechanically determine if the facts fit the statutory definition of the crime and impose the prescribed sentence? To her, how a trial judge performed this duty went to the very heart of judicial responsibility.

Scene 12: Beatrice Davis Monitors Judge Lacasa

From the time Judge Lacasa sentenced her son to three years in prison, Beatrice Davis and MAMM monitored Judge Lacasa's rulings. By getting on the Clerk of the Court's e-mail list, she was able to receive the dockets of each of the judges and the outcome of each case. Over a four year period she saw a predictability in Mario's sentencing that bothered her greatly: He never challenged minimum mandatories, even those involving non-violent offenses, and never searched for ways to get around them no matter how unjust their imposition might be in a particular case. Despite Lacasa's encouraging comments at his investiture about the need for judges to have courage, he never got beyond the black and white letter of the law with minimum mandatories, and justice suffered.

It was frustrating to Beatrice that the only people upset about this practice were families that had been devastated by its implementation. Occasionally she would manage to receive a little media attention for the cause, but the public was largely unconcerned. Cheap-talking politicians drowned her out, and some even belittled her. Inevitably it wasn't until someone was personally affected by such an injustice that a convert was made.

Beatrice was especially disappointed in the judiciary itself. Privately, many judges expressed to her their support for what she was doing, but they never conveyed these feelings to state and federal legislators. They, more than anyone, would have the credibility to begin the debate on the policy and force change. Yet, they stood silently by, hiding behind the "separation of powers" argument that policy was the prerogative of lawmakers, and the law could not be ignored.

As a general rule, no one disagreed with this, of course, not even Beatrice, but she knew more was at play. She understood that trial judges ran for election, and advocating the elimination of minimum mandatories would make them appear soft on crime. In addition, lawmakers funded the court system, and many lawmakers wouldn't take kindly to being told their policies were wrong and intellectually shallow. Still, in the face of this disillusionment, she carried on her crusade.

Scene 13: Judge Mario Lacasa is Nominated for the Appellate Court

No one was surprised when Judge Lacasa applied for appointment to the Third District Court of Appeals to become an appellate judge. He was still ambitious and the appellate court was the next logical step for his career.

To be appointed to the appellate court by the governor, one must be nominated by the "Judicial Nominating Commission" (JNC). The JNC interviews applicants and sends three names to the governor for consideration. The governor picks one of these three. The JNC is comprised of lawyers and a few lay people. The public has the chance to comment to the JNC on the applicants, so Beatrice Davis used this opportunity to oppose Judge Lacasa's application.

"My son made a mistake. He purchased fifty dollars worth of marijuana – enough for only a couple of cigarettes – less than 1,000 feet from a school. He admitted it in court. He had never been in trouble before. In fact, he had been a model student and was admitted to the Naval Academy. Then his father contracted liver cancer and died. My boy was distraught. He fell into a depression, and seemed inconsolable…until he got mixed up with a girl. She sent him to buy the drugs. He was caught and arrested.

"My son's lawyer and a very courageous state attorney agreed to a plea that would have punished my child but still given him a chance to fulfill his dream of attending the Naval Academy. Judge Lacasa would have none of this. He sentenced my boy to three years in prison, and there went his dream of attending the Naval Academy. All over a lousy fifty dollars of pot. With all due respect, Judge Lacasa doesn't deserve to be on the appellate bench. Come to think of it, he doesn't deserve to be a judge at all. I'm asking that you not recommend his name to the governor. Thank you."

"But Mrs. Davis, wasn't your son convicted under the minimum mandatory statute?" a JNC member asked. "How could Judge Lacasa have done anything else?"

"By having the courage to stand up to a bad law," she replied. "And it's not just my son that has been ruined. Judge Lacasa has a pattern of adhering to minimum mandatories so rigidly that injustice is the result in far too many cases. He routinely fails in the most basic of all judiciary responsibilities: administering justice."

The members listened politely, and two attorneys even voiced sympathetic comments, but, when the vote was taken, Lacasa was selected as one of the three names to be sent to the governor. Whether Lacasa received the appointment or not, he would still be a judge. It was hard for attorneys who might be appearing before him to oppose the forwarding of his name to the governor.

Beatrice contacted the governor, opposing Lacasa's selection, but the governor was a conservative, and he, too, supported minimum mandatories. He wasn't a lawyer and had never witnessed the injustice Rosa described. A few of his programs had been declared unconstitutional by activist judges, to boot. It was clear that he liked Lacasa's rigid deference to the legislative and executive branches as it related to policy. Lacasa received the appointment.

Act III, Scene 1: The Lacasas Have Problems at Home

Despite his dogmatic adherence to minimum mandatories, Judge Mario Lacasa was otherwise a good jurist and his career continued to climb. Unfortunately, life at home wasn't as good. His oldest child, Luis (named after Mario's father), was having trouble. By the end of his junior year in high school his grades had fallen so much that without a stellar senior year he might not graduate. His parents suspected he was doing drugs, and he was hanging out with several guys who had had serious encounters with the police and the court system. Since these friends were juveniles, they had been given several breaks. However, Judge Lacasa and his wife knew it was just a matter of time before these "friends" would do something so serious that they would be treated as adults and the consequences would be much more severe. Judge Lacasa had seen similar cases from his days as a circuit court judge, and he was determined to see that his son didn't go down with them.

Over Luis' vehement protests, Judge Lacasa and his wife decided to enroll him in Wellington College Preparatory School in New Jersey for his senior year. They had read about Wellington in a catalog of private schools, and it had a reputation of being a great place for students like Luis who were on the verge of getting into serious trouble.

The trip to New Jersey was terrible. Luis rarely spoke to his parents and didn't even say goodbye when they left to return to Florida. Still, Judge Lacasa was certain they were doing the right thing.

Luis' start at Wellington was rocky. His poor attitude caused him to receive several referrals to the Disciplinary Office, and he even got into fights. His parents were contacted on numerous occasions, and Luis was on the verge of being expelled. But just when his behavior was about to buy him a one-way ticket back to Miami, a coach took a special interest in him and he discovered the sport of lacrosse.

School suddenly became fun. He made friends with several of the guys on the lacrosse team, and he couldn't wait for practice. Luis had played baseball and football in Miami and enjoyed them, but lacrosse was something new. He loved the sport and the camaraderie of his teammates. He also loved the beer parties after the games, a Wellington tradition. Of course, the legal drinking age was 21 so the parties were secret, but that was part of the fun, sneaking around and hiding from the administrators.

One of the persons on the team, Rufus Hightower, was from the southern New Jersey area. His family owned 8,000 acres of land there, and, since most of the property was wooded, it was prime habitat for woodcock. Rufus' dad was a fanatic about hunting "timberdoodles," as woodcock were often called. And to him, the hunting experience wasn't complete unless it involved a good dog, so he had some of the finest English setters in the northeast. With Rip and Dash at his side, Mr. Hightower was content to roam the property all day long looking for the long-billed birds. He loved introducing someone to the sport, so when Rufus showed up at the property with Luis for a weekend of hunting, he was very pleased.

Luis was no stranger to the shotgun sports, having shot many rounds of skeet, trap and sporting clays with his father in South Florida, but he hadn't done much hunting. He took to it like a duck to water, though, and soon was bugging Norman to take him to the property nearly every weekend. Nothing was as exciting to him as walking up to a pointing dog and experiencing the flush of the bundle of brown feathers, and nothing was as challenging as trying to hit the bird as it darted between the trees. More often than not, the only thing that would rain down after the shot was a tuft of leaves cut from the trees by the shotgun pellets.

Between lacrosse and woodcock hunting, Luis had a great late fall and early winter. His contentment came across in his voice in his conversations with his parents, and they couldn't be happier or more relieved. Taking their son to New Jersey had been very difficult, but now he was doing well, and they were looking forward to a fantastic Christmas. Luis was their oldest child – their only son – and the first Lacasa to be born in America. He would be very successful; they just knew it.

Mario was so pleased with how things were working out for Luis that he decided to go all out for Christmas by buying him two special presents. The first was a slightly used Ford Explorer with four-wheel drive, the second a Kreighoff .20 gauge over-and-under shotgun that he had bought from an acquaintance at the local skeet club. Actually, the gifts were birthday presents too, since Luis' 18th birthday was the first week in January. Luis had gotten by without a car at school and had used one of Mr. Hightower's shotguns during their woodcock hunts, but the Explorer would allow Luis to share in the driving, and the elegant smoothbore would match nicely with the classy setters used at the Hightower property. The school, which had many students who were hunters, maintained a locked safe for the storage of any hunting firearms they wished to bring with them.

The hunting season went until the middle of January, so there would be time for a couple of hunts when Luis returned to the school. Nevertheless, Luis was certain he would be back a time or two next year, regardless of where he would be attending college; reunions of this sort were a Wellington tradition. Besides, the Hightowers had a sporting clays course set up on their property, so he was sure he and Rufus and their friends would make frequent trips there in the late winter and spring.

The lacrosse team practiced year-round. Even though they didn't have regular season games, they had plenty of scrimmages with other teams from the area. That was fun, but it was also a good excuse for more partying. A keg of beer was the usual libation, but a few of the guys would occasionally bring pot. Luis was mostly a beer drinker, but one time he hatched a crazy idea. Worse yet, he acted upon it. As he was rolling a joint from a bag of dope, he discreetly collected a dozen or so marijuana seeds and dropped them into his shirt pocket. The next day he took an egg carton and filled the egg slots with soil and planted a seed in each. He placed the egg carton on his windowsill, watered the seeds, and two weeks later 12 marijuana plants popped through the surface of the dirt.

The next weekend he and Rufus went to the Hightower land. Luis carried along the egg carton and showed it to Rufus on Friday evening. Only the two of them were there, so Luis felt comfortable suggesting that they plant the plants in a secluded part of the 8,000-acre property. At first, Rufus was furious that Luis would bring such a thing to his family's land. As the night wore on, though, and as they had a few more beers, Luis' idea of growing their own pot grew on him. They wouldn't sell it but would grow it for their own use and maybe for a few select friends.

By Saturday morning, Rufus had consented. They went to a quarter-acre clearing in a remote part of the Hightower land. In all the years the Hightowers had owned the property Rufus had never been to that spot, so he was certain their few plants would not be discovered. The clearing was near a small stream where the plants could be easily watered. Rufus was sure his father wouldn't recognize the plants as marijuana even if he saw them, but the chance of them being seen by anyone was extremely unlikely. No one but the Hightowers and their guests were ever on the land, and Mr. Hightower did not hunt in this area. Besides, in 120 days, long before the start of the new hunting season, the plants would be cut down and no one would ever know they had been there.

Every two weeks Rufus and Luis would go to the property to shoot sporting clays. At some point they would discreetly slip away and check on their plants. They had been able to get a few more plants started from leaf cuttings, so they had a fair-sized patch growing. The unusually warm spring and frequent rains helped the plants grow quickly, and towards the end of the 120-day growing period they were ready for harvest.

Traveling in Luis' Explorer, he and Rufus left one Friday afternoon for the Hightower property. Luis had his shotgun and a case of shells in the back, fully intending to shoot several rounds of sporting clays. Also in the back were a set of long-handled branch clippers, a role of jute twine and a bag of heavy-duty plastic garbage bags.

Friday afternoon they shot a round of sporting clays. Saturday they shot two; Sunday morning they shot one. No one else had arrived, so they loaded their gear as though they were about to drive back to school, but instead of turning right to head towards the front gate, they turned left and headed to their marijuana patch.

When they arrived, they worked quickly. Luis cut the stalks and Rufus folded them in half. Once an armful was tightly bundled, the stalks were tied together with the jute twine. In less than 15 minutes, they had four small bales that they stuffed into the plastic garbage bags. They then loaded the bales into the Explorer for transport to a hole they had dug behind the equipment barn on the property. There the pot would be stored so that it would be available when needed. They would cover the hole with plywood, and then place old feed bins that were never used on top.

They never made it. At the moment they got into the Explorer and closed the doors, 14 agents from the Drug Enforcement Agency (DEA), the Bureau of Alcohol, Tobacco and Firearms (BATF), and the Federal Bureau of Investigation (FBI) exploded from the woods, carrying guns and wearing bulletproof vests. No sooner had Luis looked up than he was being dragged from his vehicle and pushed to the ground onto his stomach. The same thing was happening to Rufus. As they were being handcuffed they heard a roar above them as a DEA helicopter hovered over the tree line of the clearing. As it was landing, agents in three dark blue Chevrolet Suburbans drove up to the edge. Soon about 25 people were scouring the area, gathering various items and taking photographs. One person was videotaping the entire scene.

Luis and Rufus watched in disbelief and horror. In short order they were placed under arrest for several drug-related crimes, put in one of the Suburbans and driven away. An hour later they arrived at a federal building in Newark and were led into a single jail cell.

The agents had been staking out the property since Thursday, the day before Luis and Rufus had arrived. They had been planning the raid since the cameras of a DEA satellite had first spotted the marijuana plants on a routine sweep of the rural landscape of that part of New Jersey. The satellite was one of several used by federal authorities to find marijuana fields.

Luis and Rufus were each given a telephone call, so they called their fathers. It was the toughest call either of them had ever made. Rufus' parents were at the federal building in an hour; Mario and Carmen Lacasa arrived late that night after taking the first flight to Newark out of Miami. They were not able to visit with Luis when they arrived, but they were in the courtroom early the next day, waiting on Luis to appear before the judge.

Luis and Rufus and all the others who had been arrested the day before walked into the courtroom at 9 o'clock for their "First Appearance" proceeding. The charges were read and bond was set. The federal judge began figuring the amount of bail in light of the charges and his estimation of their flight risk. When he set bond at $500,000.00, a gasp could be heard from Carmen who was seated in the courtroom. Mario, experienced in these matters, knew the judge would have no choice but to impose a high amount when he learned the seriousness of the charges.

The amount of marijuana Luis and Rufus had grown was just over the volume needed for them to fit the definition of drug "kingpins," the term given to those who trafficked in large quantities of drugs. Mario was very familiar with the term because he had passed a similar statute in Florida while in the Senate.

He had also been stunned to learn that Luis' shotgun and six boxes of shells had been in the back of the Explorer because he knew what that meant. Trafficking in such a large quantity of marijuana and also being in possession of a firearm triggered another layer of escalating penalties. With these higher penalties would come an obligation for the judge to set bail accordingly. It made no difference that Luis and Rufus never intended to sell the drugs, or that the gun and ammunition were for sporting clays; those were arguments for another day. What mattered at the First Appearance proceeding was the amount of marijuana and the fact that the boys had been in possession of firearms.

Mario was not focused on the amount of bail, however. That was inconsequential compared to what was going through his mind. State legislatures were not the only legislative bodies to have enacted minimum mandatory penalties for various crimes. Congress had passed its share, too. As he had done when he was in the Florida Senate, congressmen had held hearings on the problems caused by drug use and trafficking and had responded similarly. And it wasn't just these federal charges that would likely be brought against his son. State legislators from Newark, under pressure from constituents to find a quick fix to the drug problem of that major urban area, had sponsored many drug-related minimum mandatories. Mario had done the same when he was a legislator from Miami and he was sure the state of New Jersey would soon file charges based on state statutes. Between state and federal charges, he was certain that his son, his beloved Luis, would receive a minimum of 15 years in prison if convicted. And because he had recently turned 18, he would be sentenced as an adult, not receiving the breaks often extended to minors.

Scene 2: A Lawyer is Hired

Judge Mario Lacasa hired John Townsend Morrall, one of the best criminal defense lawyers in the country. J.T., as he was called, had represented countless people, including many celebrities and sports stars who had been charged with drug-related offenses. Years before, at the time J.T. was helping his clients beat drug charges, Mario had been a state senator using J.T. as an example of why minimum mandatories needed to be enacted. "Lawyers like J.T. Morrall are helping lawbreakers beat the system by getting off light," he would say. "That's why we need minimum mandatories!"

Mario had won that debate in Florida, and similar debates had played themselves out all across America. Now criminal defense lawyers like Morrall, and judges for that matter, had very little to do with the length of sentences prescribed for many offenses. Mario had accomplished exactly what he'd intended: minimum mandatories had taken sentencing out of the hands of those in the courtroom and placed it with legislators in the state capitol and they had gotten tough with criminals. But now, here in New Jersey, it was his own son who would feel the sting.

Scene 3: The Negotiating Begins

In the next few months, Rufus' attorney was able to get the gun-related charge against Norman dropped because the only firearm in the vehicle belonged to Luis. J.T. argued that the charge against Luis should also be dropped because neither boy had intended to use the gun for a criminal purpose. But the United States District Attorney, Stanley Steinberg, the prosecutor in this case, refused to drop the charge against Luis because it was his gun that had been in the car when the boys were caught transporting a "kingpin" quantity of marijuana. The facts fit the literal definition of the crime, so he was "left with no choice," he said.

This was maddening to Mario. It was obvious the gun was not going to be used in furtherance of a crime. This was "form over substance," he believed. The irony of his thinking this, given the many times he had done the same thing in the face of testimony from those similarly situated, escaped him.

For Rufus, this left the federal trafficking charge that carried a five-year minimum mandatory for the quantity of marijuana they were "transporting." In the time leading up to trial, the district attorney agreed to allow this charge to be prosecuted only under a state law charge of possession. This would still carry a three-year minimum mandatory, but it was the best Rufus could do, so he took the deal and agreed to plead guilty and accept the three-year penalty. But this was devastating enough. He would be forced to drop out of school and would forever carry the mark of being a convicted felon. Three years in prison would not be easy, and there was no telling how it would change him.

For Luis, the district attorney refused to drop or modify the charges. The entire enterprise had been Luis' idea, and his actions had caused Rufus to go to prison for three years even though he had never been in trouble with the law. Because he was facing a five-year minimum mandatory sentence for drug trafficking and a gun crime that carried 10 years, Luis had no choice but to go to trial. He would have to beat the charges if he didn't want to spend a very long time in prison.

Scene 4: The Trial Begins

After the jury was selected, it was time for each side to present its case. This portion of the trial began on a raw winter Newark day. It was windy and cold, and sleet was forecast for later.

When Mario and Carmen Lacasa, Luis and J.T. walked up the stairs of the federal court building, the Lacasas were struck by how powerful the building seemed. Built of granite, it was majestic and old, with tall columns on all sides. A statue of Lady Justice holding a scale, the "Scales of Justice," was located near the entrance. Inside, the ceilings were high. Inscriptions from great judicial opinions written by early jurists lined the walls. The courtroom was paneled in mahogany. The dais from which the judge would preside was raised, allowing her to stare down in an imposing fashion on the trial's participants.

Mario and Carmen took a seat on the first pew reserved for the audience. Judge Mario Lacasa, a Cuban immigrant who had risen to a position of high authority, a crusader against crime and drugs, was not used to being on this side of the bench. He was also in shock at the scene before him. Seated at the defendant's table was his only son, on trial for serious criminal charges that could bring a long prison term. Next to his son was J.T. Morrall, a flamboyant criminal defense lawyer that Mario had once held up as an example of shameless lawyers who tried to beat the law. At the prosecution's table was District Attorney Stanley Steinberg. Mario could tell that Steinberg was ambitious. The position of District Attorney was a good place from which to launch a campaign for United States Senator. Mario had once felt the same pull of higher office and knew how intoxicating it could be.

At 9 o'clock sharp, the members of the jury walked in through a side door and took their seats. As J.T. had told him, Luis looked at each one directly in the eye, but didn't hold the look for long. Luis was shaking. These 12 people would decide his guilt or innocence.

"All rise," the bailiff called out. As everyone in the courtroom was standing, in walked Judge Virginia Moore, an experienced federal judge who had been on the bench for 22 years.

"Good morning everyone. We are here on the trial of Luis B. Lacasa. Are the People ready?"

"We are, Your Honor," Steinberg answered.

"Is the defense ready?"

"We are, Your Honor," said J.T. Morrall.

"Then let's begin. You may make your opening statement, Mr. Steinberg."

Steinberg showed little emotion. He explained the charges clearly, listed what would have to be proven in order for Luis to be found guilty, and briefly led the jury through what Luis had done.

J.T., on the other hand, was flamboyant. He began by asking the members of the jury if they had ever done anything stupid. He then said that his client had, and that was why he was on trial…for doing something stupid. "It sounds strange, that a smart person could be on trial for doing something stupid, but that's why we're here." He explained that the charges carried long prison sentences, and "what a shame it would be if a bright young person lost his future because of doing something stupid." Steinberg objected because any discussion of the penalty could prejudice the jury in determining guilt or innocence, their sole responsibility at this point in the proceedings. The objection was sustained, but J.T. had gotten in his point.

J.T. talked a lot about intent, and said that he was going to prove that his client didn't have the requisite intent to commit the crimes for which he was charged. "He didn't intend to sell marijuana, and without mens rea, or criminal intent, you must acquit. Without criminal intent, you must acquit," he said over and over again.

The district attorney then got into the body of his case and laid out the facts well. Testifying were law enforcement personnel who had been involved in staking out the field and making the arrest. Their testimonies, along with photographs and videotape that they had taken, were powerful. Judge Lacasa, who was seated in the courtroom, could tell from the faces of the jury members that they were swayed.

For his part, J.T. Morrall did a good job explaining that Luis was growing marijuana for his own use. He called Rufus as a witness who pointed out that the drugs were being "transported" only to the hole they had dug near the barn, and that they weren't taking it back to school with them for sale.

Rufus also stated that the shotgun was to be used in sporting clays, not in the drug operation. He said that Luis was simply taking the shotgun back to the check-in locker at the school safe.

On cross-examination, Steinberg forced Rufus to concede that he couldn't have known with absolute certainty what Luis intended. Rufus may have thought they were growing the marijuana for their own use, but he couldn't say that Luis wouldn't have tried to sell it later. "Isn't it true that Luis might have intended to sell the drugs, that he might have told you the marijuana was for your own use just to get you to go along? Isn't it true that he might have taken some to be sold? Isn't it true that you don't know for sure what Luis intended to do with his share? And isn't it true that if Luis had intended to sell the marijuana he might have wanted to have the gun along for protection? Isn't it even possible that he would have used the gun to escape capture if that's what it had taken?"

On balance, Rufus' testimony helped Luis significantly, but Steinberg had succeeded in getting the jury to understand that there was no way to know for certain what Luis intended. If Steinberg could create enough confusion, the jury was more likely to simply look at the cold hard facts of the case and make a quick determination. If so, they would return a verdict of guilty, he was sure of that.

But then J.T. made a big mistake. He called a former member of Congress, Ruth Wells, to testify about the legislative intent behind the passage of the statutes that created the crimes for which Luis was charged.

"When the statutes were passed, Congress only intended to capture true drug kingpins, not people like Luis," Congresswoman Wells said.

"People like Luis?" the district attorney asked during his cross. "You mean people who aren't black or *poor* Latinos? People who aren't going to an expensive college preparatory school? Are these the only people who can be drug kingpins? Are you suggesting that *'people like Luis'* can't be drug kingpins?"

J.T. objected, but he had "opened the door," or made admissible evidentiary items that would otherwise not have been allowed into the record. Whether the witness intended to or not, she had insinuated that drug kingpins were not white people from wealthy backgrounds. Nine of the 12 jurors were minorities, and the district attorney had just been allowed to inject race into their thinking.

The witness's comment could also have implied that small-scale drug pushers were not much of a threat to society, so the judge allowed the district attorney to present evidence of the toll that drug use took on society, and how we were all victims in one way or another.

"How could you claim that Congress was not trying to capture someone like Luis when they passed the law, because he's from a wealthy family? Are you suggesting that pushers who peddle smaller amounts of drugs aren't a problem?" asked Steinberg. By the time he was finished, Mario knew the jury had been whipped into a frenzy because he had done the same thing to others while in the Senate. He was beginning to see his actions as a former senator and current judge in a different light.

In his re-direct examination, J.T. did his best to rehabilitate his witness and help her clarify what she had said but the damage had been done.

Because Mario was a sitting appellate court judge, the trial had attracted a fair amount of media attention. An opportunistic New Jersey state senator,

William "Billy" McGee, had been staging nearly daily press conferences outside the courthouse decrying the influence of drugs on society. He had been involved in passing many of New Jersey's minimum mandatory penalties for drug-related offenses, and his new cause was abolishing parole for those sentenced to any offense where a minimum mandatory penalty didn't apply. Mario often passed Senator McGee on his way into the courthouse, and he couldn't help but think of similar press conferences that he had held when in the Florida Senate.

After nearly two weeks, including two days for jury selection, both sides rested their cases. The judge set closing arguments for 9:00 a.m. the next day.

In the morning, when Luis and the attorneys walked in, Mario and Carmen were already seated on the front row. They all stood as the presiding judge walked in. As they were sitting down, Mario looked back and was stunned to see Beatrice Davis, the mother of the young man he had sentenced to prison for three years for buying $50.00 worth of marijuana so many years ago, sitting on the back row.

Their eyes met for several seconds. For the next few minutes, he would occasionally turn and look at Beatrice, obviously confused at why she was there. Beatrice sat stoically, obviously taking no pleasure in Luis' predicament. She knew, and Mario would later learn, that she was there to show support for Luis and his parents.

Scene 5: Closing Statements

Beatrice had heard of this case from several media reports that had appeared in South Florida newspapers. She didn't even know Luis, but she knew what his parents were going through, and one of the mission's of her support group, Mothers Against Minimum Mandatories (MADD), was to be with the family members facing such agonizing times. New Jersey was a long way to travel, especially since she was there for the man who had robbed her son of his future, but there she was nonetheless.

The district attorney would speak first, then J.T.. Steinberg would be allowed to speak again, addressing the arguments made by J.T.. Many believed that giving the prosecution two chances to speak was unfair to the defendant, but that's the way it was done.

As in his opening statement, Steinberg listed the offenses against Luis, laying out the factual case to show how the facts satisfied each of the elements of the crimes. He did not get excited or emotional; he simply made the case based on the facts.

J.T., on the other hand, was very emotional. He said the facts pointed to an entirely different outcome, and he addressed each charge in order.

"Did Luis Lacasa do a bad thing?" he asked. "Yes, no question about it. He shouldn't have been smoking pot at the party where he got the seeds; he shouldn't have collected them, planted them or grown them.

"Should he have been growing a supply for his own use? No, absolutely not. That was illegal and wrong.

"Should he have gotten Rufus Hightower involved? Of course not, that was very bad.

"Was all of this criminal behavior? You bet, and I am not asking you to excuse it."

The jury seemed a bit puzzled by this last comment, but J.T. had a plan.

"Was there a shotgun in Luis Lacasa's Explorer? Yes, there was," he continued.

"Had he used it that weekend? Yes. Would he use it again? I imagine so, for sporting clays, anyway."

He then got to the point.

"Everything I've said is true. My client did some things he shouldn't have done, and I'm not asking you to overlook them, but he has been charged with the wrong crimes! Luis Lacasa isn't a drug kingpin! He wasn't growing pot to sell to anyone. He and his friend were growing it for their own use. They were taking it to a hole they had dug near a barn to store it! They weren't trafficking. They were taking the marijuana to hide it, not sell it, and how can that be trafficking?

"And the gun charge? With all due respect to the district attorney, this charge is outrageous! Luis Lacasa was doing nothing more than taking his shotgun back to the school safe as he had done many times before. And the shells? With shooting sports like sporting clays it's common to fire a hundred rounds over one trip through the course. It is ludicrous to think that his shotgun and shells were with him because of the drugs. This law regarding drugs and guns exists to catch those who use the gun for protection, or for prosecution of the drug enterprise. This gun was not being used for that. In fact, it wasn't being used for anything. It was being taken back to the school safe for safekeeping."

Mario was very pleased with J.T.'s closing. Surely the jury would conclude that, while Luis might have technically violated the statute, this was not the kind of criminal activity the statute was intended to address. They would see that Luis had his whole life ahead of him, and, even though he shouldn't have been growing marijuana, it would not serve the interests of justice for him to be in prison for the long period of time they must know he would serve if convicted. Surely they would see that. Then he turned and saw Beatrice Davis, and he thought of her son. His stomach churned when he thought of how Trent Davis' attorney had made the same argument at Trent's trial. He remembered how he had ruled.

The district attorney approached the jury. It was apparent from the look on his face that his calm, unemotional demeanor was gone. When he began, there was no doubt.

"Mr. Morrall would have you believe that the statutes creating the offenses of which Luis Lacasa is charged were not passed with him in mind. Interesting. So, of whom would he have you believe Congress was thinking when the statutes were passed? The poor black or poor Latino who comes from the other side of the tracks?" Pointing to Luis, he asked, "Should this defendant be treated differently because he is going to a fancy preparatory school? Of course a conviction will interrupt his college plans, but do poor blacks and poor Latinos not have plans, too? If one of them were on trial would we even be hearing the argument? The law must be colorblind. There cannot be disparate treatment of those whose actions fit the definition of the crimes as outlined in the statute. You must treat everyone equally."

Mario had heard this argument before…from himself.

"Yes, the defendant is young, but he is a legal adult so he must be treated as one. I regret that he has had his life interrupted, but he did this to himself. This is not juvenile court, but adult court, and he committed adult offenses. He is 18 years old…he is no longer a minor."

Mario could feel Beatrice Davis' presence in the courtroom. Her son was 18 years old and headed to the Naval Academy when Mario had sentenced him to prison. His future had been even brighter than Luis' had.

"You must not concern yourself with the penalty given to the defendant,"

Steinberg continued. "You must concern yourself only with his guilt or innocence. You must determine if his actions satisfy the elements of the crimes. The law will determine the penalty. These statutes spell out the penalties; Congress has done that for you."

Mario thought back on his own advocacy for minimum mandatory penalties.

"And why has Congress done that for you?" Steinberg continued. "Because they were representing their constituents, people like you who were demanding a response to the scourge that drugs have brought upon this land. I don't need to tell you the toll drugs have taken on society. Crime, poor educational performance, teenage pregnancy, prostitution, low productivity in the workplace…it all goes back to drugs."

Mario thought of speeches he had given over the years in which he had said the same thing.

"If you are wondering if the members of Congress intended a defendant like this one to be seriously punished, don't. They must have known that some defendants would be more culpable than others, but they didn't carve out any exceptions. Congress rightfully concluded that the penalties must be tough in order to become a deterrent. All that matters is whether or not Luis Lacasa's actions satisfy the elements of the crimes for which he is accused. It is not your decision to determine if the penalty in this case might be too severe. That is a decision for Congress, and Congress has made it.

"I want to say this carefully. Don't over-think this case. Determine only if the elements of the crime have been proven. Don't think too much about what happens after you render your verdict. Congress has already done that thinking for you."

Mario looked around and didn't see a single member of Congress in the courtroom. The 435 members of the House of Representatives and the 100 members of the Senate were not listening to the facts of this case. "How could they presume to know what should happen with my son," he thought. "His very future is at stake. They didn't hear that Luis never intended to sell the marijuana, or that he was just transporting it for storage to a hole he and his best friend had dug. They didn't know that the gun was not part of the criminal enterprise, but only a Christmas present he was taking back to the school locker for safekeeping. All these things they didn't know, yet they had already passed judgment on what should happen to him if the jury found him guilty."

Mario felt dizzy and was only vaguely aware of the jury being directed to the jury room for deliberations. As he and Carmen walked from the courtroom, Beatrice Davis was waiting for him.

"Would you like to get some lunch?" she asked. He nodded "yes," and he and Carmen followed her to the cafeteria.

"Why are you here?" Mario asked, as they sat down.

"I read about the case in the Miami Herald and I knew what you were going through," Beatrice answered.

"But, your son...after what happened."

"Judge, by sending my boy to prison for three years you killed a dream. He's doing okay now, but every day he thinks about what could have been. If I dwell on that, it paralyzes me. I've learned to channel my energy into changing the policy, everything from the statutes to the mindset of judges."

"But why are you here?" Mario asked again. "Are you here to see me suffer the pain you had to endure now that I'm facing something similar?"

"Of course not; that's not it. Believe it or not, I'm here for the right reason: I understand what you're going through. You remember my organization, Mothers Against Minimum Mandatories? One of the purposes of MAMM is to be there for families in situations like yours. It's unlikely that I can do anything tangible to help, but I've found that there may be some comfort in having someone close by who has been there. At least that's been true for others, but the last thing I want to do is add more stress. If you want me to leave, I will."

"No. Don't go. I want you here. In fact, I want to tell my wife your story..."

For two hours Mario and Beatrice explained the case of Beatrice's son to Carmen, and talked of minimum mandatories and the role of the judiciary.

"What was it like when you heard the sentence, that your son had been sentenced to three years in prison?" Carmen asked.

"It felt like someone had socked me in the stomach. For several seconds I couldn't breath. If I hadn't been sitting, I know I would have passed out."

"How long did it take to get over it?"

"Get over it? You never get over it. I think about it every day. I can remember every word spoken, every action taken at the hearing."

"How have you coped?"

"I turned my grief into positive energy, trying to change the law and opposing judges I thought were blind to the injustice of minimum mandatories. Remember, Judge?" Beatrice said, thinking of her testimony against Mario before the JNC.

"Oh, I remember," he said. "At the time, I thought you were way off base. Now I'm not so sure."

Beatrice smiled. She was beginning to see the transformation in Mario that she had seen in others who had a family member caught in the unfairness of the law.

"I'm here to help, not make you feel guilty," Beatrice said.

"But you know what I think about the most, Carmen?" Beatrice continued. "It's a question that goes through my mind constantly. 'For what?' For what was my boy's dream taken from him? For buying fifty dollars worth of pot? No. That wasn't the reason. My son's future was taken from him because of politicians trying to score political points. They wanted to sound tough on crime, so they did what was easy."

"But minimum mandatories have their place," Mario interjected, although not as strongly as he might have before his son was arrested.

"Maybe with certain violent offenses, but even then I'm not so sure. We're far better off giving the judge the flexibility to do what's right. Don't you wish the judge had this flexibility in your son's case?"

"Yes, I do," he answered. "But when the public is looking for a solution, lawmakers must give it to them, and being tough on criminals is a quick fix to crime."

"And that approach has its place. I'm not advocating coddling the bad guys, but lawmakers should build a system that allows a judge to distinguish between those who need to be punished severely and those who need to be shown a little mercy.

"And judges need to find a way to reach a fair outcome even in the face of a statute that doesn't allow it. Justice demands it."

Mario tried to speak forcefully about the role of the judiciary and how judges were not free to ignore the law, but his arguments lacked conviction, as though he was re-thinking his entire philosophy.

"Again, I'm here to support you," Beatrice said. "I'm not here to re-live my son's case or to give you a hard time. We can talk about this more later. Besides, I have a good feeling about this judge. She understands justice; I can sense it."

"But if the jury convicts, there is little the judge can do," replied Mario dejectedly. "Minimum mandatories, remember?"

"That is a problem, no doubt about it."

Scene 6: The Jury Speaks

The day wore on. Mario, Carmen and Beatrice talked a lot about many things. Mario was especially interested in Beatrice's son.

"Let him know that I'm glad he's doing well. He may not want to hear from me, but I do care." Mario stopped short of apologizing, but Beatrice could tell he was thinking about it.

Late in the afternoon, the bailiff suddenly announced that the jury was back. Mario took his wife's hand, and with Beatrice alongside, they walked towards the courtroom. This time, Beatrice sat next to Carmen.

When the jury came in, Mario noticed that they didn't look at Luis. That was not a good sign. Few jurors looked at a defendant who was about to be found guilty.

"All rise," the bailiff called out as Judge Moore entered the courtroom and took her seat.

"Ladies and gentlemen of the jury, have you reached a verdict?"

"We have, Your Honor," answered the jury foreman.

"You may hand me the verdict," she said, as the bailiff took the verdict from the foreman and gave it to the judge.

She read it and remained expressionless. She gave it to the bailiff who returned it to the foreman as she said, "Luis Lacasa, would you please rise?" He stood. His father took his wife's hand. Beatrice put her arm around Carmen's shoulder.

"On the first count of trafficking in narcotics, how do you find?" the judge asked the foreman.

"We find the defendant guilty."

"On the second count of using a firearm in the commission of a drug-related offense, how do you find?"

"We find the defendant...guilty."

Luis slumped to his chair. His mother began crying softly and put her face in her hands. Steinberg smiled contentedly, satisfied with the complete victory.

"Ladies and gentlemen of the jury, thank you for your service. You are excused. However, I direct the parties to remain in the courtroom," the judge stated. Steinberg sat forward, concerned. This was unusual. Typically the judge would announce the date of the sentencing hearing and tell the bailiff to take the defendant into custody.

When the members of the jury had left the courtroom, Judge Moore began speaking to the parties.

"Before the trial started I studied the record of this case. I read the law enforcement reports, the pleadings and the depositions. For five days of trial I've listened closely and watched the defendant. I also read the sentencing provisions that would apply in the event of conviction.

"For days I've been playing various scenarios through my mind, thinking of what my actions should be, depending on the decision of the jury, trying to determine the best outcome. I've thought long and hard about the concept of justice, an ideal born of the spirit of high-minded people."

Mario looked up, wondering what Judge Moore was doing.

"I recognize that my primary obligation is to the people of this federal judicial circuit," she continued. "For their protection, criminals must be punished for their criminal acts. Despite what some say, I believe that the fear of punishment deters criminal conduct. The deterrent effect should be part of the thought process of any judge considering sentencing options."

When he heard the word "options," Steinberg leaped to his feet.

"Your Honor, I don't know where you're going with this," the district attorney said as he stood, "but, with all due respect, you have no options. The jury has returned a guilty verdict on both counts. The statutes are clear about sentencing. A minimum mandatory for five years on the trafficking charge and 10 years on the gun charge are your only options."

"Keep your remarks, Mr. Steinberg. You haven't even heard what I'm going to do." The district attorney sat, obviously displeased.

"I also have an obligation to follow the law, and the law seems pretty clear here. A plain reading of the statute would indicate a five-year sentence for the trafficking charge and a 10-year charge for the gun charge, just as Mr. Steinberg stated. Nevertheless, it is clear that other factors like legislative intent can be used to clarify statutory meaning, and it is here that I find the testimony of Congresswoman Wells interesting. She explained legislative intent, indicating that Congress was trying to increase the penalties on those who truly were drug 'kingpins.' Your cross-examination, Mr. Steinberg, was clever because it made the jury think Congress may have been motivated by thoughts of race and class. Clever, yes, but not something that serves the interests of justice. Regardless, how much weight her testimony should be given is debatable. My guess is other members of Congress might have a different view. Still, it is something to consider. At the very least, it is a good example of why flexibility is needed in order to find justice."

"Judge, first you use the word 'options' and now you use the word 'flexibility?'" Steinberg said sternly. "Respectfully, for the same reason you have no options, you have no flexibility!"

Mario's mind was now swimming. Seven months ago, before this had happened to his son, he would have been saying the same thing as the district attorney. He had made a legislative and judicial career thinking the same way and saying the same things. Now, he found himself angry with Steinberg for advocating positions that impeded justice.

Ignoring Steinberg, Judge Moore turned her attention to the gun charge.

"There is no question that the law attaches significant penalty to those who would use a firearm as part and parcel of a drug trafficking operation, and rightly so. The combination of the two could easily turn a situation deadly. Still, to believe that the shotgun in Luis Lacasa's car was there because of his personal drug enterprise turns the truth on its ear. I know what the statute says, and some would argue that having a firearm in the presence of drug activity is so dangerous that the two simply cannot be mixed, regardless of how unrelated the two may be. However, at least in this instance, to send a young man to prison for 10 years for an offense he didn't even know he was committing would be a perversion of justice. Luis Lacasa was returning to school where he was going to legally check his shotgun into the school safe for safekeeping. No one contended that he had the gun in his SUV as part of the drug enterprise. To say that the punishment must be this severe in order to deter future crime ignores the unique dynamics of this case, and I'm not going to do it.

"So, this is what I'm going to do. I accept the verdict of the jury as it relates to the drug trafficking charge. You did a dumb thing, Luis, and your actions hurt another person, Rufus Hightower. His life, as well as yours, will always be stained because of your misdeeds. You must be punished. Sentencing will be in three weeks. While I may question the five-year minimum mandatory, it is within the realm of the reasonable. You claim that you had no intention to sell the pot, but you could have changed your mind, so your burden of overcoming this penalty will be great. I will, in all likelihood, defer to the clear language of the statute, but I'll listen with an open mind.

"Regarding the gun charge, however, it would be a miscarriage of justice to allow this conviction to stand. You did not have the gun in your vehicle as part of the criminal enterprise. Regardless of the language in the statute and the jury's obvious technical interpretation thereof, I therefore set aside the jury's verdict on this count and this charge is dismissed."

"But, Your Honor…"

"Save it, Mr. Steinberg. Take me up on appeal if you'd like, but I'm not going to send this young man to prison for 10 years under these circumstances. That would not serve the interests of justice."

"We'll let the appellate court decide that," an angry Stanley Steinberg said.

"I'm sure you will," the judge replied. "I suggest that a better use of your time would be on the sentencing for the drug charge. I'll decide that in three weeks. And Mr. Steinberg? Don't ever again speak to me in that tone while you're in my courtroom.

"Bailiff, take the defendant into custody. I'll see you all back here in three weeks. We stand in recess until we reconvene for sentencing."

Luis Lacasa was led from the courtroom. His parents sat back down as the full import of what had just happened hit them. All Carmen could think of was her son going away to prison for five years. All Mario could think of was the 10 years Luis had just avoided. He heard Beatrice Davis say quietly, "Now that's a judge."

As they left the courthouse, Mario noticed that Stanley Steinberg and Senator Billy McGee had already convened a press conference, decrying the actions of Judge Virginia Moore, "that activist judge," as Senator McGee called her. "She totally disregarded the clear language of the statute," he said. "Does she not know that drugs and guns are wreaking havoc on society?" he said to the reporters.

Beatrice could only shake her head. "Cheap talking politicians are everywhere," she thought. "Lord, help us."

Mario, on the other hand, stood and listened. He could easily have been looking at himself 10 years ago. He thought of the many witnesses he had heard testify in legislative hearings, witnesses who had only been trying to get him to implement policy that would allow the court to do what made sense. He was ashamed to admit that he and other legislators had been demeaning, patronizing and, at times, rude to them.

And he thought of cases over which he had presided, cases like Trent Davis', where, because of a stupid mistake that was totally out of character for him, his life was changed forever and his dream of going to the Naval Academy was dashed. Mario had used reasons that now made little sense to him.

"How could I not have seen it?" he thought to himself. "Maybe I did, but perhaps I put my career ahead of justice. Maybe I hid behind what I considered principle because it was good politics. If it had been bad politics, I wonder if I would have used the same principles to base my decisions? Probably not, and that means I failed as an impartial judge."

Beatrice Davis knew exactly what he was thinking. She put her arm on his shoulder and said, "It's okay, Judge. Your journey is one that most must travel before they understand. What matters is that you have."

[1]The historical context of the discussion of Fidel Castro and the Bay of Pigs invasion was derived from two articles: 1. "Castro, Fidel," Microsoft Encarta Online Encyclopedia, 2004. 2. "Bay of Pigs Invasion," Microsoft Encarta Online Encyclopedia, 1997-2004. Some paraphrasing is included.

[2]"The Bay of Pigs and the CIA," by Juan Carlos Rodriguez, pg. 55.

[3]Note: Courts of Equity have been abolished in states that have adopted Rules of Civil Procedure.

[4]www.hklaw.com, Chesterfield Smith biography

Author's Note:

Mandatory sentences prevent judges from imposing punishments tailored to the facts of each case. Instead of imposing a sentence after weighing the evidence, reading the demeanor of the defendant, factoring in the impact to the victim, and thinking of society's welfare, judges are bound by the penalty prescribed in the statute as written by legislators.

Prior to 1983, judges in Florida had wide latitude in sentencing. Also, inmates were eligible for "parole," a discretionary early release mechanism. The Florida Parole Commission was the governmental entity that made parole decisions.

Concern grew that this system allowed disparity in sentencing, meaning that sentences weren't uniform. That is, two criminals guilty of the same offense might receive prison terms of different lengths. A common complaint was that this disparity was often based on race. A second concern was that because of "gain time," another early release mechanism where inmates could "earn" time off their sentences, prisoners rarely served for as long as they were sentenced. Advocates for change wanted to create "truth in sentencing," meaning that an inmate would serve for as long as the judge prescribed.

In 1983, my first year in the House of Representatives, under the leadership of a skilled and dedicated state representative named Elvin Martinez (now a retired circuit court judge in Hillsborough County), the Legislature passed "The Florida Sentencing Guidelines Act." I voted for the measure even though I had philosophical misgivings. I don't remember specifically why I voted "yes," but I was young and inexperienced and not very trusting of my instincts. I also thought very highly of Rep. Martinez and knew that he well understood the criminal justice system.

Under sentencing guidelines, judges were required to apply all the variables of a case to a matrix, with the variables prioritized and weighted by the Legislature. This formula prescribed the sentence. There were ways for a judge to sentence above or below the guidelines, but the judge had to put the reasons in writing and it was often appealed, so it was rarely done. The act also abolished parole for offenses committed after the effective date of the bill, partially addressed the "truth in sentencing" issue by eliminating this early release mechanism. The Parole Commission wasn't abolished, though, because of the high number of parole-eligible inmates still in prison; the courts wouldn't have allowed these inmates to be treated differently than how they were originally sentenced, so the Parole Commission had to remain to deal with these inmates.

Sentencing guidelines were controversial from the start. State attorneys didn't like them because they believed some offenses and some offenders were not treated harshly enough. Judges complained about the increase in paperwork and loss of sentencing flexibility. Consequently, it wasn't long before the Legislature began chipping away at guidelines with the passage of additional minimum mandatory sentences. With more inmates sentenced to mandatory sentences, however, there was less prison space for other inmates, so "gain time" was used more aggressively to release inmates early, thereby freeing up space for newly sentenced inmates. Alas, much of the "truth in sentencing" component of sentencing guidelines was lost.

The Legislature reacted by passing a significant change to sentencing guidelines in 1994. The reality of limited prison space also drove the passage of the bill. Offenses were again prioritized to ensure that violent or repeat offenders received the first tickets to prison. This resulted in offenders who would previously have gone to prison not going because their crimes were less serious compared to others. In the Legislature's defense (and mine too, since I voted for it as a member of the Florida Senate), legislators didn't have a choice. With inadequate prison space, there was no alternative other than to make sure there was room for the most serious offenders. That is why, at the same time this law was passed, the Legislature embarked upon a crash prison construction program.

The 1994 changes also repealed basic gain time. With this "early release" mechanism gone, the Legislature was forced to fund a prison construction program that was adequate to house the inmates sentenced.

These changes to the guidelines came under immediate attack as being too lenient. I recall a negotiating session the next year, in 1995, when the state attorneys, a very powerful lobbying force, were arguing for tougher penalties. The Legislature deferred, and penalties were increased.

In 1998, sentencing guidelines for all offenses committed after October 1 were repealed. Taking its place was a system that created uniformity in the weighing of sentencing criteria. A minimum sentence for each sentencing decision was required, and greater ability was given to the judge to deviate upwards in sentencing. This is the system we have today.

The Law: Definitions and Explanations:

Sentence: The judgment formally pronounced by the court or judge upon a defendant after his conviction in a criminal prosecution, imposing the punishment to be inflicted, usually in the form of a fine, incarceration, or probation.

Black's Law Dictionary, Sixth Edition, p. 1362

Mandatory sentence: Statutes in some jurisdictions require a judge to sentence a convicted defendant to a penal institution for a prescribed time for a specific crime and furnish little or no room for discretion. These statutes generally provide that the sentence may not be suspended and that no probation may be imposed, leaving the judge with no alternative but commitment.

Black's Law Dictionary, Sixth Edition, p. 1363

Sentencing: The post-conviction stage of the criminal justice process in which the defendant is brought before the court for imposition of sentence...

Black's Law Dictionary, Sixth Edition, p. 1363

Courts of Equity: A court which has jurisdiction in equity, which administers justice and decides controversies in accordance with the rules, principles, and precedents of equity, and which follows the forms and procedure of chancery; as distinguished from a court having the jurisdiction, rules, principles, and practice of the common law. Equity courts have been abolished in all states that have adopted Rules of Procedure; law and equity actions having been merged procedurally into a single form of "civil action."

Black's Law Dictionary, Sixth Edition, p. 356

Notable Quotes:

"Being 'at the mercy of legislative majorities' is merely another way of describing the basic American plan: representative democracy."

Judge Robert Bork / www.brainyquotes.com

"You sit up there (as a judge), and you see the whole gamut of human nature. Even if the case being argued involves only a little fellow and $50.00, it involves justice."

Honorable Earl Warren, Chief Justice,
United States Supreme Court
www.brainyquotes.com

"In a constitutional democracy the moral content of law must be given by the morality of the framer or legislator, never by the morality of the judge."

Judge Robert Bork / www.brainyquotes.com

"You'll have a young man, and he shouldn't be doing this, but he's raising marijuana in the woods. That makes him a distributor. And he's got his dad's hunting rifle in the car, he forgot about it and he wants to do target practice, that makes him armed. He's looking at 15 years. An 18-year old doesn't know how long 15 years is. And it's not so much the sentencing guidelines, it's the mandatory minimums. That's the problem."

Supreme Court Justice Anthony Kennedy,
testifying before Congress as reported on www.CNN.com,
April 9, 2003

"When a judge assumes the power to decide which distinctions made in statute are legitimate and which are not, he assumes the power to disapprove of any and all legislation, because all legislation makes distinctions."

Judge Robert Bork / www.brainyquotes.com

"A law is valuable not because it is the law, but because there is right in it."

Henry Ward Beecher / www.worldofquotes.com

"Judges are but men, and are swayed like other men by vehement prejudices. This is corruption in reality, give it whatever other name you please."

David Dudley Field / www.quotegarden.com

"The right to keep and bear arms has justly been considered as the palladium of the liberties of a republic; since it offers a strong moral check against usurpation and arbitrary power of rulers, and will generally, even if there are

successful in the first instance, enable the people to resist and triumph over them."

Honorable Joseph Story, Associate Justice,
United States Supreme Court
www.worldofquotes.com

"The greatest menace to freedom is an inert people."

Honorable Louis D. Brandeis, Associate Justice,
United States Supreme Court
www.worldofquotes.com

"The jury, passing on the prisoner's life, May in the sworn twelve have a thief or two Guiltier than him they try."

William Shakespeare,
"Measure for Measure," as attributed in
www.quotegarden.com

"Equal justice under law is not just a caption on the façade of the Supreme Court building. It is perhaps the most inspiring ideal of our society...It is fundamental that justice should be the same, in substance and availability, without regard to economic status."

Honorable Lewis Powell, Jr., Associate Justice,
United States Supreme Court
www.equaljusticeupdate.org (November 21, 2005)

Georgia Bobwhite

SLICK AS ICE
Negligence: Duty, Breach, Proximate Cause and Injury

Preface: Most advertising by attorneys is intended to get "personal injury" cases into the law firm. Personal injury cases involve, as the name suggests, physical injury to a person's body or mental pain and suffering. Most personal injury cases involve negligence, where the tortfeasor (the one who committed the negligent act) acted negligently or was negligent by failing to act.

To be found liable for injuring someone, one must have violated the "standard of care" required in the community. The "standard of care" is that level of care expected of a "reasonable person." This is known as the "reasonable person standard," and the one accused of acting negligently will be judged against what others in the community would have done in the same situation.

CIRCLE D HUNTING PRESERVE was an 8,000-acre commercial hunting operation owned by the Charles Yarborough family. Located in southwestern Georgia between the towns of Dawson and Plains, the property was a wonderful mix of river swamp, farm fields, pastures and planted pines.

Whitetail deer were abundant, and every year at least a dozen monster bucks were havested, each with racks scoring more than 160 points (inches), a size that qualified them as Boone and Crockett deer, the official record book of trophy animals. The body sizes of these animals were big, too. With a partial diet of soybeans that were grown on 900 acres of the property, bucks weighing more than 200 lbs. were not uncommon.

Turkeys were plentiful, and spring gobbler season was always exciting because it was a time when tom turkeys gobbled and strutted up a storm. Old birds with 11-inch beards and one and a half-inch spurs were common.

In the early fall, dove hunting on the property was fast and furious. Since the Yarboroughs farmed corn on approximately 1,100 acres, there was ample food to attract the sleek gray birds.

Circle D was also a working cattle ranch. Four hundred brood cows spread over 3,000 acres kept the ranch hands busy.

The Kenchenfunee River ran through the property north to south. Thick river swamp was nearly impenetrable, providing excellent refuge for the deer. Only the most committed hunter had the discipline to hunt in the few small open areas the swamp provided. Tree stands allowed the hunter to cover only a single game trail or small opening in the brush, and most hunters became bored with such limited visibility or were too fidgety to do it well.

As good as the deer hunting was, quail hunting was actually the bread and butter of the hunting operation. Hunters from across the country came to hunt quail in the farm country of southwestern Georgia, and Circle D had developed a reputation as one of the best places of all.

The excellent hunting was the direct result of good habitat management. Wide game strips of natural cover were left around all the farm fields so the birds would have places to hide from the hawks and other predators. Food plots were planted throughout the property to supplement the food the quail found from native sources, insuring that there would be many coveys of wild birds.

Pen-raised birds were also used at times, but it was the wild quail that drew the true sportsman. Most anyone could hit the slow-flying pen-raised quail, but when a hunter came upon a covey of wild birds she knew it. Wild quail flushed in a hurry, and the thunderous sound of their wings as they took flight rattled even the most experienced nimrod.

Circle D had some of the finest English pointers in the South. All the dogs were from the Elhew Kennel line, generally recognized as one of the best in the United States. These dogs had it all: great noses, intelligence and unparalleled natural pointing instinct. They were as fast as lightning but could still be controlled by the handler, as though the dogs knew the job would never be completed if they got crazy or strayed too far away. What really set them apart, however, was their *style*. They had a regal way about them, and when they locked up on a point, well, there just wasn't anything as elegant in all of hunting. Totally focused on the bird, a front foot raised and bent, tail held high and hard…many hunters have joked that they could leave and come back the next day and the dog would still be there, not having moved a muscle.

It was this vision of the classic quail hunt that had Joel Brantley so excited. He and his father, Bo Brantley, were leaving their home in Tampa, Florida the next day for Circle D and three days of bird hunting. The trip was coming at a good time because Joel was having a tough time in school. It was just the second week in December and he had already received two in-school suspensions, one for cussing at a teacher and the other for acting up in class.

The last few weeks had been better, however. Joel had been diagnosed with Attention Deficit Disorder (ADD), and been put on medication that had really helped. The drug allowed him to focus on his studies more completely, and his teachers had noted a marked improvement.

Joel's parents had also noticed that he was better. They had been worried about him for some time, his father especially since he had also suffered from the same affliction when he was in school. Back then, ADD wasn't even recognized and there was no medication to treat the symptoms. Mr. Brantley had barely gotten through high school. He never went to college; instead he went to work as an air conditioning repairman. Life had been tough, but he had worked hard and now owned his own business. He was proud of what he had accomplished, but determined to see that his son would have other opportunities. He was thrilled that two pills a day was all it took for Joel to have a shot at a better life.

To celebrate Joel's improvement, his dad had suggested the quail hunt for the weekend that school let out for Christmas break. Neither of them had been on a Southern quail shoot with dogs, but both were experienced hunters and were very excited about this chance to hunt like the guys they'd seen in magazine stories and Saturday morning outdoor television shows.

Bo and his son left early in the morning: North on Interstate 75 to Tifton for four hours, west on State Road 82 for one and a half hours to Albany, Georgia, then north for a half-hour to the Yarborough property just north of the small town of Bronwood.

It was a magnificent early-winter day. The sky was a deep rich blue, and the air was cold, about 50 degrees right after lunchtime. It would get much colder when the sun set.

They checked into their lodging place at Circle D, an earthy-smelling log house structure they had all to themselves, and then went for a stroll around the grounds. They couldn't wait to see the prized dogs of Elhew ancestry so they headed to the dog compound first.

The 18-run kennel was shaped like a horseshoe, and it was full of animals. Each run had a gorgeous English pointer. The dogs were mostly white so they could be seen more easily in the woods, with lemon, brown, black or orange-colored spots. Their hair was short and slick so it wouldn't pick up burrs, and each dog had a majestic profile with its snout curving ever so slightly upwards. The nostrils were moist and widely flared. Their necks were thick and their chests were deep. Each dog was as straight as an arrow from the shoulders to the hips. Their tails were long and broad at the base. These dogs were built exactly for their purpose: to hunt long and hard, and to find, point and retrieve birds. They weren't lapdogs or family pets, but finely tuned hunting machines.

The last run contained a whelping crate, with six cute puppies sleeping soundly. Momma was lying down, teats pulled long and sore, keeping a watchful eye on the visitors.

A few of the dogs barked, but most simply stood and studied the Brantleys, wondering if this was a chance to go afield. Such manners on the part of kenneled dogs were rare, but these dogs were gentlemen and ladies who didn't make a fuss unnecessarily.

Leaving the kennel, Bo and Joel wandered to the main lodge where the guests ate their meals. On the front porch were a dozen massive rocking chairs. Inside were mounted deer heads and turkeys in full strut. A quail was mounted in the real-life situation of flying to escape the extended claws of a mounted bobcat.

The furniture was of oak wood constructed "mission-style" – sparse but sturdy – with green leather cushions. A bar made of pecky cypress had well-worn barstools in front of it. Off to the side was a giant fireplace with a mantel made of a slab of solid mahogany. Above the mantel, towering over the entire room, was the mounted head of an imperial bull elk with a rack that had scored 393 points.

On the walls were original paintings of sporting dogs by Bob Abbot. Old posters from Remington Arms, "Field and Stream Magazine," Federal Ammunition and Browning Firearms filled in the remaining spaces. On the coffee table were several outdoor books like "A Hunter's World" and

"Sporting Craftsmen of the South."

A flight of stairs angled upwards, and, as the Brantleys were looking around to see where it might lead, in walked Charles Yarborough .

"Hello there. I'm Charlie Yarborough."

"Nice to meet you, Mr. Yarborough. I'm Bo Brantley and this is my son Joel."

"Call me Charlie, and follow me if you *really* want to see something," he said matter-of-factly.

Up the stairs they went. When Charlie began unlocking three deadbolt locks, the Brantleys knew they were in for a real treat.

When the heavy door swung open, Joel and his dad gasped, but each for a different reason. Lining the walls were 120 guns, all either Winchester Model 12 shotguns or Winchester pre-64 Model 70 bolt action rifles. These guns were genuine collectors' items.

"I'm not bragging, but these guns are worth more than a quarter of a million dollars," Charlie said. Bo went straight to them, thinking of days gone by.

"These were the guns of my boyhood," Bo said. "My dad had a model 12, and on rare occasions he let me use it. The best Christmas of my life was when I got my own, an old .16 gauge. The gun was stolen from our house years ago, but I remember getting it like it was yesterday.

"And those Model 70 rifles? My uncle had one, a 30-06, and it shot like a dream. He harvested many deer with it, and I can remember skinning them out with us all gathered around. What wonderful memories."

"Best rifles ever made," Charlie added. "Your uncle had good taste."

Joel's attention was drawn to a huge electric train set that was positioned on a giant board in the middle of the room. A landscape of mountains, valleys, trees, lakes, streams and tunnels had been constructed on the board, and when Charlie flipped a switch, the train jumped to life, lunging forward as it began traveling over the tracks. Around the mountains and through the valleys the train traveled, occasionally blowing its whistle.

Joel was totally enthralled. He liked machines and gadgets and had always been fascinated with trains. Charlie saw his reaction and explained that this was a replica of an actual train, "The Buffalo Express," that had run from Buffalo, New York to Erie, Pennsylvania in the late 1800s. Powered by coal, it was one of the last trains of its kind ever built.

"Thanks for showing this to me, Mr. Yarborough."

"My pleasure, Joel. She was a real beauty in her day. The actual train is on display in Merimack, New York. I saw it one day and had to have a replica. Few trains had the character of this one," Charlie replied.

They went back downstairs and Charlie invited them to shoot a few rounds of sporting clays, a shooting game where the gunner shoots clay pigeons in situations that simulate hunting. "Good practice for tomorrow," he said.

After directing them to the sporting clays field, he left and told them he would see them at dinner. "And wear dinner jackets. We run a high-class place here," he said with a wink.

Joel and his dad had a wonderful time shooting sporting clays. The blue sky and cold air made for a great day to move from station to station. Before they knew it, they'd each burned through several boxes of shells.

"I've had enough. Let's fly up for a nap," Bo said. "We've had a long day already and it's not even four o'clock."

An hour or so later, the Brantleys got up and prepared for dinner. The guests had been instructed to meet around the bar at six. Everyone was in a good mood, and the camaraderie borne of mutual appreciation of fine dogs and guns, enhanced by the elixir of old Scotch for the adults, made for a most enjoyable cocktail hour.

Dinner was baked quail served on white rice with brown gravy. Yeast rolls, squash and cheese casserole, and fresh large Brussels sprouts rounded out the meal. Homemade peach ice cream atop a slab of buttery pound cake finished the feast in fine style.

Over dessert, Charlie Yarborough officially welcomed his guests, and then directed their attention to a seven-minute videotape on gun safety. "Hunting alongside someone poses special risks," the narrator said. "When walking up to a covey, keep the safety of the gun on. When the birds rise and you bring the gun to your shoulder, only then should you take the safety off. This is one of two cardinal rules we have at Circle D.

"The second rule is to shoot in your assigned space. We only allow two hunters to walk up on the dogs. The hunter on the right should shoot only those birds flying directly ahead or to the right. The hunter on the left should shoot only those birds flying directly ahead or to the left. That prevents a hunter from swinging the barrel sideways to a point where it is pointing at another hunter or the dog man."

After the videotape, Charlie held up a gun and went through other safety measures like keeping the breech of the gun open or broken, depending on the type of gun, when not actually walking up on the covey. "And don't shoot the dogs," he emphasized time and time again. "Many of our quail, especially the pen-raised birds, fly very low, and sometimes a dog will run after the bird when it gets up. The last thing I want is for you to shoot one of my dogs." It was apparent that Charlie Yarborough wanted his guests to have a good time, but he was serious about safety…for his guests *and* his dogs.

The evening wound down, and one-by-one the hunters retired to their rooms. As Joel lay in bed he had visions of strong-hearted pointers working the fields in front of him and then squaring-up on point as the scent of the covey gave away the birds' presence. He had shot quail before but only when he happened to stumble onto a covey by accident, never by design. He wondered if he would have the nerve to stay composed when the sudden thunder of the birds' wings exploded during the covey rise. It was a pleasant thought to ponder as he slowly drifted off to sleep.

The hunters were awakened at 6:00 a.m. and served coffee and juice in their rooms. They then gathered in the main dining room at seven o'clock and feasted on a hearty country breakfast of scrambled eggs, grits and spicy-hot venison sausage.

At 7:30, the hunters were assigned their guides. The Brantleys would be hunting with Denmark Jones and Samuel Walker. Denmark would be on horseback working the dogs, and Samuel would lead a pair of matching dun-colored mules as they pulled a wagon carrying the hunters, dogs and gear.

One-by-one the parties left the lodge for their assigned hunting area. It was cold – 19 degrees to be exact – and ice was everywhere. There would be no need for snake boots today. The timber rattlers that were common in the area would be tucked away under logs or settled in their rock dens.

The Brantley's party traveled over a dirt road that led alongside a long cornfield and then crossed a dim creek that flowed through a thick swamp. Emerging from the bog, the wagon went uphill until it stopped at the edge of 40 acres of soybeans. At various points around the field were one-acre plots of Japanese and brown-topped millet. The birds in this area would be well fed and apt to gather in large coveys.

Denmark dismounted and let out two of the five dogs he had brought. "Their names are 'Trouble' and 'Sally.' It won't take you long to figure out which one is which," he said matter-of-factly.

The dogs began working back and forth across the field. One was wearing a shock collar, but Denmark was very judicious with the switch on the control box he was carrying. It was only when the dog charged into the swamp that he zapped him. The dog yelped and immediately came back to them.

"That's Trouble," Denmark said. "He's still a puppy, only about 11-months old, and he hasn't quite figured out what we're doing. Can't decide if he wants to hunt quail or rabbits, but he'll get it. I want him to run with Sally for 20 minutes or so, then I'll put him up. Sally's as good as a dog can get, and I want Trouble to see how it's done."

Sally was a thing of beauty: strong, stout and proud. She had a distinctive large brown spot on her forehead that made her stand out. The Brantleys were mesmerized, watching her crisscross the field in front of them. When Sally locked up, Denmark, who had been following the dogs, trotted his horse back to the wagon and said, "Gentlemen, we have a point."

He dismounted and told the Brantleys to load their guns. They climbed out of the wagon, took their shotguns from the side compartment and began loading them as they walked towards the dog. Denmark caught Trouble and put him on a 10-foot cord. He told Bo and Joel to halt, and then led the dog to Sally. When Trouble caught the scent and saw Sally, he, too, locked up on point. Denmark kept hold of the cord so the dog couldn't break when the birds flushed.

He called for the hunters to walk up, and Joel noticed ice crushing beneath his feet as he walked through the grass and soybeans. It was still below 30 degrees and the ice from the cold night had not begun to melt in the morning sun.

They approached the dogs, not knowing exactly where the birds were hidden. Denmark told Joel to walk up from his right and Bo to walk up from his left. "Remember your shooting zones," he said. "We'll get plenty of shooting today; no need to crowd anyone. And don't shoot the dogs!"

No sooner had he said that than the covey exploded from the ground and the birds blew out in all directions. Joel swung to his right and fired three times. One bird fell. His father hit two. One bird fell with a tuft of feathers floating away in the breeze. The other glided a hundred feet with one of its legs hanging down, a sure sign that it had been hit. Everyone hates to lose a wounded bird, but there was still a good chance this bird would be recovered.

"Dead bird, Sally. Dead bird," Denmark said as he walked towards the area where Joel's bird had fallen. She sniffed around a little and then rammed her nose into the base of a soybean plant. She came out with a quail; the light brown stripe across each cheek indicating it was a female.

"Good girl, Sally. Good girl," Denmark said, petting her on the head.

He took Trouble in to find the first of Bo's birds. The dog picked up the scent quickly and went straight to it. Holding the bird lightly in his mouth, he delivered it to Denmark. Trouble was catching on.

The second quail that Bo had hit proved more difficult. Denmark took both dogs into the area where he thought the quail would be, but they couldn't find the bird.

"Only one thing left to do," Denmark said. He walked back to the wagon and opened the dog pen under the bench seat used by the hunters. Out leaped a stocky British-style black Labrador retriever named "Jet."

"There has never been a bird dog with the sniffer of a good Lab," Denmark said plainly.

Denmark put the dog on a short leash and led it over to the area where the quail was believed to be. Turning the dog loose, he said, "Dead bird, Jet. Dead bird."

Jet immediately put his nose down and began walking straight towards a stand of maiden cane on the edge of the creek. When he neared the cane he accelerated, disappearing into the bushes. Shortly thereafter he emerged with a dead quail in his mouth and brought it to Denmark. The bird had obviously run from where it had glided but the bad leg had prevented it from getting too far before it expired.

"Good boy, Jet." Denmark exclaimed excitedly. "In two seasons I've lost only three birds using this dog," he said as he put the Lab back into the wagon, this time on the floor where the hunters rode. Jet had earned the right to ride with the people.

They worked several more coveys, taking extra time to hunt up the singles. It was a glorious morning, and the Brantleys had the time of their lives. The air stayed cold, however, and little of the ice thawed.

"Let's see if we can find one more covey before breaking for lunch," Denmark announced, and just before noon, the fifth dog the Brantleys had hunted over, a dog named "Babe," scented birds. She turned sharply to her right and worked her head back and forth as she tried to pinpoint the covey. When the smell became stronger, she quickened her pace to the bottom of a hill. Where the cornfield stopped and the brush began, she froze, her neck stretched out, her right leg raised and her tail pointing to the sky. Denmark dismounted from his horse and the Brantleys climbed from the wagon. They walked downhill, easing in behind the dog. When they were in position, Denmark moved up, slapping the brush with his leather buggy whip in an attempt to flush the birds. "The birds will probably fly into the swamp," he said. "You'll be shooting downhill so be especially careful about not hitting the dog."

The hunters stood with their shotguns at chest level, ready to shoulder them. Denmark slapped once, then twice. On the third slap the quail thundered to the sky, the whirring of wings against air making a deafening "thrrrrrr" sound. Instead of making a beeline to the swamp, though, birds went in every direction, with most of the covey going back over the heads of the hunters.

Joel had been covering the right flank, so when the birds flew back over him, he swung to the inside as he spun around to shoot at them going away. When he did, his right foot slipped on the ice as he took his safety off. His foot went far out from under him, and he lost his balance. He fell backwards. When he did so, his right arm pulled back instinctively to catch his weight. When his hand came away from the neck of the gun his trigger finger hit the trigger and the gun fired.

He heard his father scream. The side of his father's knee had absorbed most of the load of #8 birdshot. A shotgun at close range is a devastating weapon, and Mr. Brantley's leg was almost totally severed.

"Oh, Dad! Oh, Dad! Oh, Dad!" was all Joel could say as he ran to his father who was writhing on the ground.

"Out of the way, boy," Joel heard as he felt a strong hand on his shoulder. It was Denmark pulling Joel aside. "Let's see what we have here." Joel could not believe how composed and calm Denmark was.

Kneeling beside Bo, Denmark cut off his pants leg above the injury. It was bad. The knee bones were shattered, and the leg seemed to be held on by only a few muscles in the back of what used to be a knee.

"Is he going to lose his leg?" Joel asked.

"I'm not worried about the leg. The leg's gone. I'm worried about losing *him*," Denmark replied. "If we don't stop this bleeding, he can bleed to death." (Joel would later learn that Denmark had been a medical assistant in Vietnam and was very familiar with serious wounds, especially those caused by gunshots.)

Denmark quickly cut off the handle of his leather whip, allowing the straps to be unbraided. Using one of them, he tied a single overhand knot a couple of inches above the knee. He then laid a stout stick across the knot and tied another overhand knot above the stick.

"Take this stick, Samuel, and turn it slowly until the bleeding stops."

"I don't know Mr. Denmark," Samuel replied. "I'm not feeling so good. All this blood…and I ain't never seen no bone with live meat on it." He was pale and visibly shaken.

"I'll do it. You get my radio out of the wagon."

By turning the stick, Denmark could increase the pressure of the constriction around the thigh, thereby enabling him to better control the flow of blood down the leg. This improvised tourniquet did the trick, and within seconds the bleeding stopped.

Soon Denmark was speaking with Charlie Yarborough on the radio. Charlie called for an air ambulance to airlift Bo to a hospital in Albany.

When the helicopter arrived, the paramedics gave Bo fluids intravenously and Joel thought he saw a little color return to his father's face. Nevertheless, his dad was still in grave danger. Twenty minutes later, as the chopper lifted from the ground, he was alive but in serious shock.

Joel was not allowed to travel with his father, so he, Charlie and Denmark left for the hospital in Charlie's Suburban. When they arrived, Bo was already in surgery.

Three hours later, the surgeon emerged from the operating room with a solemn look on his face. He told the group that Bo would live, but that he had not been able to save the leg. "The bones were so shattered there was no piecing them back together. Not only was much of the bone missing, but what was there was not strong enough to accept a screw even if I had the bone to put it in. I'm sorry."

"How high up did you have to go, Doctor," Joel asked.

"Midway between the knee and hip," the doctor answered. "I was able to leave enough of a stump to connect an artificial leg if that is your father's desire."

The enormity of the situation settled on him, and Joel collapsed in tears.

Joel's father was in the hospital for five days. After returning home to Tampa, he was relegated to bed rest for another 20 as the stump healed. Throughout this time, Bo had frequent nightmares where he imagined the birdshot from the shotgun blast tearing through his knee in slow motion. The dreams were so lifelike that he would awaken in a sweat, knowing that he would find his knee bloody and mangled.

Strangely, Bo often thought he could feel pain in his leg below where it had been amputated. Sometimes it itched even though there was no leg there. This was a common occurrence for amputees, and very hard to figure.

During all this time at home, he watched a lot of television. In nearly every commercial break there were various attorneys telling the viewers, "If you've been injured, call me; you may have a compensable claim. The initial consultation is free, and if there is no recovery, you will owe nothing." These ads struck him as charlatan at first, but the more he saw them, the more he began to feel like a victim. He began asking himself questions like, "Should the guide have put us in that situation? Should we have even been hunting if ice was on the ground? Were we given proper instruction before being sent out?" He didn't dwell on these questions, but he did find himself thinking about them frequently.

His medical bills were significant. He had health insurance, but was still required to pay 25 percent and that came out to roughly $20,000.00. These financial pressures had the effect of making him think more and more about the television commercials. One day he saw a personal injury attorney say in one of the ads, "If you're mugged in the parking lot of a hotel, it may be because the hotel created an unsafe condition. Call me. Let our experienced team help you hold the business accountable for your injury."

Bo's first reaction was "How could the *hotel* be responsible? It wasn't a hotel employee who did the mugging. How could a business be responsible for the criminal acts of others?" But this concept of responsibility intrigued him. If a hotel could be liable for the criminal acts of total strangers, could a hunting establishment be liable for an injury that happened to one of its guests?

Three days later, curiosity, as well as the financial pressure of paying his medical bills, got the best of him and he called the attorney he used in his air conditioning business. The venue for any lawsuit would be in Georgia since that was where the accident occurred, so this attorney put him in contact with Brian Lapinski, a South Georgia personal injury lawyer. After Lapinski heard the extent of Bo's injury, he scheduled an appointment for him to come in. "Oh, and, bring your son and your wife. I'd like to hear how life has been for them since the accident." Lapinski knew that a way to drive the amount of the claim higher was to show that family members were suffering, as well.

The Brantleys made the long haul to Albany, Georgia. When they entered Lapinsky's office, they noted the elegant furnishings. The chairs and receptionist's desk were made of mahogany. The top of the coffee table was a slab of multicolored granite. A tall antique armoire was against the wall. The floor was dark Italian tile.

"This guy must make some serious jack!" Joel exclaimed.

"Don't talk that way, son. It's bad manners." Bo was still unsure about being there, and his nervous energy caused him to snap at Joel.

"So you must be the Brantleys," they heard from behind them. Turning, they saw a slight man with slicked-back black hair and a thin mustache. He was wearing a white shirt with gold cufflinks, yellow silk tie, black and white checked pants, black sport coat, and black Italian loafers. On his left little finger was a gold ring, and a gold chain bracelet with large links was around his left wrist. He sported an elegant gold Gucci watch on his right wrist.

"I'm Brian Lapinski. It is *so* nice to meet you. Come back with me, won't you?"

Lapinski led them into a large conference room.

"May I get you some coffee? Perhaps you'd like a soda or water. It's a little too early for the hard stuff" he joked, "even for me!"

"I'd like a glass of water," Annette Brantley, Bo's wife, said.

"Of course. Ms. Walker? Please bring Mrs. Brantley a glass of water," Lapinski said into the telephone to his receptionist. "And tell Ms. Brown we're ready for her.

"Ms. Brown is my paralegal. She'll be doing much of the work," he said. "It's a way to hold down costs." Bo didn't object to the paralegal being involved but thought that it was an odd comment. All the television commercials had said there would be no costs to the client; whatever expense was incurred would be paid by the law firm.

When Ms. Brown arrived, the business started. On the subject of fees, Bo learned that the firm would be paid a percentage of any recovery. Called a "contingency fee," this seemed too good to be true. He had occasionally hired lawyers in his business but always paid them by the hour regardless of the outcome. With a contingency fee, the law firm would front the costs of the litigation totally. He wouldn't have to come up with a single dollar, so he didn't have to weigh the likelihood of prevailing before deciding to proceed. He couldn't help but think, "Why not roll the dice and see what happens? What do I have to lose?"

Still, Bo asked, "What are our chances?"

"Remember, there might not be a lawsuit. We'll send Circle D a few demand letters and give them a chance to settle without litigation...a chance to do the right thing. The owner won't want the negative publicity of a high-profile lawsuit; it would be bad for business, so he'll want to get the matter behind him. Of course, the claim would be turned over to Circle D's insurance company, so the insurance company's lawyers would be doing the negotiating. Any settlement would be the decision of the insurance company, not the owner's, but he could encourage the insurance company to end the matter quickly."

"But if we do go to trial, what are our chances?" Bo pressed.

"That's hard to say. The theory of 'comparative negligence' would apply, meaning the percentage of responsibility would be apportioned among the parties."

"What does that mean?" Bo asked.

"To use a round number, let's just say the jury decides your injuries are worth a million dollars. (Lapinski liked using the word "million" or "millions" when discussing the cases he wanted because those injured were more likely to decide to proceed.) Then the jury would decide what percentage of responsibility for the accident was your son's, and what percentage was the defendants'. If the jury decided your son was half at fault, it would reduce the amount of money you would receive by half, leaving him with $500,000.00. This would come from the defendants, each paying whatever the jury determined was its percentage of responsibility. It's all up to the jury."

"But you think we'd get something, right?"

"Mr. Brantley, you suffered a serious injury. I've been doing this for 18 years, and the insurance companies *always* offer something, even when they believe the plaintiff was 100 percent at fault. If you're willing to take less than you might get if you go to trial, you'll get something."

"But my son slipped," Bo said. "How do we get around that? I still don't understand. And why did you say defendants? Aren't we talking about suing only Circle D?"

Chuckling, Lapinski said, "Mr. Brantley, I'll guarantee you the insurance company is scared to death of this claim. It involves a gun and that always brings scrutiny from the anti-gun crowd. It involves hunting, and many people are against hunting. It involves a minor, and many people are going to wonder why a hunting establishment would allow a kid to use a gun. There are a lot of reasons why the insurance company and Circle D would want to get this over with.

"Mr. Lapinski, you didn't answer my question. Why did you say defendants?"

"Well, there might be other defendants. For example, I intend to bring the gun manufacturer into this too. Cracker Arms is not going to want the attention that will come from one of their shotguns being involved in such a terrible accident, so we can probably get money from them."

"The gun manufacturer?" Bo asked. "Didn't the gun operate exactly as it was supposed to? My son took the safety off and the gun fired when the trigger was pulled."

"You don't understand," Lapinski continued. "We may let the manufacturer out at a later date, but at the beginning of the process we must bring everybody in. It may sound heartless, but that's just the way it's done. We don't know who should be in and who should be out at this point. We'll bring them in and see what we find. After we establish the facts, if the gun operated properly the manufacturer will have nothing to worry about. But don't prejudge anything. For all we know, the stock was too long for a kid and you should have been warned about that before you gave the gun to your son."

"That's ridiculous!" Bo said strongly. "I knew everything about that gun when I bought it."

"I'm sure you did. I'm just saying, let me ask some questions before we rule anything out. That's what our judicial system is about: finding the truth and then being fair."

Bo thought for a moment and then said he'd have to think about it. He took Lapinski's contract, his "Letter of Engagement," with him and promised to decide within a day or two.

He and his family left the office and returned home. When he arrived, he found four medical bills, each containing language that suggested the creditors were losing patience. Soon they, too, would be speaking with lawyers, he was sure, so he did what he didn't really want to do: He signed Lapinski's contract and the litigation game began.

The first step was for Lapinski to send a letter to Circle D informing Charlie Yarborough that he was representing Bo Brantley and his family for injuries sustained while he was hunting at Circle D. Charlie immediately called Bo, asking what this was all about.

"Your son slipped on ice!" Charlie shouted. "I didn't do anything wrong. God created the ice, not me! And not only that, my employee saved your life! Did you hear that? Denmark saved your life!"

"I hear what you're saying, sir, but I'm not allowed to speak with you. My attorney told me to refer any calls to him."

"I can't believe you went to a lawyer before even talking to me about this. I read you differently, Brantley. You're a business owner, for crying out loud!

You know what we're up against with these junk lawsuits. My insurance has gone out of sight because the company is scared of phony claims like this."

"I'm sorry, Charlie, but I'm not allowed to speak with you." And Bo was glad of it because he would have agreed with everything Charlie was saying if the shoe had been on the other foot.

"You might not be allowed to speak with me, but you'll hear from me. I'll guarantee you that!" he yelled as he hung up the phone.

Bo was left staring at a dead telephone, a sick feeling growing in the pit of his stomach. "This is not right. I shouldn't be doing this. Charlie Yarborough did nothing wrong." Bo was filled with doubt. His inner voice was encouraging him to end the game. He dialed his attorney's number.

"Mr. Lapinski, this is Bo Brantley. Bo Brantley…the guy who was shot· while hunting at Circle D?" It took a while for Lapinski to recognize the name of his client, but he clearly remembered the injury.

"I can't go through with this. I want to drop the case," Bo said.

"Tell me what's going on. Something has you rattled," Lapinski responded.

"Well, I just talked to Mr. Yarborough at Circle D and he said…"

"You did what? I told you not to speak with anybody from Circle D or its insurance company!"

"I know, but he called me, and…"

"Do not talk to anyone about your case. All they'll do is fill your head with garbage. Do you hear me?"

"Yes, but…"

"No buts about it. You suffered a devastating injury. It's not up to you to decide who was at fault; that's why we have juries. If Charlie Yarborough didn't do anything wrong, he won't pay a cent. Now don't let him or anyone else spook you. You have significant medical bills that must be paid. If you've incurred that expense because of someone else's negligence, *they* should pay, not you. It's as simple as that. And you've lost a leg for goodness sake! Isn't that worth something?" One thing about Brian Lapinski, he knew how to get a client to focus on the bottom line.

"Look, Bo. Let *me* do the talking; that's what I get paid for. Focus on documenting how the accident has changed your life. Make a list, just like I told you. That'll make you feel better and help you remember why you're doing this."

"All right," Bo said, thinking of the challenges he would surely face as he learned to live with his injury.

"The jury system works, Bo," Lapinski added for good measure. "Sometimes it's not pretty and it gets a little uncomfortable, but it's the best system of justice ever devised. Juries end up doing the right thing. Jurors take their jobs seriously. Believe me; whoever is responsible for your injuries will receive the blame."

With a sigh, Bo Brantley hung up the receiver.

The first hurdle the Brantleys had to clear was prevailing in a Motion to Dismiss hearing before Judge Edward Mills, the judge assigned to this case. Circle D's insurance company lawyer and the attorney for Cracker Arms would argue that the defendants had no legal responsibility whatsoever for the injury suffered by Bo, so the action should be dismissed.

To prevail in this negligence action, a "tort" in legalese, the plaintiff would have to prove four things: 1. The defendants had a duty to the plaintiff to exercise reasonable care. 2. The defendants breached this duty. 3. The breach was the "proximate cause" (not too far removed in time or place) of the accident. 4. And finally, the breach caused an injury to the plaintiff. If the plaintiff failed in proving even just one of these elements, the defendant would win. At the Motion to Dismiss hearing, the defendants would attempt to convince the judge that the evidence, when viewed in a light most favorable to the plaintiff, a requirement for this hearing, would not support the plaintiff's position in this four-pronged test.

Judges are reluctant to grant Motions to Dismiss since they occur early in the process and discovery (the methodologies used to determine the facts of the case) has been limited. More will be learned about the case as it progresses, so, unless it has no merit whatsoever, judges will usually allow cases to sort themselves out through voluntary dismissal, settlement or jury verdict. Mr. Yarborough and the other defendants would have their work cut out for them.

Walking into Judge Mills' hearing room, the Brantleys saw that a court reporter was already present. They sat with Brian Lapinski on one side of a rectangular table. A moment later the attorneys for the defendants walked in. At their side was Charlie Yarborough. He stared at Bo with contempt, never offering to shake his hand.

A side door burst open and a green-uniformed bailiff walked in and said, "All rise." Everyone stood, and in walked Judge Edward Mills.

Judge Mills was a south Georgian through and through. Raised in Moultrie, he grew up hunting and fishing and experiencing all the outdoors had to offer. He was a no-nonsense guy who wasn't afraid to call it like he saw it, and he wouldn't put up with specious claims clogging his docket or the court system. Brian Lapinski wasn't pleased that he would be the judge in this case.

Addressing the attorney for Circle D, Judge Mills wasted no time in getting to the heart of the matter. "Okay, Mr. Lester, we're here on your motion, so tell me why I should dismiss this case."

"Your Honor, the plaintiff's case fails to satisfy the elements of a negligence action. Yes, the defendant, Circle D, had a duty to exercise reasonable care to protect the plaintiff from harm, but only for *foreseeable* risks! That's the test. The risks *must* be foreseeable. Because the risk was not foreseeable, the defendant could not have breached the duty. Because there was no breach, the proximate cause issue is moot. Yes, there was an injury, but it was not because my client breached his duty. The risk was not foreseeable so there was no breach. Therefore, this case should be dismissed."

"What about that, Mr. Lapinski," the judge asked.

"Anyone who has ever walked on ice knows it's slippery," Lapinski began. "It was foreseeable that one walking on ice, especially someone holding a shotgun, could slip and that's exactly what happened. Joel Brantley, a *minor*, slipped while shouldering a shotgun and nearly blew his father's leg off. Circle D employees had a duty not to put him in a position where this could happen. It's not even clear if they warned him! They put him in this position, and as a result his father suffered a devastating injury. The elements of an actionable claim are present: Circle D employees had a duty to protect Bo Brantley from foreseeable injuries, but they did not, and the duty was breached. "But for" the breach, the injury would not have occurred; therefore the breach was the proximate cause of the accident. And the plaintiff suffered an injury. All four elements of actionable negligence are present. The case should not be dismissed."

"But Judge," Mr. Lester retorted, "Mr. Lapinski just said that anyone who has ever walked on ice knows it's slippery. He's right! Joel Brantley knew it was slippery to walk on ice. Besides, they had been hunting for nearly four hours, walking on and off ice all morning. Joel even remarked that he noticed the ice crushing beneath his feet! We also have learned that he suffers from ADD, an illness for which he takes medicine. He was medicated at the time of the accident. Maybe that had something to do with it too."

"That's an argument for comparative negligence, Your Honor," Lapinski said. "If Mr. Lester wants to concede the elements of the negligence claim and begin arguing percentage of responsibility, that's fine with me!"

Judge Mills just shook his head and sighed.

"Ms. Tomlinson, you're representing Cracker Arms. You've also moved to have this case dismissed. What's your argument?" the judge asked.

"Your Honor, we're at a loss to understand why we've even been dragged into this lawsuit. When the trigger of a loaded shotgun is pulled, the gun fires. That's what it's supposed to do! This was a tragic accident, but *not* the fault of the gun."

"What do you say, Mr. Lapinski. Sounds like a good argument to me," said Judge Mills. "Why shouldn't I dismiss the claim against them."

"Because there's a chance the trigger pull was too light. Safety requires that a certain amount of pressure be exerted before the gun fires. Hair triggers cause a lot of injuries every year."

"Do you have any evidence that Cracker set the trigger too lightly?" Judge Mills asked.

"Not at this time, Your Honor, but we haven't had the gun tested."

Directing the question to the lawyer for Cracker Arms, Judge Mills asked if the "pound pull" of the trigger was tested before guns left the factory.

"Every one, sir. Twice, in fact," the attorney answered.

"I've heard enough and I'm prepared to rule unless anyone has anything else to say." No one spoke.

"Mr. Lapinski, this kind of case grates on me. Your client had been on ice all morning so he had either become comfortable with the risks of hunting in those conditions, or he didn't know it was possible for his son to slip, in which case he would have been acting as a complete idiot. However, at this point in the proceeding, viewing the evidence in the light most favorable to the plaintiff as I must, I can't dismiss this claim. It's impossible for me to know how much danger was present. If danger was present, maybe Circle D didn't know about it, or maybe the employees even discussed it, I just don't know. Therefore, I can't dismiss the claim at this time. However, I'm going to strictly scrutinize this case as it proceeds, and I won't be afraid to dismiss it later if it appears that Circle D had done what it could to create a safe hunting environment.

"Judge, may I say something?" asked Charlie Yarborough.

"Not at this time, Charlie. I'm sorry. A Motion to Dismiss hearing is just for the lawyers. Often the clients aren't even present, but your being here is fine. Otherwise, I wouldn't have allowed it."

Charlie again stared so hard at Bo that Bo could feel it, even though he was looking down.

"The case against Cracker Arms is different," Judge Mills continued. "There is not a scintilla of evidence that anything was wrong with the shotgun. Guns discharge when the trigger is pulled; that's what they're supposed to do, just like Ms. Tomlinson said. For that reason, the case against Cracker Arms is dismissed, but 'without prejudice,' so if you find evidence of a negligent design, I'll let you re-file. But you'd better have something solid.

"That's my ruling. The case against Circle D is not dismissed at this time. The case against Cracker Arms is dismissed without prejudice. Gentlemen, Ms. Tomlinson, have a good day." With that, the judge stood and left the room.

Mr. Brantley and Mr. Yarborough made hard eye contact. Mr. Yarborough just shook his head. Mr. Brantley looked away quickly.

"What happened?" Mr. Brantley asked as the parties and their attorneys filed out of the courtroom.

"What happened? You just made a lot of money," Lapinski answered, grinning.

"I don't understand."

"The case against Circle D is alive!" Lapinski explained. "We survived the Motion to Dismiss and the litigation game has begun! The insurance company will soon offer a small amount of money to settle, but that number will grow significantly the closer we get to trial. If you'll stay patient and not quit until I tell you to, we can get the amount up pretty high. But when I tell you it's time to take the offer, you should take it."

"But what about the judge's negative comments?"

"I'm not worried about that. The insurance company will still offer good money. But in all likelihood the case against Cracker Arms is over. We'll still test the shotgun and see if the trigger is set too lightly, but my guess is it's not. In the meantime, I'll see if other cases have been filed against the company alleging the same thing. If we can find a pattern, we may be able to get Judge Mills to allow us to re-file. And all we have to do is re-file and survive the Motion to Dismiss, and Cracker Arms will put some money on the table, too. You've had a good day, Bo."

Bo Brantley wondered why he didn't feel as though he had.

Just as Lapinski had predicted, in three weeks he received an offer from the insurance company to settle the case for $25,000.00.

"It's an insulting offer. Don't even think about accepting it," he told Mr. Brantley.

"I don't know. It would pay a lot of these medical bills."

"Look," Lapinski said. "We'll end up with a lot more if you'll just trust me." Lapinski didn't emphasize the pronoun 'we,' but it was clear he was thinking of himself, as well.

"All right, but I sure wish I felt better about this."

"Believe me, you're doing the right thing. We'll take a few depositions and probably discover that the guides talked about the ice and slippery conditions before going out that morning. My guess is the insurance company won't want to take this to trial." In truth, Lapinski didn't want to take this to trial either. It would be a very difficult case to win, and he rarely tried cases anymore anyway. He would play tough with the insurance company and get the offer as h as possible before the company walked away, and then he'd tell Bo it was to take it.

positions were taken, and Lapinski searched a trial lawyer database for against Cracker Arms. He learned that two previous cases had been ist the company, alleging the same thing: triggers that were set too r case had gone to trial, but Lapinski contacted the lawyers for the ose cases and learned that the company had paid money to "make ·" Confidentiality agreements precluded the attorneys from disclosing the amounts, but Lapinski had learned what he needed. He sent the company a letter, saying he knew of the other cases and intended to ask Judge Mills for permission to re-file this case unless "they could work something out." Fearful of stories about light triggers and the cases they would surely spur, Cracker Arms decided to settle the case for $27,000.00. They considered this "blood money" because they were certain nothing was wrong with their guns. However, they made a business decision to get the case over with because they couldn't afford the notoriety of a trial.

Bo couldn't believe it. To him it was like finding money on the street because he didn't believe there was anything wrong with the gun. He reminded Lapinski of his own words, that he had said the manufacturer would have nothing to worry about if it was found that there was nothing wrong with the gun. Still, Bo took the cash, accepting Lapinski's contention that he must "trust the system," and that Cracker Arms viewed claims of this sort as simply a "cost of doing business."

The case against Circle D dragged on for a few more months. When Charlie Yarborough's deposition was taken it was learned that he and the guides *had* discussed the ice on the ground before getting the hunters up that morning. He had told them to be careful. He was certain the hunters would have chosen to go out even if specifically warned of the slippery conditions. In fact, he was sure they would have been livid if the trip had been cancelled because of ice.

It was also learned that the guide, Denmark Jones, the one who had saved Bo Brantley's life after the accident by applying first aide, had *not* warned the hunters about the "dangerous condition," as Lapinski described it. It made no difference to Lapinski that common sense would tell anyone who was walking with a shotgun on ice to be careful.

Still, this information was the hook Lapinski needed to extract a significant offer from the insurance company to settle. Bo's injuries were serious. A significant amount of medical expense had already been incurred, and a lawyer could come up with a very high number when describing to a jury what losing a leg was worth to a middle-aged man who was still active. The insurance company knew this, and was also aware that once a jury began apportioning fault as required by the doctrine of comparative negligence it was anyone's guess what would happen. Going through the four-part test for negligence, Lapinski would first state that Yarborough had a duty to protect Bo from foreseeable threats, and that slipping on ice was foreseeable. Since Yarborough had actually discussed this with his guides, there was evidence to support this assertion. Next, Lapinski would claim that because Bo was not warned about the threat or protected in any other way, the duty was breached. Addressing the third element, clearly "but for" his son slipping, the accident wouldn't have occurred, so the proximate cause requirement was met. Finally, Bo Brantley suffered damages as a result.

The measure of anyone's action in a negligence case is what a "reasonable person" would have done in similar circumstances. A person is required to do what a "reasonable person" would have done, nothing more and nothing less. The insurance company attorneys would argue that Yarborough and his guides acted reasonably, that in fact it would have been *unreasonable* not to go out. What's more, they were sure the Brantleys would have thrown a fit if the trip had been cancelled. Furthermore, a warning about not slipping on ice would have warned the hunters of something they already knew: that when walking on ice one might slip.

They would bring up the fact that the Brantleys were experienced hunters, and that they knew it was cold and that ice was on the ground. Joel Brantley's condition of suffering from ADD would be entered into the record for consideration, and that the medicine he was taking could have had something to do with the accident.

Most important, they would demonstrate the culture of safety Charlie Yarborough had created at Circle D. They would show the jury the videotape on safety that Yarborough had shown the night before and introduce other evidence showing the high emphasis he placed on safety. This was the only gun accident ever to occur on Yarborough property, and the attorneys felt certain they could get the judge to allow that information to be presented to the jury.

As Lapinski walked Bo through the arguments he would make, Bo couldn't help but laugh. That Lapinski could say this with a straight face was comical. He quit laughing, however, when Lapinski told him the insurance company had raised its offer to $75,000.00.

"You must be kidding," he said with an astonished look on his face.

"No, I'm not," Lapinski replied. "And I think they'll make one more move before choosing to go to trial."

"Why would they put so much money on this case?"

"It's not that much money, really. A jury could easily say your injury is a $600,000.00 injury. If they determined your son to be two-thirds responsible, that's $200,000.00 from them. But the jury might even split it 50/50, that's an easy thing for a jury to do, and that gets the number to $300,000.00."

Bo could only shake his head, thinking of the look of disbelief and outrage that Mr. Yarborough would feel if he learned of such settlement discussions. It was probably a good thing that his insurance company was handling this.

"What do you recommend?" Bo asked.

"Authorize me to accept $90,000.00. That keeps it under a hundred grand, which I think is important to the insurance company representative. Anything over $100,000.00 probably triggers a review by senior level adjusters.

"I'll tell them we'll take $105,000.00. My guess is they will ask if we can split the difference. I'll indicate that I doubt it, but I'll check with my client. The next day, I'll call them back and accept the $90,000.00.

"Between the insurance company and Cracker Arms, that's $117,000.00. Not a bad day's work." When he said this, Lapinski was actually thinking of the $38,610.00 he would make as his one-third contingency fee.

Bo thought for a moment or two, and finally said, "Do it, but the whole thing smells to high heaven to me." Brantley was thinking in terms of a businessperson. His son had slipped while hunting on ice and nearly shot his leg off. Neither Charlie Yarborough nor the guides had forced his son to hunt or pull the trigger that fired the shell, yet Circle D was paying nearly $100,000.00. Cracker Arms, maker of a perfectly fine shotgun, was paying $27,000.00 to avoid publicity that would have the perverse effect of costing the company more money because of the lawsuits it would spur even though a trial would prove the gun had worked exactly as it should.

Lapinski had seen this with many clients, and he always said the same thing, perhaps to assuage his conscience even though he knew the answer: "It's your case, Mr. Brantley. We can go to trial and I'll do my best. There are no guarantees, of course, but we can go to trial."

"No, make the deal," Brantley said. "Just like the defendants, I want to get this over with, and I'm tired of making these trips to Georgia." Lapinski wasn't surprised; he knew Bo Brantley would take the money when it got right down to it.

And so it was that Lapinski made the deal with the insurance company for $90,000.00. Bo Brantley paid his medical bills and had enough left over for the first two years of his son's college. He continued operating his air conditioning business, but met frequently with his insurance agent to make sure he had more insurance than he thought was needed. After seeing how claims could be essentially manufactured, he knew that *he* might someday be the businessperson in the crosshairs of contrived lawsuits aimed at him.

Charlie Yarborough was spitting mad when he heard about the settlement. He knew his insurance costs would go up as a result of the case and for doing absolutely nothing wrong. What really chapped him, however, was a condition imposed on him by his insurance company. The company required the safety film he showed to hunters the evening before the hunt to include a warning to "walk carefully if hunting on ground covered with ice." That always drew chuckles from his guests and actually hurt the credibility of the rest of the film, but the insurance company wouldn't insure him without it, so there it was, a warning telling hunters carrying a loaded shotgun to be careful when walking on ice.

Brian Lapinski made out the best of anyone. Through clever advertising, he used the case to develop a reputation as *the* Georgia personal injury attorney to see in any accident involving a gun. He had yet to try one of these cases, but the name of the game was getting the clients in the door.

Author's Note:

Many lawsuits involve acts that were clearly negligent, while others involve acts where the negligence was specious at best. A lot of cases, though, are close calls, and there is honest disagreement over how these cases should be handled. The challenge is fashioning a legal system that ferrets out cases without merit – or without enough merit (and how do you define that?) – without denying access to the courts for meritorious cases. This is perilous because if people believe there is no redress for grievances or accountability for those who have wronged them, a very unstable societal situation is created. Still, there are too many lawsuits and many defendants find themselves paying money to plaintiffs for questionable cases just to get the matter behind them.

The effort to change the laws governing civil liability is called "tort reform." The stakes are high because the welfare of people is involved; missteps can result in very real damage to people in very dire straits. Tort reform is complicated legally and treacherous politically.

There have been several tort reform efforts by the Florida Legislature. One involved Florida's workers' compensation law, the law that determines how injured workers are compensated. The exercise illustrates the difficulty in creating limits in any judicial or quasi-judicial system.

The year was 1993. The high cost of workers' compensation was a huge issue, and Gov. Lawton Chiles had toured the state drumming up support for change. I was asked to file and handle the changes he thought were necessary. I had heard from many of the employers in my Senate district and was convinced that change was needed, so I agreed.

A select committee on workers' compensation in the Senate was chaired by Senator Toni Jennings, now our lieutenant governor. Toni was very thorough, scheduling many hearings and countless speakers as we discussed wholesale reform. The system was so broken that the intended beneficiaries of the system – injured workers and employers – had become the victims. Health care providers, insurance companies and attorneys seemed to be the only ones benefiting from the law.

I was convinced that there had to be limits in the system. For example, we learned there were workers who had been going to chiropractors every week for two years, or workers receiving palliative care that didn't seem to be making them well. Consequently, I began pushing provisions that would limit the number of such visits. Needless to say, many health care providers didn't like this, so they had their patients write to complain. I wrote a detailed response back and many of these patients came to understand my point of view. A few didn't, obviously, but these contacts helped me grow to appreciate that these visits were making these patients feel better, even if they weren't making them well. It was clear that the brief relief of their chronic pain meant a great deal to them. Still, believing the system had to have limits, the Legislature agreed to cap the visits at 18 (this has since been changed to 24 with more treatments allowed under certain circumstances).

I'll never forget a meeting between myself, Senator Jennings, Senator W. D. Childers and Governor Chiles. We had been knocking this bill around for months, and in this meeting we finally came to an agreement on our last remaining differences. Toni is a tough negotiator, and I'll never forget how she and Governor Chiles batted several provisions back and forth. I wrote out the main provisions on a legal pad and we all signed it. I'd love to be able to find that piece of paper.

As it turned out, the agreement was well received by the Senate. It was a massive bill. Some of the changes had the effect of reducing benefits for workers. I remember Senator Jim Hargrett saying he didn't want to go back home to Tampa only to find that there had been a "lynching" in Tallahassee, and the ones being lynched were injured workers. He asked me if this bill was a lynching. I told him I did not believe it was, and that I would work to restore benefits if the cuts were too deep. The bill passed.

When it was implemented, it soon became apparent that the benefits for more seriously injured workers had been cut too much. Remembering my commitment to Senator Hargrett, I spoke with him about reinstating some of these benefits. I believe we even filed legislation together to do it, but I don't recall that part so clearly. My recollection is that the Legislature restored some of these benefits the next session, but I honestly don't remember. The benefits should have been restored, though, if they weren't. The basis for workers' compensation is that, in exchange for taking away the right of injured employees to sue their employers for injuries incurred in the workplace, workers would be properly cared for when injured. If that doesn't happen, it's effectively a breach of contract.

The story points out the difficulty in enacting tort reform. Virtually all changes to the laws governing civil liability result in persons being hurt, and once rights are lost, they are very difficult to restore.

This story mentions that the main character, Bo Brantley, was being told by his "inner voice" not to file the lawsuit. The concept of an "inner voice" communicating with a person was not my creation, but something I often heard Governor Lawton Chiles discuss. I had a conversation with him about my inner voice one day, and it was when I told him I had decided to run for governor.

The meeting was in the small anteroom next to the governor's office. The room was comfortable and arranged in a way to give it the feel of the outdoorsman that Governor Chiles was. We shared mutual interests in hunting and fishing, and one of his sons was a fraternity brother of mine, so we usually started our business meetings with discussions of these pursuits and of his son.

I felt that I owed Governor Chiles the courtesy of telling him that I was going to run before he heard it from someone else. His lieutenant governor, Buddy MacKay, was already in the race, so I feared it would be an uncomfortable meeting. It wasn't. I made it clear that my candidacy was not borne of any animus towards Buddy, and that, in fact, I considered Buddy to *be one of the most capable elected officials in Florida's history. (As it turned out, I ended up accepting Buddy's invitation to become his running mate later in the campaign.) Governor Chiles asked me what my "inner voice" was telling me about running. I had previously heard him refer to his "inner voice," but had never been asked about my own or even thought about it. He said we all had one, and that we should listen to it. He explained that, over the years, the decisions he regretted the most were ones where he ignored what his inner voice was telling him. I told him I was at peace with the decision to run and that it felt right. He didn't encourage me to run or not to run, only to listen to what my inner voice was telling me.*

Fine English pointers are prominent in this story. I'd always wanted a bird dog, so I made the plunge in the mid-1990s. Joe Brown, Secretary of the Senate at the time and an institution in Florida political history, was the proud owner of an English pointer that had a beautiful litter of puppies. Joe gave me one, and it had a distinctive spot right on top of its head, just like one of the dogs in this story. I convinced Dr. William Steele, a retired physician in my hometown of Winter Haven, Florida, to be my partner. He had a kennel, about six other dogs, and the expertise to train the puppy. Not only did I love the idea of owning a pointer, but I also loved the idea of getting to know Dr. Steele better and spending time with him.

I named the dog "Dr. Pete Brown" after Dr. Steele, Pete Clemons (the owner of the Okeechobee Livestock Market, former world rodeo champion, and one of my favorite people) and Joe Brown. I called him "Pete." Unfortunately, Dr. Steele and I couldn't do much with the dog. Pete had little hunting instinct and just wasn't "birdy." Maybe we quit on the dog too soon, but two years later we gave it to a bird dog man on the West Coast of Florida. I hope the dog "switched on" to hunting and is having a happy life.

THE LAW: *Definitions and Explanations:*

Negligence: The omission to do something which a reasonable man, guided by those ordinary considerations which ordinarily regulate human affairs, would do, or the doing of something which a reasonable and prudent man would not do.

Black's Law Dictionary, Sixth Edition, p. 1032

Duty: ...Obligation to conform to legal standard of reasonable conduct in light of apparent risk. An obligation, recognized by the law, requiring actor to conform to certain standard of conduct for protection of others against unreasonable risks.

Black's Law Dictionary, Sixth Edition, p. 506

Breach: The breaking or violating of a law, right, obligation, engagement, or duty, either by commission or omission...

Black's Law Dictionary, Sixth Edition, p. 188

Proximate Cause: ...The proximate cause of an injury is the primary or moving cause, or that which, in a natural and continuous sequence, unbroken by any efficient intervening cause, produces the injury and without which the accident would not have happened, if the injury be one which might be reasonably anticipated or foreseen as a natural consequence of the wrongful act.

Black's Law Dictionary, Sixth Edition, p. 1225

Injury: Any wrong or damage done to another, either in his person, rights, reputation, or property. The invasion of any legally protected interest of another.

Black's Law Dictionary, Sixth Edition, p. 785;
Restatement, Second, Torts, Section 7

Notable Quotes:

"To obtain a just compromise, concession must not only be mutual, it must be equal also. There can be no hope that either will yield more than it gets in return."

Honorable John Marshall, Chief Justice,
United States Supreme Court,
in "The Life of John Marshall," by Albert Beveridge, as attributed in
"Quotes From Supreme Court Justices," home.att.net/~midnightflyer/supreme.html

"Law is not justice and a trial is not a scientific inquiry into truth. A trial is a resolution of a dispute."

Edison Haines / www.quotegarden.com

"We must distinguish between the sound certainty and the sham, between what is gold and what is tinsel; and then, when certainty is attained, we must remember that it is not the only good, that we can buy it at too high a price."

Honorable Benjamin Nathan Cardozo, Associate Justice,
United States Supreme Court, in his paper, "The Growth of the Law," Yale University Press (1924), as attributed to him in
"Quotes From Supreme Court Justices," home.att.net/~midnightflyer/supreme.html

"This is a court of law, young man, not a court of justice."

Honorable Oliver Wendell Holmes, Jr., Associate Justice,
United States Supreme Court
home.att.net/~midnightflyer/supreme.html

"Litigation is the pursuit of practical ends, not a game of chess."

Honorable Felix Frankfurter, Associate Justice,
United States Supreme Court
www.brainyquotes.com

"I consider trial by jury as the only anchor yet imagined by man which a government can be held to the principles of its constitution."

Thomas Jefferson, 1789 / www.erodid.org

"It is not only the juror's right, but his duty to find the verdict according to his own best understanding, judgment and conscience, though in direct opposition to the instruction of the court."

John Adams, 1771 / www.erowid.org

"If the juror accepts as the law that which the judge states, then the juror has accepted the exercise of absolute authority of a government employee and has surrendered a power and right that once was the citizen's safeguard of liberty."

Justice Theophilus Parsons, 1788 / www.erowid.org

Impartial Decisions

YOU NEVER KNOW...
Right To Privacy: Abortion

"All persons born or naturalized in the United States, and subject to the jurisdiction thereof, are citizens of the United States and of the State wherein they reside. No state shall make or enforce any law which shall abridge the privileges or immunities of citizens of the United States; nor shall any State deprive any person of life, liberty, or property, without due process of law; nor deny to any person within its jurisdiction the equal protection of the laws."

Article XIV, Section 1, Constitution of the United States
(Fourteenth Amendment).

Preface: The United States Supreme Court, in the case of Roe v. Wade, 410 U.S. 113 (1973), declared that a woman had a limited constitutional right to an abortion via a "privacy" right guaranteed by the Due Process Clause of the Fourteenth Amendment. Many hailed the decision as an example of how the Constitution was to be a "living" document, interpreted in different ways to keep up with the times. Others agreed with Justice Rehnquist in his dissenting opinion, that it was inappropriate for the Court to establish such policy, believing instead that the legislative branch was the proper forum for abortion policy to be established. This story explores these perspectives and explains the complicated legal reasoning expounded by the Court. It's tedious stuff, though, better suited for morning reading when the caffeine is fresh. You'll need to concentrate on this one.

THE FIRST YEAR of law school is stressful and difficult, and students who endure this time together forge a special bond that lasts a lifetime. Hilda Summers and Randy Redd had been first year classmates at the University of Florida law school, and they had returned to Gainesville for their 10-year class reunion.

It was also Homecoming Weekend, and the Gators were playing the University of Miami Hurricanes. A game between these two powerhouse teams was always a war, but this year the Hurricanes were ranked number two in the country and the Gators number six, so there was special electricity in the air. Hilda and Randy had met for a late breakfast before going to the football field that afternoon. Other friends were going to join them soon.

"It's really good to see you," Randy said, as she sat down at his table. "Has it really been 10 years?"

"Yes it has. Hard to believe, but it has," Hilda answered. "How's your family?"

"Everyone is great. My son's a handful but an awful lot of fun; my daughter's as sweet as she can be."

"And your wife?"

"Marie is fine. In fact, she'll be here in about a half-hour."

"Is she still working?"

"Yes, but only three days a week until two in the afternoon. That's enough to keep her current on her accounting skills but leaves a lot of time for the kids. She's also able to pick them up at school every day. What about you? How's your practice going?"

"The practice is going well. I even have an oral argument before the state Supreme Court in January. And you're not going to believe what kind of case it is – a Constitutional Law case! Can you believe it, me having a Con. Law case? As much as I struggled in our Constitutional Law class, Professor Franklin would be proud of me – and shocked!"

"Ah, Professor Ronald Franklin," Randy said wistfully. "He used to keep me so tangled up in my own underwear that I didn't know *what* I'd learned when I left his class. But you know, looking back on it, I think he was the best professor I had. Those questions, though! They just kept coming and coming, didn't they? He'd never give us the answer to anything; he'd make us bumble through until we discovered it ourselves."

Hilda laughed. "Do you know he once made me so nervous I developed a case of the hives?"

"You're kidding! You never told me about that."

"Well he did. It was during the discussion of Roe v. Wade."

Randy was not surprised. "That was a complicated case. Couple that with the strong feelings we had about that subject, and it made for a stressful couple of days."

A faraway look came into Hilda's eyes. "You know, I remember those three days like it was yesterday..."

"But it's *not* life," Hilda Summers said emphatically. "It's just a clump of cells."

"Aren't cells alive?" responded Professor Ronald Franklin. "If they are, wouldn't it be life!"

"The cells are alive, but they're not a person. Not yet, anyway."

"Really? Then when *do* they become a person? Three months, six months, when?" asked Franklin.

"Oh, I don't know," answered Hilda. She was feeling exasperated and embarrassed.

"What did the Court say, Ms. Summers?"

"They said they didn't know; that if all the theologians and scientists and philosophers and doctors couldn't reach consensus, they didn't need to answer that question."

"Mr. Redd, was that wisdom or cowardice?" Professor Franklin asked, turning his attention to Randy.

"I think it was cowardice," Randy answered. "The Supreme Court is there to answer tough questions."

"Even if they don't feel qualified to answer? Even if they knew there was a good chance they'd be wrong?"

"Yes. Even if they knew there was a good chance they'd be wrong. The basic question of when life begins *must* be decided before abortion policy can be decided."

"What if the court decided life didn't begin until 40 days *after* birth?" Franklin said.

"That would be ridiculous! They wouldn't do that," Randy said angrily.

"No? Some ancient theologians thought 'ensoulment' took place 40 days after birth, so that's when life began. In their view, until the body received its soul, it wasn't alive. Again, Mr. Redd, what if the Court ruled that life didn't begin until 40 days after birth?"

"I'd, I'd…I'd be furious!"

The class laughed, as did Randy at his lack of a law-related answer.

"So you can understand how people would be *really* upset about the Court deciding the abortion issue differently than they believed?" Professor Franklin asked.

"Of course I do. In fact, *I'm* upset with the Court. I don't agree with current abortion law. Since no one can answer the question of when life begins, shouldn't the law err on the side of life, and say life begins at conception? There clearly is a union of live cells at that point. To decide otherwise, the Court is sanctioning the killing of innocent life, if life is what it turns out to be."

"What do you think about that, Ms. Summers?" Franklin asked, turning the discussion back to her.

"I don't think the court should impose that view on all of us when there is no consensus. Let everyone make the decision for themselves," she answered.

"But aren't our governmental institutions *supposed* to make tough decisions and establish policy?" Franklin asked. "They decide the death penalty, and many people are opposed to that. They decide when our country goes to war, whether we have an income tax, a lot of things people disagree with strongly. What's so special about abortion that the Court wouldn't answer such a basic question?"

"But abortions *should* be legal," Hilda said emphatically.

"You didn't answer the question, Ms. Summers. Let me ask it a different way. The court chose not to answer the question of when life begins because there was no consensus. *All* cases that get to the Supreme Case have a lack of consensus on major points or they wouldn't have gotten that far. If the court didn't decide cases where there was a lack of consensus, it wouldn't decide many cases. Was it right for the court to defer on the question of when life begins just because there was no consensus? Wouldn't the answer to that question drive the policy? Shouldn't it?"

"If the court had decided when life begins, it might have made abortions after that point illegal," Hilda answered.

"So the ends justify the means?" retorted Professor Franklin.

"No, but…"

"And should those who disagree with the Court's decision have a chance to change it?"

"I suppose so."

"How could they? The Supreme Court declared a right to an abortion to be a constitutional right, so legislative bodies couldn't infringe upon it. Was that right?" Franklin was not letting up.

"But some legislative bodies wouldn't have made it legal!" Hilda exclaimed. She was still focused on the result of the Court's decision, not its reasoning.

"Would you agree that the people of this country are supposed to be in charge of the affairs of this country?" The answer to Franklin's question seemed so obvious, Hilda was almost afraid to answer.

"Of course," she responded, after thinking for a moment. "It's *their* country."

"Then which governmental body are the people more in charge of, the Supreme Court where justices are appointed for life, or a state legislature or Congress where the representatives and senators run for re-election every couple of years?" Franklin asked.

"The latter, I guess," Hilda replied.

"You guess? Have you ever voted for or against a United States Supreme Court justice?" Franklin asked tersely.

"No, I haven't," Hilda conceded. "Okay. The people are more in charge of a legislative body." She wanted to crawl under her desk.

"So why shouldn't the *legislative* branch be in charge of abortion policy? If enough people didn't agree with what their legislators did, they could elect new representatives and senators to change it. Isn't that how the people stay in charge?"

"Yes, but this is such an important thing. It's so personal," Hilda answered.

"Keep going," Franklin encouraged.

"Well, the woman carries the baby to term, delivers it, cares for it, raises it. The woman can't walk away like the man can, or shouldn't anyway. Not many mothers do, that's for sure. It's just such a fundamental thing."

"Ah hah! Now we're getting somewhere," Professor Franklin exclaimed. "That word 'fundamental', where have we heard that before, Mr. Redd?"

"Well, let me see," Randy stammered. "There was the First Amendment right to free speech, the Fourth Amendment right against unreasonable searches and seizures, and the Fifth Amendment right against self-incrimination. All those rights are fundamental."

"Good. And there are others. But the point is," Franklin continued, "in these cases the Court declared the protections to be fundamental, basic rights; rights that were essential to liberty. Is that what the Court did here, Ms. Summers?"

"Yes, it was," Hilda said with a faint smile. She was finally beginning to see the rationale for the Court's decision. Professor Franklin didn't stop, though.

"So receiving a legal abortion was declared a constitutional right, correct?" Franklin asked.

"Yes."

"But where in the Constitution does it say anything about abortion? Is the word even in there?"

"Um, no. It's not."

"So the Court just created a new constitutional right?" Franklin asked incredulously.

"I...guess so."

"What do you think the Founding Fathers would have thought about that?"

"They probably wouldn't have been too happy," Hilda replied.

"I think you're right, so how'd the Court get there? How'd they do it?"

"They just did it!" Hilda blurted out. "They're the Supreme Court, you know." The class laughed. Professor Franklin scowled.

"*Think*, Ms. Summers."

"I don't know, Professor. I thought I was starting to understand it; now I'm not so sure."

"Then let's walk through it – Wednesday," Franklin said. "That's enough for today. But before you go, I want to encourage you to think like lawyers and judges when you read these cases. Don't simply memorize conclusions; the Court may change its mind tomorrow. I want analysis and rationale! Tell me *how* the Court reaches its decisions. With this case in particular, don't focus on the Court's decision, but how it was reached. Dissect the decision. Figure out the roadmap. That's how you learn to become a lawyer!"

Hilda Summers left the class feeling whipped and discouraged. It was the first time in law school that she had been questioned in that fashion, and she felt like everyone had been laughing at her under their breath. She had seen others get the same treatment because it was, in fact, part of law school and the Socratic teaching method used there. Rarely did the students receive a lecture; most of the time it was a series of questions with few answers from the professor. "It's all about teaching you how to think!" the dean had told the first-year students in their orientation session. Still, it shook Hilda's confidence.

"Don't let it get to you," she heard. Turning, she saw Randy Redd behind her. "I was grilled the same way the first week in Torts, so I know how you feel."

"Hi Randy. I feel like everybody was laughing at me."

"They weren't. They were too busy worrying if they were going to be called on next."

"I guess you're right. I don't know what it is about Constitutional Law. It's really interesting, but I just don't seem to get it. How the Court should rule seems so obvious to me, I can't figure out why they have to go through such gyrations to get there."

"It's because the Constitution doesn't specifically address many of these situations," Randy replied. "The Court has to invent ways to reach an outcome that seems obvious. But I know what you mean. The justices do back flips with twists to justify what they're doing. That's why all this stuff should be left to legislative bodies, but that's just my opinion. Come on, let's go to Wilbert's and get a Gatorade or something."

"Sounds good, although after that class, I'll need something stronger than Gatorade!"

Wilbert's was a small convenience store next to the law school. It had a lunch counter and a few tables, and was the hub of activity for many students. Open from early in the morning until late in the evening, one could always get a great sandwich and cup of coffee there or find a copying machine in working order. It was a great place for students to gather and talk.

Hilda and Randy were opposites in many ways. Hilda was a South Florida girl from Ft. Lauderdale with bleached blonde hair and a dark tan who had grown up surfing and playing beach volleyball. She considered herself a liberal Democrat who supported abortion rights.

Randy was from the small North Florida town of Two Egg, right in the heart of the Bible Belt. Randy was a conservative Republican who, because he believed life began at conception, thought abortion was murder.

Regardless of their differences, they were part of a six-student study group of first-year students and had become quite close. The group met every morning at 7:30 to go over the cases they had read and "briefed" from the previous night. Briefing cases – writing a short statement of the facts, stating the issue, explaining the Court's rationale, and declaring the legal principle of the case – was the bane of a student's existence during the first year of law school. Reading and briefing cases constituted at least 80% of their time.

Before class on Wednesday, Hilda found herself as nervous as a cat. She just knew she was going to be in Professor Franklin's crosshairs again, and the thought made her mouth go dry. When class began, however, it wasn't her, but Randy, who was the focus of the professor's questions…at least at first.

"Mr. Redd, on Monday we saw that the Supreme Court created a constitutional right to an abortion in the Roe v. Wade case. Thankfully for Ms. Summers, time ran out before we could explore the basis for the Court's decision, so I'll ask you. If the word "abortion" was not even in the Constitution, how could the Supreme Court conclude that a woman had a right to one?"

Randy stole a look at Hilda. She smiled. Now *he* was on the hot seat.

"The Court declared an abortion to be a what?" Professor Franklin asked.

"A 'privacy' right," Randy answered.

"And where is the privacy clause found?"

"Professor Franklin, I couldn't find it, and I looked!"

"You mean, there is no right to privacy in the Constitution?"

"No. I sure couldn't find it, anyway."

"You mean the government can control what consenting adults do in the privacy of their bedrooms?"

"Well, no," Randy answered.

"What about searches and seizures?" Franklin asked. "Can the police come barging into your home for no reason?"

"No, sir. They can't."

"Hasn't the Court declared in those cases that citizens have a right to privacy?" Franklin continued.

"Yes, sir."

"Then how did they do it?" the professor inquired.

Randy felt hot. Sweat was forming on the palms of his hands and his upper lip.

"I actually agreed with Justice Rehnquist's dissent," was all he could conclude.

"All right," Franklin said. "Then let's figure it out through the dissenting opinion. What did Justice Rehnquist say?"

"He said the right to privacy didn't include an abortion."

"In other words, he thought there was a right to privacy, it just didn't include abortion?" Franklin asked.

"Yes, sir. He agreed there was a right to privacy for some things, but not for an abortion."

"Interesting. Even though there wasn't a right to privacy clause in the Constitution?"

"Yes, sir."

"So where did the right to privacy come from in the cases where he believed one existed?" the professor wondered.

"The Fourteenth Amendment. The right to privacy clause of the Fourteenth amendment, even though there's not one there," Randy replied. Many in the class laughed.

"How can there be a right to privacy clause if there's not one there?" the professor questioned.

"I guess he was saying there really wasn't a right to privacy clause per se, but there was still a right to privacy." Randy answered.

"Okay. So he agreed there was a right to privacy?"

"Yes."

"Then why didn't he say the right to privacy applied to abortion?" Franklin pressed.

"He didn't think it was the Court's place to overturn what he considered to be a legislative decision."

"But didn't he say that if a legislative body passed a law outlawing abortions necessary to save the life of the mother that the court could properly intervene?"

"Yes, but…"

"But what, Mr. Redd?"

"I…don't know. I'm sorry."

"Don't be sorry. Look it up! What did he say?"

Fumbling through the pages of his book, Randy finally found it.

"Okay. Here it is. He said, 'If the Texas statute were to prohibit an abortion even where the mother's life is in jeopardy, I have little doubt that such a statute would lack a rational relation to a valid state objective under the test stated in Williamson, supra.'"

"Second-graders can read, Mr. Redd, but what does it *mean*?"

"It means that there *are* times when a statute outlawing abortion could be unconstitutional," Randy replied.

"And when would that be?" Franklin asked, tapping his pen on the lectern.

Randy was unsure, but he still answered confidently: "If it lacks a rational relation to a valid state objective."

"And what's the state objective?" Franklin asked. "In simple terms, please."

"I guess not forcing a woman to carry on a pregnancy that might kill her."

"Okay. So what did Justice Rehnquist say about a statute that would outlaw abortions in the first trimester?" the professor continued.

"He didn't say."

"Sure he did! *Think*, Mr. Redd."

"I guess he said that a statute outlawing a first-trimester abortion *would* have a rational relation to a valid state objective."

"Is that what he was saying?" Franklin asked. "Read on."

"Well, let me see…here it is: 'But the Court's sweeping invalidation of any restrictions on abortion during the first trimester is impossible to justify under that standard, and the conscious weighing of competing factors that the Court's opinion apparently substitutes for the established test is far more appropriate to a legislative judgment than to a judicial one.'"

"So what's he really saying, Mr. Redd? Did he say outlawing first-trimester abortions was a valid state objective?"

"Actually, he didn't say."

"Bingo! So what *did* he say?" Franklin asked strongly.

"That outlawing abortions necessary to save the life of the mother would lack a valid state objective, but it's not so clear with first-trimester abortions. In those cases, it's best to leave it up to the legislative branch."

"Yes! That's what he was saying," Professor Franklin said. He seemed genuinely pleased that Randy had gotten it. "Mr. Redd, nice work; I know this is difficult. I'll see you all back here on Friday."

Walking to Wilbert's store after class, Hilda congratulated Randy on his performance. "Professor Franklin doesn't give out many compliments," she said.

"No, he doesn't. My guess is he evens out the score over time, though."

Hilda laughed. "Maybe, but you're off the hot seat for now."

"Hilda, do you really believe a fetus is not life?" Randy asked.

"I don't know, but that's the point. Since we don't know, let women decide!"

"But what if we learn later that it *is* life?"

"You mean like when we're standing before God," she said, smiling. Hilda was not a very religious person. She believed in a Supreme Being of some sort, but was pretty ambivalent about religion. Randy, on the other hand, was deeply spiritual and believed his faith required him to point out where he thought Hilda was wrong.

"Yeah, something like that," Randy responded. "What if it turns out that God views abortion as murder?"

Hilda was a taken aback by the question, but she liked Randy. She could see that he wasn't being judgmental.

"I guess it would be considered a sin and treated accordingly. If a woman who had received an abortion was repentant, my guess is God would forgive her. If she weren't, she'd be held accountable, like with other sins. But Randy, aren't children entitled to be wanted? How many abortions have occurred since Roe v. Wade, 40 million? What if 40 million babies who were not wanted had been brought into the world? What would that be like?"

"If abortion were not legal, many of those pregnancies wouldn't have occurred; I'm convinced of that," Randy answered. "I think a lot of people are casual with sex because they know there's a way out of an unwanted pregnancy."

"That's probably true," Hilda said. "But you still haven't answered my question. Aren't babies entitled to be wanted?"

"As opposed to what, being murdered? I'm sure they'd rather be wanted, but if the choice was not being wanted or not being here, well, the answer seems obvious to me. And what about adoption? There is a waiting list for parents wanting to adopt," he said.

"Maybe for blonde-haired, blue-eyed white kids, but not for minority babies," Hilda came back fast, obviously with strong feelings. "Randy, I respect your point of view, but I don't think any of us know how we'd react if faced with an unwanted pregnancy. It's one of those things that, until confronted with it, we just don't know what we'd do."

"I know what I'd do," Randy replied. "To me, having an abortion would be no different than killing someone who was walking around. It's murder in both cases."

Hilda tried to understand, but she couldn't. "The two seem qualitatively different to me, but we just don't know. And that's exactly why I think it should be the mother's choice: we just don't know."

On Friday morning, Hilda and Randy were visiting before class. They both thought they'd be off the hook and not called on since they had been the ones getting the grilling in the prior classes, but they didn't know Professor Franklin very well. He walked into the class, arranged some papers on the lectern, and jumped right in.

"Wednesday we were discussing Justice Rehnquist's dissenting opinion. He said there would be a valid state objective in not forcing a woman to continue with a pregnancy if it might kill her. Let's stay with that. What did he state as the basis for such a decision, Ms. Summers?"

Hilda's heart sank as she realized she was going to be the focus of Franklin's questions. But she had studied hard, and was ready. "The Due Process Clause of the Fourteenth Amendment."

"What does the Due Process Clause say?" the professor asked.

"No State shall make or enforce any law which shall abridge the privileges and immunities of citizens of the United States; nor shall any State deprive any person of life, liberty, or property without due process of law; nor deny to any person within its jurisdiction the equal protection of the laws," she read.

"Ms. Summers, that's how it *reads*! What does it *say*...about abortion?

Hilda felt a knot growing in her belly.

"Actually, Professor, the Due Process Clause doesn't say anything about abortion."

"And wasn't that Justice Rehnquist's point?" Franklin asked pointedly.

Hilda was experiencing that familiar feeling of panic that accompanied her in this class. She knew she disagreed with Justice Rehnquist's conclusion, but she couldn't argue against his legal reasoning.

"Well...I guess it was," she said weakly.

"Was it?" the professor asked. "Analyze it. What was he arguing against?"

"Justice Rehnquist was disagreeing with the majority's ruling that the Due Process Clause of the Fourteenth Amendment gave women a right to have an abortion," Hilda said.

"But we said yesterday that he thought an abortion *should* be allowed for the purpose of saving the life of the mother, Franklin stated. How does that square with his opposition to the Court's ruling?"

"Actually, Professor, that's not what we said he said." Hilda couldn't believe she had corrected Professor Franklin. There was no telling where this might lead.

Professor Franklin looked at Hilda over his glasses with half lenses. "Then what did we say he said, Ms. Summers?"

"That Justice Rehnquist was saying that such a state statute would undoubtedly satisfy a valid state objective," she replied.

"Okay, that *is* what we said," Franklin answered. "You *were* listening." Hilda grinned.

"Furthermore," Professor Franklin continued, "wasn't Justice Rehnquist saying that, because a policy of legalizing first-trimester abortions didn't have a clear rational relation to a valid state objective, it should be left to the legislative branch?"

"Yes!" Hilda shouted triumphantly, prompting laughter in the class. She was smiling big-time now. She understood.

"Let's talk about the privacy right," Professor Franklin said. "Mr. Redd, it's your turn."

Hilda breathed a big sigh of relief and looked at Randy, thinking of his comment about Professor Franklin getting even. Randy told her later that his heart skipped a beat when he heard his name called.

"Mr. Redd, do you recall the case of Griswold v. Connecticut?"[1]

"Yes, sir."

"And what did it hold?"

"It struck down a state law that made it illegal for married couples to buy contraceptives."

"Yes, but why? I want analysis, not conclusions!"

"Well, let me see." Randy was thumbing back through his notebook to find his brief on Griswold. "Okay. Here it is. The Court ruled that some rights were so 'fundamental to the principles of liberty' that the government couldn't restrict them. Even though contraception wasn't mentioned in the Constitution, the Constitution contained a 'penumbra' of other rights, and the general right to privacy was determined to be one of them."

"So the right to privacy was *implied?*" Professor Franklin asked.

"That's what the Court said."

"Does the Constitution contain other rights that aren't mentioned specifically?" Franklin continued.

"According to the Court it does, but I don't agree," Randy answered.

"No?" asked the professor. "How could the Founding Fathers have imagined every conceivable scenario and addressed it in the Constitution?"

"They couldn't," Randy replied. "And that gets back to my basic point, sir – and Justice Rehnquist's: These are matters for the legislative branch, not the judicial branch. The Connecticut state legislature should have changed the law, not the judiciary. It wasn't the place for the U.S. Supreme Court to declare it unconstitutional."

"I see. And if the State Legislature won't act, Mr. Redd?"

"If the pressure builds high enough, they'll change it," Randy retorted.

"Very well," Franklin said. "That's a credible position, but I submit that throughout history a lot of injustice would have occurred in many areas of the law if the people had been forced to wait on the legislative branch for change, but that's a topic for another day. Let's get back to Roe v. Wade. What did the Court do with the 'right to privacy' as articulated in Griswold?"

"They used it," Randy said angrily.

"Why are you so angry, Mr. Redd. Isn't that what courts are supposed to do, use precedent?"

"I guess so," Randy responded, a little embarrassed.

"So what was so reprehensible about what the Court did here?" Franklin asked. "Why is it such a big deal to you?"

"Who cares if married couples buy contraceptives!" Randy blurted out. "But in Roe, the Court used the right to privacy to allow innocent babies to be killed!"

"I like your passion, Mr. Redd. It'll make you a good trial lawyer someday, but let's stay focused on the analysis. What did Justice Blackmun say about the right to privacy?"

"He cited Griswold and a number of other cases and said a right to privacy existed under the Constitution," Randy answered.

"*Under* the Constitution. I wonder why he didn't use the word 'in' the Constitution?" Franklin asked.

"Because it's not *in* the Constitution!" Randy exclaimed.

"Fair enough," Professor Franklin said, smiling. "But was the right to privacy, as enunciated in Griswold, enough?"

"I don't know, but I doubt it. Justice White saw a difference between the privacy of contraception and the privacy of abortion, so I'd say it wasn't enough."

"Good guess, Mr. Redd, but what else was required? There had to be another argument to receive the support of a majority on the Court. What was it?"

There was a long silence.

"I'm at a complete loss, Professor," Randy said, shifting uneasily in his seat.

"Think about Justice Rehnquist's arguments. A dissenting opinion takes issue with the majority's ruling, so the same points are discussed. Where did he say the majority erred?"

"With…a…liberty interest?" Randy answered shyly.

"Exactly! And what did Justice Blackmun say about a 'liberty' interest?"

"Honestly, Professor, I don't know."

"Yes you do. Where does the liberty interest come from?"

"The Fourteenth Amendment," Randy said.

"Right. And where is the liberty interest specifically found?"

"The Due Process Clause."

"Good. So do the analysis." Franklin was encouraging Randy now.

"Well," Randy said tentatively, "all the justices agreed that the Due Process Clause of the Fourteenth Amendment made the fundamental protections of the Bill of Rights applicable to the states."

"You mean, that wasn't always the case?" the professor asked.

"No. The Bill of Rights was a restriction on the *federal* government, not the states. Then the Fourteenth Amendment came along, and the Court slowly made the rights that were 'essential to liberty' applicable to the states."

"Good," replied Franklin. "And what did Justice Rehnquist say in Roe v. Wade about a 'liberty' interest?"

"He said a law that would prohibit an abortion to save the life of the mother would violate her liberty interest."

"Okay, what else?"

"He said that the liberty interest of the Fourteenth Amendment wasn't inviolate, only that liberty couldn't be denied without due process of law."

"That's right," Franklin said. "Now finish the circle. What was the test according to Justice Rehnquist? How would the Court determine if the law denied liberty without due process of law?"

Randy was really unsure of himself now, but remembering something from the previous class, answered, "If it has a rational relation to a valid state objective?"

"Very good, Mr. Redd! So wasn't Justice Rehnquist saying that a statute allowing an abortion to save the life of the mother would *not* deny due process of law because it would have a rational relation to a valid state objective?"

"That's right!" Randy said with astonishment. He was seeing how the justices came to their conclusions.

"Let's get back to the Bill of Rights," Professor Franklin said. "We are closing in on the Court's decision. I know this is tough sledding, but stay with it a little longer. Was there anything in the Bill of Rights having to do with abortion?"

"No, and that was Justice Blackmun's dilemma," Randy answered. "Everyone agreed there was a general right to privacy, but making it apply to abortion was the challenge."

"So how did he do it?" Franklin asked.

Fumbling through the pages, Randy found a relevant paragraph. He read it to himself quickly.

"Mr. Redd, are you still with us?"

"Yes, sir. I am. One thing he said were there were rights 'implicit in the scheme of ordered liberty.'"

"There's that word 'implicit' again," Franklin said. "So these rights aren't mentioned specifically?"

"No, sir. They're not."

"So what was Justice Blackmun saying? Do the analysis!" Professor Franklin implored.

"I guess he was saying the Due Process Clause created rights implicit with the liberty interest that went beyond those found just in the Bill of Rights."

"Like what?" the professor asked loudly.

"Like...abortion?"

"Precisely! Congratulations, Mr. Redd, you've just broken the code. But there's more. What was the liberty interest Justice Blackmun was speaking of?"

Randy thought he was off the hook, but apparently not.

"I guess it had something to do with having a baby," Randy replied.

"Apparently you've never had one!" a female classmate said not too quietly. Many laughed.

"Actually, that remark might be more on point than you think," Professor Franklin said. "Keep going, Mr. Redd. What did Justice Blackmun say about that?"

"He talked about the 'unwanted child' causing the woman psychological stress, and imposing family responsibilities and economic hardships."

"Do those things impair liberty?"

"Yes, I suppose they do. But if you play, you have to pay," Randy said, trying to be funny, but not many people laughed at that one.

"What about all the 'rational relation to a valid state interest' stuff that Justice Rehnquist spoke of," Franklin asked. "How did Justice Blackmun deal with that?"

"There was a lot of discussion about trimesters. Is that what you mean?"

"*I* ask the questions, Mr. Redd." The class *did* laugh at that.

"But now that you've brought it up, let's talk about trimesters," Professor Franklin said. "Why did Justice Blackmun place such emphasis on them?"

"He made some convoluted point about the mortality of abortion in the first trimester being less than the mortality of normal childbirth."

"And what was the point he was making with that statement?"

"He said everything about abortion during the first trimester was between the woman and her doctor."

"And what happened at the end of the first trimester, legally speaking?" Franklin inquired. "What was so special about the end of the first trimester?"

"At that point, he said the State's interest became 'compelling.'"

"And what's the magic of the State's interest becoming 'compelling?'" Franklin asked.

"The State could regulate aspects of the abortion procedure like the qualifications of the doctor and the facilities where the abortions could be performed."

"Good. And by the way, Mr. Redd, what was the State's interest the Court was trying to protect?"

"I didn't see any state interest involved," Randy answered honestly.

"You're thinking too narrowly," Franklin responded. "Don't think of the State as a state. Isn't the State also its people? Doesn't the State have an interest in protecting its people?"

"I...guess so."

"Of course it does. So what – or who – was the Court saying the State had an interest in protecting?" Franklin asked again.

"Women?" Randy guessed.

"Yes! Women!" Franklin said loudly. "And what about women specifically? It's right there on the printed page. Read it out loud."

"He said, 'With respect to the State's important and legitimate interest in the health of the mother, the 'compelling' point, in light of present medical knowledge, is at approximately the end of the first trimester. This is so because of the now-established medical fact...that until the end of the first trimester mortality in abortion may be less than mortality in normal childbirth. It follows that, from this point, a State may regulate the abortion procedure to the extent that the regulation reasonably relates to the preservation and protection of maternal health.'"

"Yes!" Professor Franklin said. "So it's not until the State's interest becomes 'compelling" that the State may regulate the abortion procedure, and even then only to the extent that the regulation is reasonably related to maternal health. What do you think about this, Mr. Redd."

"I think it's terrible. All the focus is on the woman, but the baby is totally ignored!"

"Is it?" Franklin asked with surprise. "The Court uses the word 'fetus', but fetus or baby, whatever you wish to call it, is it *really* ignored totally?"

"Well, the Court does seem to say that at some point what's growing there has to be taken into consideration," Randy conceded.

"When is that first mentioned?"

"On page 160. Do you want me to read it?"

"Yes. Read it," directed Franklin.

"...The pregnant woman cannot be isolated in her privacy. She carries an embryo and, later, a fetus, if one accepts the medical definitions of the developing young in the human uterus...As we have intimated above, it is reasonable and appropriate for a State to decide that at some point in time another interest, that of health of the mother and that of potential human life, becomes significantly involved. The woman's privacy is no longer sole and any right of privacy she possesses must be measured accordingly."

"Ms. Summers. Have you been following all of this?"

Hilda was jolted from her silent focus on the case. Randy sat back in his chair, glad to be off the hot seat.

"Um, yes. Professor, I have," she replied.

"Good. What does the Court seem to be setting up at this point in the case?"

"What does the Court seem to be setting up?" Hilda asked, not sure of the question.

"Yes. Any good piece of writing builds upon itself. What is the Court doing," Franklin asked again.

"There seems to be a progression of some kind developing," she answered.

"Keep going."

"Well, the Court started with a historical discussion of abortion. Then it got into legal issues like privacy and the Due Process Clause."

"Yes, but those were elements of the decision that were freestanding. What elements were linked yet separate components of the same whole?"

"Trimesters?" Hilda said weakly, almost guessing.

"Yes! Trimesters. Why does the court deal with trimesters? It's obvious."

"Because trimesters are part of the continuum of the pregnancy?"

"Is that a question or a statement, Ms Summers?"

"Both." Again the class chuckled. Even Professor Franklin smiled.

"From conception to birth, pregnancy is certainly a continuum," Professor said, "but how's the Court reacting to what's growing in the uterus?"

"The Court is shifting," Hilda answered.

"What's shifting?"

"The emotion to what's growing there."

"The stodgy Supreme Court justices are showing emotion?" Franklin wondered.

"It's not emotion really, but they're showing greater sensitivity to what's growing in the uterus the longer the pregnancy goes on," Hilda replied.

"So you would disagree with Mr. Redd when he says the Court is ignoring the fetus – or baby – as he calls it?"

Hilda looked at her friend. "I don't think the Court is *ignoring* the fetus, but it does give priority to it later in the pregnancy than Mr. Redd would."

"Priority. That's an interesting choice of words, Ms. Summers. What is a reason for why one would give a higher priority to something?"

"I don't understand," she replied.

"If you give one thing a higher priority than another, you could be said to have a greater 'what' in it?"

"Interest?" Hilda guessed.

"Very good! So the Court's interest in the fetus is shifting?" Franklin asked.

"Yes!" Hilda was feeling very proud of herself. She was sure she had gotten it correct.

"And you *were* doing so well, Ms. Summers," Professor Franklin said disappointingly. Hilda felt like she'd been sucker punched.

"The Court doesn't speak of its *own* interest in cases, does it?" Franklin asked. "In this case, whose interest is the Court speaking of?"

Hilda fumbled through the pages of the case, and looked at her notes.

"We've spoken of it already, Ms. Summers."

Hilda could think of only one thing. "The State's interest," she said without any confidence.

"Of course! The State's interest! And the State's interest is in what?" the professor asked.

She found it now. "Potential human life!"

"Yes! Potential human life. And when does the Court say the State's interest in potential human life is paramount?"

"Viability!" Hilda was ripping along now.

"And what happens to the State's interest at fetus viability?" Franklin asked.

"It becomes 'compelling.'"

"Right! It becomes 'compelling.' And once it becomes 'compelling,' what is the State allowed to do?"

"Outlaw abortion," Hilda said confidently.

"Yes. But did the Court say the State could outlaw abortion subsequent to viability in all cases?"

"No. Not when an abortion was necessary to preserve the life or health of the mother," Hilda responded.

"So, outline the finding in Roe v. Wade, and tell the legal reasons why the Court found as it did," Professor Franklin said.

Hilda cleared her throat, and began. "Okay, I'll try. The Court ruled that a woman may receive an abortion because she has a privacy right via her liberty interest under the Constitution, and for the State to outlaw abortion except for the purpose of saving the woman's life would violate the Due Process Clause of the Fourteenth Amendment. From conception to approximately the end of the first trimester, the abortion decision is between the woman and her doctor. At approximately the end of the first trimester, the State's interest in preserving the health of the mother becomes 'compelling', and, as such, the abortion procedure may be reasonably regulated as to matters such as ensuring that doctors are qualified and facilities are adequate. After viability, the State's interest in potential life becomes 'compelling', and an abortion is legal only to preserve the life or health of the mother."

Hilda held her breath. Several moments passed. After what seemed like an eternity to her, Professor Franklin finally said, "And that, class, was the ruling in Roe V. Wade. Ms. Summers and Mr. Redd, you did very well these last three classes. Congratulations. This was extremely difficult material. I will see you all on Monday when we'll begin a new topic."

"Those were some days, weren't they?" Randy asked, smiling as he stabbed at his eggs. "Hilda, what's wrong?" Randy said. "Are you okay?"

Hilda had grown silent. Her bottom lip was quivering and tears had welled in her eyes. She couldn't talk.

Randy put his hand on her arm. "Tell me what's going on."

Hilda covered her face with her hands, trying to compose herself. The mention of that case, and her thoughts of it, had put her in a different zone emotionally.

Slowly, a terrible story unfolded…

"It was six years ago. I was still with the state attorney prosecuting sex crimes in Broward County.

"I stayed late one night, as I often did, getting ready for a trial that was to start in two days. At 10:15 I called it quits and headed to my car.

"The parking garage was lighted well enough, so I wasn't scared. Still, I was hurrying; it was eerie.

"Using my remote control, I unlocked my car when I was about 20' away. The lights came on inside the car like they always did, but I remember thinking the noise of the locks unlocking wasn't nearly as loud as normal. As it turned out, the doors were already unlocked. I thought little of it, though; I was tired and ready to get home.

"As I put the key into the ignition, I glanced in the rearview mirror. Sitting in the back seat was a man wearing a dark sweatshirt, the hood pulled over his head. He was wearing narrow sunglasses.

"I spun around, but his strong hands were around my neck in a split second. He was so powerful he dragged me over the front seat. I managed to push the car horn with one foot as I was being pulled to the back. I could only hope it had been heard and someone would come.

"He was on top of me in a flash, squeezing my throat with one hand and tearing my clothes off with the other. I had no air. I couldn't scream. I was kicking but had no strength.

"He raped me. The next thing I remember was a flashlight shining into the car. The security guard had heard the horn. He saw a guy running away.

"Three weeks later I missed my period. I was pregnant."

"Hilda, I...I don't know what to say," Randy replied. "I'm so sorry! What did you do?"

"I did what I always thought I'd do. I got an abortion."

Randy couldn't swallow. He could barely breathe.

"You probably don't remember me telling you this," she said, "but I remember a discussion we had after one of the Con. Law classes on Roe v. Wade. I told you I didn't think anyone knew how he or she would react if faced with this kind of decision. As it turned out, that was wrong, at least for me. There was never any question about it. I was *not* going to have that baby."

Randy's heart was beating hard. He was rubbing his temples, trying to absorb what he was hearing. He was also having difficulty sorting out his own thoughts. "How has it been?" he asked. "Since the abortion, I mean."

Hilda began to again lose her composure. She took a sip of water. It took her several seconds to answer.

"Rarely does a day go by that I don't think of the rape; sometimes I even smell his rancid breath. And once I think of the rape, I think of the abortion."

"Do you regret getting it?" Randy asked.

"No, I don't, but I often wonder if it would have been better to have had the baby, maybe put it up for adoption."

"That may have brought you other problems, like wondering how the baby was doing," Randy said, surprised that he would say something that sounded supportive of her decision.

"I know," Hilda said. "I've thought of that. Still, it's pretty bad how it is; very bad, actually. I don't know. Maybe I do regret it."

Randy was quiet, deep in thought. Abortion had always been something he had been able to discuss academically, but this was real, and he was not nearly as confident in his position as he had been when the issue was an abstract hypothetical. Was this murder? He certainly didn't think of Hilda as a murderer, but what she had aborted was life, he was sure of it. Suddenly, though, he didn't feel qualified to tell her he thought she had made a bad choice.

"Choice," he thought. "That word sums up an entire position on the most volatile issue of our day. But what was it really a choice between?"

[1]Griswold v. Connecticut, 381 U.S. 479 (1965)

Century Tower
Gainesville, Florida

Author's Note:

Even though I supported choice during my days in the Legislature, at least in the early stages of pregnancy and under limited circumstances thereafter, I sympathized with those who disagreed with the existing policy and how frustrated they must have felt with five non-elected Supreme Court justices deciding the question. Unable to recruit candidates and change policy by resorting to the ballot box, as we are taught in ninth grade Civics as the way to effect change, their frustration builds.

Roe v. Wade placed much of abortion policy off limits to legislators. However, there were a number of instances during my time in the Legislature when we dealt with various aspects of the abortion issue.

In the late 1980s, when I was in the Florida House of Representatives, the United States Supreme Court issued a ruling that allowed the states to get back into the abortion debate after a long absence. It was within the context of whether the parents of a minor seeking an abortion had to give their consent to the procedure. Suddenly, the abortion issue was one that legislators had to deal with, and the Health Care Committee was the committee that would be the committee of reference for any abortion-related bill. I was the vice-chairman of that committee. I remember my father and me talking about how my job as a legislator had just become less fun.

In the wake of the Supreme Court decision, Governor Bob Martinez called a special session to deal with this issue. The discussion wasn't limited to just parental consent, however. One thing led to another, and before we knew it, we were having hearings on the full range of abortion-related issues and the abortion procedure itself.

Advocates from both sides swooped into Tallahassee by the thousands. For security reasons, we held our committee meetings in the House Chamber because bulletproof glass separated the gallery from the legislators and those who were testifying. Guards escorted us through the hallways and our staffs were instructed on how to handle suspicious looking mail and packages. It was quite a time, but it pointed out how strongly people felt about the issue.

The testimony during these meetings was quite compelling. We heard from doctors who performed abortions and women who had received abortions. Clergy spoke on theological matters related to abortion and on issues like when a person received his or her soul. Legal scholars testified, as did *representatives from advocacy groups. Even those who might have disagreed with the ultimate outcome of our deliberations must admit that we did not duck the issue.*

Before these meetings, I was invited to attend a gathering in a constituent's house to discuss my views. I knew those in attendance would not share my position and that it would be an uncomfortable time. Yet, how could I not go? They were entitled to their meeting and it was my obligation to tell them my beliefs and receive their input.

The only other member of our county's legislative delegation who was there was Representative Charles Canady. As one who shared their position right down the line, Charles was a hero to this group. That left me in the hot seat, and hot it was. The house was packed. Charles and I had to stand halfway up the stairs so we could be seen and heard. I spoke honestly and directly; they had a right to hear my views. It was a long night.

Years later, when I was in the Senate, there were other issues on abortion. One proposal would have imposed a waiting period before a woman could receive an abortion after first visiting an abortion clinic. I don't recall the details, but I believe the proposal required that a woman seeking an abortion be given materials explaining the abortion procedure and its risks, and the stage of fetus development. A period of time – perhaps 24 hours after receiving the materials – would have to pass before she could receive the procedure. Advocates for the bill claimed that women often received an abortion without being fully informed of the procedure and its ramifications, and without time for consideration of this information before having it. I had a hard time believing this, so I made arrangements to visit an abortion clinic. I looked at the materials given, watched the film on the abortion procedure that women were shown beforehand, and walked through the process from start to finish. I spoke with personnel at the clinic and learned what I could about what was involved in having an abortion. I became satisfied that women were given enough information to make an informed decision and voted against the bill.

Minutes later we considered a bill that would have abolished "partial birth abortion." From my study I had concluded that this was an especially abhorrent procedure – perhaps even borderline infanticide – so I voted to outlaw it.

I've always tried to stay open on issues, including abortion, but it poses an age-old question of legislators: Should they vote the majority view of their constituents or what they believe is correct? I always felt that on "moral" matters or matters of philosophy I had a special obligation to vote my personal convictions because my constituents were entitled to know my morals or philosophies, and that was best evidenced by how I voted. On run-of-the-mill matters I was more likely to cast my vote as I determined the majority view in the district. Tempering this always, though, was the fact that legislators were exposed to more information on issues than voters because they attended committee hearings and meetings. I would always ask myself, "If my constituents knew this, what would their position be?" It's important to remember, however, that state legislators represent the entire state and members of Congress represent the entire nation. They don't represent just their own districts. Finding the right balance between a state or national perspective, and a parochial district perspective, is sometimes difficult.

THE LAW: *Definitions and Explanations:*

Excerpts from Roe v. Wade, 410 U.S. 113 (1973), the United States Supreme Court case that created a limited constitutional right to an abortion via the Due Process Clause of the Fourteenth Amendment. Justice Blackmun, writing for the majority:

"...We forthwith acknowledge our awareness of the sensitive and emotional nature of the abortion controversy, of the vigorous opposing views, even among physicians, and of the deep and seemingly absolute convictions that the subject inspires. One's philosophy, one's experiences, one's exposure to the raw edges of human existence, one's religious training, one's attitudes toward life and family and their values, and the moral standards one establishes and seeks to observe, are all likely to influence and to color one's thinking and conclusions about abortion.

"Our task, of course, is to resolve the issue by constitutional measurement, free of emotion and predilection...We bear in mind, too, Mr. Justice Holmes' admonition in his now-vindicated dissent in Lochner v. New York, 198 U.S. 45, 76 (1905): 'The Constitution is made for people of fundamentally differing views, and the accident of our finding certain opinions natural and familiar or novel and even shocking ought not to conclude our judgment upon the question whether statutes embodying them conflict with the Constitution of the United States.'" (supra, 116, 117)

"The Constitution does not define 'person' in so many words...But in nearly all of these instances, the use of the word is such that it has application only postnatally. None indicates, with any assurance, that it has any possible pre-natal application...All this, together with our observation, supra, that throughout the major portion of the 19th century prevailing legal abortion practices were far freer than they are today, persuades us that the word 'person,' as used in the Fourteenth Amendment, does not include the unborn. (supra, 157, 158)

"...The pregnant woman cannot be isolated in her privacy. She carries an embryo and, later, a fetus, if one accepts the medical definitions of the developing young in the human uterus. See Dorland's Illustrated Medical Dictionary 478-479, 547 (24th ed. 1965)...As we have intimated above, it is reasonable and appropriate for a State to decide that at some point in time another interest, that of health of the mother and that of potential human life, becomes significantly involved. The woman's privacy is no longer sole and any right of privacy she possesses must be measured accordingly.

"...We need not resolve the difficult question of when life begins. When those trained in the respective disciplines of medicine, philosophy, and theology are unable to arrive at any concensus, the judiciary, at this point in the development of man's knowledge, is not in a position to speculate as to the answer." (supra, 160)

"...In view of all this, we do not agree that, by adopting one theory of life, Texas may override the rights of pregnant women that are at stake. We repeat, however, that the State does have an important and legitimate interest in preserving and protecting the health of the pregnant woman...and that it has still another important and legitimate interest in protecting the potentiality of human life. These interests are separate and distinct. Each grows in substantiality as the woman approaches term and, at a point during pregnancy, each becomes 'compelling.'

With respect to the State's important and legitimate interest in the health of the mother, the 'compelling' point, in light of present medical knowledge, is at approximately the end of the first trimester. This is so because of the now-established medical fact...that until the end of the first trimester mortality in abortion may be less than mortality in normal childbirth. It follows that, from this point, a State may regulate the abortion procedure to the extent that the regulation reasonably relates to the preservation and protection of maternal health.

"With respect to the State's important and legitimate interest in potential life, the 'compelling' point is at viability. This is so because the fetus then has the capability of meaningful life outside the mother's womb. State regulation protective of fetal life after viability thus has both logical and biological justifications. If the State is interested in protecting fetal life after viability, it may go so far as to proscribe abortion during that period, except when it is necessary to preserve the life or health of the mother.

"Measured against these standards, Art. 1196 of the Texas Penal Code, in restricting legal abortions to those 'procured or attempted by medical advice for the purpose of saving the life of the mother,' sweeps too broadly. The statute makes no distinction between abortions performed early in pregnancy and those performed later, and it limits to a single reason, 'saving' the mother's life, the legal justification for the procedure. The statute, therefore, cannot survive the constitutional attack made upon it here.

"To summarize and to repeat:

A state criminal abortion statute of the current Texas type, that excepts from criminality only a life-saving procedure on behalf of the mother, without regard to pregnancy stage and without recognition of the other interests involved, is violative of the Due Process Clause of the Fourteenth Amendment.

For the stage prior to approximately the end of the first trimester, the abortion decision and its effectuation must be left to the medical judgment of the pregnant woman's attending physician.

For the stage subsequent to approximately the end of the first trimester, the State, in promoting its interest in the health of the mother, may, if it chooses, regulate the abortion procedure in ways that are reasonably related to maternal health.

For the stage subsequent to viability, the State in promoting its interest in the potentiality of human life may, if it chooses, regulate, and even proscribe, abortion except where it is necessary, in appropriate medical judgment, for the preservation of the life or health of the mother. (supra, 163, 164, 165)

Selected excerpts from Justice Rehnquist, in a dissenting opinion in Roe v. Wade:

"...I have difficulty in concluding, as the Court does, that the right of 'privacy' is involved in this case. Texas, by the statute here challenged, bars the *performance of a medical abortion by a licensed physician on a plaintiff such as Roe. A transaction resulting in an operation such as this is not 'private' in the ordinary usage of the word. Nor is the 'privacy' that the Court finds here even a distant relative of the freedom from searches and seizures protected by the Fourth Amendment to the Constitution, which the Court has referred to as embodying a right to privacy. Katz v. United States, 389 U.S. 347 (1967).*

"...I agree with the statement of Justice Stewart in his concurring opinion that the 'liberty,' against deprivation of which without due process the Fourteenth (41 U.S. 113, 173) Amendment protects, embraces more than the rights found in the Bill of Rights. But that liberty is not guaranteed absolutely against deprivation, only against deprivation without due process of law. The test traditionally applied in the area of social and economic legislation is whether or not a law such as that challenged has a rational relation to a valid state objective. Williamson v. Lee Optical Co., 348 U.S. 483, 491 (1955). The Due Process Clause of the Fourteenth Amendment undoubtedly does place a limit, albeit a broad one, on legislative power to enact laws such as this. If the Texas statute were to prohibit an abortion even where the mother's life is in jeopardy, I have little doubt that such a statute would lack a rational relation to a valid state objective under the test stated in Williamson, supra. But the Court's sweeping invalidation of any restrictions on abortion during the first trimester is impossible to justify under that standard, and the conscious weighing of competing factors that the Court's opinion apparently substitutes for the established test is far more appropriate to a legislative judgment than to a judicial one. (supra, 172, 173)

"...The decision here to break pregnancy into three distinct terms and to outline the permissible restrictions the State may impose in each one, for example, partakes more of judicial legislation than it does of a determination of the intent of the drafters of the Fourteenth Amendment.

Notable Quotes:

"America needs no words from me to see how your decision in Roe v. Wade has deformed a great nation. The so-called right to abortion has pitted mothers against their children and women against men. It has sown violence and discord at the heart of the most intimate human relationship. It has aggravated the derogation of the father's role in an increasingly fatherless

society. It has portrayed the greatest of all gifts – a child – as a competitor, an intrusion and an inconvenience..."

Mother Theresa of Calcutta, in an amicus curiae brief
filed in the case of Alexander Loce v. The State of New Jersey,
U.S. 93-1149 (October Term, 1993)

"Morality is not merely different in different communities. Its level is not the same for all the component groups within the same community."

Honorable Benjamin N. Cardozo, Associate Justice,
United States Supreme Court
"Paradoxes of Legal Science," by Benjamin N. Cardozo, published in 1970

"I believe the Court has no power to add to or subtract from the procedures set forth by the founders...I shall not at any time surrender my belief that the document itself should be our guide, not our own concept of what is fair, decent, and right."

Honorable Hugo L. Black, Associate Justice,
United States Supreme Court
"The Supreme Court and its Great Justices," by Sidney H. Asch, 1971,
as attributed in "Quotes From Supreme Court Justices,"
home.att.net/~midnightflyer/supreme.html

[Justices do not have the right to declare] "*a law unconstitutional simply because they consider a law unwise." [The court] "is not to decide whether the view taken by the legislature is a wise view, but whether a body of men could reasonably hold such a view."*

Honorable Louis D. Brandeis, Associate Justice,
United States Supreme Court
"The Supreme Court and its Great Justices," by Sidney H. Asch, 1971,
as attributed in home.att.net/~midnightflyer/supreme.html

"We do not sit as a superlegislature to weigh the wisdom of legislation."

Honorable William O. Douglas, Associate Justice,
United States Supreme Court
www.brainyquotes.com

"Tact, respect, and generosity toward variant views will always commend themselves to those charged with the duties of legislation so as to achieve a maximum of goodwill and to require a minimum of unwilling submission to a general law. But the real question is, who is to make such accommodations, the courts or the legislature?"

Honorable Felix Frankfurter, Associate Justice,
United States Supreme Court, dissenting in West Virginia
State Board of Education v. Barnette, 319 U.S. 624, 651 (1943)

"A word is not a crystal, transparent and unchanging. It is the skin of a living thought and may vary greatly in colour [sic] and content according to the circumstances and time in which it is used."

Honorable Oliver Wendell Holmes, Jr., Associate Justice,
United States Supreme Court
www.brainyquotes.com

"It is the part of wisdom, particularly for judges, not to be victimized by words."

Honorable Felix Frankfurter, Associate Justice,
United States Supreme Court,
dissenting in Shapiro v. United States, 335 U.S. 1, 56 (1948)

"Americans revere both the Constitution and an independent Court that applies the document's provisions. The Court has done many excellent things in our history, and few people are willing to see its power broken. The difficulty with all proposals to respond to the Court when it behaves unconstitutionally is that they would create a power to destroy the Court's essential work as well."

Judge Robert Bork / www.brainyquotes.com

"If the performance of the Court changes, it is to be hoped that liberal revisionism will not be replaced by conservative revisionism. The two are equally illegitimate. The Constitution is too important to our national well being and to our liberties to be made into a political weapon. Departure from its actual principles, whether in Dred Scott, Lochner, or Roe, is inconsistent with the maintenance of constitutional democracy."

Judge Robert Bork / www.brainyquotes.com

"The notion that Congress can change the meaning given a constitutional provision by the Court is subversive of the function of judicial review; and it is not the less so because the Court promises to allow it only when the Constitution is moved to the left."

Judge Robert Bork / www.brainyquotes.com

"I don't think the Constitution is studied almost anywhere, including law schools. In law schools, what they study is what the Court said about the Constitution. They study the opinions. They don't study the Constitution itself."

Judge Robert Bork / www.brainyquotes.com

"In a constitutional democracy the moral content of law must be given by the morality of the framer or legislator, never by the morality of a judge."

Judge Robert Bork / www.brainyquotes.com

"The Constitution is not an organism, it is a legal document."

Honorable Antonin Scalia, Associate Justice,
United States Supreme Court
Milwaukee Journal Sentinel, March 13, 2001

"If you think aficionados of a living Constitution want to bring you flexibility, think again. You think the death penalty is a good idea? Persuade your fellow citizens to adopt it. You want a right to abortion? Persuade your fellow citizens and enact it. That's flexibility."

Honorable Antonin Scalia, Associate Justice,
United States Supreme Court
www.brainyquotes.com

"The Framers of the Bill of Rights did not purport to 'create' rights. Rather, they designed the Bill of Rights to prohibit our Government from infringing rights and liberties presumed to be preexisting."

Honorable William J. Brennan, Jr., Associate Justice,
United States Supreme Court
www.brainyquotes.com

"As a member of this court I am not justified in writing my private notions of policy into the Constitution, no matter how deeply I may cherish them or how mischievous I may deem their disregard."

Honorable Felix Frankfurter, Associate Justice,
United States Supreme Court
www.brainyquotes.com

"Our Constitution was not written in the sands to be washed away by each wave of new judges blown in by each successive political wind."

Honorable Hugo Black, Associate Justice,
United States Supreme Court
www.brainyquotes.com

"We current justices read the Constitution in the only way that we can: as 20th century Americans."

Honorable William J. Brennan, Jr., Associate Justice,
United States Supreme Court
www.brainyquotes.com

"We look to the history of the time of framing and to the intervening history of interpretation. But the ultimate question must be, what do the words of the text mean in our time."

Honorable William J. Brennan, Jr., Associate Justice,
United States Supreme Court
www.brainyquotes.com

"Who is to say that five men ten years ago were right whereas five men looking the other direction today are wrong?"

Honorable Harry A. Blackmun / www.brainyquotes.com

Destination Destin

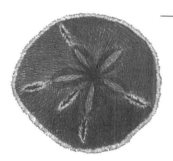

CAREFUL WHAT YOU SAY
Defamation: Libel and Slander

Preface: Free speech is fundamental to our democracy and American way of life. Consequently, just because a statement about someone is false doesn't make it defamatory. For the tort of defamation to occur, a false statement must also be communicated to a third person and injury must result. If the false statement was made about a public figure, however, recovery in a defamation action requires that the false statement be made with "malice," a concept we'll learn about in the pages that follow.

This tale also touches on whether a reporter can protect the identity of a confidential news source. The United States Supreme Court spoke to this in 1972 in the case of Branzburg v. Hayes, 408 U.S. 665 (1972). Florida later passed a "shield law," as have 48 other states, which outlines the parameters within which the identity of sources may be protected.

LUCY MYERS was beside herself, so angry she was shaking. In her hands was a newspaper story that quoted an unnamed source: "Myers is known to sleep around, and once even had a girlfriend, if you know what I mean." This story, on top of everything else she had been going through, would cause big trouble for her. She'd be lucky if she were able to hold on to her job as principal of Blue Springs High School in Marianna, Florida. She loved her students and was distraught over what they would believe about her personally, and how that might affect her ability to be their principal even if she were able to keep her job.

Lucy was born in Chipley, Florida. Her father was a Methodist minister, and her mother an elementary school teacher. She had two younger brothers, one a football star at Florida State University, and another who was in residency at the University of Miami Medical School.

Lucy was always driven to succeed in whatever she attempted. In sports, even though she didn't have great natural ability, she practiced hard enough at tennis to earn a scholarship to Florida State University and played Number One her last two years there. She then went to a tennis camp for aspiring tennis professionals in Sarasota, Florida. But, after a year of punishing practice and training, she realized she didn't have the talent to compete with the top players on the professional circuit.

While in Sarasota, she met a special man, Ben Fuller, and fell madly in love. She followed him back to Tallahassee when he started law school at FSU, but their romance cooled by the time he graduated. Unsure of what to do next, she returned to her hometown of Chipley and took a job as a physical education and history teacher at Chipley High School, and soon discovered that she *loved* teaching. Nothing gave her more satisfaction than working with students who had little self-confidence and getting them to "switch on" to learning. Once a desire to learn was established, it was easy for students to set goals and begin to believe they could actually achieve something worthwhile in life. Being a part of this wonderful education process was what Lucy came to enjoy the most.

She was equally fascinated with how an entire school responded to leadership from the top. If the principal was tired and satisfied with the status quo, the teachers tended to be lethargic and rarely strayed from whatever teaching methods they had learned when they first began teaching. On the other hand, if the principal was full of energy and encouraged the teachers to experiment with different teaching methods, the teachers carried that enthusiasm to the classroom and tried new teaching techniques. Lucy's goal became to be a principal of a school and lead it to greatness. This led to her eventual certification as an administrator, and, after teaching for seven years, she left the classroom for a job as an assistant principal at a high school in a neighboring county. Again she excelled, and in four years, at the young age of 35, became the principal of Blue Springs High School.

Lucy hit the ground running, a dynamo full of energy and youthful enthusiasm. She encouraged her teachers to attend seminars to improve their teaching skills and gave the School Advisory Council, a committee comprised of parents with children attending Blue Springs, real authority to share in the decisions of where school funds were spent. She expected her teachers to experiment with new teaching methods and was a firm believer in Mark Twain's quote: "The only thing that spoon-feeding teaches is the shape of the spoon." Teachers were told to give students their home telephone numbers and be willing to meet with them after school if they needed additional help. Lucy also wanted them to attend extracurricular activities. Her goal was to build the most progressive school in North Florida and to develop an ethos of hard work and commitment to learning that was second to none.

Most teachers, mainly the new teachers and those approaching retirement, bought into the program. They found it exciting and challenging, and liked the idea of being part of something unique and special. There were others though, usually teachers in the middle of their careers, who resented her methods. They were set in their ways, teaching on "auto-pilot," using the same lesson plans and tests they had used on their first day of teaching. Actually, they resented her early success and found it hard to take guidance from someone so young. These teachers grumbled in the lunchroom and in faculty meetings, badmouthing her efforts where and when they could. Lucy wouldn't tolerate this negativity for long, but assumed they would "get with it" sooner or later. She wanted to give them ample opportunity to become a positive force in the school.

One teacher in particular, Luther Flood, was unusually obstinate. Long before Lucy appeared on the scene, he was constantly complaining about teacher pay and quality of life issues. He had a point, certainly, but would rather grouse about it than take positive steps to bring about change. His negative energy brought people down, and his demeanor was reflected in the classroom. He didn't particularly enjoy teaching but wouldn't move on to try something else. Instead, he had been a marginal teacher for 17 years, too long in the system to leave, but still so many years before retirement that his lackadaisical ways would deprive countless students of the good education they deserved. He was mired in self-pity, upset about his low pay and resentful of those who were daring to excel in the classroom.

When Lucy Myers began prodding her teachers to stretch and take chances, it hit Luther the wrong way. He was at the point in his career where he wished to essentially "run out the clock," and the last thing he wanted to do was attend a class on Saturday to learn new teaching methods. Lucy's enthusiasm made him uncomfortable, and when she suggested that he give her approach a try, he took it as a personal affront to his professional experience. "One day she'll get hers," he thought.

The only time Lucy Myers had ever been knocked back on her heels was when her boyfriend, Ben Fuller, the one she had followed to Tallahassee from Sarasota, told her he was leaving her. He was graduating from law school in three months and had accepted a job with a big Atlanta law firm. Lucy had fully expected they would be married and that she would go to Atlanta with him to start their married life together. Instead, Fuller simply announced over dinner one night that he thought they should "go their separate ways." After three years of dating, Lucy thought this was a terrible way to end their relationship. She deserved more. When he had nothing more to say, she threw her glass of water in his face, causing quite a scene in the Tallahassee restaurant.

When Lucy moved back to Chipley, she lived with her parents for a year. She didn't have a single date, not because she didn't get a few offers, but because she knew Ben Fuller would come to his senses and ask her back. Her refusal to accept these dates was a polite "No thank you, but I appreciate your asking."

Lucy's father encouraged her to forget Fuller and move on with her life. Lucy knew her father was right, but it was hard. She had three years invested in her relationship with Ben, and she was hurt deeply. However, when a fellow teacher, Charlotte Manley, offered to lease her a room in her house, Lucy saw a way to slip back into a routine that was more normal for her age, so she took it. Lucy had heard the rumor about Charlotte – that she was a lesbian – but it didn't matter to her. Charlotte was a nice person who saw the opportunity to rent a room to Lucy as something that worked well financially for each of them – nothing more.

She lived with Charlotte for two years before buying her own place. By then, Lucy had begun to date, but never found "Mr. Right." She remained single, much to the chagrin of her boyfriends. Lucy was attractive, smart and energetic, and her suitors were unhappy when she broke up with them. With *these* relationships, though, unlike the one with Ben Fuller, she was the one walking away.

Luther Flood's slow boil against Lucy continued. He wanted her gone, but how? He couldn't publicly attack her style because he suspected most people would agree with her. There were also limits on how personal he could get with his criticism; teachers were allowed to speak out about education issues, but they couldn't cause disruption at their schools. He decided on a strategy of becoming a frequent critic of school policy generally and of School Board members specifically, hoping it would reflect badly on Lucy or cause her problems somehow. His Letters to the Editor in the local newspaper – the Jackson County Herald, known locally simply as the "Herald," – always prompted calls from the school superintendent to Lucy, telling her to quiet Luther. Lucy, in turn, encouraged Luther to work *with* her for change, instead of battering school district authorities in the newspaper. It didn't work. Luther continued his barrage, and Lucy was under increasing pressure to silence him. She tried everything she could think of, but to no avail. Finally, after many polite conversations that were unsuccessful, Lucy made a mistake. She told Luther that if he didn't stop, he would be transferred to another school. Luther saw this as extortion, pure and simple, and was sure the public would see it the same way. He now had the hook he needed to criticize Lucy personally.

"Teacher Threatened for Criticizing School Policy," the headline read in the Herald. Luther had gone to the press. The reporter, Bill Pelosi, was new to the area and saw this story as a way to make a big splash. He quoted Luther extensively, portraying him as a dedicated teacher who was simply trying to improve life for all teachers or prevent the wasting of taxpayer money with his criticism of School Board policy. "In exchange for speaking out, Flood was threatened with transfer to a middle school that was farther from his home," Pelosi wrote in a sentence better suited for the editorial page than a news story. "Not only would he no longer be teaching in a high school, but his work would be 30 miles from his house, 60 miles a day roundtrip."

It was curious that the Herald would run such a one-sided story, or that it would run it at all. In truth, the newspaper was in a fight for its survival. Subscriptions were dropping as more and more people received their news from the Internet or television, and competing newspapers new to the area were adding extra pressure. The publisher, Theodore Stuart, had been given an ultimatum by the paper's parent organization to stem the tide or he would lose his job. Consequently, he told his editors to take chances and if in doubt, "print it!"

The story hit a nerve with the community. It had become almost fashionable to criticize public education, especially by those who hadn't set foot in a school for years. The public was quick to side with Luther. "Of course the schools waste money," was their reaction. "And they have the gall to blister some poor teacher who has the courage to tell the truth? Outrageous!"

The story also quoted Luther on Lucy's approach to teaching: "She calls these methods 'progressive,' but I call them weird," Luther said. "Get back to basics is what I say we should do."

Such simplistic statements appealed to a populace nostalgic for a simpler age like the one when they were growing up. Never mind that today's teachers were forced to be surrogate parents to kids who were totally unprepared for learning because of rotten family situations. Never mind that the classroom lessons students learned in school weren't reinforced at home. Never mind that the popular culture made it more difficult than ever to teach. Still, "get back to basics" was the fashionable solution that many school critics believed was needed.

The newspaper story led to a follow-up article by Pelosi on what was going on at Blue Springs High. Lucy had her defenders, certainly, but the story used words like "exotic" and "liberal" to describe the teaching methods, instead of "innovative" and "progressive." Words like these unnerved many in this conservative area of the Panhandle. Pelosi also made sure to point out that Lucy was 40 years old and unmarried, injecting a salacious and provocative angle to the story. Soon the entire community was having a dialogue on Lucy Myers – her personal life as well as her approach to education.

Luther Flood's habit was to go to the public golf course after school each Friday to have a few beers. This day, he had no sooner taken his first swig when a man sat down next to him and introduced himself.

"My name's Shaw Johnson, and I used to date Lucy Myers. I read your comments about her."

Luther looked up. He wondered if this guy was getting ready to sock him, but intuitively he knew he had hit pay dirt.

"Then have a seat, by all means," Luther said.

"I dated Lucy for eight months. I loved her and wanted to marry her. We traveled together occasionally, but she never stayed over at my place, and I never stayed over at hers. She knew how it would look if the high school principal were caught leaving a man's house early in the morning."

Luther listened, growing more excited by the minute at Shaw Johnson's words, sensing that he was hearing news that could be devastating to Lucy.

"But I loved her," Johnson continued, "and I thought she loved me. But one night she dropped me like a hot rock. Gave me no warning whatsoever; just said she thought it was best for us each to move on. I've since learned there are other guys she's treated like this. It didn't add up, but then I found out she once lived with Charlotte Manley. Then things began to make sense."

Luther knew about Charlotte Manley. She had taught at Blue Springs for a year before transferring to an elementary school. He had heard the rumors about her.

"Are you saying you believe Lucy Myers is gay?" Luther asked.

"I'm not saying that; I'm just wondering it," Shaw answered.

Neither could see the convoluted logic of the suggestion, but each wanted it to be true, even if for different reasons, so they bought into the idea. It provided Shaw with a rationale for being dumped, and Luther with a surefire way to get her replaced as principal. Luther was downright giddy.

"Would you be willing to tell this to a reporter?" Luther asked.

"Not if my name would be in the story. Why can't you tell the reporter?"

"Because you're the one with personal knowledge," Luther responded. "It's just hearsay coming from me."

Shaw scratched his chin and thought for a moment. "Okay, I'll do it. But only if the reporter promises not to use my name."

"I know the perfect guy. I'm sure he will," Luther said. "I'm sure he will."

Bill Pelosi was more than willing to go off the record with Shaw Johnson and speak on "background." The newspaper had just authorized Pelosi to investigate Lucy further, and this was intriguing information.

Shaw Johnson led Pelosi through the series of Lucy's relationships that he was aware of and ended with a discussion of her living with Chalotte Manley. Of course, he had to explain the prevailing thinking about Charlotte's sexual orientation for Pelosi to understand the significance.

The resulting story was so outrageous that it was more appropriate for a tabloid than a serious newspaper, but to Lucy, it didn't matter. The damage was done, and she was in the fight of her life to save not just her job, but also her reputation.

The story was strictly an expose' of her personal life and had nothing to do with her goals as an educator. How Pelosi discovered some of the stuff he reported was a mystery. He mentioned a couple of unpaid parking tickets from her days at FSU, and even told of the incident at the restaurant when she and Ben Fuller broke up and Lucy threw water in his face. As luck would have it, a student reporter for the FSU school newspaper who wrote a weekly gossip column on campus life had witnessed the incident and had written about it. He recognized Lucy from her days on the FSU tennis team. Clearly the most damaging, however, was the discussion of her series of romantic relationships and the two years she had lived with a woman "widely thought to be a lesbian." The newspaper editors were smart enough not to mention Charlotte Manley's name, but for Lucy it didn't matter. Shaw Johnson's quotes, attributed to a "former boyfriend," openly speculated that "Lucy might like gals more than guys." The way the issue was framed, even objective readers couldn't help but wonder.

The story set off a torrent of Letters to the Editor, equally split between those who were outraged at the way the newspaper had treated Lucy, and those who were furious that "a homosexual was allowed to be the principal of a public high school." Teachers who supported Lucy signed a Petition of Support. Those in opposition demanded that the School Board replace her. The community was split down the middle, and sitting back, enjoying it all, was Luther Flood.

"It's just a matter of time, now," he thought.

For her part, Lucy decided to take her fight directly to the people. She spoke at any civic club that would have her, sent letters to the parents of the kids in her school explaining her approach to education, and wrote her own Letter to the Editor, explaining her goals for the school and how she intended to meet them. What she refused to discuss, however, was her personal life. These attacks didn't deserve a response, she believed, and they were irrelevant anyway. "I'm not going to dignify the remarks by commenting on them," she said to friends.

At Blue Springs High School, things were tense. The faculty was generally supportive of Lucy, but even her strongest backers could see divisions beginning and chaos developing. Teachers who had been allies were not so sure anymore, torn between their support of Lucy's approach to education and their strong religious beliefs and feelings about homosexuality. Unless the controversy died down soon, only a change in leadership would return the school to normal.

Few teachers would speak to Luther, blaming him for getting all of this started by criticizing education policy. But he didn't care. Outside the school he was viewed as a hero, and no one saw through his manipulation of this whole thing. There was no way he would be transferred now; he was secure.

One Friday afternoon, just as school was letting out, the school superintendent and the School Board attorney arrived at Lucy's office. They went in to see her and closed the door behind them. Lucy knew what that meant.

"The great majority of my faculty is happy," she stated emphatically. "And the kids are learning! Test scores are up and dropout rates are down."

"But the situation has become untenable, Lucy," Ralph Sargeant, the superintendent, replied. "It can't keep going on like this. We have to make a change."

"No, you *don't* have to make a change," Lucy pleaded. "Tell the community that as long as the school is succeeding in its core mission –

educating its students – there is no reason to change!"

"It's not that simple," Sargeant replied. "It's not about education anymore. The issue's gotten all caught up in this other stuff…"

"Like my sex life?" Lucy asked.

"Well, actually…"

"Don't answer that," the School Board attorney said strongly. "I'm instructing you not to answer that question."

"This is unbelievable!" Lucy said. "Okay. I'll say this one time, and only to you. I'll never say this in public because it shouldn't matter. I'm not gay. I like men. I'm not married because I haven't met the person I want to spend the rest of my life with. Is that what you needed to hear?"

"Ms. Myers, we're not here to discuss that," the attorney said. "We're here to tell you that you are relieved of your duties, effective immediately. You will be placed on six weeks administrative leave, with pay. There is a position open at the district office and it's yours if you want it. If not, at the end of the six-week period you will no longer be employed by this school district."

"So if I took the position at the district office, I would have no contact with kids?" Lucy asked.

"That's right. At least for a while," Sargeant said.

"I can't do that, Ralph. Working directly with teachers and students is what I want to do with my life!" Lucy answered.

"Then we must do what we must do," Sargeant replied. "We'll hold the position open for six weeks. If you change your mind, let me know. But as of now, you are relieved of your duties."

The two rose and walked out of the office. Lucy sat there, stunned.

News of Lucy's termination from the high school was the headline in the next day's paper. School authorities had released a statement, too late for the newspaper to get quotes from others, but early enough to make the next day's edition. Absent from the story was a comment from Lucy; she hadn't even been given an opportunity to respond.

Sunday afternoon, two days after being given her choices, Lucy's doorbell rang. It was Ben Fuller, Lucy's former boyfriend. He had found her address on the Internet and driven all the way from Atlanta.

"I thought you could use a lawyer," he said. "May I come in?"

Lucy was flustered and looked confused. Her eyes filled with tears. She didn't know whether to hug him or slap him. Then she motioned him to come through the door.

The Atlanta Constitution newspaper had picked up Lucy's dismissal and reported on it briefly in Sunday's paper. When Ben read it, he got in his car and headed south. Ben specialized in labor law and was familiar with circumstances that constituted permissible grounds for firing. This didn't sound right to him.

"Is that why you're really here, because you thought I might need a lawyer?" Lucy asked.

"That's really why I'm here," he replied. "But in all honesty, I've thought of you a lot over the years."

"You're not wearing a ring. Are you married?" Lucy asked.

"No. Divorced."

"Any kids?"

"One. A daughter. She lives with her mom."

Ben and Lucy talked for several hours about a lot of things, not just her dismissal. They called out for a pizza. At ten o'clock, Ben left and headed for his hotel room. They would get together in the morning to discuss the case some more.

When he left, Lucy collapsed in her bed, exhausted. The last few weeks had been a huge strain on her and with Ben back on the scene, she was seeing an emotional roller coaster developing that she wasn't sure she wanted to ride. "It has to stay totally professional," she thought. "Even if he's here for some other reason, I don't need to be dating my lawyer. How am I going to have the energy for this?" Closing her eyes, she was out like a light.

"The big question in the suit against the newspaper is whether the cour will consider you a 'public figure,'" Ben said to Lucy over coffee the ne morning. "If so, we'll have to prove malice."

Lucy and Ben were discussing the possibility of filing a "defamation" lawsuit against the newspaper and a "wrongful termination" suit against the school district. That was the last thing Lucy wanted, but her ability to get another job in education had been severely compromised by the controversy, and she wasn't going to take that lightly.

"I know what 'malice' means generally, but what does it mean within this context?" she asked.

"That the one making the statement knew it was false, or that it was said with a reckless disregard of whether it was false or not," Ben answered.

"And if I'm not considered a public figure?"

"We don't have to prove malice," Ben responded. "All we have to prove is that a false statement was made, it was communicated to a third person, and you were injured as a result."

"Well, we know a false statement was made. All this stuff about my sex life…it makes me furious. And it was communicated to a third person. I'd say publishing it in the newspaper is communicating it. And I have most surely been injured. Losing my job is enough, isn't it?"

"It is, but there's something else in your favor. A suit for defamation is all about damage to *reputation*. Since that's hard to prove, the courts have determined that certain things are 'libelous per se.' In other words, injury is assumed without proof of actual damages."

"Is this one of those cases that are libelous per se?" Lucy asked.

"Yes. Accusing a woman of being of 'unchaste character' is libelous per se, and that's what they did when they accused you of sleeping around. Throw ⟩ the speculation that you're a lesbian, and I think we have a strong case. ⟩re's one other thing that helps the case. Because they put these accusations ⟩e newspaper – in writing – we have a stronger case. Technically their ⟩e is 'libel' because the defamatory comments were written. If they had ⟩mmunicated the statements, it would have been 'slander.' The courts ⟩reater injury if the accusations are in writing."

"⟩rstand that," Lucy said. "There *is* something worse about seeing ⟩omments in writing than just hearing them."

"⟩ht. It also creates a record that remains long after spoken words ⟩ it's treated more seriously by the courts," Ben added.

"⟩ious business to the judiciary?" Lucy asked.

"⟩t it is!" Ben answered. "You're considered to have a

'property' interest in your job and in your ability to work, and defamation affects your ability to work. When that's taken from you, the courts view it as though you've lost something tangible, because you have."

"It can't be this easy," commented Lucy.

"It's not," replied Ben. "Those accused of defamation have a defense, and it's almost totally absolute."

"What's that?"

"The truth. If the accusations are true, it will be hard to nail those who said them," said Ben, looking straight into Lucy's eyes.

Ben waited for Lucy's answer.

"I've had several boyfriends since we broke up, Ben. Some were serious relationships."

"And the story about Charlotte Manley?"

"I've already answered that. I'm not gay. You know that."

Lucy was angry now. She was seeing a situation developing where she would have to say publicly that she wasn't a lesbian. Charlotte's name would then somehow leak out, and she'd get dragged into this for no reason other than she'd offered Lucy a place to live. For all Lucy knew, this could jeopardize Charlotte's job, given the way the community had reacted to her and the way the School Board had reacted to the community.

"So what do we do, counselor?"

"File the most strongly written lawsuit I can write," he answered. "Hit the newspaper and the school district right between the eyes. No courtesy calls to the other lawyers, and no meetings beforehand to try to work it out."

The newspaper had done a hatchet job on Lucy, and the school district had forsaken her when she needed them the most. She was mad and ready to fight back.

"What do you say, Lucy?"

She was thinking of how she once would have followed him anywhere.

"Do it!" she said resolutely.

Ben spent the next few days preparing the lawsuit. When it was ready, he and Lucy scheduled a press conference to announce its filing. To show her determination, she even held the press conference in front of the administration building of her high school. Her replacement didn't dare stop her; a dozen reporters, including three from television stations, were there. The story was attracting attention from around the state.

"One week ago, I was presented a choice," Lucy began. "I was told by the school superintendent, Mr. Sargeant, that I could either take a job at the district office or be fired. Notwithstanding that test scores are rising at my school and most of the faculty is happy, as evidenced by this three-year history of test scores and petition signed by the teachers, I was told that my employment had become 'untenable.'" Lucy held up a small packet of papers. "The school district attorney would not let Mr. Sargeant elaborate, but I'm convinced that if he had, he would have told me I was being removed as principal because of the rumors regarding my personal life. I have not – and will not – confirm or deny the allegations because they aren't relevant. What matters is what kind of job I'm doing as principal. If the allegations had been that I broke the law, then certainly I would have to respond. But these allegations are salacious and voyeuristic, not at all related to my fitness to be a principal.

"Because they have no bearing on my ability to fulfill my responsibilities as a principal, the allegations shouldn't have appeared in the newspaper. My reputation has been hurt, and my ability to work in this field has been impaired. I'm suing the newspaper and school district, and my attorney will answer any legal questions you may have about the lawsuits."

As Lucy sat down, Ben stood and walked forward. He turned and faced the reporters.

"My name is Ben Fuller. I'm from Atlanta, but I'm licensed to practice law in Florida as well as Georgia.

"The school district denied my client procedural and substantive due process in violation of the 14th Amendment to the United States Constitution. She was dismissed without a hearing, and treated differently from other employees similarly situated.

"She was also wrongfully terminated. Even if the allegations regarding her personal life were true, one's sexual orientation should not be a legal basis for terminating employment. Neither should the assertion, if true, that she was physically intimate with those of the opposite gender whom she may have dated. Simply put, neither scenario should be legally relevant.

"Our claim against the newspaper is based on the theory of defamation, specifically libel. We must satisfy a three-part test, and we do: (1) The newspaper published a false statement. (2) By publishing the false statement, it was communicated to a third person. (3) Because of the publication of the false statement, Ms. Myers suffered damage. Additionally, the statements were libelous on their face. They imputed that Lucy Myers – a woman – was of an unchaste character and immoral, and that's libelous per se."

The press conference was short. After hearing the statements from Lucy and Ben, the reporters were off to the school district office and the newspaper for reactions. Later that day, they received them.

The school district attorney walked into the lobby of the district office, noticeably ill at ease. He said very little, commenting only that all principals served at the pleasure of the superintendent and could be replaced for any reason. "The element of 'just cause,' a legal requirement for dismissing most public employees, is not required for administrative positions like principal," he said. "Nevertheless, the superintendent *had* cause to dismiss Lucy. The school was in turmoil, and credible reports of Myers' moral fitness for the office had arisen, reports she did not *publicly* deny." A barrage of questions came from the reporters, but the attorney remained tight-lipped, repeating only what he had said. However, one question did pull from him the statement: "It is legally permissible to fire a principal for the reason that she is gay."

This was exactly what Ben Fuller had hoped to hear. He wanted the question of a person's sexual orientation as a reason for Lucy's dismissal to be put squarely before the Court. He was aware that, in Florida, sexual orientation was not legally protected behavior, especially for educators, and that one could be fired for being gay. Still, he thought the time was right to challenge it.

From the district office the reporters hustled to the address of the newspaper where they were handed a written statement: "The newspaper stands behind its story. The truth is an absolute defense to a charge of defamation. Regardless, Ms. Myers' burden is even higher because she is a public figure; she must prove malice, and that most certainly isn't present in this case."

Ben knew the question of whether Lucy was a public figure would have to be decided by the Court. He also knew the answer: she *would* be considered a public figure, at least within this context, and they would have to prove malice in order to prevail. To show a reckless disregard for the truth, and to prove it with "clear and convincing evidence" which was the standard required, would be difficult. Therefore, he settled on a novel legal strategy. He intended to assert that, even if the reports of Lucy's sexual orientation or sexual history were true, they had no "news" value whatsoever. Consequently, publishing them could only have been to satisfy a "prurient interest" in sex, portrayed sex in a "patently offensive" way, and did not have any serious literary, artistic, political or scientific value [Roth v. United States, 354 U.S. 476 (1957)]. In other words, the article fit the legal definition of "obscenity" and, as such, was not protected speech. He was essentially asserting that the newspaper had published pornographic material about his client, something that, if established, would be deemed malicious, or so he thought. This was a long shot, but it was the only way he could think of to get around the requirement of proving malice.

Luther Flood was downright giddy about recent events. The district's decision to replace Lucy, her lawsuits, the press conference…it was more than he could have hoped for. Apparently he had never heard the adage, "Pigs get fat, hogs get slaughtered," and proceeded to make a big mistake: he piled on. He couldn't help it; it was just too delicious not to. Luther called his own press conference and detailed "liberal" teaching strategies Lucy had encouraged her teachers to try. He told of an English teacher who took her students outside, blindfolded them, and had them feel the rough bark of an oak tree and then the smoothness of the tree's leaves. She then made them write about how two parts of the same thing could be such opposites, yet each was vital to the other, and whether the students saw parallels between this example in nature and racial diversity in society. He told of a mathematics teacher who allowed students to teach the class for a day. "Can you imagine that?" Luther asked. "A teacher allowing a student to teach the class?"

Luther gave several other examples, distorting the context and misrepresenting the goals of each method. The resulting newspaper story was perfect in Luther's eyes: it made it seem that what was going on at Lucy's high school was totally loony. Everything was going his way. This was a fact not lost on Ben Fuller.

"Tell me about Luther Flood," he asked Lucy one evening.

Lucy told him all she knew and pointed out that Luther was the one who got the ball rolling against her.

"Does he have any friends? What does he do in his time away from school?" Ben asked.

"I don't have a clue. He's pretty much a loner. I know he doesn't have any friends in the school. All I know is that he goes to the local golf course every Friday afternoon for a few beers."

"Hmm. Interesting. Maybe I'll have somebody go out there and see what he does...or who he talks to."

Ben returned to Atlanta the next day, but made plans to travel to Tallahassee when necessary to prosecute the lawsuits. When he left, he gave Lucy a lingering hug. It was more than just a simple goodbye to a friend. He knew it, and Lucy did too.

"It's been good seeing you, Lucy."

"I've enjoyed seeing you, too, Ben. Don't be gone so long this time."

"I won't," he said with a smile. "I have a client to represent."

For the next couple months, Lucy's toughest opponent was boredom. There was little for her to do with the lawsuits other than to attend the few hearings. She read every deposition transcript and helped Ben where she could, but mostly she was simply waiting for the next court proceeding.

She took advantage of this time to travel some, but it was hard to relax with the lawsuits pending. She found that adventure travel was a good distraction, so she took several great trips. She flew to Maine and hiked to the top of Mt. Kataydin, and later rode horses from an outpost near Cody, Wyoming to Bridger Lake in the Grand Tetons and back.

During this time, Lucy suffered several setbacks with the lawsuits. First, the Court gave her a double-dose of bad news in the action against the school district. Not only did the judge rule that a principal serves totally at the pleasure of the school superintendent and that "just cause" is not required for termination, but he also stated clearly that "homosexuality was a valid reason for employment termination in a school setting." Ben was disappointed, but not surprised. The one silver lining was that the ruling that homosexuality was a valid reason for termination in a school setting set up a straightforward question of law for the appellate court to consider. Naturally, Ben would have preferred to defend a trial court ruling instead of trying to get a ruling overturned, but at least the question of law was squarely framed for the appeal.

The lawsuit against the newspaper wasn't going much better. As expected, the newspaper argued that the story was truthful, forcing Lucy to do what she had said she wouldn't: discuss her own sexuality. She said publicly that she wasn't gay, and then, to address the charge that she "slept around," had to go through the indignity of stating that she didn't believe sex was to be entered into casually, and that she "wasn't that kind of person."

During these months, Ben and Lucy were either together or spoke on the telephone nearly every day. Often their conversations were about things other than the lawsuits. Their personal relationship was growing; each felt it and was happy about it. It felt right.

Late one afternoon Ben flew in from Atlanta. Over dinner that night, Lucy spoke of her frustration with their legal position. "Every time I respond, it puts this whole mess back in the newspaper," Lucy said. "People don't read or remember the entire story. A headline that reads: 'Teacher Denies She's Gay,' does me in no matter what the rest of the story says."

"I know," replied Ben. He knew they were losing not only the lawsuits, but also the public relations battle. "But I don't know what else to do. We have to show that the allegations are untruthful. Of course, there is one other way, but I know what you're going to say about it."

"Don't even think it, Ben. I'm not going to ask Charlotte Manley to come forward and say we were just roommates and nothing more. She doesn't deserve to be dragged into this."

"You're right. But it *would* be a way to set the record straight."

"But then they'd ask her if she were gay, and I'm not going to do that to her."

"I thought that's what you'd say, but I had to bring it up. We still have two more moves: the Court hasn't ruled on the idea that the newspaper story was essentially pornography; and I will soon be asking the Court to order the newspaper to disclose its source. If we can find out the source of the story, we may be able to show that the whole thing was concocted."

"But isn't that close to impossible?" Lucy asked. "Aren't reporters allowed to protect their sources?"

"It's tough, no doubt about it. But reporters do *not* have a constitutional right to protect their sources, at least not to conceal the criminal conduct of others or facts relevant to a criminal investigation. The Court weighs the need for the information against the public's interest in maintaining a free press. The courts are much less likely to require a reporter to disclose information if a crime's not involved, and it's not in this case, but we can try. There's also the problem of Florida's 'shield' law, which grants a qualified privilege to journalists to protect the identity of their sources. There are some exceptions, but it is another hurdle to overcome."

"All of this seems like such a long shot to me, Ben. No one is going to think the article was pornographic, or that the reporter should be required to reveal his sources. This is not going well."

"It's your case, Lucy. If you want to throw in the towel, I will, but my gut is telling me to hang in there a little longer."

Lucy was silent for a few moments. Tears filled her eyes.

"Those were the exact words I said to you when you broke up with me, to 'not throw in the towel, to hang in there a little longer.'"

"Well you know what, Lucy? Maybe I should have listened to you. Maybe I did throw in the towel too quickly."

She looked up at Ben. He took her in his arms and kissed her softly. She looked into his eyes.

"If you're telling me to hang in there a little longer, I will," she said.

The strategy of "hanging in there a little longer" worked, but not because of anything Ben did in court. On the contrary, his motion to have the column declared obscene was summarily dismissed by the judge. Ben's attempt to get the judge to compel the newspaper to disclose its source was faring only slightly better. The judge had not yet ruled, but from his questions it was apparent he was leaning the other way.

Something else happened to change the tide. Ben hired a private investigator to go to the golf course on Friday afternoons to watch Luther Flood. On two consecutive Fridays he saw him drinking with Shaw Johnson, Lucy's former boyfriend. Later, the investigator asked the bartender about them. The bartender said he overheard a conversation they were having about a teacher who was supposed to be a lesbian, and about a principal who was in some kind of trouble. When the investigator reported this to Ben, and Ben asked Lucy about Shaw, the source of the lurid speculation about Lucy's sex life was discovered. This was valuable in two ways: It showed that Luther was actively undermining his boss (Lucy), and it gave a "scorned lover" motive to what Shaw told the reporter. This would be helpful only if it got out, however, and that meant finding a reporter who would be willing to give the matter the time it would require to do it correctly.

They found their person in Vicki Morgan, a seasoned reporter for a competing newspaper, The Panhandle Times. She had been at Lucy's press conference when she announced the lawsuits and had been on the story ever since. Morgan had a good heart and possessed a strong sense of right and wrong. She also was brave and tough as nails, not afraid to take on the establishment to defend an underdog or expose a corrupt public official.

Vicki agreed to check into the information Ben and Lucy gave her. When she called back a few days later and said no one would talk to her, Lucy was discouraged.

"So I guess you're not going to do anything with it?" Lucy asked.

"What are you talking about?" Vicki replied. "This is what gets my juices going. I'm on it! I know injustice when I smell it."

The next Friday afternoon Vicki Morgan walked into the golf course bar and sat down at the table with Luther Flood and Shaw Johnson. She introduced herself and put her tape recorder in the middle of the table. She pushed the button and turned it on. Then she said: "Which one of you wants to go first?"

Shaw Johnson turned as white as a sheet and hustled out of the room, getting in his car and driving off. But Luther Flood's arrogance and inflated ego got the best of him. He was convinced that he could match wits with this or any reporter. "Keep your cool, Luther," he thought to himself. "That's all you have to do."

Vicki Morgan was so good she talked Luther right out of his story and he didn't even know it. Luther thought he was being coy, cool and vague, but he was really implicating himself with his non-answer answers.

The story that appeared a week later was a masterpiece. It connected all the dots, and all trails led to Luther Flood. Things began happening quickly then, but not until the Herald made one last attempt to blister Lucy, and this turned out to be its undoing: They 'outed' Charlotte Manley as the "suspected lesbian" with whom Lucy had lived. Theodore Stuart, the Herald's publisher, should have known better, but desperate to not be upstaged by Vicki Morgan's paper, authorized the story.

The decision cost him dearly. Charlotte brought her own defamation action and won $150,000.00 against the paper. Unlike Lucy, she was not a public figure and didn't have to prove malice. She convinced the jury that she and Lucy were housemates and nothing else, and there was no civic value in the public knowing her sexual orientation. Stuart was fired the next day.

When the truth behind the stories came out, Lucy was reinstated as principal of Blue Springs High by the superintendent in exchange for dropping the appeal of her lawsuit against the school district. With the lawsuit over, Ben would not be able to argue before the appellate court the question of whether a school principal could be terminated because she was gay, but at least Lucy had her job back.

Lucy lost her lawsuit against the newspaper and elected not to appeal. She had done so poorly at the trial level that she couldn't convince herself it was worth the energy.

She did better with Ben, however. They began dating again, and this time he followed her, leaving Atlanta for the small-town charm of Marianna, Florida. They were married six months later.

Justice triumphed in the fate of Luther Flood. Teachers are allowed to speak their minds about school issues, but they may not undermine their superiors. It was sweet indeed when Lucy called Luther into her office.

"Luther, it was obvious to me from the first day we met that you didn't want to be a teacher. You fought me every step of the way, refusing to believe there might be a better way to educate students. Why? Why did you do it?"

"I've been doing this for 17 years, and you come in and start telling me how to teach?" he said. "No way. We had a good thing going before you arrived, but you wanted to make it better. What was wrong with what we had?

So I'll ask you. Why did *you* do it?"

"All I wanted was to build a better mousetrap," she answered. "My motivation was solely to help the students. Perfection is never reached...not with teaching, not with anything."

"But what we had was good enough," Luther responded.

"And that's the difference between us, I suppose," Lucy said. "I wanted more for the students, Luther, and I still do. That's why you're fired, effective immediately."

"You can't do that," Luther protested. "I have tenure."

"It doesn't matter," Lucy replied. "Even tenured teachers can be fired for cause. You embarrassed and humiliated me, but that wasn't your undoing. Your fatal offense was purposefully undermining me in my responsibilities as principal. That is not allowed in any school district, even for tenured teachers. The vice principal will escort you to your room for you to clean out your desk."

After 17 years of being a mediocre and unenthusiastic teacher, Luther Flood was finally given a chance to do something else with his life, a chance he had been unwilling to take on his own. He began a new career as a real estate salesperson selling condominiums sprawling over the pristine sugar-sand beachfront land outside Destin. Who knows? Maybe his treachery saved him from being forced to lead the virtuous and truly rewarding life of a teacher.

"Wedding Room"
Florida Caverns State Park,
Marianna, FL

Author's Note:

During my time in the Legislature, bills involving "gay rights" were occasionally considered. One such bill prevented gay marriage by defining marriage as a legal union between a man and a woman. It passed, and I voted for it.

Later, during my race for governor, I met with the leadership of the gay and lesbian community of Broward County. They represented a sizable voting block in a Democratic primary. My travel aide asked me how I was going to explain my vote on gay marriage. I told him I was going to say that I believed a marriage was a holy union between a man and a woman. He knew that wouldn't go over very well, and encouraged me to come up with a different answer. I said, "No, that was how I felt." Besides, those I would be meeting with had the right to know my reasoning.

After I made a few introductory comments about my candidacy I opened the floor up for questions. As expected, the first question was about my vote on gay marriage. I answered as I had told my travel aide I would, although I dropped the word "holy" from the explanation, either consciously or unconsciously. Needless to say, they disagreed, but we had a respectful and dignified discussion about it. I also mentioned that in the legislative district I was from I hadn't received many calls to oppose the measure, but many calls to support it, so I could argue that I was just representing my district.

From a legislative standpoint, inherent in any discussion of an issue such as this is the question of whether one is born gay or whether homosexuality is a lifestyle choice. If one is born gay, it makes a stronger case for creating greater civil rights protections. My own view is that sexual orientation is mostly contained within one's DNA, so I would lean towards more civil rights protections. A friend noted that of those who were born with a predisposition towards homosexuality, only a percentage of that group actually adopted that orientation as an identity, pointing out that some people were more likely to act upon the orientation than others. This creates even more of a gray area from a legal point of view.

This story mentions the affirmative defense of truth as a defense against a defamation claim. When an affirmative defense is asserted, a defendant is claiming that even if everything the plaintiff is saying is true, there is a defense to it so there is no liability. An example would be the defense of "duress."

There, the defendant would assert that, assuming the facts claimed by the plaintiff were true, the defendant was under duress at the time of the incident so liability couldn't attach.

Perhaps the most discussed affirmative defenses in modern Florida jurisprudence occurred in the "tobacco litigation," a lawsuit filed by Florida Attorney General Bob Butterworth and Florida Governor Lawton Chiles on behalf of the state to recover Medicaid tax money spent to treat indigents for tobacco-related illnesses. Before the suit was filed, however, there was legislative drama of the highest order that set up the lawsuit.

In 1994, the Florida Legislature passed a bill that was an amendment to the Medicaid Third-Party Liability Act. Medicaid is a joint federal/state program that pays for health care costs of indigents. The Medicaid Third-Party Liability Act authorized the state to seek reimbursement of these costs from the parties responsible for the injuries to the indigents under the theory that it was fairer for the responsible parties to pay these costs than for the taxpayers to pay them.

The bill that passed in 1994 received little debate and few legislators realized its true import at the time of its passage. I clearly remember when it happened. I had left the floor of the Senate for the Senate president's suite. There I saw Fred Levin, a very successful trial lawyer from Pensacola and close friend of Senator W.D. Childers, who was also from Pensacola. I knew Fred, but not well. We greeted each other briefly and I wondered what he was doing in the president's suite. I then noticed that Senator Childers was presiding over the Senate, having taken the place of Senate President Pat Thomas a few moments before. I had a feeling that something might be up, so I went back to the floor just in time to hear Senator Childers recognize Senator Ken Jenne to explain the next bill being considered. I picked up my copy of the bill from my desk and saw that it was a short amendment to the Medicaid Third-Party Liability Act. It seemed innocuous and non-controversial, and I hadn't heard from anybody about it, so I didn't think much of it. Senator Howard Forman then raised his microphone and was recognized for a question. Senator Jenne turned quickly and gave Senator Forman an impatient look. Senator Forman asked for clarification on the bill, and Senator Jenne said it would make it easier to seek Medicaid reimbursement from third parties. Senator Forman seemed satisfied. Senator Childers moved things along and called for a vote. I believe it passed unanimously.

By the next day we were hearing that the bill was quite significant. It soon passed the House and went to Governor Chiles. Later, Senator Thomas told me that when the bill passed the House he immediately received a telephone call from Governor Chiles. Senator Thomas was presiding over the Senate at the time, but telephones at the dais allow one to speak to the governor or Speaker of the House. Governor Chiles said to Senator Thomas, "The rocket has launched, the rocket has launched, the rocket has launched!"

Indeed it had. As it turned out, the bill prevented tobacco companies from asserting affirmative defenses if sued by the state for expenses incurred in treating Medicaid patients for tobacco-related illnesses.

Governor Chiles signed the bill into law and it was immediately challenged in court as being unconstitutional. It went all the way to the Florida Supreme Court where it was upheld by a 4-3 vote. Attention then shifted back to the Legislature where opponents passed a bill repealing the first. Many legislators, including myself, were upset with how the first bill had passed and felt a bit snookered. It also struck us as unfair to deprive a particular set of defendants the affirmative defenses allowed other defendants.

To no one's surprise, Governor Chiles vetoed this repeal bill, setting up a legislative battle of gargantuan proportion as the tobacco companies and much of the business community sought to override Governor Chiles' veto. Billions of dollars were at stake for the tobacco companies so their interest was obvious. Other industries were engaged because they thought they could be next. Governor Chiles argued that tobacco was the only consumer product that killed when used as directed, and even signed an executive order stating that he would not seek reimbursement from any other industry. Still, it did little to allay their concerns.

A lawsuit against the tobacco companies was soon filed. Without the benefit of affirmative defenses, the companies were in a much more difficult legal position. Two affirmative defenses in particular, assumption of risk and another involving how liability could be apportioned among the various cigarette manufacturers, were the most important.

The tobacco companies had been sued countless times by smokers for smoking-related illnesses but had always prevailed under the theory that the smokers had assumed the risk by choosing to smoke. General Butterworth and Governor Chiles argued that assumption of risk shouldn't apply in the state's lawsuit because the state hadn't made the decision to smoke, yet it had to pay for the smoking-related illnesses of Medicaid patients.

The affirmative defense involving apportioning liability among the various cigarette manufacturers was also very important to the tobacco companies. The companies contended that the state must identify which brands of cigarettes each Medicaid patient had smoked and for how long, or a particular company would be paying for the injuries caused by another. This would be nearly impossible, so when the bill denied the companies this affirmative defense the state was allowed to use market share to apportion liability among them. That is, if the companies were found liable for the smoking-related expenses of Medicaid patients, each company's percentage would be whatever its market share was.

The lobbying effort to override the veto was unbelievably intense. Lobbyists and tobacco company lawyers were everywhere. I must say, though, that I was impressed by the professionalism of these individuals. Lobbyists have a bad reputation in some circles, but they and the lawyers who spoke to me were totally focused on the merits of the issue and the equities involved. I never saw a hint of expectation of support from any legislator because that legislator might have received campaign contributions from tobacco companies, as has been suggested.

Governor Chiles was giving it all he had from the other side, too. I spoke with him many times about this matter. I remember a one-on-one visit with him in his office where we talked frankly about my concerns. I had written a long paper outlining the positions of each side to help clarify my thinking, so I was ready for the meeting. In fact, I had numerous questions for him. We went back and forth over the legal issues, how we felt about tobacco products, and how the attorneys hired by the state had been hired and how they would be paid. I consider much of this conversation private, but he could see that I was genuinely concerned about the legal implications of a bill that deprived defendants of affirmative defenses. He asked if I would work with Mallory Horne, an attorney and one of Florida's most capable former legislators, on a bill to cure many of the defects. Mallory had been hired to help sustain the veto. Governor Chiles didn't agree to support a bill that would reinstate the affirmative defenses of assumption of risk and the one involving market share, but he agreed to negotiate in good faith on everything else.

The vote on the override was not too far away, so Mallory and I got together for the first time that afternoon. He was a delight to work with, and totally respectful of my opinions. Over the next five days or so, including a weekend where we spent a lot of time over the telephone with each other negotiating, we developed what became Senate Bill 12. This bill reinstated much of the due process that had been eliminated by the first bill, and reduced the attorneys' fees to a proportion akin to what attorneys typically made in class action lawsuits against the state. On the personal word of Governor Chiles to actively support passing this bill, I agreed to vote to sustain his veto. We convened a hastily called press conference and made the announcement.

As it turned out, Senate Bill 12 became the bridge that several senators needed to vote to sustain the veto. Without it, I believe the veto would have been overridden. As it was, the veto was sustained and SB 12 passed the Senate. I'm not crowing though. In fact, my vote to sustain the veto is one of a half dozen votes that have stayed with me over the years. I'm not sure I would do it differently if I could go through it again, but it gnaws at me nonetheless. I understood fully the state's theory of the case, but depriving defendants who manufactured a legal product of the affirmative defenses that were available to other manufacturers of legal products bothered me then and it bothers me now. Also, some of the state's lawyers made hundreds of millions of dollars off the case and that wasn't right, even though I recognize the talent of the attorneys and the risk they took in fronting the costs of the lawsuit. However, after the law was changed depriving the tobacco companies of their affirmative defenses, prevailing in the lawsuit was made much easier. Indeed, the day before the trial was to begin, the tobacco companies settled the case by agreeing to pay 11.3 billion dollars to the state of Florida so they must have felt the same way. Finally, I had a special relationship with Governor Chiles and was convinced that his governorship would have been over for all practical purposes if he had lost this issue, but how much such broader considerations should play in a legislative decision is debatable.

Senate Bill 12 never passed the House, despite Governor Chiles' advocacy for it. Do I feel played? To some extent, but I know Governor Chiles was sincere in his support for it. Had it passed, it would have been a reasonable compromise for a very controversial and significant matter, and, for better or worse, that's the legislative process.

THE LAW: Definitions and Explanations:

Defamation: An intentional false communication, either published or publicly spoken, that injures another's reputation or good name.

Black's Law Dictionary, Sixth Edition, p. 416

Libel: A method of defamation expressed by print, writing, pictures, or signs.

Black's Law Dictionary, Sixth Edition, p. 915

Slander: The speaking of base and defamatory words tending to prejudice another in his reputation, community standing, office, trade, business, or means of livelihood.

Black's Law Dictionary, Sixth Edition, p. 1388

Malice: The intentional doing of a wrongful act without just cause or excuse, with an intent to inflict an injury or under circumstances that the law will imply an evil intent. A condition of mind which prompts a person to do a wrongful act willfully, that is, on purpose, to the injury of another, or to do intentionally a wrongful act toward another without justification or excuse...

Black's Law Dictionary, Sixth Edition, p. 956

Procedural due process: The guarantee of procedural fairness which flows from both the Fifth and Fourteenth Amendments due process clauses of the Constitution.

Black's Law Dictionary, Sixth Edition, p. 1203

Affirmative defense: In pleading, matter asserted by defendant which, assuming the complaint to be true, constitutes a defense to it.

Black's Law Dictionary, Sixth Edition, p. 60

Substantive due process: Doctrine that due process clauses of the Fifth and Fourteenth Amendments to the United States Constitution require legislation to be fair and reasonable in content as well as application. Such may be broadly defined as the constitutional guarantee that no person shall be arbitrarily deprived of his life, liberty or property. The essence of substantive

314

due process is protection from arbitrary and unreasonable action.

Black's Law Dictionary, Sixth Edition, p. 1429;
Jeffries v. Turkey Run Consolidated School Dist., C.A. Ind., 492 F. 2d 1, 3

"Congress shall make no law respecting an establishment of religion, or prohibiting the free exercise thereof; or abridging the freedom of speech, or of the press; or the right of the people peaceably to assemble, and to petition the Government for a redress of grievances."

Article I, Constitution of the United States.

"A rule compelling the critic of official conduct to guarantee the truth of all his factual assertions – and to do so on pain of libel judgments virtually unlimited in amount – leads to a comparable 'self-censorship.' Allowance of the defense of truth, with the burden of proving it on the defendant, does not mean that only false speech will be deterred...Under such a rule, would-be critics of official conduct may be deterred from voicing their criticism, even though it is believed to be true and even though it is, in fact, true, because of doubt whether it can be proved in court or fear of the expense of having to do so...The rule thus dampens the vigor and limits the variety of public debate. It is inconsistent with the First and Fourteenth Amendments...The constitutional guarantees require, we think, a federal rule that prohibits a public official from recovering damages for a defamatory falsehood relating to his official conduct unless he proves that the statement was made with 'actual malice' – that is, with knowledge that it was false or with reckless disregard of whether it was false or not."

N.Y. Times v. Sullivan, 376 U.S. 254, 279-280 (1964)

"First Amendment rights, applied in light of the special circumstances of the school environment, are available to teachers and students. It can hardly be said that either students or teachers shed their constitutional rights to freedom of speech or expression at the schoolhouse gate." Tinker v. Des Moines Independent School District, 393 U.S. 503, 507 (1969). "...Under our Constitution, free speech is not a right that is given only to be so circumscribed that it exists in principle but not in fact. Freedom of expression would not truly exist if the right could be exercised only in an area that a benevolent

government has provided as a safe haven for crackpots. The Constitution says that Congress (and the States) may not abridge the right to free speech. This provision means what it says. We properly read it to permit reasonable regulation of speech-connected activities in carefully restricted circumstances. But we do not confine the permissible exercise of First Amendment rights to a telephone booth or the four corners of a pamphlet, or to supervised and ordained discussion in a school classroom."

(supra, at 514)

"The problem in any case is to arrive at a balance between the interests of the teacher, as a citizen, in commenting upon matters of public concern and the interest of the State, as an employer, in promoting the efficiency of the public services it performs through its employees." Pickering v. Board of Education, 391 U.S. 563, 568 (1968)... "Teachers are, as a class, the members of a community most likely to have informed and definite opinions as to how funds allotted to the operation of the schools should be spent. Accordingly, it is essential that they be able to speak out freely on such questions without fear of retaliatory dismissal."

(supra, at 572)

..."Thus, we cannot seriously entertain the notion that the First Amendment protects a newsman's agreement to conceal the criminal conduct of his source, or evidence thereof, on the theory that it is better to write about crime than to do something about it."

Branzburg v. Hayes, 408 U.S. 665, 693 (1972)

Notable Quotes:

Judge Learned Hand, speaking of the First Amendment, and, parenthetically, the free speech clause therein, said that the Amendment "presupposes that right conclusions are more likely to be gathered out of a multitude of tongues than through any kind of authoritative selection. To many, this is, and always will be, folly, but we have staked upon it our all."

United States v. Associated Press, 52 F. Supp. 362, 372

"Those who won our independence believed that the final end of the state was to make men free to develop their faculties, and that in its government the deliberative forces should prevail over the arbitrary. They valued liberty both as an end and as a means. They believed liberty to the secret of happiness and courage to be the secret of liberty. They believed that freedom to think as you will and to speak as you think are means indispensable to the discovery and spread of political truth; that without free speech and assembly discussion would be futile; that with them, discussion affords ordinarily adequate protection against the dissemination of noxious doctrine; that the greatest menace to freedom is an inert people; that public discussion is a political duty; and that this should be a fundamental principle of the American government. They recognized the risks to which all human institutions are subject. But they knew that order cannot be secured merely through fear of punishment for its infraction; that it is hazardous to discourage thought, hope and imagination; that fear breeds repression; that repression breeds hate; that hate menaces stable government; that the path of safety lies in the opportunity to discuss freely supposed grievances and proposed remedies; and that the fitting remedy for evil counsels is good ones. Believing in the power of reason as applied through public discussion, they eschewed silence [274 U.S. 357, 376] coerced by law-the argument of force in its worst form. Recognizing the occasional tyrannies of governing majorities, they amended the Constitution so that free speech and assembly should be guaranteed."

Whitney v. California, 274 U.S. 357, 375 (1927)

"Free speech is not to be regulated like diseased cattle and impure butter. The audience that hissed yesterday may applaud today, even for the same performance."

Honorable William O. Douglas, Associate Justice,
United States Supreme Court

"In the realm of religious faith, and in that of political belief, sharp differences arise. In both fields, the tenets of one man may seem the rankest error to his neighbor. To persuade others to his own point of view, the pleader, as we know, at times resorts to exaggeration, to vilification of men who have been, or are, prominent in church or state, and even to false statement. But the people of this nation have ordained, in light of history, that, in spite of the probability of

excesses and abuses, these liberties are, in the long view, essential to enlightened opinion and right conduct on the part of the citizens of a democracy."

Cantwell v. Connecticut, 310 U.S. 296, 310 (1940)

"In the First Amendment the Founding Fathers gave the free press the protection it must have to fulfill its essential role in our democracy. The press was to serve the governed, not the governors. The Government's power to censor the press was abolished so that the press would remain forever free to censure the Government. The press was protected so that it could bare the secrets of government and inform the people. Only a free and unrestrained press can effectively expose deception in government. And paramount among the responsibilities of a free press is the duty to prevent any part of the government from deceiving the people and sending them off to distant lands to die of foreign fevers and foreign shot and shell."

New York Times Co. v. United States, 403 U.S. 713, 719 (1971)

"Make no laws whatever concerning speech, and speech will be free; as soon as you make a declaration on paper that speech shall be free, you will have a hundred lawyers proving that "freedom does not mean abuse, nor liberty license"; and they will define freedom out of existence."

Voltarine de Cleyre / www.erowid.org

"A function of free speech under our system of government is to invite dispute. It may indeed best serve its high purpose when it incites a condition of unrest, creates dissatisfaction with things as they are, or even stirs people to anger. Speech is often provocative and challenging. It may strike at prejudices and have profound unsettling effects as it presses for understanding."

Honorable Potter Stewart, Associate Justice,
United States Supreme Court
"Free Speech and Political Protest,"
by Marvin Summers (1967)

"The Framers of the Constitution knew that free speech is the friend of change and revolution. But they also knew that it is always the deadliest enemy of tyranny."

Honorable Hugo Black, Associate Justice,
United States Supreme Court
www.brainyquote.com

"The mind of a bigot is like the pupil of the eye. The more light you shine on it, the more it will contract."

Honorable Oliver Wendell Holmes, Associate Justice,
United States Supreme Court
www.brainyquote.com

"[I]mperative is the need to preserve inviolate the constitutional rights of free speech, free press and free assembly in order to maintain the opportunity for free political discussion, to the end that government may be responsive to the will of the people and that changes, if desired, may be obtained by peaceful means. Therein lies the security of the Republic, the very foundation of constitutional government."

De Jonge v. Oregon, 299 U.S. 353, 365 (1937)

Grove Patrol

THE "D" WORD
Dissolution of Marriage: Divorce

Preface: The National Center for Health Statistics reported that in the year 2003, the last full year that data was available as of this writing, 155,240 couples were married in Florida. That same year, 151,344 couples were divorced. It is a sad fact that in today's society, there are nearly as many divorces as marriages.

Certainly there are marriages that should be dissolved. No one should have to endure physical or emotional abuse, for example. But an elderly man once told me that when he was younger, getting a divorce was very difficult from a legal standpoint. As a result, when couples began having problems, they had to find a way to work it out. More often than not, they did. He believed that too many couples bail out too quickly these days.

I don't have enough experience in divorce cases to judge whether many couples "bail out too quickly," but I do know that it is pretty easy to get a divorce these days. A also know that few couples appreciate the legal consequences of a divorce until they get one, and that each spouse usually greatly underestimates the ongoing involvement they will have with the other if there are children involved.

AFTER 16 YEARS OF MARRIAGE, Peter Carter's world crashed in around him. When his wife told him over breakfast that she wanted a divorce, he was stunned at first, but his shock quickly turned to disbelief, then anger.

"I just don't love you anymore," Sheila said.

"What do you mean, 'You just don't love me anymore?' That doesn't happen overnight. Why didn't you say something sooner if that's how you were feeling?"

"I tried to, over and over again. But you weren't listening, and you didn't want to talk."

"Well I'm listening now, and I'm ready to talk, so let's talk."

"No, Peter, I've made up my mind. I want a divorce."

"Is there another man? Is that it?"

The hesitation in her voice answered his question.

"Oh, Sheila. How could you?"

"Peter, you haven't been here for the last five years, and I don't just mean traveling with work. Your mind has been elsewhere, too. We rarely talk, and I'm an afterthought to everything else in your life. We've grown apart.

"And by the way, there is not another man in my life, not now anyway, but I did have an affair two years ago. It didn't last long, but it made me think about what our lives together have become, which is not much."

"So you *did* have an affair! With who?"

"It doesn't matter. A more important question is 'Why,' but you haven't asked that, and that speaks volumes."

Peter stood and walked around the kitchen, his hands pressing tightly behind his head, which was pounding.

"It does matter! Who did you have the affair with, Sheila?"

"It doesn't matter! You don't need to know."

"But I want to know. Who was it with?"

"Do you really want to know? Are you sure?"

"Of course I'm sure. Otherwise I wouldn't have asked. Who was it with?"

Sheila looked at him for several seconds before answering.

"Royce Baxter."

"Royce Baxter! You had an affair with my most important employee?"

"You were gone so much, Peter. I was at the office one night as he was leaving, and one thing led to another. The affair lasted only three months. We both realized how stupid it was, and we ended it."

"How could you have done this? I've *never* cheated on you!"

"You just don't get it, do you? I'm sorry about the affair, but that's not the reason why I want out. This marriage is dead; it's not working!"

"What do you mean, 'It's not working?' What's not working? I'm making a fortune. The kids are doing well…"

"You think the kids are doing well? How would you know? You haven't had a face to face conversation with them in years. They hardly know you."

"But that can change. And speaking of the kids, what about them? They will be devastated!"

"I'm not so sure. I've thought about that…a lot…but they know we're just going through the motions here. Maybe it would even be good for them."

"*Good* for them! How could it be? Divorce is never good for the kids," Peter said incredulously. "And how would they know we've just been 'going through the motions?' They're kids for goodness sake. Divorce will be terrible for them!"

"It doesn't have to be. How the kids handle it will depend on how we handle it."

The full measure of Sheila's resolve was sinking in with Peter. He was reeling, but he maintained the presence of mind to slow down and think rationally. He had not become successful in business by making rash decisions.

"This is happening too fast. Don't do it Sheila. We can work it out. We'll go to counseling…whatever it takes. I've met my goal with the business. I'll slow down."

"Peter, the business will get even more taxing. You won't be satisfied unless you maintain the volume you've built up, and that is going to take an awful lot of work. Getting someone's business is only the beginning. Keeping it can be just as tough."

"But Sheila, we have too much time invested in this marriage to give up. I can get over your having the affair. It will be hard, I'll admit that, but I can do it. Don't quit on this marriage. Give it another chance. Give *me* another chance. Please!"

Sheila paused for a moment, looked down, and then said, "I'm sorry Peter. It's over."

Peter and Sheila had been high school sweethearts from Zellwood, Florida. They enjoyed great times on nearby Lake Apopka, fishing and boating on Peter's small skiff. In the summers, he made spending money by running trot lines to catch softshell turtles and catfish. She would sometimes go with him early in the morning to bring in his catch, and the sunrise became as special to them as the sunset was to others.

The beauty of the day breaking over the vast expanse of Lake Apopka was a good place to fall in love, and they thought they would marry and live happily ever after. Their bliss was interrupted, though, when Peter left for college at the University of South Carolina in Columbia. Sheila stayed home and attended the University of Central Florida in Orlando. They tried maintaining a long-distance relationship, but by the end of the fall it was apparent that it wouldn't work, and they broke up.

They were apart for five years. After college, Peter returned to Apopka, near Zellwood where he had grown up, accepting a job as a plant wholesaler for a huge ornamental plant nursery. Sheila became a bookkeeper for CDC Golf Course Management Company, also an Apopka-based company.

Neither knew the other was close by until Peter bid on a plant contract for a golf course under construction near the city of Windermere, just a few miles from where they were both located. CDC was soliciting the bids and would manage the course.

Peter scheduled a lunch meeting with the president of Sheila's company to discuss his offer. The president brought Sheila along to explain the scheduling of the payments in the event that Peter received the contract.

"Sheila! What are you doing here?" Peter exclaimed when he saw her.

"Hi, Peter. I'm with CDC. I guess you're trying to sell us some plants."

"You know each other?" the president asked when they met at the table.

"We do," Peter responded. "From a long time ago."

"We used to date," Sheila added, smiling. "Gosh it's good to see you."

On the way out the door after the meeting, Peter asked Sheila if she would like to meet him after work for a glass of wine.

"Of course I would," she answered, laughing.

"What's so funny?" he asked.

"The last time we went out we weren't old enough to drink!" she answered.

They began dating, and a year later they were married.

Soon afterwards, Peter went out on his own using $5,000.00 given to him by Sheila's father for start-up capital. The business, Carter's Wholesale Plants, struggled for a year or so, but with Sheila keeping her job with the golf course management company and doing the books for Peter's business in the evenings, they were able to get by. Peter's big break came when he landed the account of a national chain of home improvement stores, and his plant business increased tenfold overnight.

Sheila quit her job but continued to do the books for Peter's company. When the workload became too much for her, and the services of a certified public accountant were needed, she left the business entirely. This was fine with Peter because Sheila was pregnant with their first child, a boy they would name Daniel. Two more children followed in the next four years: a son, Mark, and a daughter, Mary.

Carter's Wholesale Plants grew like kudzu vines. In 10 years the business was grossing 10 million a year, but it was in year 11 that Peter decided to roll the dice and become a big-time national player in his industry. His goal was to triple his sales in the next five years. This required him to throw himself into his work like never before. He traveled every week and typically put in 14-hour days.

The schedule took a toll on him and his family. Sheila tried to get him to slow down, but he was obsessed with reaching his goal. He pushed himself harder and harder, missing Little League games and dance recitals. He called his kids when he was away, but it wasn't the same as being there.

He and Sheila did little more than pass in the night. Sheila knew only a few of the details of what was going on at the business, and he knew nothing of what was going on in her life. They lived together, as strangers.

Peter met his financial goal. His business reached the 30 million mark five years after he started this torrid pace. Peter was very proud, and thought his family would be too. But, ironically, it was five days after reaching this milestone that Sheila told him over breakfast that she wanted a divorce.

Sheila was determined to see the divorce, or "dissolution of marriage" as it was legally called, through. By the time she told Peter she wanted out she had already hired an attorney. His name was Richard Conan, and he was tenacious in the way he represented his clients. Peter knew Conan's reputation, and when he heard that he was the divorce attorney Sheila had hired he realized she was serious about splitting up. Still, for the next two weeks Peter begged Sheila to go to counseling and give the marriage one more chance. But when he was served the divorce papers at work, he knew the time had come to hire an attorney. He also knew that he had to move out. It would be untenable for them to live in the same house while the divorce was pending.

Explaining to his kids why he was moving into an apartment was the hardest thing Peter had ever done.

It was Sunday afternoon. The kids were in the family room watching television, and Sheila and Peter were on the porch outside. Peter was trying one last time to convince Sheila to tough it out, to give reconciliation a chance. She would have nothing to do with it, though, so the time came to talk to the kids.

"But why, Daddy?" Mark, the youngest son, asked through his tears. He and Mark were especially close.

"Mommy and I have decided that we need to live apart for a while."

"But why?" he persisted.

"It's just best for now that I do this." As much as he wanted to tell his kids that it was Sheila's decision, he didn't want to poison their relationship with their mother.

"When are you coming back?" Mark said, tears running down his cheeks.

"I don't know, sport. But you can be sure that I won't be far away, and I'll see you every day, you can count on that. Everything else will be the same. I just won't be living here."

Daniel, the oldest son, and Mary, the daughter, were watching their father intently.

"Mom, are you making Dad do this?" Daniel asked. At age 13 he could tell that his father wasn't telling them everything.

"Daniel, this is complicated," Sheila replied. "Things have changed between your father and me. It's not like it used to be between us."

"What's changed?" Daniel continued.

"Your dad's been gone so much lately, and…"

"But he said a couple of weeks ago that he wasn't going to have to travel as much. He said he had finished what he had been working on."

"Yes, but during the time he was away, I started thinking it might be better if we lived apart."

"So *you're* the one doing this! *You're* making him leave!"

Peter was glad Daniel had figured it out, and that the other kids had heard. He was also glad to see that, despite the time he had been away, they still loved him and wanted him around.

"Daniel, the love I once had for your father is not there like it once was."

"You don't love Dad anymore?"

"I still care for him, but I can't say I love him anymore."

"What a thing for a mother to say to her kids," Peter thought.

"It's going to be okay," Sheila said. "He's not going to quit being your father, are you Peter?" She looked at Peter, needing some help.

"No way! I love these kids too much for that." He grabbed the kids and hugged them. "But now I have to go."

He picked up his bag and began walking out the door. Mary, his daughter, had not said a thing, but she took his leg with both arms and held on with all her might. Sheila had to peel her away from her grip on her father. It was now time for Peter to cry.

Peter hired an attorney named Greg Waters who was experienced in family law. He had a calm and thoughtful demeanor like Peter's. He didn't particularly enjoy court, instead preferring to work out settlements that made sense for both parties. He knew the law thoroughly, and their first meeting was a time to give Peter a general overview of it.

"Unless the court finds that the marriage is 'irretrievably broken,'" the judge won't grant the dissolution," Greg explained. "Do you believe it is?"

"No, I don't. But Sheila wants out. Does that make it irretrievably broken?"

"Nope, but if one spouse says it is, most judges assume the same."

"Can I contest it?"

"Yes, and we should if you are totally opposed to the dissolution and if you believe the marriage can be repaired. Sheila's attorney will have to present evidence that the marriage is irretrievably broken, but, unfortunately for you, that evidence does not have to be corroborated. In other words, her saying she can't reconcile with you is most likely all that will be required. If the judge determines that you are unsuited for each other, he'll grant the dissolution."

"But I am totally opposed to the divorce. Can the judge end it if there is no fault on my part? Doesn't Sheila have to prove that I've done something wrong?"

"Not in Florida, or in most other states for that matter. Ours is a 'no fault' state. As such, a reason for wanting out of the marriage doesn't have to be asserted and proven, only that the marriage is irretrievably broken."

"But that's not right. That makes it too easy to break up. Couples aren't required to hang in there and tough it out."

"That's the effect in some cases, no doubt. But lawmakers decided it was best not to make a spouse prove the other caused the breakup. When that was required it made for wild accusations, blackmail and very unsafe family situations. The Legislature decided it would be better to just allow a spouse out if he or she wanted out."

"And if the other spouse didn't want the marriage to end, or he thought divorce was morally wrong?" Peter asked.

"He'd be out of luck as long as the court determined that the marriage was irretrievably broken."

"So Sheila can end the marriage regardless of what I want. That's pretty amazing. I still think this marriage can be saved if Sheila would just try."

Greg had heard such statements from clients before, so he stayed quiet and let the import of his words sink in. The reality of modern-day divorce and the ease with which a marriage could be ended was hard for many people to comprehend.

Peter then broached the most important subject to him.

"Who gets the kids?" he asked resolutely. He'd been away for a good part of the last five years, but the last few weeks had caused him to realize what was most important to him.

"The statute has changed," Greg answered. "It says you each have equal status in that regard, but the reality is, all things being equal, the mother still usually gets them."

"But she's the one splitting us up, and the kids know it! In fact, I bet they'd rather stay with me. Does what they want matter?"

"It does. It's something the court is required to consider, but it's totally within the discretion of the judge. Most people still believe kids should live with their mother, and judges feel the same way."

"But I could still end up with them, couldn't I?"

"Yes, it's certainly possible. Not probable, but possible. I'm assuming Sheila wants them, though. If she doesn't, we'll get them. What does she want?"

"I think she wants them."

"You *think* she wants them?" Greg asked. "It doesn't sound like you're sure."

"Actually, I'm not," Peter replied. "My guess is she would; I mean, what mother wouldn't? Then again, Sheila has always been very unsure of herself as a mother. She was never close with her parents, and always kept her distance from our kids. She didn't like making decisions about them, always deferring to my judgment. I can't remember a single time when she had a strong opinion about anything involving the children. So, I don't know for sure that she'll want them."

Talking of his kids as if they were chattel – mere possessions – was repugnant to Peter. The thought of him wanting to take them from Sheila, and Sheila wanting to take them from him, nearly made him sick.

"Well I want the kids. Now what's next," Peter asked.

"There must be an 'equitable distribution' of the marital assets," Greg answered.

"What in the heck does that mean?"

"The court attempts to divide the assets of the marriage in an equitable and just manner. It's a laudable goal, but very difficult to accomplish when significant assets are involved, as they are here."

"Are we talking about a 50/50 split?"

"Not necessarily. The Court starts out with the idea that it should be equal, but equitable distribution is based on fairness, and that doesn't always mean an equal split. With non-liquid assets like homes and other real property, it's impossible to split things right down the middle. Besides, there are always fights over what are marital assets and what are not."

"So everything we have doesn't belong to both of us?"

"No. Just those assets considered 'marital assets.' If an asset was brought into a marriage by a spouse it is a 'nonmarital asset.' Also, if an asset was acquired from nonmarital assets, the asset will be deemed nonmarital. It gets complicated, though, because if the asset was relied upon by the parties or treated as a marital asset, it may be deemed as such."

"Why does this matter?"

"Because a nonmarital asset goes to the party that brought it into the marriage. When it comes time to split everything up, the nonmarital assets will be determined first, and they will go to the party that brought them into the marriage. Whatever is left – the marital assets – will be subjected to an equitable distribution."

"Is that the end of it, after we do that?"

"Probably not. Sheila will undoubtedly ask for alimony, and because it's a 16-year marriage, she'll probably want permanent, periodic alimony, meaning you'll pay her whatever amount the Court mandates every month for the rest of her life unless she remarries."

"Every month for the rest of her life? She should have to work. She has skills," Peter said angrily. "She always said women should have equal rights. That should cover the bad as well as the good."

"I understand, and the Court is required to consider factors such as age, earning ability, education and the standard of living enjoyed during the marriage. A 16-year marriage is a close call. It's right on the edge of when courts grant permanent alimony, so just because she asks for it doesn't mean she'll get it. We'll fight it, but she'll probably end up with some type of alimony."

"So there are other kinds?"

"Several. To provide short-term assistance, there is 'bridge-the-gap' alimony that lasts for less than two years.[1] Then there's 'rehabilitative' alimony which is given to assist a party prepare to become self-sufficient. Maybe the person needs additional education, that kind of thing."

"Something like that would be reasonable. Sheila could study for the CPA exam. She's always wanted to do that, and she's already a darn good bookkeeper. She did my business's books for years."

"*My* business?" Greg asked. "What makes you think it's *your* business?"

"Because I'm the one who built it! You mean it might not be my business?"

"It depends on whether it's considered a marital asset, and it probably is."

"But I'm the one who busted his rump all these years, not her!" Peter was starting to lose his cool. "Are you telling me that Carter's Wholesale Plants is not my business?"

"She'll say it belongs to both of you, that it is a marital asset, because that's where the big bucks are in this marriage."

"But *I* own all the stock. She doesn't have a single share!"

"Didn't her father put in $5,000 to get you started?"

"Yes. To get *me* started, not us!"

"And didn't she put in a lot of time with the business, doing the books and other things?"

"In the beginning, yes, but we hired a CPA after just a couple years."

"And wasn't she taking care of the kids so you could spend your time building the business?"

"Well, yes, but..."

"All of this gives her a claim for a 'special equity.' Because of these contributions, her lawyer will argue that the business is as much hers as yours, that there wouldn't have been a business if she hadn't done what she did."

The way things were going, Peter was afraid to ask, but he had to.

"Is she going to win?"

"She'll win something. Some portion of the value of the business will go to her side of the ledger. It was a business grown during the marriage, and that's what supported the family. Part of it is hers, maybe even half."

The enormous consequences of the battle he was about to wage began to sink in. Peter knew how determined Sheila could be, and he now understood he would have to fight with everything he had to defend his position. This was a call to arms. She would be after the things in his life that he cared the most about: his kids and his business. Lost on him at this moment was the fact that his marriage was absent from the list. If he had spent more time nurturing his relationship with Sheila, perhaps this wouldn't be happening.

Richard Conan, Sheila's attorney, lived up to his reputation: pushy, mean, and uncompromising. He was that, and more, totally determined to squeeze every penny he could from Peter. Early in the divorce proceedings he succeeded in getting the Court to direct Peter to pay $10,000 for his attorney's fees. He then requested information about everything related to the value of anything remotely connected to the marriage and filed every conceivable motion. He made life so miserable for Peter that Peter felt himself losing his resolve to fight, becoming more willing to give Sheila more than she was entitled to receive.

Conan hired appraisers, all paid by Peter, to appraise the value of the Carters' biggest assets: Carter's Wholesale Plants, the home in Apopka and the oceanfront house at New Smyrna Beach. Conan estimated a value – high, of course – for the Carters' cars, boat, furniture, clothes, guns, rods, reels and jewelry.

Conan totaled all values and proposed a settlement. He demanded that Sheila receive custody of the children, one-half of all marital assets, and one-half of Carter's Wholesale Plants. For the equitable distribution, Sheila would get the house in Apopka, all furniture and household goods, her clothes and jewelry. Peter would get the beach house at New Smyrna Beach, his clothes, guns, rods, reels and boat.

Peter's lawyer, Greg Waters, was sitting at his desk as he read Conan's proposal. "The numbers are high, but the concept's pretty reasonable," Greg thought to himself. But then he choked when he read that Conan was demanding a lump sum payment of five million dollars for Sheila's interest in Carter's Wholesale Plants, and $12,000.00 per month in permanent, periodic alimony. On top of that, she would receive child support of $2,800.00 per month.

Greg did some figuring on his yellow pad to get a sense for where the final dollar figures might really land. He then asked his assistant to schedule a time for Peter to come in.

"Let me get this straight," Peter fumed. She would get the income from five million dollars, *plus* $12,000.00 per month in alimony, *plus* $2,800.00 in child support?"

"That's right. That's the proposal, at least."

"If she earned just five percent on the five million, that's nearly $21,000.00 a month! Add that to the alimony and child support and it's close to $36,000.00! All that for just staying home and watching TV? That's ridiculous! Let's go to court."

"If the Court awards permanent, periodic alimony it's going to be a high number, so just going to court doesn't necessarily solve your problem. The Court will attempt to maintain the standard of living Sheila enjoyed during the marriage."

"But Greg, that's $432,000 a year! That supports a lifestyle much higher than what we actually had."

"Really? Your tax returns for the last three years show annual income of around $600,000."

"But we lived on far less. Because the business was growing so fast, there was a lot of income to distribute at the end of the year. It's a Subchapter S corporation, so the income flows through the corporation to the shareholders. Since I'm the sole shareholder, all the income came to me."

"I understand, but the Court will rely predominately on your tax returns to set the amount, and they show this much income. Unless there is some sort of changed circumstance that shows your earnings will be less, the Court will assume this will hold true in the future. It will then assume that Sheila was enjoying a lifestyle that required this much money and make an award accordingly."

"But what about *my* lifestyle? If she gets this much money, and my income stays the same, I'm the one who will suffer!"

"You're right, and the Court is required to take that into consideration. That's why I'm confident she won't end up with this much money, not even close to it, but it is a remote possibility. Conan is just trying to bully and intimidate you. He's trying to make you believe it could be this bad if you go to court, hoping you'll settle for a little less. He'll still want a lot for his client – and him – but he knows these numbers aren't realistic."

"What do you suggest?"

"Let them know we intend to fight for custody of the kids, and that you won't pay permanent alimony. We also must not concede that she has any interest in the business, at least not yet."

"What do you mean, 'At least not yet?'" Peter asked.

"We've been over this, Peter. Her father gave you start-up money. Sheila did the books for a while and took care of the kids so you could work."

"Yes, but I made the business what it is today!" Peter was having a difficult time accepting the fact that the business effectively belonged to both of them, even though Sheila didn't own a single share of stock. "A measly five thousand bucks, a year or two of work and staying home with a few kids shouldn't entitle her to half of a business that grosses 30 million dollars a year!"

"And that's the last time you will ever say that, okay? Don't ever denigrate Sheila's contribution to the family or you'll regret it. Courts place high value on maintaining a good home life."

"But you know what I mean, Greg. I was the one making the sales calls, not her."

"I know, but you and Sheila will be viewed as having been a team, growing the business together. She'll be compensated for everything the Court views as her contribution. Some percentage of the value of the company will be credited to her because she stayed at home, taking care of the kids, freeing you up to make the sales calls and do all the things necessary for the business to be successful."

Peter scowled, but was resigned to ask, "What do you suggest we do?"

"Accept their proposed split of the marital assets, minus the business; agree to pay three years of rehabilitative alimony while Sheila prepares for the workforce; and pay the $2,800 for child support until Sheila begins working. That figure is required under the statutory child support guidelines, so you can't get around that anyway. Once Sheila begins working, we can re-calculate it; she'll have to contribute her proportionate share based on how much she is earning."

"How much would the rehabilitative alimony be?"

"Let's offer $3,000 per month. That gets the total of child support and alimony to nearly $6,000 per month for three years. That assumes, of course, that the Court awards the kids to her. If we get them, she would receive only the alimony. Conan won't let her accept this, but it's a starting point."

"All right, do it. In the meantime, I'll prepare myself for World War III."

World War III was what he got. Conan came at Peter with everything he had. If Peter suggested a value for a marital asset that was different than the value claimed by Conan's appraiser, it was automatically challenged, necessitating the hiring of another appraiser, all paid for by Peter. Conan had psychologists perform psychological evaluations on the children, trying to get the kids to say something that would hurt Peter's chances of receiving custody. This infuriated Peter and concerned Sheila, but Conan convinced her it was "a necessary part of the proceedings," so she didn't back him off. Using actuaries to estimate Peter's life expectancy and earning capacity, he came up with greatly inflated claims of the value of the business and what Peter could expect to make, thereby driving the alimony figure higher. After six months, Peter was exhausted physically and emotionally and running low on cash. Between paying two attorneys and all the "experts," Peter had laid out nearly $80,000.00.

"This is crazy," he said to his attorney, Greg Waters. "Just let me talk to Sheila. We'll work it out."

"She's represented by counsel. You can't talk to her. Besides, if she had wanted to talk she wouldn't have hired Richard Conan."

"But there has to be a better way. This is draining me dry and we're not getting anywhere."

"We *are* getting somewhere, Peter. It just takes a while to establish the values of the assets we intend to divide, and we're going into mediation in two weeks. Maybe we can work it out there. It's a process ordered by the Court, and the parties are required to negotiate in good faith."

"But the mediator can't force the parties to settle, can she?"

"No, she's there simply to facilitate a discussion that might lead to a resolution."

"From what I've seen of Richard Conan, that's unlikely."

"Maybe so, but let's not pre-judge it. Besides, I've never seen a mediation that wasn't helpful, even when the case didn't settle on the spot."

"I hope you're right, but I'm not going to hold my breath."

The mediation session was one of the few times Peter had actually seen Sheila since the dissolution proceeding began. She was thinner and harried, looking as though she hadn't had a good night's sleep in a long time. She greeted Peter nicely enough, but then never looked him in the eye for the rest of the mediation.

Mediations are informal proceedings where a neutral third party – the mediator – leads a discussion between the parties aimed at reaching a settlement. In her opening statement, the mediator, Elizabeth Tanner, outlined her role and the process they would be following.

"Good morning. My name is Elizabeth Tanner, and I will be serving as your mediator. I'm certified by the Florida Supreme Court, and it's my hope that we can find a resolution to this case that works for each of you.

"I'm also an attorney, but I won't be serving in that capacity today. My job is not to give legal advice – you have excellent attorneys who can do that. My job is to facilitate a discussion that will lead to a settlement so you don't have to go through all the heartache and expense of a full blown trial. This case has been churning along for a while already, and you've already gotten a taste for how difficult and expensive litigation can be. My goal is to find a way to resolve this matter and get it behind you.

"I'm not a decision-maker in this case. I will not mandate an outcome or force you to accept something you don't want to accept. Instead, I'm going to try to help you reach a voluntary agreement.

"I'm required to be neutral, but that doesn't mean I can't ask questions that you may perceive as unfriendly. Please don't take them that way. It's my job to help you honestly examine the strengths and weaknesses of your case.

"One other thing. This is a confidential proceeding. While I may take copious notes, I will destroy them at the end of the mediation so there will be no written record of what transpired. I want you to feel free to talk candidly with me.

"At some point we may break out into a "caucus," which is really just a fancy word for a private meeting. There may be things you wish to tell me that you don't want the other side to hear. I will respect those confidences. In fact, I won't disclose anything to the other party that you don't authorize me to disclose.

"In a moment, I'm going to recognize the attorneys to make an opening statement. I know very little about the case, but that's okay; mediators frequently don't. In their openings, the lawyers will share the facts with me that I need to know so that I can be helpful. But because I know so little about the case, if I ever say anything that contradicts what your attorneys have told you, by all means, rely on what you have heard from them.

"There is coffee and water on the credenza, and bathrooms down the hall.

If you need a break, let me know. My guess is we'll go most of the day, so we may have sandwiches brought in. I'll play it by ear. Are there any questions? Good. Let's begin.

"Richard, would you like to make an opening statement and share with me what you think I need to know?"

Richard Conan treated his opening like an opening statement to a judge or jury, complete with charts and graphs. He delivered it while standing, and it was very long and overwhelming, especially his claim that Sheila was entitled to one-half of Carter's Wholesale Plants. Greg Waters, on the other hand, said very little except that they were there to negotiate in good faith and "work it out." Conan's tactic worked; it had the effect of totally deflating Peter. Peter viewed Conan's presentation as forceful and persuasive, Greg's as meek and unconvincing.

Elizabeth Tanner sensed this, so she asked a few questions to deflate Conan's position and keep the parties on a more even keel. If she was going to get Sheila to accept what Peter might be willing to pay, she had to create a little doubt in Sheila's thinking.

"Did Sheila make any of the sales calls for Carter's Wholesale Plants?" Elizabeth asked. "Was she involved in the business in any way after she left as bookkeeper? Is there anything in the record suggesting that Peter wouldn't be a good custodial father?" On and on the questions went. Conan had good answers, but Sheila couldn't help but wonder if the judge would view the issues the same as the mediator apparently had.

"Have there been any settlement offers?" Elizabeth asked.

Conan was quick to point out that there had been, but Peter's response had been "pathetic" so there was little to discuss.

"Careful with the language, Richard," Elizabeth admonished. "We're here to work it out. Let's stay respectful. Tell me about the offers, please." Conan was the kind of guy who would try to take over the mediation if he could. Elizabeth Tanner was not going to lose control.

Conan explained the terms of their initial offer. Elizabeth stayed quiet, thinking hard and writing furiously on her notepad.

"I want to make sure I understand this," Elizabeth finally said. "In your initial demand, your client would make $432,000 a year for life?"

"That includes child support which would end when the kids reach age 18," Conan responded.

"So, $432,000 minus the child support after the children become adults?"

"That's right, but it's all based on sound legal theory."

Elizabeth didn't respond. Instead she just stared at Conan and then at Sheila. She knew there was no way Peter would pay anywhere close to this, so her actions and words were intended to make Sheila realize she had to reduce her demand significantly.

"What about that, Greg. Did you counter?"

"We did," Peter's lawyer replied. "And we're willing to work something out today, but there is no way my client would or should pay such a sum. We'll go to court before we do that." Greg outlined the terms of their counteroffer.

"I'm assuming these proposals are still alive?" Elizabeth asked each side. After receiving confirmation they were, she said, "So the ball's in your court, Richard. Why don't we meet in caucus?"

"Whatever you want, Madame Mediator," he said condescendingly.

Early in the mediation, Elizabeth's goal in the caucus was to get a sense of what the attorney and client were *really* thinking, regardless of what they had said in the opening statement, so she could begin fashioning a strategy to bridge the gap between the parties. She needed to know the limits of each.

"Richard, do you mind if I ask Mrs. Gunn a few questions?" Elizabeth wanted to speak directly to Sheila, so Conan couldn't filter her answers.

"Go right ahead," he said sarcastically. Elizabeth didn't flinch.

"First, may I call you Sheila?"

"Yes, of course."

"Of everything on the table, what is the most important to you?" Elizabeth asked.

"I stayed home with the kids, so Peter could grow the business," Sheila responded. Elizabeth noted to herself that Sheila had just admitted that it was Peter who had done the work in the company. Conan picked up on it, too.

"But as you know, the law gives Sheila credit for freeing up her husband from domestic duties, so he can concentrate on the business," Conan injected.

"I understand," Tanner answered. "I'm not going to share any of this with the other side. You were saying, Sheila?"

"I might not have been in the office, but what I was doing allowed Peter to go to work and not worry about the kids. My father also gave the business five thousand dollars to get us started."

Elizabeth caught Sheila's use of the word 'us.' She also made a mental note that Sheila had not said having custody of her children was the most important thing to her.

"So you want a part of the business?"

"I do. I think I deserve it."

"Does that mean you want an ownership interest like stock, or do you want him to pay you a lump sum for what you believe is the value of your contribution?"

"The latter. He's the one who can run it, and he doesn't need me hanging around."

"That makes sense," Elizabeth commented. "What else is important to you?"

"If I'm going to be on my own, I'll need money and a place to live."

Again Elizabeth noted that Sheila had said nothing about her kids. She was after money.

"What are your long-term plans? Any intention to go back to work?"

"I've been out of the workforce for so long I don't see how I can."

"Plus, she'll have children to care for," Conan injected.

"Oh yes," said Sheila, "the kids. I can't work if I'm home taking care of the kids." The way she said it made Elizabeth wonder if she was interested in the kids only if they could help her achieve her financial goals. If Peter wanted custody of the kids badly enough, he might be willing to pay extra money to get them, and Elizabeth was getting a strong feeling that Sheila would go along.

Elizabeth wanted to go back into the room with Peter and Greg with at least one point of agreement, so she took the most obvious.

"Regardless of who gets custody, will you agree to accept the guidelines in the statute? Richard?"

"Oh, I suppose so. We could ask for more, but we'll go along with the statutory guidelines even if they are just the minimum amounts required."

"And Sheila understands that if she works, she will be responsible for child support in whatever her percentage of income is relative to Peter's?"

"Yes, we've been over that. But it really doesn't matter. We want permanent, periodic alimony so she won't be working."

"I know that's your goal. I've been listening," Elizabeth responded, smiling. "But what about the alimony amount? You know your number is high, Richard."

"I know," Conan answered. "We know we're going to have to make a move. What we want to do is consider the payment for the business and the alimony amount together. We're not going to agree on one without an agreement on the other, you understand?"

"Of course," Elizabeth said, biting her lip at the chauvinistic tone he was taking with her.

"We didn't pull the five million figure out of a hat," Conan continued. "The business grossed 30 million last year, and there's no indication it won't keep doing at least that. If Peter will give Sheila five million for her one-half interest, we'll drop our alimony demand to $9,000.00 per month. And we'll still need the $2,800.00 a month for child support."

"I understand. Let me see what I can do," Elizabeth said, walking out of the room.

Elizabeth Tanner began in the same manner with Peter as she had with Sheila.

"What do you want most out of a settlement."

"My children. This madness has made me see with perfect clarity what I care for the most. I don't want to lose my business, but more than that, I don't want to lose my kids."

"I thought that's what you'd say," Elizabeth said with a smile. "I don't know if that's going to be possible, but I'll do my best. It may cost you a little more, but I'll try. Would you be willing to pay a little more if that's what it took?"

"It would depend on everything else," Greg said, before Peter could respond.

"Of course," Elizabeth answered, but she had planted the seed.

"They've reduced their demand," Elizabeth stated. "First, though, would you agree that you'll abide with the statutory child support guidelines, regardless of who gets custody?"

"Yes, of course. Peter will be the one paying for them regardless of who gets custody, so we'd like to hold it to the minimum," Greg answered.

"Good. They've agreed too.

"They've also reduced their alimony demand to $9,000.00," Elizabeth continued, "but they still want five million for what she considers her share of the business. I did get her to agree not to seek an ownership interest, though."

"She just wants the money," Peter said angrily, "and I'm really surprised. She's not that way, at least she hasn't been. I don't know what's gotten into her."

"Probably Richard Conan," Greg answered. "I'm sure he's painted a big picture in her mind about what she's entitled to under the law. Even if it's not something she even cares about, she's begun to think she should have it. Some lawyers are like that. They won't let the client settle for anything less than what the law would allow. And getting that extra little bit is often what causes all the trauma and heartache."

"Unfortunately, that's true," Elizabeth responded, "But how do you want to respond, Peter?"

"She's not getting the kids and she's not getting the business. Everything else is negotiable," Peter said defiantly.

"Okay, so if you get custody of the kids, you won't have to pay child support. That saves $2,800 a month right there. Would you add that to the rehabilitative alimony you have already offered, raising that number to $5,800.00."

Peter looked at Greg, who nodded. "I'll do that," Peter said, "but only for three years as we first offered. She needs to work."

"Fifty-eight hundred a month for three years is not very much after a 16 year marriage, not when the two of you have been living off of $600,000.00 a year. Would you agree, Greg?"

"I would," Greg answered. "We know we'll have to pay more, but that's where we are for now."

"What about the business?" Elizabeth asked.

"I'm not giving her any of my company!" Peter said strongly.

"I hear you loud and clear, Peter," Elizabeth said. "I'm just exploring, trying to see possibilities, helping us focus on the strengths and weaknesses of the case. I'm not here to give you legal advice, but it's my opinion that a court will determine that she is entitled to something for the business."

"You're the second attorney who's told me that," Peter said, looking at Greg. "What would you suggest, Greg?"

"Give her some money for the business," Greg said. "Call it 'blood money' if it makes you feel better, but the truth is the Court is going to recognize her contribution to the company's success. I think it's more important to avoid permanent, periodic alimony. That's a check you'll write every month for the rest of her life unless she remarries. Offer the $5,800.00 rehab alimony for three years and $500,000.00 for the business. And you get custody of the kids."

Peter thought for a moment or two. "All right. Do it." Elizabeth left the room and headed down the hall to Conan and Sheila.

"I have good news," Elizabeth said to Conan and Sheila. "Peter has offered to pay a significant amount of money for your interest in the business, Sheila. He's also agreed to nearly double the amount he had previously offered for rehabilitative alimony."

"No permanent alimony?" Conan asked sharply.

"No, but that would be a tough sell for you in court, Richard. Sixteen years is not a slam dunk, you know."

"No, it's not. But I'll have a decent shot. How much did he offer for the business?" Conan demanded.

"Five hundred thousand, and he wants custody of the kids. That's very important to him."

"Important to him? He was hardly home for five years, and now he's found fatherhood? Give me a break!" Sheila retorted.

"I'm just telling you what he told me. It seemed sincere, but you would know better than I," Elizabeth answered.

"This is comical!" Conan said. "I have a good shot at permanent alimony with the judge, and a good shot at a 50/50 split on the business. It would be *malpractice* for me to allow my client to accept what they're offering!"

"Then send me back in with something else. I'm sure we'll ping back and forth several times before we get to the bottom line…for either side," Elizabeth said, letting them know that she expected them to continue coming downward.

"We talked while you were gone. Mrs. Carter will reduce her demand for her interest in the business by a million dollars. That's a pretty good move, Elizabeth. But we won't reduce the permanent alimony demand, at least not until they agree to pay some amount, and we want custody of the children. Try that. See how it flies."

Back to Peter and Greg she went with the new offer.

"Why is she so hung up on permanent periodic alimony?" Peter asked Elizabeth.

"For the same reason banks get robbed. Because that's where the money is," Greg said.

"That's pretty much it," Elizabeth confirmed. "Conan makes a big deal about having a good shot at getting it at trial, and he may be right, wouldn't you say, Greg?"

"He has a chance, but I'd rather have my argument than his. I think it's more likely the Court would require rehab instead of permanent."

"Hmm," Elizabeth said. She didn't want to confirm a position that weakened her bargaining ability if she didn't have to. Greg didn't push it.

"And she still wants the kids?" Peter asked.

"Yep, but they did reduce the demand for the business by a million dollars."

"So four million is their number," Greg said. "We came up a half-million, they came down a million. I wonder if Conan is setting up a bracket. If we stay with moves of those increments we end up at 1.5 million and they end up at two. Do you think that's where he's going?"

"I don't know," Elizabeth answered. "Send me back with another $500,000.00 and we should be able to tell."

"Okay, you have it," Greg responded. "We've also agreed to raise the rehab amount to $8,000.00 a month."

"For three years?"

"For three years, and we get the kids."

"So they're up to a million dollars for the business," Conan said, scratching his chin. "Interesting. Give me a moment with my client if you would please."

"Of course," Elizabeth answered, leaving the room. Ten minutes later, Conan opened the door and summoned her from the hallway.

"We'll go down another $500,000 for the business, and reduce our demand for permanent alimony from $9,000.00 to $5,800.00. That's an amount he agreed to pay for three years. We'll take it, but we want it for the rest of Sheila's life."

"There's a big difference, Richard," Elizabeth said.

"I know, but Peter's a big man. Take it in there and see what happens."

"And the kids?"

"Oh, of course we want the kids," Conan said with a wry smile.

"My guess is Conan's angling for a little more than two million," Elizabeth said to Greg and Peter. "He came down $500,000.00 instead of a million, and he gave me a funny smile when he said they still wanted the children."

"Do you think he was sending you a message?" Greg asked.

"Hard to tell, but it may be a good time to make a big jump and see if you can buy the kids from her."

"*Buy* the kids from her?" Peter repeated. "It's unbelievable that we're talking in these terms. We're speaking of them like they were things you'd buy in an auction! These are my children, for goodness sakes!"

"I know they are, and that was a bad choice of words," Elizabeth said. "I apologize."

Peter just shook his head. "I'm ready to get this over with. Where do you think he's going?"

"My guess is 2.5 million, although he hasn't told me."

"Let's cut to the chase. Tell them I'll pay 2 million but not a penny more. I also won't pay permanent alimony, but I'll pay the $5,800.00 for five years instead of three. But all of this is contingent on my getting custody of the children. If I don't get that, we're not moving from our last offer and we're leaving."

"Peter, it's too early for a 'take it or leave it' offer," Greg said. "Take a few more steps, smaller steps, before you do that."

"No, I'm sick of this! I don't even want the divorce, but you've told me I can't prevent it. If that's the case, I want it over with!"

"Why don't I give you two a little time together," Elizabeth said. I'll be back in a moment."

A few minutes later, Greg stuck his head out the door and called Elizabeth into the room.

"Peter still wants to make that offer," Greg said. "But make sure they know that's it. We aren't going any higher."

"I understand," Elizabeth answered. She left for Conan and Sheila.

"Don't take it, Sheila. He's bluffing," Conan said.

"I don't think so," Sheila replied. "Peter doesn't bluff. What you see is what you get."

"I do not believe he's bluffing, Richard," Elizabeth said. "Greg tried to get him to go lower, but Peter wants it over with. If you don't take it, I think he's going to walk."

"He won't walk. If he does, we'll make him pay for it. I'll cover him up with so many pleadings we'll bleed him dry just attending court hearings."

Sheila was confused. She didn't know whether to follow her instincts or her attorney's advice.

"Okay, what do we do?" She had made her choice. She was deferring to her lawyer. Conan smiled.

"Tell them we'll come down to 2.5 million for the business, but we're not coming off our last demand for permanent alimony. We also want the kids," he said to Elizabeth.

"If I can get him to 2.5 million for the business, will you allow him to have custody of the kids?" Elizabeth asked.

"And what do we do about alimony?" Conan inquired.

"I don't know. Let me see if they have a suggestion."

"Present it as a hypothetical. It's obvious that custody of the kids is important to him. I'm reluctant to give away that bargaining chip before we have an answer on alimony," Conan said.

"I'll see what I can do," Elizabeth answered. She rose from the conference table and headed out the door.

"Peter, I know you said you were leaving if your last offer wasn't accepted, but stay with me a little longer. I think we're on the verge of getting this done," Elizabeth said.

"So they didn't take it?" Peter asked.

"No, they didn't, but…"

"Nope. That's it. I'm through! Sheila knows I don't play around…not like *she* does," he said angrily.

"What do you mean?" Elizabeth asked. "Why did you say, like *she* does?"

Peter hesitated for a moment, then told her about Sheila's affair.

"The affair was with one of your employees?" she asked.

"Yes. My chief horticulturist. My main guy!"

"Is he still working there?"

"He is. I haven't had a chance to deal with him with all this divorce stuff going on. And the truth is, I'm not sure how to handle it. I want to fire him – actually I want to wring his neck – but he's still doing a good job. I plan on checking with a labor law lawyer to find out my options. I don't want to end up with another lawsuit on my hands."

"The affair she had was with your chief horticulturist?" Greg said, leaning in with great interest.

"Yea, I told you that."

"You told me she had an affair, but not with your most important employee! This changes things significantly. What she did could have wrecked the company! It was reckless, and showed a callous disregard for the welfare of the business. This might influence the judge's thinking on what he would award her. We're in a stronger position now. You should sweeten your last offer slightly, but my guess is Conan's temperature is getting ready to change. Will you go to seven years for rehabilitative alimony?"

"And get the kids?"

"You get the kids. She gets two million for the business and $5,800 per month in rehab alimony for seven years."

"Where's she going to live?"

"You'll want to stay in the big house the kids are in now, right?"

"Yes."

"And the condo at New Smyrna Beach is paid for, so give her the condo and the furniture that's there. You get the house and its furnishings. Split the $50,000.00 in certificate of deposits evenly, and you get your retirement account."

They hadn't even negotiated over Peter's retirement account, and Sheila had a possible shot at half of it.

Peter thought for a moment. He was shaking he was so angry. He knew Sheila, and he knew she would take this offer. When she took it, their marriage would be over. It was a difficult moment for any spouse, especially one who didn't want the marriage to end.

"And I can't prevent the divorce?" he asked Greg, one last time.

"We can argue that the marriage is not irretrievably broken, but the judge is going to grant the dissolution if Sheila wants out."

"She does, I'm convinced of that," Peter said. "Make the offer, get them to go along with it, and let's end this."

"It's time to take the deal, Sheila," Conan said, after hearing from Elizabeth. He had been through another divorce where a spouse had an affair with a very valuable employee, and he'd seen how it had influenced the judge. He knew so much about it because the divorce had been his own, and he was the spouse who had done the cheating. His affair with his long-time legal assistant had led the judge to award permanent, periodic alimony to Conan's spouse even though the marriage had been for only 14 years. Conan was still paying for his bad choices.

"But you told me the affair was relevant only if I spent marital money on the guy, and I didn't!" Sheila exclaimed. "Only if I 'dissipated marital assets' was how you put it."

"Normally that's true. But now that Greg has realized who your affair was with, he's zeroed in on how he can make it work to Peter's advantage. I'd been wondering all along why he hadn't brought this up before. I guess he just didn't realize it."

Conan's advice confirmed what Sheila had been feeling in her gut.

"Tell him I'll take the offer, but I want to get my clothes and things out of the house. I also want the kids every other weekend. We'll alternate holidays."

"Pretty much the standard visitation schedule," Conan chimed in.

"I'm sure that won't be a problem," Elizabeth responded.

The agreement was drafted on the spot, and the parties, their attorneys and the mediator signed it. Copies were distributed and everyone left. As Greg and Peter were walking to their car, Sheila pulled up alongside them.

"Will you get in for a minute?" she asked Peter.

"I will if I'm allowed," he answered, looking at Greg.

"It's okay with me. The agreement is signed."

Peter got in.

"I'm sorry," Sheila said. "I'm sorry for the affair, and I'm sorry for ending the marriage."

Peter stared ahead, not sure what to think or say.

"I'll tear the agreement up if…" Peter said.

"No, I still want the divorce. But I just wanted to apologize."

"Our kids need a mother, Sheila. We're going to have to get along."

"The visitation schedule we worked out will be fine."

"Maybe we can get back together after the divorce," Peter said. "That happens with some couples, you know."

"Yea, maybe, who knows?"

"That's right, who knows." Peter said, as he got out of the car.

"Peter, take care of yourself."

"I will. You too."

He closed the door, took a deep look at Sheila through the open window, and stepped out of her life. Sheila drove off, the car disappearing around a corner. It was over...or so they thought. Little did they realize that their disagreements, conflicts and involvement with each other were just beginning. They were going to come face to face on countless custody and parenting issues like pick-up and drop-off, school conferences, who pays for what, and adjusting to possible remarriages. All of that was ahead. In fact, when Sheila drove around the corner, it wasn't the end at all, but just the beginning.

[1]My descriptions of the various types of alimony I partly learned from a very informative article written by attorneys Victoria M. Ho and Jennifer L. Johnson, an article which appeared in The Florida Bar Journal/October 2004, pages 71-73.

Author's Note:

During my time in the Senate, women who wanted Florida's "no fault" divorce law changed would occasionally visit me. They were distraught over their marriages having been dissolved because they didn't want the divorce. Usually it was apparent their burden was partly caused by a spiritual concern, a conviction that the divorce conflicted with their religious beliefs. These were uncomfortable meetings for me. These good people were clearly hurting, but I couldn't commit to abolishing no fault divorce. Still, from what little I learned of their marriage situations, it did seem that the marriages might have ended too easily. It made me realize the importance of judges genuinely exploring the issue of whether a marriage was irretrievably broken, and not just accepting at face value such an assertion from only one party.

This story mentions Lake Apopka, once the second largest lake in Florida but now the fourth largest. Its reduction in size came about in 1941, when 20,000 acres of marshland were drained on the north shore to allow farming on the resulting muck soils as part of the wartime effort to feed the nation during World War II.

In 1987, as chairman of a sub-committee of the House Natural Resources and Conservation Committee, I toured Lake Apopka to see firsthand its water quality problems, which were extensive. The water smelled like rotten eggs and bubbled from the bottom as muck and other organic matter decomposed. On the day I was there, biologists from the Game and Fresh Water Fish Commission (now the Florida Fish and Wildlife Conservation Commission) were pulling in a gill net that had been set to sample the kind and number of fish in the lake. The net was full of gizzard shad and gars, but there were no sport fish. The loss of sport fish had taken its toll on businesses that depended on good fishing in the lake; there once had been 21 fish camps on Lake Apopka, but now there was just one.

The lake deteriorated from a variety of factors. For years, untreated sewage from nearby towns was dumped directly into it, and runoff from agricultural operations on the north shore brought in phosphorous and other nutrients. Alga blooms resulted, preventing sunlight from reaching the plants growing on the bottom. These plants died, creating muck. The lake was caught in a death spiral.

Slowly the cities built sewage treatment plants, stopping that source of pollution, but the nutrients coming into the lake from agriculture were more difficult to treat. The farming didn't stop after WW II, and this region continued as a major food producing area. For example, it was here that the best corn in America – Zellwood sweet corn – was grown. Few people wanted to stop the farming, but there was growing concern over the nutrients leaving the farms and ending up in the lake.

The Legislature passed the Lake Apopka Restoration Act in 1985 which set the goal of restoring the lake to Class III water quality standards, meaning that it would be suitable for recreation. In 1987, the Surface Water and Management Act (SWIM) was passed, designating Lake Apopka a priority water body of regional importance. Consequently, government officials directed a great deal of attention to the lake, attacking the water quality problems on two fronts.

First, they sought ways to reduce the nutrients entering the lake. Farmers implemented farming practices that were the least damaging environmentally, techniques called Best Management Practices. This resulted in fewer nutrients leaving the farms.

Second, governmental engineers began planning an elaborate natural filtration system on the northwest corner of Lake Apopka, just below the Beauclair Canal, to remove nutrients already in the lake. Water from Lake Apopka flowed north through the Beauclair Canal into the Harris Chain of Lakes. From there it made its way into the Oklawaha River and on into the St. Johns River. The filtration system would remove nutrients before they entered these downstream waters.

The effort to restore Lake Apopka continued. In 1996, a phosphorous criterion rule was passed, limiting the amount of phosphorous that could be in water leaving the farms on the north shore. Farmers seriously questioned whether they could meet these water quality standards. All the while, momentum for the government buying these farms was building.

At this time I was chairing the Natural Resources Committee in the Senate. Senator Buddy Dyer, the senator for the area around Lake Apopka, asked for my support for an appropriation of 90 million dollars to acquire much of this farmland. Farmers had agreed to sell, and the plan was to convert these acres back into the marsh they once were.

I met with a few of the affected farmers and they were convinced that the environmental standards on the horizon would be so stringent they couldn't be met. Reluctantly, I agreed to support the appropriation even though I had grave reservations about the government buying this land. I would have preferred to try some other way of cleaning the lake, maybe by dredging the bottom or creating filtration systems on part of the property that was targeted for acquisition, thereby keeping most of the land in agricultural production. Years before, I had toured a vegetable processing facility on one of these farms, and carrots were being brought in from the field. Truckload after truckload of carrots were lined up, waiting to dump their load. The carrots were washed and bagged and then sent off to feed families somewhere in America. It was beautiful and wholesome. Now it was heartbreaking to think this would stop because we couldn't figure out another way to clean the lake. Nevertheless, the appropriation passed, although at the much lower amount of 20 million dollars. By 1999, most of the farms had been acquired.

The trend of the government buying prime farmland and taking it out of production is one that concerns me greatly. I once had a Political Science professor at the University of Florida who said that our nation's great geo-political advantage was its ability to feed its own people. He was right, but if the government continues acquiring so much prime agricultural property and converting it back into its natural state we may find ourselves in the position of having to import food on a grand scale, and that would be disastrous.

Even though a great deal of farmland was lost, which I regret, the restoration of Lake Apopka is working. Water clarity is much better and vegetation is taking root on the lake bottom. Also, part of the filtration system planned for the northwest corner of the lake is in place and working well. I toured it to see if a comparable system could be used to clean Lake Hancock in Polk County, another degraded water body, and was very impressed. Water that came in looking like cheap dark whiskey left as clear as good gin.

THE LAW: *Definitions and Explanations:*

Divorce: The legal separation of man and wife, effected by the judgment or decree of a court, and either totally dissolving the marriage relation, or suspending its effects so far as concerns the cohabitation of the parties.

Black's Law Dictionary, Sixth Edition, p. 480

Equitable distribution: No-fault divorce statutes in certain states grant courts the power to distribute equitably upon divorce all property legally and beneficially acquired during marriage by husband and wife, or either of them, whether legal title lies in their joint or individual names.

Black's Law Dictionary, Sixth Edition, p. 538

Alimony: Comes from Latin "alimonia" meaning sustenance, and means, therefore, the sustenance of the wife by her divorced husband and stems from the common-law right of the wife to support by her husband. Allowances which husband or wife by court order pays other spouse for maintenance while they are separated, or after they are divorced (permanent alimony), or temporarily, pending a suit for divorce (pendente lite)...

Black's Law dictionary, Sixth Edition, p. 73

Notable Quotes:

"Marriage is a coming together for better or for worse, hopefully enduring, and intimate to the degree of being sacred."

Honorable William O. Douglas, Associate Justice,
United States Supreme Court
www.brainyquotes.com

"In mid-life the man wants to see how irresistible he still is to younger women. How they turn their hearts to stone and more or less commit a murder of their marriage I just don't know, but they do."

Honorable Earl Warren, Chief Justice,
United States Supreme Court
www.brainyquotes.com

"People who love sausage and people who believe in justice should never watch either of them being made."

Otto Bismark / www.quotegarden.com

"Justice is the tolerable accommodation of the conflicting interests of society, and I don't believe there is any royal road to attain such accommodation concretely."

Honorable Learned Hand, Associate Justice,
United States Supreme Court,
"The Great Judge," by P. Hamburger

"The law embodies the story of a nation's development through many centuries, and it cannot be dealt with as if it contained only the axioms and corollaries of a book of mathematics."

Honorable Oliver Wendell Holmes, Associate Justice,
United States Supreme Court, "The Common Law."
www.quotegarden.com

"Corn can't expect justice from a court composed of chickens."

African Proverb / www.quotegarden.com

Out-of-Bounds

TEMPER, TEMPER...
Contract: Offer, Acceptance, Consideration

Preface: Contracts are the basis of most legal relationships. They may be written or oral, or they may be created by conduct. All contracts, though, must contain certain elements to ensure that each party knew it was making a deal and understood what the terms were.[1] This story illustrates these elements in a fun and, admittedly, somewhat farfetched way. The drama that unfolds around a simple transaction between two men also speaks to what is required for one to be guilty of assault and battery.

BRUCE "DUFF" DUFFY loved being on the golf course just before dark. Walking the last few holes as the sun was dipping behind the trees, he would become aware of a wonderful quiet that was settling in, a stillness all too rare in a world increasingly covered over by concrete and asphalt.

By then his shirttail would usually be out, hanging over the pockets of his baggy shorts. Much of his sweat would have dried in the cooling air, and he could taste its salty residue from above his upper lip. His face would be a little red from being in the sun all afternoon. Sometimes his left cheek, along the jawbone, would be chaffed from his rough cotton shirt rubbing across it as he swung the club. Occasionally he would have a little sand in his hair from it being blown back onto him while blasting out of a sand trap.

He hit many of his best shots at this time in the round, maybe because he was so relaxed. On those rare occasions when a ball went astray, it didn't bother him much. He'd simply drop another one and swing again. There were no temper tantrums anymore, no throwing of clubs, just an appreciation for the beauty of the course and the health to enjoy it.

As a boy, he would often walk 36 or even 54 holes on a summer day. That was behind him now, but even at age 82 he could walk 18 holes. He took pride in this, and after leaving the final green he'd open the trunk of his car and sit on the bumper as he took off his golf shoes, thinking of the great and not so great shots he had hit that day. It mattered not if he had played alone, as he often did, or with others. This was his time to be with himself, and it was time he cherished. Losing these moments would be, well, too much to contemplate...

Duff fought valiantly as an Army soldier in WW II. His tour took him to fields of France for one of the bloodiest conflicts of the war. Soldier-friends fell beside him as they gave the last full measure of service to the cause of freedom. Duff was himself wounded by shrapnel as he pulled a French soldier to safety. Rarely did American and French troops fight side-by-side, but in this instance their companies were traveling together on a road when they were attacked. He returned to the United States as a war hero and was awarded a Purple Heart because of his injuries.

The war took a terrible toll on the country in the 1940s, but the nation rebounded when the war was over as Americans turned their attention to building a new life for themselves. Confidence and optimism were on the rise, and nothing could hold down anyone who was willing to work hard and play by the rules. It was the beginning of a golden age in America. Business failures were rare, and even blue-collar jobs paid enough for a single income to provide a house, two cars, and a two-week vacation for families.

Duff set out to achieve his own American dream by starting an insurance agency in Akron, Ohio. He had a wife and young son to support so he enthusiastically put his nose to the grindstone. His business grew steadily, and after a few years he opened several new offices in the Akron area. He built quite an insurance network.

He found that the golf course was a good place to get to know potential customers so he honed his game, taking weekly lessons for a year from the professional at the club where he belonged. He became an honest three-handicap player, and this made him competitive in most any match. He was invited to join teams in scramble tournaments, and this led to many friendships he would not otherwise have had. Many of these new friends would later buy insurance from him, so golf was not only enjoyable, it helped pay the bills.

His son, Bruce Duffy, Jr., graduated from college and went into business with his father. "Junior," as he was called, took the agency to the next level of excellence and the business became statewide in its scope. With such a large operation, however, came enormous stresses and strains. Even though Junior was running more of the day-to-day operations than his dad, Duff refused to slow down.

In addition to refusing to slow down, Duff had another personality trait: he had a sudden and explosive temper. Occasionally it served him well, like in the war when he got so mad at the enemy that he charged the soldiers firing at him to save the life of the French soldier. But mostly his temper got in the way, especially in business when he berated employees who made mistakes or grew frustrated with difficult customers.

One day, when he was 70 years old, his unwillingness to slow down and his temper nearly killed him. He was boiling mad at a customer who had taken his business elsewhere. He was walking around the office, angry and fussing at everyone for the most minor of things. As he left his son's desk, he grabbed his chest in pain. He was having a heart attack.

He survived, and after a brief recuperation he tried working just "half-way," but his personality type wouldn't let him. As long as he was involved in the business he insisted on being a part of everything. Finally, bowing to pressure from his son and wife, he retired when he was 72, moving to Naples, Florida, in 1994. He and his wife, Mary, bought a lot on the 10th green of the Naples Country Club. There they built a simple but elegant home, and he began playing golf four times a week.

Full-time retirement was strange at first, but Duff settled right in. He found himself thinking less of his insurance business with each passing month. Southwest Florida was wonderful, and he and Mary enjoyed exploring interesting places like the Rod and Gun Club in Everglades City, and Rookery Bay north of Marco Island.

After a few months their lives fell into a routine of doing the same things day after day, week after week. Duff would play golf every Saturday, Tuesday, Thursday and Friday. Together, they would play bridge with the same couples on Wednesday, attend church every Sunday morning, go to a movie every Monday night and eat lunch most days at the clubhouse.

Mary was fine with this. She had wanted to leave Ohio for some time so she was very happy. She managed to do some volunteer work and was involved with the church, so she found the right mix of relaxation and community service.

Duff, too, was having a ball. He had worked hard to enjoy this carefree lifestyle and he hadn't a care in the world. Little did he know, however, that this routine was causing him to grow restless and unsettled. He had always been a city leader with many community and business responsibilities, but, curiously, as the years of his retirement went by, his total focus on having fun began to take a toll on him. There were signs of penned up frustration, like the time his temper caused him to cuss out his neighbor who parked his boat in the driveway in violation of Homeowners' Association by-laws, or when he exploded on telephone solicitors instead of politely saying he wasn't interested in what they were selling.

Why he would behave like this was largely lost on him. At times he would feel discontent, but he didn't perceive that it was born of boredom. Without seeking out the source, he would, instead, charge off to the golf course or poker room at the clubhouse. It was like an itch that never got scratched, just covered over with numbing cream.

Late summer of 2004 brought the threat of several hurricanes to Southwest Florida, the first of which struck with a vengeance. A tree limb crashed through a part of the roof of Duff's home and power was out for a month. Adding insult to injury were drenching thunderstorms that came nearly every day for a week after the hurricane was long gone, flooding the interior of the beautiful home. Much of their furniture in the house was ruined. Duff's wife went back to Ohio to be with their son and grandchildren, but Duff needed to be home to deal with insurance adjusters and repairmen, so he lived in a roadside motel for three weeks. The motel wasn't air-conditioned because the electricity was off, but at least it was dry.

With no power to run the gasoline pumps, fuel was a scarce commodity. Long lines of cars extended for blocks as motorists waited at the few stations that were operational. Once Duff waited for an hour and a half only to have the pumps run dry just as he was nearing the station. He was left to fume about wasting an eighth of a tank while waiting in line. Duff found himself thinking the country was only one tank of gas away from anarchy, and maybe oil really was the essence of Middle East politics.

Federal emergency shelters of tents and trailers were soon set up, and Duff left the motel for a trailer. Despite the efforts of wonderful workers and volunteers, the first few weeks were very trying. Generators were in short supply, so there were few hot meals, no hot coffee in the mornings, no air conditioning, and no hot showers. There also was very little ice, so nothing was served cold.

As Duff and others around him were digging out from underneath the first storm, meteorologists began reporting that other hurricanes were forming off the coast of Africa and heading westward "down the alley" of the warm Atlantic tropical waters. The slow-motion drama of these storms gaining strength, churning to the west, curving northward, and finally threatening Florida was hard to believe. The anxiety caused by the very real possibility of getting hit by a second storm within weeks of the first was too much for some people to bear. The first hurricane had thrown their lives into chaos. The second, they were sure, would ruin them, so many left Florida for good. A few desperate souls, suffering from other problems, even committed suicide.

By the end of the hurricane season, this cycle had repeated itself two more times. It mattered little to Duff that the storms hit other parts of Florida. The build-up over the possibility of another hurricane over his head frazzled his nerves, and he was exhausted physically and emotionally. When his home golf course finally re-opened, playing golf was to him like an alcoholic getting a drink.

Duff's occasional golfing buddy was Pierre Toureau of France. Toureau had made a fortune importing French wines into the country from the wine-growing region of Bourdeaux. The fabulous wines of the Margaux and Petrus vineyards were his specialities, and his long customer list of serious American wine drinkers had made him a lot of money over the years.

Duff didn't care too much for Pierre. He was a bit snobby and always complained about the heat and humidity, as though Southwest Florida was supposed to be something other than hot and humid. He poked fun at the southern drawl of native Floridians and frequently commented on their "lack of sophistication." The truth was, Pierre's thin mustache and snappy dress hit Duff the wrong way, too. Still, he was someone to play golf with, and Duff always took his money when they bet on a round, so he put up with him.

One October morning Duff and Pierre teed off at 8:00 a.m., trying to beat the afternoon thunderstorms. With the recent rains and hot weather, mosquitoes were out in full force. The county had been spraying, but the spray hadn't killed them all. Actually, the issue of mosquito spraying had received a high political profile lately.

Led by Marge Mahoney, a newly elected county commissioner, the commission had doubled the county's mosquito spraying budget in the last two years. She actually campaigned on the issue. "Scratch a vote for me before you scratch a bite from them," was the tag line on her campaign materials. She even gave out miniature cans of insect repellent at campaign appearances. It didn't matter to Mahoney that the mosquito was a critical part of the food chain for most of the natural world, and that without it a link would be missing that would be devastating to many species further up the chain. "Mosquitoes bite and cause welts so they should be eliminated," was her position. She won in a landslide, and after that, the last thing the other commissioners wanted was to be viewed as being against mosquito spraying.

This began a campaign to kill as many mosquitoes and mosquito larvae as possible. But in the process, a huge amount of environmental damage was done. Snook eggs floating on the surface of the estuaries were killed as the deadly spray from helicopters and airplanes settled on the water. Fish hatchlings died because there were fewer mosquito larvae for them to eat. Because there were fewer mosquitoes, many newly hatched frogs couldn't survive. The casualties went on and on, but there were fewer mosquitoes to bite people. The commissioner considered her program a huge success.

Many of the mosquitoes Mahoney hadn't killed were biting Toureau.

Cussing these biting insects and the heat, he was almost unbearable in the golf cart. Duff tried to tune him out, but it was impossible.

"Pierre, why are you complaining?" Duff asked incredulously. "I'm from Ohio, but I'm smart enough to know that heat and mosquitoes are part of life in Florida, even in October. What's your problem?"

"*I* don't have a problem. The *county* has a problem. They won't spray enough to get all these bugs!" Pierre respondid sharply.

Pierre did have another fixation, however: his new TaylorMade r7 quad driver, a club he had just bought for $615.00. This, coupled with his graphite shafted Ping G2 irons, Vokey design wedges and Scotty Cameron putter, gave him a club set valued at more than $2,400.00. Duff was playing with an old set of Haig Ultra blade irons, PowerBilt persimmon woods, and a Bulls Eye putter. "That rich little Frenchman and his expensive clubs are about more than I can take," he thought to himself.

Pierre commented on Duff's clubs: "You're playing with dinosaurs! Get some modern sticks; they'll improve your game."

"My clubs work just fine," Duff said sternly.

"But the new clubs are so forgiving, and the ball goes a lot farther," Pierre continued. "These titanium drivers, for example; I'm sure you'd pick up another 20 yards if you'd get one. In fact, I have a Titliest 975D driver back at the house that I'll sell you for not much money. It's a fantastic club."

"Then why'd you get another one?" Duff asked.

"Because it's three years old, and the technology is changing so fast I wanted a current-generation driver."

Duff thought of his 40 year-old persimmon woods. He had, in fact, been considering getting new clubs, at least a new driver.

"How much do you want for it," Duff asked.

"It cost me $550.00, but I'll sell it to you for $400.00."

"That's a lot of money for a three year-old club," Duff said.

"$350.00 then."

"Pierre, I thought you were giving me a deal. Would you take $250.00?"

"No, but I'll take $300.00."

Duff thought for a moment. "Sold," Duff said. "I'll give you the money when we get home."

Out of the blue, Pierre then began speaking of the war in Iraq, commenting that it was the biggest foreign policy blunder in American history. Duff bristled. What did this little toad know about the United States to make such a statement?

Toureau poured it on until Duff could stay quiet no longer. He had fought to liberate France in WW II, and this arrogant sophisticate was criticizing the country that had freed his homeland.

"You know, you Frenchmen get in bed with the bad guys and then expect the rest of the world to protect you. All take and no give. You do business with the tyrants, but say you're against terrorism. The irony is that your French policy of doing business with them keeps them in power." Duff's reference to Pierre being a Frenchman chapped Pierre, but Pierre stayed quiet – for now.

"When President Bush was looking for support for the Iraqi invasion, you did nothing but kick him in the teeth," Duff continued. "You wouldn't stand with us in our time of need even though we saved you from Hitler's persecution. You sip your fancy wines and act suave and sophisticated, but you're the first to tuck your tail and run when the going gets tough."

"But it was a bad war; the French didn't agree with it!" Pierre responded, quite taken aback by Duff's vitriol. "They thought it was a huge mistake. Should they have gone along even if they didn't agree with it?"

"Well, yeah," answered Duff. "If it hadn't been for the United States freeing your country in WW II you'd be speaking German today!" He was really getting worked up, thinking of his own war experiences and his soldier-friends who had died in battle.

"So that means for the rest of time France is to do whatever the United States wants, to support it even when she believes it's wrong?" Pierre asked.

Duff didn't have much of an answer because there wasn't one. "All I know is we needed you and you weren't there," was all he could say.

"Your president makes a big deal about not ceding authority over foreign policy decisions to the United Nations," Pierre continued. Duff bristled at Pierre's use of the words '*your* president,' as though President Bush wasn't his president too. "Are you suggesting that France should cede authority over its foreign policy decisions to the United States?" Pierre asked.

"The world is a safer place without Saddam Hussein," Duff said, remembering a line often spoken by President Bush.

"That's debatable," Pierre retorted briskl, "but one thing is sure: The world is *more* dangerous as a result of the war. More people hate the West, especially the United States, than before. The war has created more terrorists than have been killed, and it's given them real-life experience in fighting an urban war and making bombs! And where are the weapons of mass destruction? The whole pretense for the war turned out to be false."

"They *were* there, and maybe they still are," was all Duff could say, something he had heard on conservative talk radio shows.

"But Duff, your own president has admitted there weren't any. You just can't accept that your president was wrong, can you? And let me remind you that the United States is now my country. I'm a naturalized citizen, and my opinion counts just as much as yours. *I'm an American, too.*"

"Then why don't you start acting like one!" Duff shouted. "Support the president! Support the troops!"

"But invading Iraq was a poor decision! We didn't attack the ones who attacked us on 9/11! I don't think President Bush lied, but it was a mistake, and we'll be paying for it for a long time to come."

"We have to take the fight to them!" Duff exclaimed emphatically. "Fight them there or fight them here, it's as simple as that." Duff was not one to over-analyze anything, totally missing that innocent Iraqis were caught in the crossfire.

"But who are we fighting?" Pierre asked. "We're sure not fighting the terrorists who brought the fight to us. And we've squandered the support we had from the rest of the civilized world in the war against terrorism after 9/11. The whole world was with us except the bad guys, but not anymore. American soldiers are dying, Duff, and for what? Is simply to rid the world of a dictator enough?"

"The war in Iraq is central to the war on terror. The president said so, and he has better information than the rest of us."

"He has better information, yes, but the in Iraq is *not* central to the war on terror, certainly not against the terrorist threat made evident on 9/11. And why do we call it a war on 'terror'? It's a war on 'terrorism.' 'Terror' is an emotion, and if we're going to fight an emotion it should be fought with psychologists. 'Terrorism' is what we use soldiers to fight against."

This disagreement over semantics really chafed Duff. It was just the kind of thing a snooty pinhead like Pierre would take issue with the president over. What difference did it make? Once again, Pierre was taking a backhanded shot at the president's sloppy use of the English language. "He's attacking my president's intelligence," Duff thought. He was boiling now.

"And one more thing," Pierre said. "Some of the bravest soldiers in the history of modern warfare were French. Do not ever challenge the patriotism or courage of my native countrymen!"

That did it. Receiving this lecture from someone who wasn't even a person born in this country was more than Duff could take. This – combined with his frustration over doing nothing productive for the last 10 years and nerves rubbed raw by the hurricanes – caused him to snap. He walked around the golf cart, took the TaylorMade r7 quad driver from Pierre's bag, raised the club and crashed the shaft against the Frenchman's head, splintering the graphite shaft into a million pieces.

When Pierre awoke, he was lying on a table in the emergency room of the local hospital, a doctor shining a light in his eyes and asking him his name. As the fog cleared, Pierre learned that he had a concussion and a cut on the back of his head that required nine stitches to close. He would spend the night in the hospital for observation, but no further treatment was expected. The stitches would be out in eight days.

Duff was in the waiting room, embarrassed, scared, apologetic and repentant. He was aware of what he had done but not why he had done it. Never before had he done anything so impulsive or crazy.

Pierre Toureau had fallen to the ground like a rock with the strike of the club, and this snapped Duff out his deranged tirade. Duff called 911 on his cell phone for an ambulance and followed it to the hospital. Now that he was there, he didn't know what to do, but that was answered when two police officers approached him. The doctor treating Pierre had called the police after hearing the explanation of his injury.

They spoke with Pierre, interviewed Duff, and then went back in to see Pierre. When they emerged from the treating room, they told Duff he was free to go. Toureau had chosen not to press charges. While the state attorney might later choose to do so, the chances were he wouldn't without Pierre's consent.

Duff wanted to see Pierre but the officers wouldn't allow it. As Duff was driving home he tried to sort out his thoughts. "How could I have done that?" he wondered.

He called his wife, and she was waiting for him when he arrived.

"What happened?" Mary asked.

"The graphite shaft of the club broke like a pretzel," Duff said.

"But why'd you do it, Duff?"

"I don't know. I just snapped. One moment we were talking about the war in Iraq, the next he was lying on the ground. I don't even remember hitting him."

"This is so unlike you!"

"I know. It doesn't make any sense. Nothing adds up. I'll be the first to admit it. I guess the rest of our family is bound to find out, wouldn't you guess?"

"I imagine so. We probably should call them."

"*I'll* call them. I did it, so I should be the one to make the call. They're not going to believe it; *I* don't believe it."

Over the next few weeks Duff called Pierre several times to apologize and offered to pay Pierre's medical expenses. Pierre took the calls but said little. Two months after the incident, Duff answered a knock on his front door. A man handed him an official looking document called a "Summons." This "process server" informed Duff that he was being sued, and that he was required to respond to the Summons within 20 days. "Have a nice day," the server said as he turned and left.

Mary walked up. "What is it, honey."

"I'm being sued," Duff answered, as he read the Summons, "by Pierre. I guess I shouldn't be surprised, the way he wouldn't talk when I'd call. I should have known something was up."

"What are you going to do?" Mary asked in a calm voice. Nothing ever rattled her. She was steady as a rock and possessed a calm demeanor born of a deep religious faith. Duff was lucky to have her.

"Well, what are you going to do?" she asked again.

"The only thing I can do: hire a lawyer and hope for the best."

Duff would learn that he was being sued for the intentional torts of assault and battery. These offenses could also be criminal charges, but the state attorney chose not to file, bowing to Pierre's wish that the incident be dealt with in civil court. Instead of being charged with a crime that could have brought jail time, Duff was being sued in civil court, and that meant Pierre was trying to get money from him.

Duff hired Vernon Hendry, an attorney with deep roots in Southwest Florida. From his insurance days, Duff had learned from many lawsuits his insurance underwriter defended that it was important to have local representation, and not offend the Court with some hotshot lawyer brought in from another area.

"Unfortunately, they have you dead to right," Vernon said. "Your actions fit the definitions of these offenses perfectly. You 'intended' to use unlawful force against Toureau; he was 'aware' of it because he saw you raise the club; and you had the 'ability' to carry out the blow. You committed an assault.

"You also committed a battery because you struck him without his consent.[2] The only thing we're going to be arguing about is the extent of his injuries."

"Does it matter that he provoked me?" Duff asked.

"It could, but not in this case. No one would agree that it was reasonable to strike him under those circumstances, and that's the test, what would an ordinary, reasonable person have done. That's the standard you'll be measured against, and reasonable people don't let arguments escalate into a physical altercation."

"But he was criticizing my president! Those are fighting words!" Duff said emphatically.

"No they're not, Duff, and you know that. We need to settle this case. Maybe Pierre will be satisfied with only his out-of-pocket expenses being paid."

"I doubt it; I've already offered to pay him that. He wants more; you just wait and see. He'll want a written apology, too; I just know it. Something he can show off and gloat about."

"And that wouldn't be the end of the world, not if it gets this behind you. Let me see what I can do," Vernon answered.

Toureau's out-of-pocket medical expenses were $600.00, but his insurance company wanted the money it had expended on his care reimbursed. This was $2,600.00, so the total medical expense claim was $3,200.00. Pierre's attorney also demanded $25,000.00 for "pain and suffering," claiming Pierre had developed a fear of being on the golf course, couldn't sleep well, and had constant headaches. Duff nearly choked. He could understand wanting something for the headaches, but the rest of it seemed ridiculous.

"That Frenchman is just taking advantage of a bad situation simply to squeeze money from me! He's not actually injured in the ways he claims," he said to Vernon.

"Maybe not, but this is not an outrageous first offer. It doesn't even contain a request for punitive damages, something they'll ask for if the case goes to trial," Vernon answered.

Duff looked exasperated and confused. "What should I do?"

"Offer $5,000.00 for starters. That'll get the attorney a decent fee for the small amount of time he has in the case and allow Toureau to put a little money in his pocket. They won't take it, but it's a good counter-offer."

"For starters? So you think I'll have to pay more than that?"

"Duff, you broke a golf club over someone's head! A jury will not excuse that kind of behavior."

"All right. Make the offer. Get this over with. I don't want to spend the rest of my retirement worrying about it."

After three months of negotiations, Duff agreed to pay $11,000.00 to settle all claims. This, plus $4,000.00 he had to pay his attorney, made his out-of-pocket expenses $15,000.00, a sum that made for a pretty expensive round of golf.

He also agreed to see a therapist and attend an anger management class. This was insulting to him, but it helped bring the case in for a landing, so he agreed.

There was one more part of the settlement that Duff had predicted. Pierre wanted a written apology. He got it, and began carrying the statement in his golf bag. Duff was never aware of Toureau actually showing it to anyone, but just knowing it was there drove him crazy.

Two weeks after the case settled, there was a knock on Duff's door.

"I wonder if I should answer it?" Duff said to his wife. "Remember the last time I answered the door. I got sued."

"Let me get it," his wife said with a grin.

When she returned, she was no longer smiling.

"Someone at the door wants to see you," she said with a concerned look.

"Who?"

"Pierre Toureau."

Duff thought for a moment and then rose from his chair. His wife followed him to the door.

Pierre Toureau was holding a golf club. For a second, Duff wondered if he had come to settle the score.

"I'm delivering the driver you agreed to buy from me," Pierre said. Duff recognized it as the Titliest 975D they had discussed when playing golf those months before. "And I'll take a check for $300.00 if you don't have the cash."

"You've got to be kidding me!" Duff responded, his heart nearly jumping through his chest. He felt his face flush and rage was welling up inside him. The last thing he wanted was any more involvement with Pierre Toureau. That Pierre would have the audacity to try to sell the driver to him after all they had been through was unbelievable. Duff took a deep breath and counted to 10 as he had been taught in the anger management classes he had taken, but it didn't work. He was on the verge of taking the club from Pierre and breaking this one over his head, too.

"No, I'm not kidding. We made a deal. I offered to sell you this club for $300.00 and you accepted. Legally speaking, there was an offer and an acceptance so there was 'mutual assent;' we had a 'meeting of the minds.' The terms of the agreement were 'definite and certain,' and no more negotiation was anticipated. We have a contract. I'm delivering the club and you owe me the money." Pierre sounded like he had researched contract law and was spouting off what he had learned. "And in case you're wondering if an oral contract is binding, it is. This isn't a transaction involving the sale of real estate or a long-term lease or something that must be in writing."

But Duff also knew something about contract law. Years of selling insurance had taught him that a contract wasn't valid unless there was "consideration," or something of value given by each party for the benefit of the other.

"Sorry, Pierre, but there was no consideration. We don't have a binding agreement."

"Consideration. What's that?" Pierre asked.

Duff knew he had him.

"We didn't seal the deal with a cash down payment or recite other consideration. I gave you nothing of value that induced you to proceed. But I'll tell you what: I'll give you $100.00 for the club. I'll give it to you right now and we'll call it even. What do you say?"

"I don't know. We had a deal at $300.00."

"That's where you're wrong, Pierre. We didn't have a deal. There was no 'consideration', so there was no contract. I'm surprised you didn't learn that when you were doing your research. Now come on. Take the hundred bucks. Frankly, I don't want to deal with you any more and you probably don't want to deal with me."

"How about $200.00?" Pierre countered.

"No, but I'll give you $150.00 if you'll take it right now."

Pierre thought for a moment. "Okay, give me the one-fifty and I'll be on my way."

Duff peeled the money from his wallet, gave it to Pierre and took the club.

"Nice doing business with you, Pierre." Duff was feeling much better after getting such an expensive club for so little.

Pierre turned and walked away. Duff closed the door.

"Very impressive," Duff's wife said with a wry smile. "I didn't realize you knew contract law."

Duff, knowing he had just bluffed Pierre, said, "I know it better than you think."

Two hours later, there was another knock on the door. Actually, it was more like a bang, not a polite knock.

"That would be Pierre," Duff said without even looking. "Don't answer it," he told his wife.

"But why would he be back?"

"Because there *was* valid consideration when we first made our deal on the golf course. My guess is he just discovered it in whatever law books he's reading."

"Duff, I know you're in there. I'm not going away," Pierre shouted.

"We could call the police," Duff said to his wife.

"That's the *last* thing I want," she answered tersely. "No more police or legal wrangling. Talk to him and get this over with."

"I guess you're right," Duff responded.

He cracked the window but didn't open the door. "What do you want, Pierre?"

"I want the other $150.00 you owe me. There *was* valid consideration in our original deal. I asked my lawyer. He said my offering to sell you the club for $300.00 and your accepting to pay it was consideration. The $300.00 was the inducement to enter into the contract."

Knowing Pierre was correct, Duff tried another tact. "But we modified the contract and changed the price to $150.00. If the $300.00 was valid consideration in the first contract, the $150.00 reduction was valid consideration for the modification."

"I knew you were going to say that, so I asked my attorney about that too," Pierre replied.

"He said you fraudulently induced me into reducing the price. You lied about there being no consideration, so the modification is void."

Duff wasn't sure about this, but what Pierre was saying sounded reasonable. He *had* said something he knew to be incorrect, and Toureau had relied upon it.

"Pierre, I'll give you another 50 bucks to end this."

"No. I want the full one-fifty. You lied to get me to come down on my price."

"I was *negotiating*," Duff said. "You sounded like you knew the law. For all I knew you'd call my bluff. Take the 50 dollars. I'm not going to pay another cent. Besides, I have the club, and you *don't* want to try to take it from me."

Thinking of what a pain and hassle it would be to try to collect the rest of the money or the club, Pierre agreed.

"Great. I'll slip it under the door," Duff responded. "And I don't ever want to talk to you about this again."

A month later, in late February, Duff was playing golf on a magnificent day. A cold front had just moved through. The air was cool and the sky was a deep cobalt blue, the kind of day that entices so many people to move to Collier County. He had finally decompressed from the hurricanes and legal wrangling with Pierre Toureau. His sessions with a therapist had actually helped, and he had come to understand that the stress of the storms had taken a much bigger toll on him than he had realized. Using a slogan from Alcoholics Anonymous, "Live and Let Live," the therapist had gotten Duff to have greater empathy for others, even Pierre, because he didn't know what struggles they might be having to overcome. Everybody had been affected by the storms, but each person had been affected differently. For all Duff knew, Pierre might have been as assertive as he was because his insurance company had refused to pay for damage to his home and he was simply lashing out because of frustration. This outlook had the effect of reducing Duff's anger at others and teaching him forgiveness. He had even mailed Pierre $100.00, making good on the original deal of $300.00 for the driver.

He also had begun volunteering as a driver for Meals on Wheels, an activity that had given him the feeling of contributing to the betterment of the community, a feeling he had been missing for several years.

In the fading light of the afternoon, walking to the tee of the 18th hole, Duff was aware of a wonderful stillness and quiet that had settled in around him. His face was a little burned from the sun and wind of the day. He ran his fingers through his hair and felt a little sand on his scalp, evidence of his downwind blast from the sand trap a few holes earlier.

His shirttail was out and a little sweat had dried on his upper lip. He tasted it as he reached into a baggy pocket of his pants and pulled out a tee.

All day he had been thinking of the bizarre months that had just passed. He had learned much about himself and others. He felt confidence, too, as though he knew he had much left to learn and to give even at this late stage in life. He actually felt youthful and vibrant like he had when he first returned from the war and was getting started in his insurance business.

"Maybe the best years of life begin at 82," he thought, smiling as he teed up the ball.

With the swing speed of a much younger man, the Titliest 975D driver that had once been Pierre's flexed on the downward stroke and the club head came square with the ball at just the right moment. With a sharp metallic crack, the club shot the ball 230 yards down the middle of the fairway.

The right side of Duff's mouth curled upward in a grin, and to only himself he said, "Perfect – absolutely perfect."

[1]The Uniform Commercial Code (UCC) has usurpted most common law contract principles. UCC theorems are similar, but generally not as rigid as those in common law.

[2]Many criminal codes now combine the offenses of assault and battery into one offense.

Author's Note:

Early in this story I spoke of a time in America when the job of one parent was sufficient for a family to have a home, two cars in the garage, a nice vacation once a year and a nice retirement. A union leader I met in Miami shared that thought with me in 1998 when I was running for governor. His first name was Gary. He was bemoaning the passing of this era, and how few families today can make it on one income.

The problem of which he spoke is symptomatic of a much larger issue. As the country continues to lose its manufacturing base, the gap between the "haves" and "have nots" becomes even greater. When unskilled or manufacturing laborers lose their job opportunities, frustration builds. Frustration often leads to hope being lost, and when hope is lost, desperation sets in. Desperate people often strike out in one way or another. The construction industry is one of the few places where well paying jobs for day laborers still exist, but cities can't keep expanding outward forever, so even this will slow at some point.

Part of the solution is to prevent trade agreements that further weaken our nation's manufacturing base. Several trade agreements have already passed, and there have been many economic losers. Among the biggest losers have been the nation's manufacturers. With unfettered free trade, in order to stay competitive, manufacturers must rush to the countries that have the least amount of environmental protection, poor labor laws, and no practice of providing health insurance for employees. It may be too late to reverse this trend, but existing agreements should be changed to give American companies a fighting chance if they manufacture their goods in this country.

Agriculture is another industry that needs to be protected. The growing, harvesting, processing and transporting of crops creates countless unskilled and skilled jobs. Agriculture also has a huge ripple effect throughout the economy, especially in the manufacturing sector, yet it too is being crippled by shortsighted trade agreements.

The hurricanes of 2004 were harrowing, but hurricanes are a part of life in Florida. In fact, my earliest memory is of Hurricane Donna when it came through Polk County in 1960. What sticks in my mind the most was a big pecan tree in our back yard that was uprooted, and how much fun it was climbing on it the next day.

My next experience with a hurricane was in 1992, when Hurricane Andrew slammed into south Florida. I was in the Florida Senate, and was appointed to a committee to help with the state's response to the storm. As damaging as the hurricane was, if it had come ashore 50 miles north the damage would have been several times greater.

Then came Hurricane Opal, which clobbered the Panhandle coastline in 1996. I was still in the Senate and flew to Pensacola from Tallahassee in a Blackhawk helicopter with Major General Ronald O. Harrison, Adjutant General of the Florida National Guard, and North Florida senators to inspect the damage and prepare a legislative response. We then rode the beach in Humvees. I'll never forget that for miles and miles, nearly all the houses built on the ocean side of the sand dunes were gone. All that was left was the concrete foundation. But the houses built on the landward side of the dunes were still there, relatively unscathed. It was a powerful illustration of the merit of growth management efforts that have attempted to prevent construction on the "wrong" side of the dunes, yet there are those who fight such common sense proposals.

THE LAW: *Definitions and Explanations:*

Contract: An agreement between two or more persons which creates an obligation to do or not to do a particular thing.

Black's Law Dictionary, Sixth Edition, p. 322

Offer: A proposal to do a thing or pay an amount, usually accompanied by an expected acceptance, counter-offer, return promise or act.

Black's Law Dictionary, Sixth Edition, p. 1081

Acceptance: A manifestation of assent to terms thereof made by offeree in a manner invited or required by offer.

Black's Law Dictionary, Sixth Edition, p. 13. K-Line Builders, Inc. v. First Federal Savings & Loan Association, App., 139 Ariz. 209, 677 P. 2d, 1317, 1320

Offer and Acceptance: In a bilateral contract, the two elements which constitute mutual assent, a requirement of the contract.

Black's Law Dictionary, Sixth Edition, p. 1082

Consideration: Some right, interest, profit, or benefit accruing to one party or some forbearance, detriment, loss, or responsibility given, suffered, or undertaken by the other."
Black's Law Dictionary, Sixth Edition, p. 306. Shaffer v. Ricci, 603 So. 2d 566, 17 Fla. L. weekly D1713 (Fla. Dist. Ct. App. 4th Dist. 1992)

Assault: An intentional, unlawful offer of corporal injury to another by force, or force unlawfully directed toward person of another, under such circumstances as create well-founded fear of imminent peril, coupled with apparent present ability to execute attempt, if not prevented.
Black's Law Dictionary, Fourth Edition, pg. 147

Battery: Any unlawful beating, or other wrongful physical violence or constraint, inflicted on a human being without his consent.
Black's Law Dictionary, Fourth Edition, pg. 193

Notable Quotes:

"The right to swing my fist ends where the other man's nose begins."
Honorable Oliver Wendell Holmes, Jr., Associate Justice, United States Supreme Court. www.brainyquotes.com

"The old idea of a good bargain was a transaction in which one man got the better of another. The new idea of a good contract is a transaction which is good for both parties to it."
Honorable Louis Brandeis, Associate Justice, Supreme Court of the United States, Commencement Address, Brown University, 1912

"All our work, our whole life is a matter of semantics, because words are the tools with which we work, the material out of which laws are made, out of which the Constitution was written. Everything depends on our understanding of them."
Honorable Felix Frankfurter, Associate Justice, United States Supreme Court www.brainyquote.com

"Unthinking respect for authority is the greatest enemy of truth."

Albert Einstein / www.brainyquote.com

"Peace hath higher tests of manhood than battle ever knew."

John Greenleaf Whittier / www.brainyquote.com

"Allow the president to invade a neighboring nation whenever he shall deem it necessary to repel an invasion, and you allow him to do so whenever he may choose to say he deems it necessary for such a purpose – and you allow him to make war at pleasure."

President Abraham Lincoln / www.brainyquote.com

"If there is no struggle, there is no progress. Those who profess to favor freedom, and yet deprecate agitation, are men who want crops without plowing up the ground, they want rain without thunder and lightning."

Honorable Frederick Douglas, Associate Justice,
United States Supreme Court
www.brainyquote.com

"Since when have we Americans been expected to bow submissively to authority and speak with awe and reverence to those who represent us?"

Honorable William O. Douglas, Associate Justice,
United States Supreme Court
www.brainyquote.com

"Emergency does not create power. Emergency does not increase granted power or remove or diminish the restrictions imposed upon power granted or reserved. The Constitution was adopted in a period of grave emergency. Its grant of power to the federal government and its limitations of the power of the States were determined in the light of emergency, and they are not altered by emergency."

Charles Evan Hughes, Associate Justice,
United States Supreme Court
Home Building & Loan Association v. Blaisdell, 290 U.S. 398, 425 (1934)

"No one is fool enough to choose war instead of peace – in peace sons bury fathers, but in war fathers bury sons."

Herodotus

Monument to an Era
Citrus Tower, Clermont, FL

CAREFUL THE COMPANY YOU KEEP
Felony Murder Doctrine

Felony murder doctrine: At common law, one whose conduct brought about an unintended death in the commission or attempted commission of a felony was guilty of murder (e.g. a homicide committed during an armed robbery). Black's Law Dictionary, Sixth Edition, p. 617

Preface: The felony murder doctrine makes the saying, "Be careful the friends you keep," very important. Prosecutors use the doctrine to charge those involved in the commission or attempted commission of a felony with murder if a person was killed, even though the death was not planned. Those charged include not only the person who actually did the killing, but also everyone else involved in the felony during which the murder occurred. One who is participating in a large drug deal, for example, may find himself facing a murder charge if someone is killed, even though he wasn't the triggerman.

CURTIS RASNAKE was a good kid. He went to church most Sundays, did his homework, was respectful to elders and worked part-time cleaning cars at a detail shop three afternoons a week.

His last name was short for "Rattlesnake," a moniker given his great-great-great grandfather, Charlie Rasnake, after the Civil War. Like many African-Americans in early America, newly freed slaves often had only first names, and such was the case with Charlie. Soon after moving to the sandy hills of Lake County in central Florida from the low country of South Carolina, he killed a giant rattlesnake, nearly eight feet long, and a picture of him and the snake appeared in a national magazine. Since Charlie had no last name, the photographer gave him one, "Rattlesnake," and this was soon shortened to "Rasnake."

Curtis' doing well was a bit miraculous. His mother had become pregnant with him when she was 16 years old, still a kid herself, and in no position to provide for him financially or emotionally. He never knew his father, and all his mother had told him was that his dad had been in his early 20s when she became pregnant.

When Curtis was three, his mother was convicted of selling drugs and sentenced to four years in prison. The job of raising Curtis fell to an aunt and uncle who were nearing retirement. Their children were raised and gone, each doing well, and the last thing Aunt Betty and Uncle George wanted was the responsibility of raising another child. But who else was there? Betty and George didn't want their nephew to become a ward of the state, supported by the taxpayers and left to bounce around from one foster home to the next. They were proud people, and their kin would pay their way and take care of themselves.

Betty and George took Curtis into their lives and treated him like one of their own. They showered him with love and good care so that when he started kindergarten, he was nearly as ready to learn as the children from stable family situations.

Curtis' love for his aunt and uncle grew strong, so much so that when his mother was released from prison, he made it clear that he wanted to stay with them. This was fine with Betty and George because he had, by then, become the apple of their eye. They approached Curtis' mother about adopting him. She didn't object; in fact, she was actually relieved. The prospect of raising a child who she barely knew overwhelmed her. The adoption was finalized in six months.

As well as Curtis was doing, he still had obstacles to overcome. His vocabulary was not as developed as other kids, and his social skills were lacking. He was quiet, small in stature, pudgy, and weak physically. He wore thick glasses and sometimes the kids teased him. Consequently, throughout elementary and middle school he spent a lot of time inside his home in the afternoons, not playing in the neighborhood like most kids. Usually he was alone and reading sports magazines, dreaming of life as an athlete, a life he knew he would never experience because of his physical limitations. Still, he poured through publications like "Sporting News Magazine," and by the time he reached high school he was a walking encyclopedia of sports trivia, especially baseball.

His reputation as a sports trivia expert grew, and members of the varsity baseball team enjoyed trying to stump him during lunch period, but they never could. This impressed the baseball coach, and he asked Curtis if he would like to become the equipment manager and batboy for the team.

Curtis jumped at the chance. Fueled mainly by population growth, Hilltop High in the city of Clermont had one of the great sports programs in Florida because it had so many students wanting to participate. Clermont's growth was accelerated after three freezes in the 1980s nearly wiped out the citrus industry. With citrus no longer profitable, growers found a sizable housing market for people retiring to the warm Florida climate who wanted easy access to Disney World and Orlando without the problems of traffic and crime that often go along with a more urban lifestyle. Where beautiful citrus groves had once covered high rolling hills, housing developments and golf courses now covered the landscapes.

This growth swelled the size of Hilltop High and provided a large pool of players to field athletic teams. Varsity sports, at least the bigger ones, were taken very seriously and the Boosters' Club made sure the athletes had facilities that were among the best in the state. The football stadium was brand new, and the field was immaculate. The basketball gym was big enough for many college teams. The baseball diamond was perfect; the infield grass didn't have a weed in it, and the clay was always dragged and smooth. It was every bit as good as the field of any Triple-A professional team in America.

Hilltop High's baseball team was a contender for the state title. They had several all-state players that Curtis admired. Being able to hang around them as a ninth grader was a treat, and it gave him a little status. Curtis wanted to accept the coach's offer, but that would mean he would have to quit his job at the detail shop, at least during the spring when the season was in full swing. Fortunately his employer was a good man, and when he saw how excited Curtis was, he told Curtis the job would be waiting for him when the season was over. Curtis became part of the team!

After Christmas break, the team began practicing for the new season. Curtis had played Little League, but to be on a regulation-sized baseball diamond was awesome. The first time he walked out to the batter's box he gazed from left field to right, trying to imagine a homerun ball disappearing into the stands. He stared at the pitcher's mound, thinking of a curveball breaking over the outside corner. He thought of a throw from right field to third base, as the deceased Hall of Fame rightfielder for the Pittsburgh Pirates, Roberto Clemente, would have done, nabbing the runner trying to get from first to third on a single to right.

In the dugout, he rubbed the pine tar rag on the bat, between the label and the spot where the upper hand would be placed. The tar was sticky and smelled strong.

On the pitcher's mound, he picked up the resin bag and tossed it up and down in his pitching hand a few times, as he had seen it done on television by major league pitchers. It made the palm of his hand and fingers squeaky dry, better able to grip the ball.

He jogged around the bases, touching the inside edge of each bag, thinking of what it would be like to hit a game-winning homerun to win a World Series game, as Kirk Gibson had done for the Dodgers in the 1988 Series.

From the shortstop position, he ran over the second base bag, dragging his right foot as he simulated a catch from the second baseman and then throwing to first, completing a double play to end the inning.

He heard the clatter of steel cleats on concrete as the team came from the dressing room to the field.

"Baseball cleats on concrete?" Curtis thought. "The players are coming out! What am I doing daydreaming? I have work to do!"

The players, led by star pitcher Juan Ramirez and all-state centerfielder Billy Bulger, ran to the outfield and began warming up. Curtis just stared. These area superstars had been written about in the sports section of the local newspaper since they were 10 years old, and Curtis knew all about them. He was in awe. He'd be sharing the dugout with them this season.

The season got underway and Curtis was in hog heaven. Some of the kids in the stands would say hurtful things like, "Look at Curtis; he couldn't make the team so now he's the batboy!" Curtis never let it get to him. He loved baseball too much for that, and he also knew that he was contributing to the team. He was much more than just a batboy; he kept the equipment together and in good working order. He also helped with travel arrangements on away games. Soon after the season began, the head coach realized he could leave many of these details to Curtis, and this was a big help.

Juan Ramirez and Billy Bulger were off to a great start. Ramirez won his first four games and Bulger's batting average was .567 with seven homeruns. College scouts and coaches attended every game to watch these stars, and that made the other players play even harder. At the midseason mark, the team's record was 9-1.

Curtis was fitting right in. The players liked him, and he was recognized as an important part of the team. It was no surprise that he was invited to a team party at a player's home one Friday night. One of the guys had managed to get a couple of cases of beer, and many of the players were drinking. A lot of girls were there and music was blaring.

Curtis had never been to a party like this, but he had a fun time and no one got out of control. One thing concerned him, though. Juan Ramirez and Billy Bulger disappeared several times into a room with a person Curtis had never seen, a shady looking character with long hair and a scruffy beard. He was too old to be a high school student.

Curtis asked a few players if they knew who the guy was, but they looked at him with a strange look. Finally, one of the team members said, "You obviously don't know much about Juan and Billy. They're not who they seem." He would say nothing more, and Curtis left the party wondering what that comment meant.

Hilltop High ended the regular season on a roll. They won their last 10 games and entered the state championship tournament the heavy favorite. They delivered, winning the state title with a 4-1 victory over a Miami team full of Dominican Republic immigrants who spoke broken English but who sure could play.

The final game featured stellar play by Juan Ramirez and Billy Bulger. Ramirez went the distance, giving up only the one run, a solo homerun in the first inning. After that, he pitched two-hit ball, hits that came back-to-back and could have led to a rally if Billy had not gunned down a runner at home plate to end the inning. Bulger also hit a thunderous homerun to put his team ahead for good.

When the team arrived back in Clermont that evening, the coach had arranged for a big celebration, providing a feast for the players and their parents: barbecue ribs, potato salad, cole slaw, baked beans, garlic bread and cherry pie. It was a grand time, a fitting end to such a fantastic season.

But after this there was a secret "post-party party" that only a handful of the players were invited to. Juan Ramirez and Billy Bulger asked Curtis if he wanted to go with them. Curtis was still a little star-struck with these guys, especially after their heroics in the title game that day, so he agreed, although he was uneasy about it. He did call his aunt to receive permission. She didn't want him to go, but when Curtis made it clear how much he wanted to spend time with Juan Ramirez and Billy Bulger, she acquiesced.

The first person Curtis saw at this party was the scruffy looking fellow he had seen at the party held at the mid-season mark, and again Juan and Billy went into a room with him and closed the door. Curtis thought of what his teammate had said at the other party: that these guys were not who they seemed.

Curtis had a terrible time. He knew only the teammates who were there, and there was a lot of drinking and pot smoking. He wanted to leave but had to wait on Juan and Billy. He did manage to find a telephone and call his aunt and uncle, and they immediately got in the car to come get him. But a minute or two later, Juan and Billy came out of the room and told Curtis it was time to go. Curtis reached his uncle on a cell phone and told him he had a ride.

"Are you sure?" his uncle asked.

"I'm sure. I'll get them to take me home right away."

"All right, but if you need me, will you call me?"

"Of course I will, Uncle George. But I'll be okay."

Curtis thought Billy was driving the car aimlessly. Sitting in the back seat, he watched Billy and Juan grow silent and restless, like something big was about to happen. His instincts were telling him to get away.

"I'm ready to go home, guys," Curtis said.

"Not yet," answered Billy.

When Juan reached into the glove box and pulled out a gun, Curtis freaked out. "I want to go home. Now!" he demanded.

"Soon, kid, soon," Billy replied.

"No, now! Please take me home," Curtis pleaded. Neither Juan nor Billy responded.

Billy parked down the street from a rundown house in a seedy part of town. He put the car in park, got out, and told Curtis to get behind the wheel.

"What? I'm only 15 years old! I don't have my license. I can't do that!"

"Oh yes you can, and you will," Juan said as he, too, got out of the car. "And leave it running. We won't be long."

He and Billy walked towards the house. Curtis was scared to death, but he reluctantly climbed behind the wheel. His high school idols were looking much less like idols, but he was lost and had no idea how to get home if he ran. He was also scared to disobey them; Juan had a gun! Nevertheless, when they returned, he would get back in the backseat. He would not drive the car.

Ten long minutes later, Juan and Billy came tearing down the street and piled into the car. Juan was carrying a briefcase.

"Drive!" Billy screamed at Curtis.

"But I don't have a license!"

"I said drive!"

"But guys, I…"

"Are you going to go or am I going to have to shoot you!" Juan said sternly, brandishing a pistol.

"Oh, man. What is going on?" Curtis asked as he put the car in gear and drove off.

"Faster!" Billy shouted. He was wired as tight as a guitar string.

As the car sped by the house, Curtis saw a woman in her nightshirt standing in the doorway, crying and screaming and shaking her fist at their car.

"What have you guys done?" Curtis asked, his voice shaking.

"Just keep driving," Juan said. "When Billy calms down he'll take over."

When they got a mile or two from the house, Juan told Curtis to pull over.

Billy got behind the wheel and began driving to Curtis' home. When they arrived, Juan told Curtis to tell no one about what had just happened.

"But what happened?" Curtis asked.

"It's best you not know. It's best that you forget everything you saw tonight, okay?"

"But the gun…"

"Curtis, you heard Juan. Forget everything you saw tonight. Will you do that? Tell me you'll do that," Billy whispered in a scary way, his face twisted into a snarl.

"Sure, Billy. I'll do that. I'll forget everything. Whatever you say."

"That's good, Curtis. Real good," Juan said. "And Curtis. You did well this year. We may not have won the title without you. You helped a lot. Don't worry about tonight. It's going to be all right."

Curtis walked from the car to his house, his legs so weak he could hardly stand. He was sure that things would definitely *not* be all right.

Curtis' aunt and uncle were waiting for him when he walked in.

"Curtis, where have you been?" Uncle George asked.

"I don't want to talk," Curtis answered. "I'm tired. I want to go to bed."

"I think we should talk now," Uncle George responded.

"Please, Uncle George. Not now," Curtis said with pleading eyes.

"Okay, Curtis. We don't have to talk now. We'll talk in the morning."

"Thanks. Goodnight."

The next morning was Saturday, and Curtis stayed in his room until noon. This confirmed to his aunt and uncle that something bad had happened the night before. Curtis was spooked.

When he finally came down, Betty said, "Curtis, whatever happened last night, you should tell us about it. If you're in any kind of trouble, it will only get worse if you hold onto it."

Curtis didn't speak.

"Curtis, tell me what happened," his uncle said.

Curtis looked at his uncle, tears in his eyes. "I can't," was all he said. "You just have to believe me. I can't, but I didn't do anything wrong. I promise."

Uncle George didn't press it. He knew Curtis would open up soon or he wouldn't have admitted that something *had* happened. His wife followed his lead.

"Whatever it is, we will always be there for you," Uncle George said, as he put his hand on Curtis' shoulder.

Monday morning the headlines of the local newspaper described the shooting of a known drug dealer named Jimmy Rainey. He wasn't a drug kingpin by any means, but was known by the police as a dealer who occasionally sold marijuana to students.

"We've had a few dealings with him," a police spokesperson said. "Mostly smalltime stuff, but it looks like things escalated."

The police were surprised by Rainey's murder. He had a regular job as a diesel mechanic, was married and had two kids. What the police didn't know was that Jimmy Rainey had a gambling addiction that had left him $30,000.00 in debt to loan sharks and they were putting pressure on him to pay. They were even beginning to threaten his children. He didn't want to deal drugs, but he had to get out of debt, for the sake of his kids.

Rainey's wife, Maddie, was distraught about the killing. She wasn't proud that her husband occasionally sold drugs, but she loved him. He worked hard, was a good father, and kept saying that he'd stop all illicit activity as soon as he had the loan sharks off his back.

Maddie told the police in detail what had happened the night of the murder.

At 1:30 a.m., two young men had pried open the back door and run in on her and her husband as they slept in their bedroom. They were wearing ski masks and one was carrying a pistol. The guy with the gun put it to Maddie's head and said to Jimmy: "You'll mop her brains off the floor if you don't give me the money. You have five seconds. One, two…"

"I don't know what you're talking about," Jimmy shouted.

"Three…"

"What are you talking about? What money? I don't have any money. Please let her go."

"Four…Four and a half. This is it Jimmy. Where's the cash?"

"Okay. I'll give it to you. Just please put the gun down. Please. Don't hurt my wife."

"Good, Jimmy. Real smart. Where is it?"

"It's in the closet."

"Get it. And no quick moves."

"All right, I'll get it. Just don't hurt my wife."

Jimmy walked to the closet and stood on a footstool. With his left hand he took the handle of a black briefcase. As he was taking it down from the top shelf, Jimmy's seven-year old son, Joshua, came through the bedroom door.

"What's going on Mommy? Who are these men?"

"Get the kid out of here!" the gun-toting man shouted.

Joshua screamed and ran to his mother. Both parents were shouting to him to leave. The thugs were yelling and the person with the gun was shaking it at the wife and kid. "Keep that kid quiet!" one of the men shouted. Pandemonium broke loose.

Jimmy was still on the footstool in the closet. He grabbed a pistol he had hidden on the top shelf next to the briefcase. In one motion he came off the stool and raised his gun, but it was too late. The gun held by the thug barked and a red spot of blood appeared on the front of Jimmy's white tee shirt. When his feet hit the ground, his body hesitated, and then he crashed to the floor.

"Jimmy!" His wife yelled.

The men pulled the briefcase from his left hand and bolted for the door. As they ran from the house, they heard Joshua shrieking in agony as he realized his father had been shot.

The last thing Jimmy's wife saw was a car speeding away with three people in it. A young boy with thick glasses was driving.

When Curtis came downstairs for breakfast, he looked at the newspaper, and froze. On the front page, next to the story of the murdered drug dealer, was a picture of the drug dealer's house. It was the same house Juan and Billy had gone into the night before. His aunt noticed his alarm.

"What is it, Curtis?" she asked.

Curtis couldn't speak. He could only stare at the paper, seeing the picture and reading the headline, "Man Murdered in Home." A subtitle read, "Son and Wife Witness Killing."

Curtis' lip was quivering. When his uncle saw what he was staring at, he knew immediately what was wrong.

"Okay, it's time to talk. Sit down and tell us what happened last Friday night," he said sternly.

By the time Curtis finished, his uncle knew there was only one thing to do: they had to go to the police. Curtis didn't want to do this. He was scared of Juan and Billy, but he also was having a hard time believing they could have done what the newspaper described. The circumstances were undeniable, however. He had seen Juan with a gun, Billy was shaking badly when he returned from the house, and the woman he had seen on the porch as he drove by looked very similar to the picture of the wife of the dead man. It had to be true, and his uncle convinced him that he had to tell the police.

Curtis cried the whole way to the police station. He didn't want to rat out the baseball team's superstars, but he knew he had to. Still, it was hard. It would never be the same for him again at school, and for all he knew, he could be in trouble with the law himself. His uncle convinced him it was a risk he had to take, and again assured Curtis that he and Aunt Betty would always be there for him.

Detective Susan Gillespie was good with kids. Having grown up with five younger brothers and sisters, she knew how to speak to them, and she knew the perils of ratting someone out.

"Tell me what happened, Curtis," she said calmly. "I know it's difficult, but it's important that we know."

Curtis stared at her, a few tears running down his cheeks. Then he looked down. He wasn't talking.

"Curtis, the only way we catch the bad guys is with help from people like you."

Curtis thought for a moment.

"But I looked up to them. At times I even wanted to be like them. I just didn't know."

"Wanted to be like who, Curtis?"

"Billy and Juan."

"What changed your mind? What did you see?"

"You can tell her, Curtis," Uncle George said. "In fact, you must. And I'll never let anything happen to you."

Taking a deep breath, Curtis began.

After speaking with Curtis, the police went to the high school and arrested Juan Ramirez and Billy Bulger. A ski mask was found in the trunk of Bulger's car. Between the mask, Curtis' testimony, and Jimmy Rainey's wife's description of the getaway car and size of the assailants, it was a slam dunk case. Ramirez and Bulger, both adults because they were 18 years old, were going to prison for a long time.

The local newspaper carried a full story of the arrest. Curtis' name was withheld because he was a minor, but it was no secret that it was he who had provided the details necessary to make the arrests. This made Curtis uncomfortable at school, but most of his classmates agreed he had done the right thing.

In the story it was clear that the state attorney intended to prosecute Juan and Billy to the fullest extent of the law. He stated that he was even going to invoke the felony-murder rule, a common law doctrine that allowed anyone who was a part of the commission of a felony to be charged with murder if a homicide resulted from the felony. It didn't apply to Billy since he was the triggerman; he was facing a murder charge anyway. But it did apply to Juan. He had not wanted anyone to be shot, but because he was part of the breaking in of a home with the intent to steal – a felony – he too would be tried for murder since a homicide had occurred.

News stories later revealed that Juan and Billy were working with the scruffy looking man Curtis had seen at the parties. This character was a major drug dealer who controlled much of the heroin traffic in central Florida. Jimmy Rainey, desperate to get the loan sharks off his back, had agreed to make one run to the Bahamas on a fast boat to bring drugs back for this guy. He made the trip and received $50,000, enough to pay the loan sharks what he owed and still have a little left over. But like most major drug dealers, once this dealer let Jimmy in, he wouldn't let him out. He insisted on Jimmy making another run. When Jimmy refused, the drug dealer made plans with Juan and Billy for them to break into Jimmy's house and steal the entire $50,000.00. The drug dealer knew Jimmy still had all the money because he knew the loan sharks and they told him they hadn't been paid. For their efforts, Juan and Billy were going to get $10,000.00 apiece.

The state attorney was very pleased to break such a large and dangerous drug ring. The story received a tremendous amount of news coverage, and, being an elected official up for election that year, the state attorney milked it for all it was worth. In his zeal, he made the worst mistake a state attorney could make: he became too aggressive, temporarily losing sight of good judgment. He had Curtis arrested, charging him with aiding and abetting Juan and Billy by driving the getaway car. Since this too was a felony, Curtis could also be charged with murder under the felony-murder rule, just as Juan had.

Many were outraged over this action, none more so than the assistant public defender, Kate Hatchett, who was assigned to represent Curtis. She threw herself into her responsibilities, first successfully arguing that the case should be remanded to juvenile court and that Curtis should be released on his own recognizance. Next she visited Curtis' home, getting to know Curtis and his aunt and uncle personally. She met with Jimmy's wife Maddie, convincing her to oppose the prosecution of Curtis. She received written statements from baseball teammates stating that Curtis had asked them who the scruffy looking guy was, proving that he didn't know him. She solicited character references from teachers and administrators who stated that Curtis was a well-behaved student, and from his minister who vouched for the fact that he was a regular churchgoer.

By the time Kate was finished, the state attorney knew he had misread Curtis' involvement and moved to have the case dismissed. Still, the experience had left Curtis rattled to the core. He had nothing to do with the crimes, yet for a while he was facing a possible murder charge, and that was enough to rattle anyone. He realized how foolish and dangerous it had been to be so awestruck of Juan and Billy. He didn't even take time to find out who they really were before becoming their "friend."

The scruffy looking drug dealer was also implicated in Jimmy's death. Juan spilled the beans on the dealer in order to avoid the murder charge brought under the felony-murder rule, a deal he cut with the state attorney. Billy was convicted of second-degree murder, however, and sentenced to 25 years in prison.

It was only after Jimmy Rainey's death that his wife had learned of the drug run to the Bahamas. She never quit believing that he did it for the good of his family, to get himself out of debt so that he could be a better father and husband. In a way, she saw it as heroic. But their son, having seen his father shot dead, began thinking of his father as just another drug dealer who died in a drug-related shooting. Thinking of it in any other way was just too painful.

The experience left Curtis determined to help disadvantaged youth avoid the pitfalls of hanging out with the wrong crowd. Throughout college and law school at the University of Florida he mentored at middle schools and volunteered at the local Boys Club. He also became an assistant public defender, committed to helping others just as a wonderful public defender had once helped him.

Author's Note:

The idea that, once a person does one job for a drug dealer, he can't get out of doing other jobs is real. A police officer told me about this around a campfire one night, as a few of us were wondering why more people didn't make just one run if there was so much money in it. I thought of that as I remembered a longtime friend who worked as a citrus caretaker for a grove of several thousand acres in size. A grass landing strip was on this property for company executives to use. My friend was approached by drug dealers who said they would pay him $80,000.00 just to be gone for one weekend so they could use the landing strip. My buddy refused, smart enough to know that if he agreed, he would never be able to say "no" again.

The area around Clermont was one of the most beautiful places in Florida when I was going back and forth to the University of Florida from 1974-1981. The citrus groves on the high rolling hills were magnificent, a spot on the trip I always enjoyed seeing.

I remember one night in particular when I was driving home. I was sleepy, slapping myself, shouting, singing...anything to stay awake. I should have pulled over, but didn't. Suddenly I saw a red fox standing on the shoulder of the road. Grey foxes were common, but red foxes were seldom seen; this was special. It snapped me out of my daze, and I was wide-awake for the rest of the trip. Who knows what would have happened if that fox hadn't been there.

Freezes came and the groves in and around Clermont were replaced with housing subdivisions. Saint Augustine grass in yards and Bermuda grass on golf courses now grow where the citrus groves once were. My guess is there aren't many red foxes there anymore, either.

Notable Quotes:

"I'm convinced that every boy, in his heart, would rather steal second base than an automobile."

Honorable Tom Clark, Associate Justice,
United States Supreme Court
www.quotegarden.com

"Temptation is not always invitation."

Erie Railroad Co. v. Hilt, 247 U.S. 97, 101 (1918).
Honorable Oliver Wendell Holmes, Associate Justice,
United States Supreme Court, writing for the majority

"The law must be stable and yet it must not stand still."

Roscoe Pound / www.worldofquotes.com

"The law is not a 'light' for you or any man to see by; the law is not an instrument of any kind. The law is a causeway upon which so long as he keeps to it a citizen may walk safely."

Robert Bolt / www.worldofquotes.com

"Somebody recently figured out that we have 35 million laws to enforce the Ten Commandments."

Attributed to both Bert Masterson and Earl Wilson
www.quotegarden.com

Key West House

403

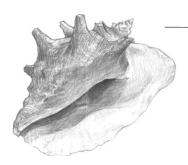

WHO'S TO BLAME?
Eminent Domain and Inverse Condemnation:
Governmental Taking of Private Property

Preface: The bundle of rights known as "property rights" is a distinguishing feature of a free society. At its core is the idea that property owners should be able to do with their property whatever they wish, within reason. However, society has a legitimate interest in seeing that the exercise of these rights doesn't hurt the general welfare. These interests are often at odds with each other, as we'll see in this story.

The attempt to balance these competing interests is the basis for growth management law in Florida. Growth management is intended to prevent irresponsible growth, but it's a relatively new concept. For most of Florida's history, government actively encouraged population growth and provided the infrastructure for it. A tool often used by government to secure the land necessary for public necessities like roads and utility lines to accommodate this growth is "eminent domain."

Eminent domain is allowed by the state and federal constitutions, and by statute. Clearly, government has the legal authority to acquire land for "public uses." However, what constitutes a public use has not always been clear, and to this day the definition is evolving. For instance, the recent Supreme Court decision in Kelo v. City of New London et al, 125 S. Ct. 2655 (2005), established that a public purpose such as creating jobs in a depressed area of a city could satisfy the Fifth Amendment to the United States Constitution. Congress is considering legislation that would override this decision.

This story is set in Key West, a place with unique and historically significant architecture. Few reasonable people would dispute that certain buildings should be preserved, but is their importance great enough to justify government taking them by eminent domain? Would such action satisfy the definition of "public use?" If not, could a city government pass an ordinance prohibiting their destruction? If so, would that be a "taking," triggering a valid claim for inverse condemnation? These are the questions explored in this story.

KEY WEST in the 1950s was a golden era. The people were rugged, wholesome and a bit quirky. The architecture of the buildings was unique; some buildings were ornate, some simple and cozy. The streets were quaint, bordered by lush tropical vegetation. The laid-back atmosphere, promoted by the cool nights and balmy days, made for an easy rhythm of the town. Fish and shrimp in great numbers in nearby waters made for fine sport and delicious food. White-uniformed sailors walking down Duval Street and visiting celebrities and dignitaries who appreciated and respected the culture added flavor and personality.

Much of that is still there, but life in Key West today is vastly different. Traffic clogs most streets and debauchery is rampant. Large modern hotels with no architectural imagination occupy choice real estate, and a landfill towers over the city. Sadly, many Key West natives, called "Conchs," have been driven from their homes because they can't afford the high cost of living. Particularly oppressive have been property taxes that have gone sky high as property values have escalated. When these Conchs sell and move out, they are often replaced by new residents with money but no sense of Key West's special history; they have no sense of place. It was this latter phenomenon that had Dan and Lisa Albury so upset and concerned.

"It's not the same, is it?" Dan asked Lisa. They were sitting on their front porch watching the traffic pass by.

"No, it's not," she replied. "My parents wouldn't believe this was their old neighborhood."

"They sure wouldn't," Dan answered. "And we're getting squeezed from all directions with all the commercial development coming in. I'm not sure we can hold out much longer; we can hardly pay the taxes as it is."

"I know. And it's not just the commercial stuff that's driving the increases. Can you believe how much residential properties are selling for? That little bungalow down the street just sold for a million dollars! Who are these people buying these homes, and where does all the money come from?"

"Who knows? I guess they made a pile up north and now they're coming down south to spend it. At least we have a way out of the trap if it gets too bad. We could get a bank full of dough for this house."

"Maybe so, but I can hardly bear the thought of selling it. Remember when we bought this house?"

"I sure do," Dan said with a smile. "It was right after our wedding. I was doing carpentry work with Dad and running lobster traps on the side, remember?"

"How could I forget? Those were tough times. We were living from paycheck to paycheck."

'Yes we were, and that's why Dad thought we were crazy when we paid forty-four thousand for this house. That was a fortune in 1958."

"What do you think it's worth now?" Lisa asked.

"I have no idea. This house is a little bigger than the one down the street, and the lot is much larger. It's also on the corner, so it could probably be re-zoned to commercial or professional use."

"I'd hate to see that,' Lisa said. "This is where we raised our kids."

"But they've moved away, sweetheart, and they aren't coming back, not at these prices."

"Probably not, but they love it down here when they visit, especially the grandkids."

"But loving Key West and being able to live here are two different things. Even if the kids could borrow the money to buy a place, the property taxes would be based on the selling price, and I don't know what kind of job they could get that would allow them to pay that much. Our increases have been limited to three percent a year since 1994 because of the 'Save Our Homes' initiative passed by the voters of Florida, but as soon as the property sells, the taxes re-set at the selling price."

"Yes, but the tax system was never supposed to drive people from their homes or prevent them from buying a modest house." Lisa replied. "It isn't right! Our families have been here for generations, but it's our generation being forced out."

"I know, but that's what's happening." Dan watched several neighbors passing by, waving. Dan nodded in return. "This has been a good house though, hasn't it?"

"It sure has," Lisa said. "It sure has."

The Alburys' home was a medium-sized house in Classical Revival "eyebrow" style. It was called an "eyebrow" house because the second story windows seemed to peer out from underneath the ceiling of the front porch that stretched the entire width of the house, like eyes beneath eyebrows. Actually, the second story was more like a half story in the front, and sloped to one story in the back. The style probably originated in either Louisiana, as many of the Key West homes did, or New England.

The home was built in 1888, the second on that lot, the first having burned to the ground in 1886 in a massive citywide blaze that burned much of Key West. When the Alburys purchased their home, it had fallen into disrepair, all the more reason Dan's father thought they paid too much for it. Dan and Lisa didn't mind, though; in fact, they received much satisfaction restoring it to its previous splendor.

The house was located on Truman Street, within walking distance of the dock where they kept their boats. They'd had many boats over the years, but currently had two: a 22' Albury center console open fisherman built in Man 0' War Cay, Bahamas, by distant relatives, and a flats skiff. The larger boat didn't get much use, but when the kids were growing up they took trips of several days to Fort Jefferson, loading up on fish the whole way down and back. With the kids gone, Dan and Lisa's fishing patterns had changed. Now they usually took the skiff to the flats south of Key West, and sometimes slightly farther away to the Marquesas Islands. The emerald green and brown colors of the water and flats were breathtaking, and there was no place Dan and Lisa would rather be. Their quarry was the elusive permit, a flat silver fish that was as hard to catch on a fly as any in the sea. The difficulty of catching them was matched only by the excitement of trying; when a permit would break from the cuts surrounding the flats and head across the shallows towards the angler, it was one of the great moments in all of fishing.

The last thing the Alburys wanted to do was sell their house, but they were tiring of the street noise and their high property taxes. With a tax bill of nearly $15,000.00 a year, a big part of their income was eaten up just paying taxes, and Dan would have to retire soon. Physical ailments were already preventing him from taking on the kind of home repair jobs he once did, and pulling lobster traps was out of the question. Social Security and his modest savings wouldn't go very far shelling out this kind of money for property taxes. When an unsolicited offer of 2.5 million dollars came in from RNP, a national pharmacy chain, they knew it would be foolhardy to ignore it.

"Take the deal," said Skip Pinder. He and his wife, Janice, were having dinner with Dan and Lisa. They had all been great friends for years, and were discussing the offer from RNP.

"But what will the neighbors think?" Lisa wondered.

"Don't worry about it," Skip advised. "I'll guarantee you they'd take the deal if they could."

"Maybe so, but I'm sure they aren't going to like it," Lisa answered.

"Probably not," Skip replied. "I wouldn't want to live next door to a retail store that size, especially one that would be open 24 hours a day. But two and a half million dollars is a lot of money. You'd be dumb to turn it down."

"I guess you're right, but it's going to break my heart to see them tear down this house," Lisa said wistfully.

"Mine too," Dan chimed, "but we're not to blame for all this growth. Maybe no one's to blame; it just happened. You can't blame people for wanting to live here. I'll call the guy from RNP tomorrow."

"Now you're talking," Skip said encouragingly. "And don't think twice about it."

The retail giant intended to knock down the Alburys' house and build a modern drug store on the 1.5-acre lot, but that would require a zoning change, and the community was in an uproar.

People were generally split into three camps. The first didn't want to lose the "eyebrow" house and demanded that the government intervene. By and large, these people had only recently moved to the area and were intent on protecting what remained of the laid-back lifestyle they had moved to Key West to enjoy. They were also keenly aware that the value of their homes would be best protected if the area was not commercialized to the point that it looked no different than countless other waterfront communities throughout Florida. Others in this group were motivated for a different reason. They were craftsmen and craftswomen who years ago had poured their creativity into many of the homes on the island, saving them from ruin and decay. Losing a historical structure was like losing part of the legacy they had helped save.

The second camp couldn't care less. They were either aimless with few high-minded thoughts like legacy, or were so focused on day-to-day living that they didn't have time for such musings.

The third was sad, but resigned to what was happening all around them. Most of the people in this camp were Conchs, heartbroken about the disintegration of the life they had known, but by nature conservative folks who didn't think the government should get involved in a matter between two private parties.

The Alburys were stuck in the middle. It hurt them to sell, but Key West had changed. They would have preferred a neighborhood apothecary that might have been able to remodel the house and operate out if it, but the economics of that didn't warrant a second thought, and they hadn't received any offers. Now that they were resigned to selling, they wanted to get as much for their home as possible.

At first, it didn't seem that the zoning change would be difficult or that many people would oppose it. Key West was large enough to need a drug store that would be open 24 hours a day, seven days a week. The two pharmacies in town had been there for a long time and were owned by long-time Key West residents, but they were never open on Sunday, much less 24 hours a day. The pharmacists in these stores actually supported RNP, envisioning working for them as they neared the end of their careers. They were tired of the worries and stresses of running their own businesses.

The issue changed when those in opposition hired Irma Pasternak, a local historian who had begun working as the city librarian when she moved to Key West 12 years ago. During her time there, she had read everything she could find on Key West history, and she had a special interest in its buildings. She wrote a story for the newspaper about the Alburys' home and its unique Keys' architecture and colorful past. She explained that the house was built of resin-laden pine framing from Charlotte County in Florida to withstand termites, and that the exterior horizontal clapboard was from the Upper Keys' cypress trees. The interior siding of mahogany had been salvaged from a ship that ran aground sailing from Honduras. The house was particularly unique because it still had wood shingles. (Wood shingles from most houses had been replaced with galvanized steel because of fire concerns, and the steel shingles collected water in the cisterns more efficiently.)

Mrs. Pasternak described how – because of the rarity of nails in 1888 – the wood of the house was bound together with tenon joints (wooden projections from boards that were inserted into holes drilled into other boards to form a secure fitting) and wooden pegs. These were stronger than nails so the house was better able to withstand hurricanes. She described how the Alburys' "eyebrow" home was unique in that it had elaborate trim normally found only on Queen Anne-style homes. It was most surely modeled after a New England "saltbox" house, not from a Louisiana home as most were, and that added to its special character. The builder, who was a ship's carpenter hired by the captain to build his retirement home, was from Gloucester, Massachusetts, so the "saltbox" home was familiar to him. The captain was Captain John Summerlin, son of a Confederate general who had been at General Robert E. Lee's side at Appomattox. Summerlin retired to Key West and lived in this house for 18 years. There was an abundance of history bound up in this "eyebrow" house.

Pasternak ended her story with the tantalizing prospect that Clarke Williams, a Hollywood movie star, had considered buying the house in the mid-1950s. Williams was a Key West regular back then, and liked the large lot of this home. Large lots were rare. At the time most homes in the historic part of Key West were built, there was still a concern about Indians, so settlers figured they'd rather have a neighbor close by than a big yard where Indians could hide. "The bravery Captain Summerlin showed during the war was ample evidence that he was not the sort of man to be afraid of Indians," she concluded.

Her newspaper story created quite a buzz around town. Pasternak then shaped the story into an interesting 20-minute speech and hit the streets, speaking to civic clubs and other groups. Listeners were fascinated, and soon the movement to stop the zoning change for the Alburys' home was gaining steam.

Dan and Lisa were amazed to find themselves in the middle of all the hoopla. Other houses that were equally historic had been felled by the crushing growth in Key West with hardly a whimper from anyone, but theirs took on a political life. The Old Building Restoration Commission weighed in, encouraging the city to deny the request. The Commission was a not-for-profit organization of local citizens created several decades before to help preserve old buildings in Key West. Additionally, a state legislator energized the Department of State to begin the process of placing the Albury house on the State Registry of Historic Places, a move that, if realized, would make it nearly impossible for the home to be destroyed. The county commission even passed a resolution encouraging the city to "protect and preserve any residential structure older than 100 years."

From the other side of the issue, a pro-property rights organization from Oklahoma swooped in and took up defending the Alburys as a call to arms for all property owners. "If they can do it to them, they can do it to you!" was their tagline to the public. Dan and Lisa didn't want the attention or the help, but it didn't matter; the organization was receiving publicity and that was good for its membership, so they stayed at it.

Indeed, the situation was becoming messy in a hurry. A public hearing before the City Zoning and Planning Commission, the first step in the rezoning process, drew 230 people, the most ever in Key West. A land planner for the Alburys presented their case. Dan and Lisa sat on the front row, aware of the glares they were receiving from locals who thought that selling their house to a national pharmacy chain in the historic neighborhood ran counter to the Key West values they all loyally supported. More than 36 people from the community spoke during the "Public Comment" portion of the agenda, all opposing the change. The only supporters were representatives from the Oklahoma property rights association and an executive from RNP drug stores.

Despite the overwhelming public opposition to the change, the Zoning and Planning Commission passed the motion to rezone unanimously, forwarding their recommendation to the city commission. The members of the

Commission expressed many of the frustrations with growth articulated by those who had testified, but could see no legal reason to oppose the change. Utilities had the capacity to service the store and RNP promised to make road improvements that would actually better the flow of traffic in the area.

After this, the matter really heated up, receiving a great deal of media coverage from the Miami television stations. This one zoning case took on a life of its own, a perfect symbol for everyone who was against growth. The public was sick and tired of their piece of tropical paradise becoming despoiled by so many people moving in, and they mobilized. The fact that RNP pharmacy chain was a faceless adversary made it easier. Other than the Alburys, the only RNP supporters were their out-of-town lawyers and corporate executives and representatives of the Oklahoma property rights' association. For Keys residents who opposed the change, it was a classic "us against them" battle, and they found their champion in Ron Weider, mayor of Key West.

Weider was a loose canon and a bit crazy. He was also politically savvy. He sensed that the tide was turning against the Alburys, and he wanted to be credited with leading the opposition to victory. He scheduled a press conference in front of one of Key West's most historically significant houses, the "Southernmost House" on Duval Street, to announce his opposition to the zoning change.

The local newspaper carried the story on the front page, and Weider was called a "hero" by many. The ranks of those opposing the change swelled, and soon Weider was leading a movement, a wave of opposition to change in the Keys that went far beyond the issue of the Alburys' home.

Even Mayor Weider was surprised, but he basked in the limelight nonetheless. His campaign morphed into more than just defeating this particular zoning change; the goal became passing a citywide ordinance that prohibited any structure in the Keys deemed "historically significant" by the Old Building Restoration Commission from being willfully destroyed. The zoning change was tabled by the city commission, and the ordinance became the focus. Weider had shrewdly shifted the issue. By targeting *all* historically significant buildings, the media coverage increased and advocates for historical preservation from all across South Florida weighed in.

Four hundred people attended the city commission meeting when the ordinance was considered. The meeting room was not big enough to accommodate such a large crowd, so they spilled out of the room all the way around the block. Anticipating such a turnout, Weider had directed the city manager to broadcast the meeting on large-screen televisions outside. When someone spoke in favor of the ordinance, the commissioners inside could hear the crowd outside cheering. Likewise, when someone spoke against the measure, the commissioners could hear them booing.

Before the vote, the city attorney warned the commissioners of the legal consequences. "This measure will subject the city to lawsuits and financial liability," he said, but he was ignored. The city commissioners wilted under the pressure and approved the measure unanimously. A great cheer went up from the crowd. The city commission adjourned. Mayor Weider held an impromptu press conference, television cameras beaming his gloating face all across South Florida.

"Can they do this?" Lisa asked Dan as they hustled to their car.

"They just did," he answered.

"What do we do?" Lisa retorted anxiously.

"We do what everyone does in a situation like this," Dan remarked casually. "We hire a lawyer."

"We fight this on four fronts," said Sandy Horan, attorney for the Alburys. Dan and Lisa were in his Duval Street office, discussing their legal strategy.

"Our first argument is that the ordinance is unconstitutional because it violates substantive due process," Horan continued, "and it violates substantive due process if it's arbitrary, unreasonable and discriminatory. If the Court finds that the ordinance is 'rationally related to a legitimate governmental interest,' it won't find it unconstitutional. 'Vagueness' is another basis for finding an ordinance unconstitutional, so we'll argue that, too.

"The second argument is that the ordinance is unconstitutional because it violates your equal protection rights. Laws may not treat a person or class of persons differently from everyone else. You're being treated differently from other homeowners just because your house is considered 'historically significant.' Unfortunately, if the Court finds that the ordinance is 'rationally related to a legitimate government interest' we'll lose on this count. Again we'll argue that the ordinance is arbitrary and irrational, but Courts give a lot of deference to elected bodies on legislative matters.

"Next we'll contend that the ordinance violates the Harris Act (Florida's private property rights law). Under this law, the Court will have to find that the ordinance creates an 'inordinate burden' on you. The challenge will be that the Harris Act was intentionally written to allow government to regulate in ways that were reasonable, but if the line is crossed, the affected party is entitled to compensation."

"All of these sound like tough sells to me," Lisa said. "Can we win?"

"Yes, but none of these arguments are slam-dunks," Horan answered. "We have another basis for relief, though, and it's a good one."

"Then let me hear it," Lisa replied. "I could use some encouraging news right now."

"We'll file an 'inverse condemnation' action against the city," he said. "We'll assert that the ordinance is arbitrary and capricious, and that it effectively takes your property without compensation."

"Is that like eminent domain?" she asked.

"They're related concepts, but different in a fundamental way. With eminent domain, the government initiates the action and physically takes possession and title to the property. With inverse condemnation, the individual initiates the action, claiming that a governmental action has effectively taken property from him. The argument is that even though the government hasn't taken title to or possession of the property, it has 'taken' it nonetheless."

"I wonder why they didn't just deny the zoning request." Dan said.

"Because that would have denied Weider the broader political issue of trying to protect *all* the historically significant properties in the city," Horan answered. "It was pure politics, but count your blessings. Courts generally allow zoning decisions to stand, concluding that if the public disagrees they can elect new commissioners to get it changed. If we were fighting an adverse zoning decision, we'd have a tougher fight on our hands."

"Why didn't the city simply file a condemnation action against us and acquire the property through eminent domain?" Lisa wondered.

"It would have cost them money, for one thing. They can't take it without paying full compensation for it," Horan replied, "and we know it's worth at least 2.5 million because you have a contract for that amount."

"There's no way the city commission would pay that kind of money," Dan added. "I know those guys."

"It's not just money, either," Horan said. "It's not clear that the city even has condemnation power for historic preservation. There is a general catch-all phrase in the statute that allows eminent domain for '...good reason connected in any way with the public welfare or the interests of the municipality and the people thereon,' but that's a stretch here. The test is whether the property acquisition is for a 'public use.' Preserving a historically significant house promotes more of a 'public purpose' than a 'public use,' and the courts are less likely to allow eminent domain for a public purpose. It has been done, but it's a tougher sell."

"What about the state condemning it? Our great state representative has gotten them all juiced up," Lisa said facetiously.

"The state has the power to condemn properties for historic preservation, but typically that power is used to acquire historically significant land, not buildings," Horan responded.

"Does it matter that it's our house, our homestead? Could the state even condemn that?" Dan asked.

"Yes, even for a homestead."

"Do you think we should approach the state about condemning it?" Lisa wondered.

"I don't think we should do that yet," Horan answered. "We might at some point, but let's get a little farther down the road with the lawsuit first. If it looks like we're going to win, the city may become our biggest ally with the state."

"If we file this lawsuit, how are you paid?" Lisa asked.

"You don't have to worry about that if we win on the inverse condemnation action," Horan replied. "The government would have to pay my fees and all of your costs, subject to approval by the Court, of course. There's even a fee schedule in the statutes. But if we lose, or even if we win on the substantive due process or equal protection actions, I'll charge you $225.00 per hour. There are ways to try to get your attorneys' fees paid in constitutional matters like this, but you can't count on it."

Lisa and Dan looked at each other and nodded.

"Then file it," Dan said with determination. "We're fourth generation Conchs, but we're being victimized by our own city government, and blamed for things that were not of our doing. I'd love to turn the clock back 40 or 50 years and encourage city leaders to better control growth in Key West, but that can't happen."

The lawsuit was filed, but the city commission remained defiant, instructing their attorney to fight it with all he had. Soon, several parties filed amicus curiae briefs. ["Amicus curiae" means "friend of the court" in Latin. It is a way for interested groups or individuals who are not parties to a lawsuit to have input before the Court.] The Oklahoma property rights organization that had moved in when the ordinance was proposed submitted a brief in support of the Alburys. Sunshine State Historical Preservation Society filed in support of the city commission.

The judge who would be hearing the case was the Honorable Wilhemena Russell, a resident of Duck Key. She was a fifth generation Florida Keys resident, and had seen the Keys grow and develop. She well understood the frustration of seeing the laid-back way of Keys' life slip away. She, too, longed for a simpler time when she might be the only one on the water, or the traffic was not so bad.

Mayor Weider and his supporters were pleased that she was the judge assigned to the case. They thought that, as a longtime resident of the Keys and one who appreciated its special history, she would naturally lean their way. The Alburys weren't as concerned, though. They had known the judge and her family for years and knew she would listen and rule with impartiality.

As the trial approached, the issue grew in public profile, even attracting attention from the national media. Those supporting the Alburys did what they could to advocate their position, but the real interest was in the local residents who opposed them. Led by Mayor Weider, bizarre afternoon rallies were held at Mallory Square, a place where tourists from all over the world gathered to watch the sunset. Joining the tourists were supporters of the ordinance, and the combination of the two groups made for an odd scene. The tourists were there to see the remarkable illusion of the sun melting into the sea. For them, this was a time for quiet reflection. Mayor Weider's followers, on the other hand, were raucous and loud, quickly turning the serenity of the late afternoon into a display of irrationality, ignorance and garishness. Some supporters were genuinely concerned about the loss of a house that had historic value and what it would mean if all such homes were lost. Others, many of whom were not even from the Keys, saw the Albury house as a symbol of what was being lost from so much growth. But plenty in the crowd were merely troublemakers who saw the rally as an excuse to be rowdy or dress decadently. They knew nothing about the issue, and even if they did, they could care less; they were there because of the excitement of a buzzing crowd. There was palpable energy from the group of people coming together and cheering speakers. There was no telling what could happen!

Watching this from afar were the Alburys, astounded that it was their home, a house that was in the direct line of commercial development, that was the focus of such a brouhaha. Add the irony that it would be the actions of fifth generation Conchs who were pillars of the community that would trigger such a movement, and it was downright amazing.

"This is unbelievable." Dan said. "What do these people expect? We'd be foolish not to sell."

"Dan, I'm tired of everybody looking at us like we're pariahs. It's like we haven't been here for all these years."

"What are you saying? Do you want to throw in the towel?"

"I don't know. Maybe," Lisa answered. "I'm just tired of it, that's all."

"I'm tired of it, too, but we're not quitting," Dan said resolutely. "These protesters would do the same thing if they were us. We're not backing down."

In an inverse condemnation action, the judge decides all issues except value, which the jury determines. Judge Russell would decide all legal and factual issues. "This is a good thing," Sandy Horan, the Alburys' attorney, explained as he was discussing last minute legal strategy with them.

"Why is that?' Lisa asked.

"Because your property achieves its highest value only with the zoning change, and we'd rather have a judge determine the likelihood of that being successful than a jury. If the judge decides that the change would have occurred, then there was a 'taking' because the ordinance prevented you from realizing the benefit of the change. If the judge decides that the zoning change wouldn't have succeeded, you're no worse off now than you were before."

"Assuming we get to the jury, tell me again how compensation will be determined," Lisa requested.

"You are entitled to 'just' compensation, and that's defined as 'full' compensation," Horan responded. "With inverse condemnation, the jury would look at the property's worth before the ordinance, taking into account the value with the new zoning, and its worth afterwards. That's different than an eminent domain action, where the jury would give a value to the property taken. Here, the government is not taking title to your property as it would in an eminent domain proceeding. Instead, they are taking an action that reduces the value of your property, and that's what the jury would determine."

"So, we would get the difference in value and still own the land?" Lisa asked.

"That's right. You'd get the difference in value and then be able to sell your home as residential property."

"Or stay in it if that is what we decided," added Dan.

"Correct," answered Horan.

"But what if the judge says the change is too speculative and rules against us?" Lisa asked nervously.

"We appeal, but I'm not very worried," Horan said confidently. "Your house is in a perfect location for the zoning change. If you were in the middle of the block, I'd think differently, but you're not. You're on the corner, and there is no lawful reason to deny the request. The commissioners were operating solely on emotion when they passed the ordinance. It was pure politics."

Judge Russell allotted two weeks for the trial, although she didn't think it would take that much time. The claim that the ordinance violated the Alburys' substantive due rights, and the claim that it denied them equal protection were essentially just questions of law, requiring few witnesses. She suspected that she might even take "judicial notice" that the home was historically significant. Judges take judicial notice of matters generally accepted as true, thereby eliminating the need for them to be established at trial. She wouldn't do this if the attorneys objected, but she doubted they would.

The substantive due process and equal protection actions were heard first.

"Since the ordinance applies to 'historically significant' buildings, first we must determine if the house is historically significant," Howard Saunders, the attorney hired by the city to serve as special counsel, stated.

"If neither of the parties objects, I'll take judicial notice that it is," Judge Russell said. "I've read enough about this house to know a great deal about it." Sandy Horan, the Alburys' attorney, didn't object, but, curiously, Howard Saunders did.

"*You* object, Mr. Saunders?" Judge Russell asked. "Don't you believe the house is historically significant? Isn't that the heart of your case?"

"It is, and we do believe it is historically significant," Saunders replied. "But we assert that it is critical for the record to reflect in detail *why* it is historically significant."

Horan smelled a skunk in the woodpile. "That is not necessary, Your Honor. Mr. Saunders merely wants to inflame public sentiment and create more sympathy for his case. Allowing a recitation of what we already know is prejudicial."

"Oh, I don't know about that, Mr. Saunders," Judge Russell answered. "It may be a waste of time, but I don't see how it would be prejudicial. I won't take judicial notice if Mr. Saunders doesn't want me to. There's no need to create points of appeal unnecessarily."

Saunders then called Irma Pasternak, the local historian who had started the entire controversy with her newspaper columns and talks about the history of the Albury house. The reporters covering the trial would again write and speak about the unique architecture of the home and the interesting characters who had lived there. Saunders' strategy worked perfectly, and the masses of people supporting the ordinance grew.

In presenting the claims that the ordinance deprived the Alburys of substantive due process and violated their equal protection rights, Horan asserted that the judge should use "strict scrutiny," meaning that Judge Russell would be required to strike down the ordinance unless she determined that it satisfied a "compelling" governmental interest or purpose. Horan contended that preserving historically significant buildings, while worthy and admirable, was not compelling.

"I disagree, Your Honor," Saunders replied. "Strict scrutiny is allowed only when fundamental rights like free speech and voting are involved. A fundamental right is not involved in this case, so the appropriate standard is one of 'rational basis.' If you find a rational basis for the ordinance, you must uphold it." Saunders knew that the rational basis test was met if the ordinance was 'rationally related to a legitimate interest,' and preserving historically significant buildings was certainly a legitimate interest for government.

"What could be more fundamental than home ownership?" Horan responded. "Our Constitution even protects one's homestead from forced sale. You can owe someone a million dollars, but he can't take your home."

"Mr. Horan, courts assume that legislative bodies pass rational laws," said Judge Russell. "We know that's not always true, but that's the assumption. Courts typically defer to legislative bodies and assume that laws are rational. I'm going to rule that the standard for interpreting this ordinance is one of 'rational basis.'"

"In that case, Your Honor, I assert that the ordinance is arbitrary and irrational," Horan said. He knew that even if the rational basis test were used, the ordinance would still be stricken if it were either arbitrary or irrational.

"So you're getting into the substantive due process argument, I take it?" Judge Russell asked.

"I am, Your Honor."

"What do you say about that, Mr. Saunders?" said Judge Russell.

"This ordinance does not violate substantive due process. It would be a due process issue only if the ordinance applied to *all* persons and this one doesn't. It applies solely to those who have historically significant structures."

"But doesn't it apply to *all* persons who have historically significant buildings?" the judge asked.

"Yes, but..."

"And if that's the case, doesn't that get us into the equal protection issue?"

"I suppose it does, but..."

"I think it does, but let's stay with the due process argument for a while," Judge Russell said.

"Very well," Saunders said, a bit ruffled. "Assuming that the class of affected persons for due process considerations is defined as only those with historically significant structures, the ordinance is not arbitrary," Saunders said. "It applies to *all* structures deemed historically significant, not just a few. The ordinance doesn't 'pick on' the Alburys. They just happen to be the first ones affected. And the ordinance isn't irrational. In fact, what could be more rational than a city wanting to preserve its past?"

"And your response, Mr. Horan?" the judge asked.

"The ordinance declares that if one owns a particular kind of property – historically significant structures – it shall remain in that state forever. That's arbitrary and irrational. Tastes may change, yet the Alburys will be forever locked into a land use that already doesn't fit the surroundings. Add to the mix that non-elected persons – the members of the Old Building Restoration Commission – will be making the determinations of which buildings are historically significant, and the potential for arbitrary abuse is very real. What's more, the ordinance is legally vague. There's no definition of what constitutes 'historically significant structures'. How are people to know? If the ordinance had, for example, sought to preserve all properties that survived the fire of 1886 – a fire that burned down most of Key West – people would be on notice about what structures were historically significant. As it is, property owners have no idea what buildings are captured by the designation, and that's arbitrary, irrational and vague."

"This gets to the heart of the substantive due process argument," Judge Russell said. "I'm going to reserve judgment until all claims are presented. Do you wish to make your argument on the equal protection claim, Mr. Horan?"

"Yes, Your Honor. This ordinance discriminates against the Alburys, as it does with all persons owning 'historically significant' structures, because it treats them differently than everyone else. Under the ordinance, they do not have the same development opportunities as those whose buildings are not historically significant. Their freedom is restricted relative to other persons, hurting them financially. They are adversely impacted solely because they own historically significant properties, and the ordinance was passed *after* they became owners, so the argument cannot be credibly made that they bought the properties with full knowledge of the restriction. This ordinance came from out of nowhere, clobbering them economically by violating their equal protection rights."

"Mr. Saunders, what's your response?" asked Judge Russell.

"There *is* something inherently different about these buildings, Your Honor," Saunders said. "They are truly special, and how we treat them will partly define our character as a people and as a community. They help tell the story of who we are, and how can we know who we are if we don't know who we have been? If the ordinance applied to only a portion of the historically significant properties, Mr. Horan might have a point. But the ordinance applies to *all* historically significant properties, so there can't be a violation of equal protection."

"So you would define the class of persons against whom the ordinance is to be measured as only those who own historically significant structures, not all property owners?" Judge Russell asked.

"That's right!" Saunders answered. "It is in the best interest of society that historically significant buildings be protected. As you ruled earlier, the standard is whether there is a rational basis for the ordinance, and there most surely is in this instance. Once it is determined that the ordinance has a rational basis, as long as all similarly situated property owners are affected the same way, there is no violation of equal protection."

"Do you have anything to add by way of response, Mr. Horan?" Judge Russell asked.

"Not about equal protection, Your Honor, but Mr. Saunders' argument leads right into our contention that the ordinance violates the state's private property rights act. If you believe, as he contends, that these properties are so important to society that they should be preserved, is his client willing to pay for the impact to my client? He'd better be willing, because that is the requirement under the Harris Act. The uses for the property that my client is left with are unreasonable, causing him to bear a disproportionate share of the burden imposed for the good of society. Indeed, the burden is 'inordinate' as envisioned under the Act, so the city must pay for the impact. I would add that surely there are other property owners who are affected the same way, so the city needs to be prepared to compensate them, too."

"The ordinance does *not* create an inordinate burden, Judge," Saunders injected. "The plaintiffs have been living in their house since 1958, and nothing about the ordinance prevents that. By all accounts, the value of their investment is worth exponentially more than it was when they moved in, notwithstanding this ordinance! Regardless, there is nothing unreasonable about preventing historically significant buildings from being destroyed.

Society has decided that wetlands are important, so property owners aren't allowed to destroy them. What's the difference? There isn't one. If there can be a legal prohibition on destroying wetlands because of their intrinsic value, there can be a legal prohibition on destroying historically significant buildings because of their intrinsic value. As a matter of public policy, society has decided that historically significant structures should be preserved, and I have little sympathy for those who would attempt to destroy them!"

'No editorial comments, Mr. Saunders," Judge Russell admonished. "Mr. Horan, do you wish to respond to Mr. Saunders' argument?"

"Only to point out that wetlands help sustain ecosystems that help sustain ourselves. As nice as historically significant buildings might be to some people, they aren't critical to our survival, which gets me into my final argument: inverse condemnation.

"There is no question but that the city has effectively taken my clients' property. The ordinance 'takes' *all* economic uses of their property. They are left with only the current use – residential. It unjustly reduces the value of the property, and the law is clear: there must be compensation paid!"

"The ordinance does *not* take all economic uses of their property, Your Honor," Saunders injected. "In fact, it doesn't take any."

This raised the judge's eyebrows. "Explain that, Mr. Saunders."

"All the ordinance does is prohibit the building from being destroyed," he replied. "If the pharmacy wanted to move into the current building, it could, if the zoning were changed. There is no end to the economic uses the building could be used for, as long as the zoning would allow it."

"Your Honor, that is not a credible argument," Horan exclaimed. "In fact, it's absurd! RNP pharmacy, and most other businesses I would guess, would need a new building in order to operate. The ordinance effectively shuts them out."

"Judge, Mr. Horan just implicated his argument," said Saunders. "He used the word 'most' other businesses. To prevail in an adverse condemnation action, *all* economic uses must be precluded."

"Your Honor, Mr. Saunders is parsing words," replied Horan. "I'll concede that a brothel could operate out of the building, but that doesn't prevent a successful inverse condemnation claim."

The attorneys were getting worked up with each other.

"All right, gentlemen. That's enough from you, and that's enough for today. Closing arguments tomorrow, beginning at 9:00 a.m. Good day." With that, Judge Russell slammed down her gavel and left the courtroom.

The next morning it was a circus. Outside the courthouse Jimmy Buffet music was blaring; Mayor Weider was leading his minions in cheers; street vendors were set up alongside the sidewalks selling everything from hot pretzels to tee shirts; and media tents and television trucks lined all side roads leading to the courthouse. When Dan and Lisa arrived, escorted by their attorney, they were booed as they entered the courthouse.

"Can you believe this?" Dan asked incredulously. "Who do these people think they are, booing us like we were common criminals? We're the ones with standing! Most of them are carpetbaggers or misfits who just showed up for the party! They haven't had a long-term commitment to Key West." He was incensed. He turned to confront the hecklers when Lisa pulled him away by the arm.

"Let's just get in the courtroom. Let Sandy do the talking."

Lisa and Dan took their seats alongside Sandy Horan, their attorney. Mayor Weider and Howard Saunders, the city's attorney, came in next and were seated. The first four rows of the seating area in the courtroom were reserved for journalists, and there wasn't an empty seat in the house.

"All rise,' the bailiff called out loudly. Everyone rose as Judge Russell entered. She took her seat, and, after reviewing a short stack of papers on her desk, looked up.

"Mr. Horan, are you ready to present your closing argument."

"I am, Your Honor."

'Then you may begin."

Sandy Horan strode to the lectern with his head back and a disdainful look on his face. He wanted the judge to see that he thought the Alburys were victims of their own government.

"Your Honor, we all know that the history of a city is important. My clients know that, and they love their city. They've been here for generations, longer, in fact, than most of those who have taken issue with their plans for their home." Horan looked over his shoulder at the audience. Some guy hissed. "Like him," Horan smirked.

"Stay with your argument, Mr. Horan," Judge Russell said firmly.

'In fact, my clients are a part of the history of this city. In some ways, they're heartbroken over how Key West – the whole Keys, actually – have changed. But change it has and my clients are not to blame. Because they are not to blame, it would be patently unfair to force them to pay the price for the new-found love many in the community have apparently developed for 'historically significant' buildings." Horan then led the Court through all the arguments he had made during the eight days of the trial. His comments were sharp and to the point, relying heavily on statutory and case law. Skillfully he went through each of the bases upon which he was requesting relief, ending one argument with a perfect lead-in to the next. From substantive due process, to equal protection, to the Harris Act, to inverse condemnation he laid out a powerful and authoritative case. When he finished, the courtroom was silent, each observer contemplating the persuasive presentation and wondering how Howard Saunders could counter such a well-stated recitation of the law and how it related to the facts at hand.

Saunders walked slowly and dramatically to the lectern. He knew that the constitutionality of the ordinance was questionable at best. He also knew that the Alburys' house was in the direct line of commercial development. Consequently, he did what most lawyers do when the law and facts aren't with them: he hollered and screamed and ranted and raved. First, though, he quietly appealed to emotions by conjuring up sentiments of nostalgia and outrage. He addressed the judge, but he was really speaking to the audience.

"Your Honor, we've all felt the effects of Key West. The natural beauty of he surrounding water, the flowers, the smell of sea breezes at night...it's hypnotic. The atmosphere created by its wonderful and curious mix of people, the boutiques downtown, the charm of a city alive with diversity and charm...it's captivating. Who among us hasn't gazed in awe at the magnificent buildings, some quaint and some dramatic, but all with personality and unique style. And that's why we're here today, because some among us would destroy these wonderful buildings. I'm sure the Alburys are good people; they've been here a long time, no one disputes that. But money makes even good people do bad things." When Saunders said this, Dan Albury almost came out of his seat after him. Lisa put her hand on his leg, encouraging him to stay down and keep calm.

"What we've seen throughout this whole process," Saunders continued, "is a community trying to preserve its past. Using the Civics lessons we were all taught in the ninth grade, supporters of this ordinance rose up against a governmental action they opposed and sought change to prevent it from happening. They used the process exactly as our democratic model prescribes, yet they are criticized!" Saunders was pounding his fist on the table by now, angry that supporters of the ordinance would be ridiculed "for simply wanting to preserve historic structures. How wholesome their motives, how pure, yet they are ridiculed!" He ended by portraying the proponents of the ordinance as patriots, ordinary citizens who were trying to save what remained of a community that was losing the battle against forces beyond its control. When he finished, several people could be heard sniffling and could be seen wiping their eyes. Howard Saunders had reduced them to tears. He turned and walked back to his seat.

"I will render my written ruling within a week," Judge Russell said. "Hearing nothing more before the Court, we are adjourned."

When the Alburys got to their car, they found that it had been egged. As they drove off, they saw several television reporters selectively interviewing some of the emotional folks from the courtroom who had been crying at the end of Saunders' closing argument."

"People like that make good interviews for the evening news," Lisa said.

"Yeah," Dan answered dejectedly. "I guess they do."

Lisa looked up, surprised at how defeated her husband sounded. "Let's hop on the skiff and run out towards the Marquesas," she said. "The water and sun will do us both some good."

"Sounds like a good idea to me," Dan answered.

It was a bluebird day, and the bright sunlight would make it easier to see any cruising permit. They headed southwest for 30 minutes, almost to the seven-mile crossover to the Marquesas Islands. A good current was washing across the grass flats, and Dan knew the fish would be feeding into it, catching unsuspecting critters as they drifted along. He positioned the boat to take advantage of this tendency of fish, and tried to keep the sun at his back to better enable him to see into the water. It wasn't long before he saw two permit dart up from a deeper channel and head across the flat.

"Fish at two o'clock, Lisa."

"I got 'em," she said, as she started the first of two false casts she would make with the 'Sid Camler' brand nine-weight rod. She dropped the fly five feet in front of the first fish. The crab-like Merkin fly settled in the grass.

"Strip it!" Dan said. From his perch high on the poling platform at the stem of the boat he could see what was going on in the water better than Lisa could.

Lisa gave the fly a little twitch, causing it to bob up out of the grass before settling back down. The first fish darted towards it, stopped, and then stood on its nose.

"He's got it!" Dan shouted.

Lisa expertly pulled the line with one hand and gently swept the rod to the side with the other, setting the hook. In less than a second the fight was on!

Line peeled from the reel as the fish made a mad dash for the deeper water of the channel. Crossing the channel, it came up on another grass flat, stirring up mud as it blitzed across the 18-inch deep water.

Twelve minutes later, Lisa pulled the tired fish to the side of the boat. Dan reached over and "tailed" it, grabbing its sickle-like tail at the base. The silver sides of the magnificent creature sparkled in the sunlight as Dan expertly removed the hook without taking the fish from the water.

"There aren't many fish as pretty as this one," he said as he gently moved the fish back and forth through the water, washing water over its gills to help it recover.

"No, there aren't," Lisa answered. "The yellow on its throat is *so* delicate."

After 15 seconds or so, he released the fish, and it slowly swam away.

They both sat on the bow of the boat. "That was fantastic!" Dan said.

"The fish or the trial?" Lisa joked.

"The fish, of course," Dan said, smiling. "The trial was torture. Can you believe what we've just been through?"

"No, I can't," Lisa answered. "It was a lot worse than I thought it would be."

They rolled up towels to use as pillows and stretched out. The sun sucked the tension and stress of the last few months from them. They were so tired. Drifting slowly along, they heard only the soft and quiet slap of the ripples of the water striking the side of the boat.

They both dozed off. A half-hour later, Dan stirred. He wanted to fish but didn't want to waken Lisa. But when Dan's cell phone rang, their solitude was interrupted anyway.

"Really? That's pretty unusual. I wonder what it means?" Lisa heard Dan say. He hung up.

"Who was that?" she asked.

"Sandy. He said the judge's assistant just called him and said Judge Russell has made up her mind. She's called a meeting tomorrow to go over her decision."

"That didn't take long. I don't know if that's good or bad."

"Me either, so I guess there's nothing to do now but fish!" he said with a grin.

"You can fish if you want," Lisa replied, "but I'm too tired to pole. I'm going to stay right here and close my eyes. Wake me up if you get anything on."

The next morning, Dan and Lisa walked into the courthouse holding hands. With them were Sandy Horan, their lawyer, and their friends, Skip and Janet Pinder. Walking into the courtroom, Sandy greeted Howard Saunders, the attorney for Key West, who was accompanied by Mayor Weider and the city manager. They all took their seats in Judge Russell's courtroom. Every seat in the audience was filled with press people and observers.

"All rise," the bailiff called out as Judge Russell walked in. "Take your seats, please," she said.

"I've made my decision," she began, "and I was up a good part of the night writing the Order. It's too long to read, but you'll receive a copy of it as soon as we adjourn today.

"Given the profile of this issue, I thought it was important to have this meeting to publicly announce my findings. I'm going to ask that you hold your questions or comments until after I finish. Needless to say, anyone in the audience who is disruptive will be removed from the building." Judge Russell was in charge of her courtroom.

"Key West is one of the most unique communities in the country," she began, "and one of the things that makes it so unique is its architecture. Few places in America have such wonderful and old buildings."

"We're cooked," Dan thought to himself.

"Certainly preserving historically significant structures is a laudable goal and one that is rationally connected to a legitimate governmental interest," she continued, "but the ordinance as written contains no definition of what constitutes an 'historically significant' structure. Furthermore, it places unbridled discretion with the Old Building Restoration Commission to determine which structures are deemed historic. Therefore, the ordinance is vague, arbitrary and discriminatory, and violates the plaintiffs' substantive due process rights. I find that the ordinance as adopted by the City of Key West is unconstitutional, and render it null and void."

The crowd stirred. One person jumped up and screamed, "How could you!" She then ran out of the courtroom before the bailiff had to take her from the building.

Judge Russell next addressed the question of whether the ordinance violated the equal protection rights of the plaintiffs. "As I stated earlier, preserving historically significant structures is rationally connected to a legitimate governmental interest. An ordinance otherwise constitutionally written could legally treat all owners of historically significant structures differently from owners of other properties. For that reason, I conclude that the ordinance does not violate the equal protection rights of the plaintiffs."

Lisa and Dan looked at each other, not sure of what was happening. It sounded as though they had won one argument and lost another.

The judge moved to the next issue, the Harris Act and private property rights. "The plaintiffs allege that the ordinance violates the Harris Act by 'inordinately burdening' them. However, I do not have to decide this question. The ordinance is unconstitutional because it violates the plaintiffs' substantive due process rights, so I am withholding judgment on the Harris Act claim, but I would offer this dictum. If the City wishes to protect its historically significant buildings, it may legally do so if the ordinance used satisfies the constitutional parameters outlined within this ruling. However, it *is* possible for the ordinance to be so restrictive that it would amount to an 'inordinate burden' on the affected property owners, in which case compensation would have to be paid.

"Likewise, because I am striking down the ordinance, there is no longer a basis for an inverse condemnation claim. That is, because there is effectively no ordinance, there is nothing to restrict the value of the property. Nevertheless, should this ruling be overturned on appeal, or should the ordinance be repealed and another passed that causes a similar effect on the plaintiffs, the City should know that I believe the plaintiffs would have a valid claim for inverse condemnation. The zoning request initially sought by the plaintiffs was reasonable and consistent with sound planning. Therefore, since the ordinance made the zoning change moot, it amounted to a taking, and compensation would have to be paid. Testimony valued the plaintiffs' home at 1.1 million dollars as a residence. They had a contract for 2.5 million, contingent on the zoning change. Therefore, if I were calculating the value of an inverse condemnation claim it would be the difference between 2.5 million and 1.1 million, or 1.4 million, payable by the City to the plaintiffs.

"That's my ruling. Do you have any questions of comments?" The attorneys had none; they understood perfectly.

"Hearing no questions or comments, court is adjourned." She rose and left the courtroom. The audience was strangely silent. They didn't understand the intricacies of the legal arguments, but they knew intuitively that the judge had issued a well-reasoned ruling.

"What does it mean?" Lisa asked Sandy Horan.

"It means she bought our case," Sandy replied. "She's giving the City another chance to do what's right. She's letting them know that it's possible to write a constitutional ordinance to preserve historically significant structures, but it'll cost them. The City gets the opportunity to allow the zoning change you originally sought, thereby avoiding any cost to the taxpayers, before she hammers them. It's a pretty clever ruling, really."

"But what does this mean for *us*?" Lisa asked again.

"My guess is your zoning change will sail right through," Sandy answered. "Mayor Weider may try to pass another ordinance that addresses the concerns raised in the ruling, but that will take a long time. He's gotten all the political mileage out of the issue anyway. He'll probably move on to other things."

"Do you think the City will appeal?" Dan asked.

"No, I don't," Sandy answered. "They know they're whipped. They'd be throwing good money after bad. Howard Saunders doesn't work for peanuts."

Dan and Lisa looked at each other, shaking their heads at how they had been so vilified by those who were really mad at a much larger issue: population growth and how it was ruining many of the last remaining truly special places on Earth. Maybe there is no solution to this problem. Perhaps it's all part of a divine master plan that leads inexorably towards the demise of the natural world. If that's the case, do we simply enjoy the party while it lasts, or do we fight it, knowing that our efforts will ultimately be unsuccessful? What a choice, and what a dilemma.

"Spectrum of Life"
Tribute to Biodiversity

Author's Note:

On the opening day of my first regular session of the Florida Legislature, in the spring of 1983, Speaker of the House H. Lee Moffitt, in his remarks to the entire House, asked this question, "How are we going to pay for all this growth?" Today, in the year 2006, we're still asking the same question.

Growth-related issues occupied more of my time than any others during my years in the House and Senate. From Everglades restoration to property rights to taxes, much of my time was spent dealing with matters attendant with population growth, like its effect on the environment and our state's infrastructure. I comment on this at length in my first book, "Under the Panther Moon," so I won't spend much time on it here. Suffice it to say, it remains the biggest issue in Florida.

If we could roll the clock back 50 years and either do or not do just three or four things, we would prevent untold environmental degradation and save billions of dollars. Today, the comprehensive plans of Florida's counties allow for 95 million people at build-out. I wonder what three or four things we could do now that would save the next round of environmental degradation and billions of dollars. I hope policymakers are thinking of such things.

THE LAW. *Definitions and Explanations:*

Eminent Domain: The power to take private property for public use by the state, municipalities, and private persons or corporations authorized to exercise functions of public character.

Black's Law Dictionary, Sixth Edition, p. 523

Inverse Condemnation: An action brought by a property owner seeking just compensation for land taken for a public use, against a government or private entity having the power of eminent domain.

Black's Law Dictionary, Sixth Edition, p. 825

"...; nor shall any person... be deprived of life, liberty or property, without due process of law; nor shall private property be taken for public use, without just compensation.

Article V, United States Constitution

Article X, Section 6, Constitution of the State of Florida: Eminent Domain -

(a) No private property shall be taken except for a public purpose and with full compensation thereof paid to each owner or secured by deposit in the registry of the court and available to the owner.

(b) Provision may be made by law for the taking of easements, by like proceedings, for the drainage of the land of one person over or through the land of another.

Substantive due process: Doctrine that due process clauses of the Fifth and Fourteenth Amendments to the United States Constitution require legislation to be fair and reasonable in content as well as application. Such may be broadly defined as the constitutional guarantee that no person shall be arbitrarily deprived of his life, liberty or property. The essence of substantive due process is protection from arbitrary and unreasonable action.

Black's Law Dictionary, Sixth Edition, p. 1429, and Jeffries v. Turkey Run Consolidated School District, C.A. Ind., 492 F.2d 1,3

Equal Protection Clause: "...nor shall any State deprive any person of life, liberty, or property, without due process of law; nor deny to any person within its jurisdiction the equal protection of the laws."

Article XIV; Section 1, Constitution of the United States

Florida Statute 70.001 Private property rights protection.-

(1)(e) The terms "inordinate burden" or "inordinately burden" mean that an action of one or more governmental entities has directly restricted or limited the use of real property such that the property owner is permanently unable to attain the reasonable, investment-backed expectation for the existing use of the real property or a vested right to a specific use of the real property with respect to the real property as a whole, or that the property owner is left with existing or vested uses that are unreasonable such that the property owner bears permanently a disproportionate share of a burden imposed for the good of the public...

Notable Quotes:

"To declare that the end justifies the means, to declare that the government may commit crimes, would bring terrible retribution."

Honorable Louis D. Brandeis, Associate Justice,
United States Supreme Court
www.brainyquotes.com

"When a legislature undertakes to proscribe the exercise of a citizen's constitutional rights it acts lawlessly and the citizen can take matters into his

own hands and proceed on the basis that such a law is no law at all."

> Honorable William O. Douglas, Associate Justice,
> United States Supreme Court
> www.brainyquottes.com

"The Constitution is not neutral. It was designed to take the government off the backs of people."

> Honorable William 0. Douglas, Associate Justice,
> United States Supreme Court
> www.brainyquotes.com

"The Fifth Amendment is an old friend and a good friend. One of the great landmarks in men's struggle to be free of tyranny, to be decent and civilized."

> Honorable William 0. Douglas, Associate Justice,
> United States Supreme Court
> www.brainyquotes.com

"Liberty implies the absence of arbitrary restraint, not immunity from reasonable regulations…"

> Honorable Charles Evans Hughes, Associate Justice, United States Supreme Court,
> 1937, "The Supreme Court in American History," by Marjorie G. Fribourg (1965),
> as attributed in www.home.att.net/~midnightflyer/supreme.html

"The right to revolt has sources deep in our history."

> Honorable William O. Douglas, Associate Justice,
> United States Supreme Court, in "An Almanac of Liberty,"
> by William O. Douglas (1954), as attributed in
> www.home.att.net/~midnightflyer/supreme.html

"A little rebellion every now and then is a good thing."

> Thomas Jefferson / www.famous-quote.net

"It is not the function of our Government to keep the citizen from falling into error; it is the function of the citizen to keep the Government from falling into error."

> Honorable Robert H. Jackson, Associate Justice, United States Supreme Court,
> American Communications Association v. Douds,
> 339 US. 382, 442 (1950).

BIBLIOGRAPHY NOTE

In researching this book, several web sites were very helpful in finding germane or provocative quotes. Among them were:

1. www.brainyquotes.com
2. www.quotegarden.com
3. www.worldofquotes.com
4. home.att.net/~midnightflyer/supreme.html. "Quotes From Supreme Court Justices."
5. www.erowid.org
6. www.fact.trib.com

Often, quotes in these sites were attributed only to the person who uttered them, not listing when or where the words were said. Through additional research I pinpointed the citation where I could, but sometimes more information could not be found. Still, the web sites were very helpful in getting me started. Another site, www.findlaw.com, was very useful in finding Supreme Court cases.

Notable Quote:
"Restriction of free thought and free speech is the most dangerous of all subversions. It is the one un-American act that could most easily defeat us."

Honorable William O. Douglas, Associate Justice,
United States Supreme Court,
in a speech given to the Authors Guild
in New York City on December 3, 1951.
www.fact.trib.com
"Famous Quotes on the First Amendment."

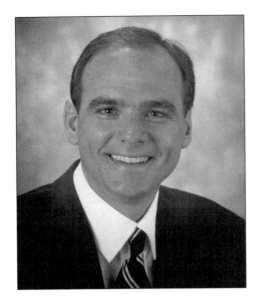

ABOUT THE AUTHOR

Rick Dantzler grew up in Florida, hunting and fishing and enjoying the natural wonders of the Sunshine State, and excelling in sports. He received his K-12 education from the Polk County Public School system, and his undergraduate and law degrees from the University of Florida.

In 1982, at the age of 26, Rick was elected to the Florida House of Representatives. He was re-elected three times without opposition and served until 1990 when he was elected to the Florida Senate. There, he was known as the "conscience of the Senate," and held many leadership positions in both Democrat and Republican administrations. He was given numerous awards and compiled an outstanding list of legislative accomplishments.

In 1998, Sen. Dantzler resigned from the Senate to run for governor. He ultimately became the Democratic nominee for lieutenant governor that same year.

Now out of public office, he is an attorney living in Winter Haven, FL. He is married to Julie Pope and they have two children, of whom they are very proud.

This is Rick's second book. His first, *Under the Panther Moon*, has been wonderfully reviewed and is a "must-read" for all who cherish the natural heritage of Florida. In addition to adventurous tales with poignant lessons suitable for all readers, Paul Schulz's magnificent artwork graces the pages of that book, as well.

ABOUT THE ARTIST

Paul Schulz also grew up in Florida and had the great fortune to personally explore many unspoiled wild habitats unique to this amazing state. In 1982, Paul graduated from Davidson College, where he majored in economics and minored in art. His first job required both marketing and artistic skills, as a " design coordinator" for Hallmark Card Company at their headquarters in Kansas City, MO. Then, in 1985, Paul returned to his hometown of Winter Haven, FL to run the family business, Florida Chemical Company, Inc., a 60 year-old company that sells citrus oils worldwide. With a capable management team and talented staff, Paul is now able to split his workweek to more fully accommodate his professional art career.

Paul produces original artwork from a large art studio at his home. This is the second project on which he and Rick Dantzler have collaborated. Paul produced the artwork for Rick's first book, *Under the Panther Moon*. Both books tested Paul's talent with a pencil, bringing the artist back to the task of creating delicate line work reminiscent of the scratchboard drawing by his late grandfather, master engraver William Pringle. Paul is best known for his vibrant paintings that capture the spectacular colors of his natural subjects.

An early love and appreciation for nature's beauty and diversity was instilled in Paul by his father, Henry "Bert" Schulz, and family friends including outdoorsman George Costello, herpetologist Ross Allen, and the founding father of sea turtle conservation, Archie Carr. The artist has traveled extensively collecting reference for his work, including several trips to the rain forests of South America.

Paul's artwork is displayed in many homes and offices around the world. A complete catalog of the artist's work for sale, including original pencil sketches and paintings featured in *Law Matters* and *Under the Panther Moon*, can be viewed on his website www.paulschulz.com.